LIBERTY
falling

NEVADA BARR

LIBERTY
falling

WHEELER
PUBLISHING, INC.
ROCKLAND, MA

★ AN AMERICAN COMPANY ★

Published in Large Print by arrangement with G.P. Putnam's Sons, a member of Penguin Putnam Inc., in the United States and Canada.

Wheeler Large Print Book Series.

Set in 16 pt Plantin.

Library of Congress Cataloging-in-Publication Data

Barr, Nevada.
    Liberty falling / Nevada Barr.
        p. (large print) cm.(Wheeler large print book series)
    ISBN 1-56895-711-4 (hardcover)
    1. Large type books.
I. Title. II. Series
[PS3552.A73184L53   1999b]
813'.54—dc21

99-18708
CIP

FOR TRISH; *once my agent, twice my editor, always my friend.*

For help on this book, I thank the staff of the Ellis Island and Statue of Liberty National Monuments, the Park Police on Ellis and Liberty (and yes, they are all handsome), the staff boat captains, and especially Becky Brock, who gave me the place and a bed to sleep in while I did my research, an individual who is too shy to be named and Charlie DeLeo, who kindly let me use him in the story.

Since the writing of this book, plans have been made to stabilize the buildings on Islands II and III, though no work has yet begun. It is hoped that if the structures can be saved, there will be funds to restore them. Contributions toward this future restoration can be made to The Statue of Liberty Ellis Island Foundation. E-mail: pr@ellisisland.org.

1

Of course Molly would live; anything else was unthinkable. But Anna was thinking it.

Concerned for her mental health—or their own—the nurses at Columbia-Presbyterian had banded together and banished Anna from the hospital for twelve hours. Once pried free of the rain-streaked monolith housing umpteen floors of misery, Anna fled the far reaches of the Upper West Side, spiraling down into the subway with the rainwater. Huddled on the Number 1 train, she rattled through the entrails of Manhattan to the end of the line: South Ferry. The subways weren't those she'd known as a young woman—a wife—living in New York City with Zach. These were clean, silver. They smelled of metal and electricity, like bumper cars at the carnival. Graffiti artists, frustrated by the glossy unpaintable surfaces, made futile attempts to etch gang symbols and lewd declarations of adolescent angst in the plastic of the windows. Vandals lacked patience and dedication.

At South Ferry, Anna sprinted up the stairs and burst from the station like a deadline-crazed commuter and across the three lanes of traffic that separated the subway from the pier. The National Park Service staff boat, the *Liberty IV,* was waiting at the Coast Guard dock, floating on the tip of Manhattan Island. Anna got aboard before they cast off. Kevin, the boat

1

captain, winked. "I wouldn't have left you."
She knew that, but she'd needed to run, to see
the planks of the pier passing beneath her
feet, to feel she'd outpaced the demons,
beaten them to the boat. Ghosts can't cross
open water.

On shipboard, she kept running. Avoiding
kindly questions from Kevin, she left the
warmth of the cabin and went to the stern.
Under the dispirited flapping of the American
flag, she watched the skyline, dominated by
the twin towers of the World Trade Center,
recede, carried away on the wake of the *Liberty IV*. Patsy Silva, the woman on Liberty
Island with whom Anna was staying, referred
to this pose, this view, as her "Barbra Streisand
moment." It was the East Coast equivalent of
Mary Tyler Moore throwing her hat into the
air in downtown Minneapolis.

Crossing the harbor, Anna tried to fix her
mind on the movie that had burned that image
into the collective unconscious of a generation of theatergoers, but could not remember
even the title.

The NPS boat stopped first at Ellis Island.
From there it would continue its endless triangle, ferrying staff to Liberty Island, then the
third leg of the run, back to MIO, the dock
shared with the Marine Inspection Office of
the U.S. Coast Guard where Anna had boarded.
Farther out in the harbor, the Circle Line
ferried its tourist cargo in roughly the same
path but docking at different points on the
islands. Anna was bunking in Patsy Silva's spare

2

room in a cozy little cottage on Liberty Island in the shadow of the great lady herself. The view from Anna's bedroom—could it be duplicated—would jack the price of a condo into the high six figures. As it was park housing, Patsy and her roommate paid the staggering sum of one hundred and forty dollars a month; recompense for living in an area a GS-7 on NPS wages couldn't possibly afford.

Loath to go "home" immediately, to strand herself amid the all too human accoutrements of coffee cups and telephones, Anna thanked Kevin, disembarked at Ellis, the *Liberty IV*'s first stop, and slunk away, keeping to deserted brick alleys.

For ease of reference, Ellis was divided into three "islands," though all three of its building complexes shared the same bit of earth and were joined together by a long windowed walkway. Island I was the facility the tourists saw. Spectacularly refurbished in 1986, it housed the museum, the Registry Hall, the baggage room and the service areas through which twelve million of the immigrants who poured into America from 1892 to 1954 had passed. Vaulted ceilings, as airy as those of a cathedral built to worship industry, intricate windows, modern baths, electricity, running water—all the state-of-the-art nineteenth-century architecture—had been lovingly restored to its original grandeur. And returned, Anna had little doubt, to its original cacophony. At Ellis's peak, ten thousand souls a day were shepherded through the "golden door" to America. Now Ellis, in season, saw eight to ten thousand visitors from all over the world each day. The raucous babble of languages must have seemed familiar to the old building.

Echoing off acres of tile in cavernous rooms, the din gave Anna a headache. She'd arrived in New York two days before. After a day of staring blindly at exhibits, she'd been driven to Islands II and III. In these crumbling urban ruins she'd found solace.

Isolated from the public by an inlet where Circle Line ferries disgorged two-legged freight, Islands II and III had been the hospital wards and staff living quarters when Ellis was an immigration station. One of the first American hospitals built on the European spa principle that light and air are actually good for people, its many rooms were graced with windows reaching nearly from floor to ceiling. The infectious disease units on Island III were interconnected by long, freestanding passages, walled in paned glass. Ellis had boasted a psychiatric hospital, two operating theaters, a morgue and an autopsy room. At the turn of the century, the hospitals on Ellis were showcases for modern medical practices. That, and the fact that at one time or another nearly every disease known to man was manifest in at least one hapless immigrant, lured students and doctors from all over. They came to Ellis to teach, learn and observe.

In the early fifties the hospitals had been abandoned. Unlike the registry building on Island

I, they'd never been restored. There had never been funds to so much as stabilize the structures. Thus Anna loved them, found in them the peace the sprawl of New York City had destroyed even in the remote corners of her famed city parks.

On these abandoned islands, as in the Anasazi cliff dwellings in Colorado, the sugar mills on St. John, the copper mines on Isle Royale, Nature was taking back what had once been hers. Brick, glass and iron were wrapped with delicate green tendrils, vines content to destroy the man-made world one minute fragment at a time. Walls disappeared behind leafy curtains. Glass, shattered by the vicissitudes of time and vandals, was slowly returning its component parts to the sand that had been dredged from the Jersey shore to build the island. Four stories above this landfill, hardwood floors, sloped with moisture, grew lush carpets of fine green moss on the mounds of litter half a century of neglect had shaken down from the ceilings.

The rain that had been an unrelenting mirror of Anna's spirits since she arrived in New York blew down through chimneys, in windows, through ragged sockets of ruined skylights. Rain worked its silent progress down walls and pipes and electrical conduits of the old structures till, days after the skies cleared, it would rain in the maze of tunnels and corridors beneath the ancient buildings.

Protected by the covered walkway connecting the islands, Anna threaded her way through the detritus of a functioning park and odd stores remaining from a long history as a public trust. When Ellis was abandoned, it was left almost as if the bureaucrats and medical personnel would return. Files, desks, furniture, dishes, beds and mattresses clogged the old rooms.

The corridor she followed curved gently, joining the three building complexes together. At best guess it was three or four hundred yards long, but the curvature warped the distance, giving a sense of an endless hallway to nowhere. Electrical cable dripped from the ceiling in knotted gray swaths, but no lights burned on the second and third of Ellis's "islands." What light there was leaked in through arched windows spaced down the walkway, each curtained in June's voracious greenery. Gouts of ivy and feathered fingers of locust broke through the glass, reached into the dim hall, greening the light and bringing in the rain. Spiderwebs caught the drops and converted them to emerald and diamond. Last year's leaves littered the floor.

Past the inlet between Islands I and II the corridor forked, the left branch leading underneath the buildings of Island II. The way was blocked by piled boxes of deteriorating manuals. Beyond, Anna could hear water—more than the hypnotic *drip drip* of creeping rain— and guessed the passage would be flooded.

Farther along the connecting passage, two wooden doors opened into a large room. The ceiling was partially destroyed, exposing bones of iron that divided the darkness above. The floor was soft with a mix of dirt, plaster and decomposing plant material. Slipping through the jam of rusted hinges, Anna skirted a frightening chunk of machinery. Once a mangle for cleaning and sterilizing hospital linens, it was now rusted immobile. Squatting over a quarter of the room, it suggested a malevolent past it had never possessed, hinted not at pink-cheeked laundresses but at inquisitors and iron maidens.

Skirting the mangle, Anna trod soundlessly, wanting to keep her whereabouts unknown, at least for a while. The back of the laundry room let into the first in the line of four-story interconnected buildings that made up Island II. The buildings were in a row: the psychiatric ward, hospital wards, living quarters and one of the islands' two operating theaters. The buildings were tied together by long hallways, one on each of the four floors. Two days' wandering had yet to bring Anna into all the rooms. From cellar to attic they enclosed hundreds of thousands of square feet of shadow and memory.

At the staircase in the psychiatric ward, she began her climb. The steps were rotting, the ceiling hanging in tatters. Walls were damp to the touch. Plaster had fallen away and choked the steps till she walked on a ramp only partly divided by treads. Eroded plaster revealed walls of red stone blocks mortared together. Time, like a cancer, had eaten away at each layer of building material till the walls had the look of leprous and decaying flesh.

Anna found it beautiful, and wondered at herself. Was it merely the twisted set of her mind, or was this mosaic of ashes to ashes and dust to dust a thing of beauty? The latter, she decided. Her heart was lifted by the tiny clutches of fragile moss, by the down of a pigeon feather on the dappled gray of old wood. The stark and perfect walls of Columbia-Presbyterian, where Molly was interred, burned her with their sterility, their stink— if not of death, then of the weapons with which humanity waged war against it. Here in the mold, in the leaves and rain and growing mountains of bird shit, life was rich, fecund, strong enough to tear down the best man had to offer.

Each floor gained brought Anna closer to the sky, to the elements. The stairwell told its story of exposure in increasing amounts of damage. The five flights of stairs, from cellar to fourth floor, ascended in an angulated corkscrew fenced on one side by the wall and on the side of the stairwell by the high iron grating that graced all public areas in the psych ward, a net of metal gridding the world into two-inch squares. On the third floor the stair treads were gone. Anna eased up on metal risers, the wood of the steps frayed away in splinters. From the third to the fourth floor even the risers had succumbed. Rust ate through bolts and metal tore away. From above rain dripped through a skylight framed in leaves—not from the massive and venerable trees outside but from the struggling, anemic upstart of an oak no more than four feet high and rooted in pigeon droppings and plaster dust on the top-floor landing.

Fingers hooked through the rusting mesh, feet reaching for stumps of metal the color of dried blood where risers had once been, Anna pulled herself toward the tree, the watery gray light of day.

When she'd gained the new-made earth on the fourth floor, she let herself stop. Walls built when labor was cheap and money plentiful shut away the high-pitched squeal of bunched humanity. Savoring a silence only made deeper by the monotonous symphony of water, she breathed deep of the moldering air. It stank with life. She had no doubt spores and microbes were thick, each breath a colloidal suspension of mist and microscopic worlds.

Turning from the silver-bright garden under the skylight, she picked her way through the remnants of what had apparently been a mess hall when the Coast Guard used the island in the 1940s. This high up, Anna had little faith in the floor and trod with great care between fallen chunks of ceiling and the inviting but treacherous stretches of greening. The far wall, facing south, away from the peopled part of Ellis, was alight with windows. Ducking through one of these glassless apertures, she breathed a sigh of relief. Resting against the stone of the window ledge, she took in an aching lungful of air. This was the place she'd found her second day in New York, the place she'd claimed for her own. A tiny private wilderness in the megalopolis that consumed the Eastern seaboard.

Her window overlooked a deep balcony the width of the room, thirty or more feet. The balustrade was of brick, laid in a lattice pattern, welcoming light and air. To the left was the red-tiled roof and green copper rain gutters of the next building in the complex. A locust tree, easily a hundred feet high, pushed branches over the balcony rail, lending this fourth-story aerie the snug mystery of a tree house. Beyond this kindly embrace, Anna could see the rain-pocked water of New York Harbor and, if she squinted through the leafy canopy, the head and upthrust arm of the lady on nearby Liberty Island.

Here Anna felt safe. From what, she would have been hard-pressed to say. Perhaps from prying eyes or well-meant inquiries, from the gabble of tourists and the strange uninterrupted hum of Manhattan across the water. Here she could let herself think, free from the fear that thoughts would overwhelm her and she would run screaming into the ocean or, worse, huddle in a closet somewhere under the pitying eyes of those not yet insane.

Human frailty was cumulative. Anna did not find safety in numbers, only the pooling of neurosis. Seldom did she feel comfort in another's arms, only the adding of their burdens to hers. To think of Molly, she needed to be alone in the pure clean air above the huddled masses yearning for God knew what ridiculous bullshit.

In April Molly had come down with pneumonia. True to form, she'd not gone to the hospital. One of her clients at the ParkView Psychiatric Clinic was a thoracic surgeon with deep insecurities about his sexuality. Halfway through a session he'd gotten off the couch—Molly did use an actual couch, a very fine one of wine-colored Moroccan leather with ebony lion's-paw feet—and diagnosed his psychiatrist. Two days later the doctors were saying the pneumonia was a blessing in disguise. Because of it, they'd found an undiagnosed heart problem: clogged arteries. Bypass surgery was recommended. When the pneumonia was cured, Molly went in for the procedure. All had gone well except that Molly's lungs would not pick up where they'd left off. Thirty years of Camel non-filters, Dewar's Black Label and considering riding the escalator at Bloomingdale's a form of aerobic exercise were taking their pound of flesh. Dye was injected to discover why her lungs were failing. The dye damaged her kidneys. At fifty-two, Anna's sister was on a respirator, a feeding tube and dialysis. The doctors, or more accurately, Dr. Madison, said there was no reason why Molly should not recover, but it would be very, very slow. Unsaid was the obvious: There was equally little reason why she should not die.

Except that Anna would not have it.

Except that Anna could not bear it.

And there was nothing she could do. Helplessness bound her in tight coils, making her muscles twitch and her lungs pinch. Guns, knives, courage, strength, cunning, wit, anger, chutzpah, stamina, skill, experience were as confetti, feathers on the wind in the face of this creeping death.

If anyone was to go mano a mano with the killer, it had to be Molly. Anna could only stand on the sidelines and cheer her on.

Too restless to retain her perch on the sill, she stalked across the rubble-strewn balcony, snatched leaves from the tree, stalked back. Face half a foot from the brick, she stood without moving for nearly a minute.

I'll wear out the fucking pom-poms, she thought. *Revenge of the Cheerleaders.* Low comedy. Life and death. The life and death of the dearest person in the world.

2

Self-medicated with a decent Beaujolais, Anna fell out of consciousness before ten p.m. The wine was searing nerve ends already flayed raw, and her sleep was infiltrated by scenes of loss. Handicapped by a dream-scape's malicious illogic, she desperately sought everything from woolen socks to the antidote for an injection that induced death by madness.

Around midnight, alcohol jangle and a pulsing jungle beat scraped at nightmare and nightmare became reality. Visceral pounding invaded her room, thudding that mimicked migraine and loosened marrow from bone. Opening her eyes did nothing to banish what sounded like the score to a Dean Koontz musical.

Patsy's spare room, only slightly larger than the single metal-framed cot Anna slept in, was piled to the ceiling with the oddments of a nomadic lifestyle. At the foot of the bed, taking up nearly the width of the wall, was an old-fashioned sash window propped open with a two-by-four Patsy left there for that purpose. Noise poured in on a damp wind.

Anna slept as she swam and bathed, most sensibly and comfortably naked. When traveling, she brought pajamas lest she frighten the natives. Pulling them on against air too cold for June, she wove her way through the boxes to lean on the windowsill.

Across a black harbor Manhattan's skyline glittered, a perfect Broadway postcard. On the water, lit up like a lantern, floated the perpetrator of Anna's nightmare: a party boat. Patsy had warned her, but she'd forgotten. From Memorial Day to Labor Day they circled Liberty Island like hungry coyotes around a newborn moose calf, pressing as close as they dared without risking life and limb. Weddings, graduations, unspecified revelry, proving, if nothing else, that disco was not as dead as it deserved to be.

The festivities would grind on till two or three hours past midnight. Anna felt her way back to bed. The teensy light on her alarm told her it was 12:03. No rest for a while. She was annoyed on principle, but knew the wine would have ruined her sleep without the advent of the floating circus. Knowing she was as isolated in the midst of one of the world's largest cities as she would have been on the mesas of southern Colorado, she slipped on moccasins, pulled a Levi's jacket over her pajamas and went out through the kitchen door.

The physics of sound waves would dictate that the noise out of doors was in actuality louder than it had been in the room, but without walls and the dull air of even a well-ventilated house, it seemed less toxic. Wind off the water was cold, heavy with moisture. Stars that, in the grand scheme, had only recently been dimmed by Manhattan's glory and would be shining still when the last light-bulb on earth burned out, showed through jagged rents in the storm. Tomorrow—today—should show a more amiable face of summer. For the nonce, the cool gusts of midnight suited her, cooled the fevered sweat of wine gone cruel and reminded her the world was a place of the senses and not only of the mind.

A twisting sidewalk led from the cluster of employee houses. Cutting through a hedge black and shining with raindrops, Anna walked onto a broad circle paved in a circular pattern of brick and gray slate. East-northeast was Manhattan, looking magical and small. Due east was the lady. Luminescent in copper aged to a fine verdigris patina, Liberty stood shoulder

14

to shoulder with the land, her face turned determinedly out to sea, her torch, newly gilded, catching the light of sixteen high-intensity lamps. Like most other Americans, Anna's ancestors had come through this harbor, passed the lady, disembarked at Ellis Island. But for her and Molly there were no stories. The only daughters of two black sheep, they'd known only one of their four grandparents and nothing—not even the names—of their great-grandparents.

Anna walked along the island's perimeter and around the remains of old Fort Wood, build in the 1800s to protect New York Harbor. The walls of the fort were shaped like the Star of David and made of solid granite. Inside, the fort had been filled in to make a base that lifted the lady's skirts twenty yards above the top of the old walls. Even without history gilding it, it was easy to imagine the impact this glorious woman would have, seen from tired and hopeful eyes in need of new dreams.

Below Liberty's left foot, set into a grassy bank separating the harbor walk from the statue, was a metal grid thirty feet long and six wide. From beneath probed the impressive beams of fourteen high-pressure sodium lights, illuminating the massive drapery of the gown and the bottom of the book and firing the underside of jaw and crown.

From the party boat anchored offshore, the music shifted to an all-bass rendition of "Staying Alive." Unable to resist, Anna ran up the grass, walked to the middle of the

15

light grid and struck the pose made famous by John Travolta in *Saturday Night Fever.* She doubted that at this hour anyone on the boat, barring the crew, would be sober enough to focus their eyes, but she amused herself considerably.

"You. Buddy. Come off of there." A deep voice, rich with the neighborhood warmth of Brooklyn, came through the blaze.

Anna shaded her eyes. A futile gesture. Full bore of the sodium lights had induced terminal night blindness. Anxious to get out of the spotlight, she leapt for the grass.

"Easy now, buddy. You take it easy. Don't want you strainin' nothing. Including my patience. You probably just got yourself lost."

The voice was not peremptory but oddly gentling, the way people talked to growling dogs and lunatics. Off the grid, Anna could see the outline of the man who had called to her. Light blue shirt, gold badge: Park Police, supposedly tough guys. Or perhaps more accurately, highly trained professionals taught to distrust. The avuncular tone seemed out of character for addressing a night intruder. Then she remembered the pajamas. She was wearing a pair of flannel PJs given to her by the Cumberland Island fire crew as a joke. They were pale pink and patterned with fat brown bear cubs.

This Park Policeman thought she was a wandering nutcase. And so she was. Anna laughed, realizing as she did that it was not the most reassuring course she could have taken. To her embarrassment, she couldn't stop. The disco pose, the pajamas and three days of too much stress and too little sleep had rendered her borderline hysterical. "It's okay," she managed.

"Sure it is, buddy, sure it is. Everything's gonna be okay. Take your hands out of your pockets now and come on down here where I can see you."

Mustering a semblance of self-control, Anna held her hands out where the policeman could see she was unarmed, and walked slowly down the grassy slope. "My name's Anna Pigeon," she said. "I'm staying with Patsy Silva." She could see him now. He moved his hand away from the butt of his pistol and his face relaxed.

"That's right. I remember a lady was visiting Pats. In that jacket with the short hair, I thought you was a guy." Respectfully, he refrained from mentioning the pajamas.

"You get a lot of weirdos out here?" Anna asked.

"Not a lot. Kids sometimes. You can land a little boat anywhere. I shoo 'em off."

Assured he was reassured, Anna stuck her hands back in her pockets and hugged her jacket around her for warmth. "Party boat woke me," she explained.

"They'll do that. You want to see the statue? Cleaning crew's gone. I thought I'd tuck her in for the night. I wouldn't mind the company. I'm Hatch. Well, James Hatchett, but it's always been Hatch."

There was a wistful air to the invitation, and Anna realized how lonely—and deadly dull—the midnight-to-eight-a.m. shift would be. "Hatch," she said. "That would be great. Just one law-enforcement person on?" she asked as she fell into step beside him.

"Just one."

"What if something happens?"

"I guess I dial nine-one-one," he said, and laughed.

No backup: Anna had worked without backup half her career, but here in the city it surprised her.

The entrance to the lady through the pedestal was in keeping with the beauty of the statue. Two bronze doors, decorated with a bas-relief glorifying industry, rose over twenty feet. Hatch pushed them and they glided quietly on metal tracks laid in the granite floor. Inside was another set of doors, more pragmatic in nature. They were of glass with modern locks. Beyond, at the entrance to a one-and-a-half-story room with a mezzanine, white security arches like those used in airports to detect metal stood sentry. Visitors had to walk through them. Security measures had begun appearing in parks and museums all over the country. A sad commentary on the times.

Hatch disappeared momentarily; then the hall was filled with light. When he returned Anna saw him clearly for the first time. He was young—somewhere between twenty-five and thirty-five—big and, she suspected, deceptively soft-looking. Olive skin, close-cropped black hair and an inky mustache suggested an Italian ancestry that clashed with the surname Hatchett. The uniform of the Park Police fit him snugly, as if night duty on Liberty had put a few pounds on what had been a football player's physique. Dark eyes under thick straight brows were his finest feature. Hatch wasn't a smiling man, yet his face was pleasant. He stood with the easy hip-shot stance of a man accustomed to easing his back from the constant weight of a duty belt laden with gun, nightstick, pepper spray, cuffs, extra magazines for the 9mm, flashlight and other items carried by choice, departmental directive or necessity.

"That's the original torch," Hatch said with pride. "Old Charlie keeps her shined up like new. Charlie's been the Keeper of the Flame forever—maybe thirty years. He keeps the torches lookin' good. Says God sent him to do it. I guess that's as good an explanation as any."

Anna walked around Liberty's first light. Polished and glowing by the good offices of God and Charlie, it was displayed in the monument's base. The torch was of stained glass. Irregularly shaped panes in pale gold, white and ocher licked up like flames. In the old days the torch had burned from within. Its light was feebler but perhaps, Anna thought, admiring the delicate craftsmanship, shone with greater warmth.

Hatch took her to the balcony of the torch room, then up again into the bottom of Liberty herself. First dreamed of in 1865, then built with a skeleton of iron, sinews of rivets and beams and a skin of glowing copper, completed in 1886, she was a greater wonder of modern technology than all the cyber-magic of Silicon Valley. Greater because the least mechanical could grasp how it could have been done and yet marvel at the magnitude of the task. The lady could be worshiped in human terms, not gigs and bytes but "How big is it?" and "What does it weigh?"

Skirting of green floated away by the ton, falling in soft folds off massive girders. Leaning back, Anna let her eyes follow the graceful infrastructure upward. An elevator for those who couldn't walk the 354 steps carried visitors to what was called 5-P—the fifth floor within the pedestal. The elevator was an afterthought, the technology born later than Lady Liberty. Piggybacked into the space next to the main elevator, accessible only by squeezing in between the main elevator and the iron girders, was a small emergency elevator pod. The pod was later still and looked it: ovoid and sleek and mostly of glass. It was a tool for law enforcement and emergency medical personnel, Hatch explained as he gallantly gestured her in first, then mashed in next to her. She in her pajamas and he in his gun, they stood close as lovers as the elevator, belying its high-tech exterior, vibrated and jolted upward. Anna was put in mind of the orgasmatron in Woody Allen's *Sleeper* and had to work at not laughing lest she be forced to explain herself.

"S-eight. See, the S is for Statue, the 8 means eight stories up," Hatch said as the elevator jerked to a stop. "From here on we're on foot."

Stepping around an I beam running slantwise across the elevator's exit, Anna eased out. From this height she could see to the lady's neck. Tightly coiled spiral stairs of iron squirreled into the gloom.

"Step aerobics," Hatch said, and started up.

In the higher reaches of the statue, girders closed in, forming partial floors and shadowed recesses joined by gridded catwalks. Anna had been to the crown once before, years back, when she'd lived in New York with her husband. Then it had been packed with people. And hot. Mostly she remembered feeling faint and claustrophobic. The journey up had taken over two hours. Tonight, running after Hatch, the climb took minutes.

Breathing hard, they stood before the row of small windows, the jewels in the crown. The room was ten feet wide and seven feet high. The windows, eye level for the five-foot-four-inch Anna, looked out over a piece of Brooklyn to the Verrazano Narrows Bridge at the mouth of the harbor. Behind Anna and Hatch, in the lady's head about where doctors say the personality is located in the human brain, were three spotlights powerful enough to push their rays out from the crown.

They lit up the room till every detail was harsh and clear. It was all of metal and spotlessly clean.

21

"Gum," Hatch said when Anna commented on it. "The cleaning crews come every night and scrape off gobs of gum. Graffiti's big too. Kids and not-mature adults get bored standing so long on the stairs and they gotta scribble or scratch on something. Lot of wear and tear, you gotta figure. In summer from ten in the morning till four there'll be twelve to fifteen visitors in this room all the time."

Fifteen. The space felt just comfortable for Anna and three quarters of the beefy policeman.

The appropriate remarks on the view, the structure and the heat of the lights having been made, they started down. Hatch pointed out the ladder leading to the torch. Access was locked; the torch was Charlie's exclusive domain. Visitors had not been allowed up for over fifty years.

At the top of the pedestal, just below Lady Liberty's feet, where the elevator stopped and visitors pooled, Anna and Hatch went out one of two double doors onto a stone balcony sixty feet above the island. The view back toward Manhattan was spectacular, and hidden as they were in the lee of the statue's skirts out of the wind, they were comparatively warm.

The balcony was protected by a parapet with shallow crenels, like the tower of a medieval castle. Hatch swung his legs through a gap and sat down, feet dangling over space. "The smoking lounge," he told Anna as she came up to lean on the wall beside him. From the breast pocket of his shirt, he removed a foil packet, the kind in which Anna used to carry joints during her misspent youth.

His blunt fingers were surprisingly dexterous, and as he uncurled the edges, Anna couldn't believe he'd be stupid enough to smoke marijuana on duty in front of a stranger.

She was right.

"My cigarette," he said, holding the forlorn crushed object up for inspection. "I used to smoke two packs a day. For the last five years I been down to a pack a month. This is my spot. One a day after I put the lady to bed. Don't smoke at all on my weekends." He looked to see if Anna was laughing at him. She wasn't. She knew the value of ritual in ordering the mind and lending meaning to lost souls. "Gauloises," he told her, indicating the cigarette. "They're French. Kevin gets 'em for me in the city. It's kind of a tribute, see. The lady came from France, and in Paris, they got a little bitty statue just like this one to welcome us when we go over there. That's really something, isn't it? These two ladies facing each other over the ocean welcoming strangers back and forth. I'm going to Paris someday just to see her sister." Hatch lit up, took a drag. Anna stared across the water at the endlessly fascinating hive of humanity that was New York City. To her, the tobacco smelled like smoldering manure, albeit fresh manure, but Hatch seemed to be enjoying it.

She kept him company till he'd smoked it down to where he was about to burn his fin-

23

gers, then watched as he took a tin the size gourmet hard candies come in from his shirt pocket and opened it. Inside was fine, white sand. "Pinched from the Waldorf-Astoria. Peacock Room, no less. First-class all the way, that's me." Hatch smothered the butt in the sand, capped the tin and put it back in his pocket.

"There go your pals." He nodded in the direction of the harbor between Liberty and Ellis Islands. The party boat was motoring away, trailing sound after it like a bad smell. "Maybe you ought to put those pajamas to work," he said, and Anna laughed. "Somebody oughta be getting some shut-eye."

"You're on till eight in the morning?" Anna asked as he locked up behind them.

"Usually. Today I've got a double shift. I'll be on till five tomorrow."

Anna groaned her sympathy and took her pajamas back to bed.

Anna was persona non grata in the ICU till noon. During the morning hours doctors would be doing things to her sister; things she had to accept on faith as benevolent or make herself crazy. Columbia-Presbyterian Medical Center was one of the best in the world, Dr. Madison one of the finest heart and lung specialists in the hospital. There she must enter into a realm where she was not particularly comfortable, that of trust.

After the nocturnal ramblings with James

24

Hatchett, she thought she would be able to sleep in, but a cloudless peach dawn had found her sitting at Patsy's dining table watching ferries drag sleepy Staten Islanders to jobs on Wall Street and beyond. Unable to remain within the house walls, she had emerged onto Liberty proper around ten a.m. Since ten-thirty she'd been pacing on the top of the old fort, watching the dock for the *Liberty IV*. Each new Circle Line ferry, bristling with tourists, full to capacity with maybe a thousand people, amazed her. Towns all over the world must stand empty so that Liberty Island might be populated from Memorial Day to Labor Day. There was nothing to "see" at the monument, nothing that in the years since Lady Liberty's completion and the first boatload of tourists hadn't been done better and more efficiently by Walt Disney. Habit and the memory of a dream Americans no longer had was keeping them coming.

But the lady was real. Even these dull-eyed, camera-wielding masses seemed to sense it. Why else would they stand three and four hours in line, inching step by step up the spiral staircase, a double helix of DNA moving along Liberty's spine, for a meager peek at the harbor through the stingy glass jewels in her crown?

Only the day before, much of which Anna had spent on her deteriorating fourth-floor balcony, Patsy had been squiring around a professor from Vermont who made studying overcrowding in America's National Parks part of his life's work; whether it's better to let a lesser number of visitors have a quality experience, or to continue in the democratic practice of letting everyone be disappointed equally. And too, how much love can a limited resource—even one made by talented and industrious Frenchmen—stand?

"Christ," Anna whispered. Perhaps it was lack of sleep that was poisoning her outlook. No; it was the crowds. Hadn't rats, packed too many to a cage, begun to devour one another and commit other antisocial acts? As the herd of tourists pushed by, portions of them or their swinging baggage jostling portions of her anatomy, Anna felt her teeth growing sharper and the urge to bite forming deep within her ratty little soul.

Challenging herself to have at least one unjaundiced thought before lunch, she turned her back on the next wave of humanity and stared over the water toward the Verrazano Narrows Bridge. The rain was gone. Sun lay on the world like a blessing. Sparkling blue, the harbor belied all rumors of pollution. Sailboats took the place of butterflies, buildings in Brooklyn and Staten Island the place of cliffs and forests, the graceful line of the bridge that of distant mountains. Grudgingly, Anna admitted it was a glorious sight, stunning and not without magic.

A sharper sound cut through the low-grade fever of noise. It moved out through the crowd like ripples on a pond, a sound every law enforcement officer becomes attuned to.

Like a shepherdess listening to her flock and knowing a predator is among them, Anna knew that something alien, hostile, disturbed the visitors. Without making a conscious decision, she ran toward the epicenter of the noise.

Dodging somnambulant tourists, she scattered "Excuse me's" and "Pardons" liberally as she ran across the pedestal. On the Manhattan side of the monument's base the crowd had separated out: a ring of those not understanding, not wishing to get involved, then a space, then a denser ring of well-wishers and ghouls packed together.

"Step back. Back, please. Give them room." Anna recited the official litany as she squeezed through to the inner ring.

Crumpled on the granite was a boy no more than ten years old, from what Anna could see of his face. His little body was sprawled in the awkward way of violent death. Mechanically, she felt for a carotid pulse. CPR didn't even cross her mind. The kid was wearing a tractor cap, slightly too large and pulled down till it bent the tips of his ears outward. Still, she could see his head had split, burst on impact. The crown of the cap was crushed flat to the eyebrows as if he'd landed squarely on his head. Blood, a single clean-looking fragment of skull bone, and gray matter had been forced out the left temple.

"He jumped," said a scrawny young man in huge denim shorts and a T-shirt that read, "Been There, Wrecked That."

"Naw, man, he was pushed." This from a disembodied adolescent voice behind the first speaker. "That cop shoved him off. I was looking when he did it."

Anna looked up. Twenty yards above them, framed in the gray stone of a shallow crenel, was James Hatchett.

3

"Step back. Back, please. Give us room." Anna looked up to see the gray and green of the monument's emergency medical technicians bearing down on her. Out of uniform, out of her own park, her EMT skills redundant, she melted into the crowd. As the medical technicians closed around the child's corpse, she glanced at the parapet sixty feet above. Hatch was gone. Curiosity egging her on, it crossed her mind to seek him out, pepper him with questions, but given the circumstances, one evening's acquaintance was not enough to presume upon. For a while—an afternoon, a week, a month, depending on what had actually happened—Hatch would be subjected to interrogation by all and sundry.

Turning her back on the hubbub, she walked toward the dock. Around her, tourists speculated in half a dozen languages as to what had occurred. A perspiring woman with a toddler in one hand and a hot dog in the other stopped Anna and asked.

"I think a water main broke," Anna told her, and moved on.

Despite the graphic and gory vision she'd been witness to, she was oddly unmoved. Training warned her of post-traumatic stress with its potpourri of delayed reaction miseries, but she doubted that was the case. Over time one did become desensitized. The child's face, the blood and brains on the stone, would be filed away with other like horrors and probably never referred to again unless a similar incident brought them to mind.

Aware of the innate selfishness of the human heart, she realized that the heaviness she was experiencing—a depression that felt more like physical exhaustion than mental disorder—was because the accident had brought death too vividly to the fore: Molly's death, Anna's young husband Zach's death, her own death. With that thought came an unsettling sense of life's being meaningless, either too short or too long.

To her relief, the *Liberty IV* was motoring up to the quay. She began to run the last fifty feet, an uncomfortable reprise of fleeing Manhattan the day before. Lest she look as haunted as she felt, she forced herself to slow to a walk.

Liberty IV was a trim little ferry with a high snug bridge above a passenger cabin, a square box with padded benches for fifteen or twenty people. A walkway ran between the rail and

29

the cabin from the bow to the flat open area in the stern. There the American flag flew, rain or shine.

Cal Jackson, a black man so skinny his considerable strength seemed to emanate from skeleton rather than muscle, made an unerring toss of the rope, lassoing the thick wooden upright that supported the dock. No one currently working on Ellis or Liberty, the two parts of the National Monument, had ever seen him miss. Cal never boasted. He just never missed. At first Anna had thought him a young man, but on talking with him had revised her opinion. He looked maybe forty, but he talked of having worked on a fishing boat off Long Island in the early fifties and hiring on as a deckhand on a boat that supplied oil rigs off the coast of Texas in the early sixties after he got out of the Navy. He had to be close to retirement age.

Today Dwight Alvers captained the *Liberty IV*. Though sunlight and relative solitude tempted her, Anna climbed the short stairs to the bridge.

"Look what the cat drug in," Dwight said, and moved amiably aside to let her squeeze by. Patsy had gotten her in the habit of riding up on the bridge for the trips from island to island. The captains never seemed to mind the company and the view was good. There were two long-legged stools in front of the instrument panel, a radar screen hanging down in the middle of the window over the bow, a walking space no more than thirty-six inches wide, then a deep, butt-high wooden shelf finishing the small cabin. This shelf, with the captain's log and his lunch box, was Anna's favorite place.

Dwight was thick and red-necked. Anna didn't know if his politics fit, but his neck was the color of old brick. Hair bristled blond from creased, burnt-looking skin. His eyes were deep-set beneath brows bleached white. The nose, decidedly too delicate for the beefy face, sat aloof above a wide mouth. Narrow lips and a frown that showed Dwight's genes more than his disposition gave him a forbidding look. The crew cut and single diamond stud in his left ear didn't help.

Today he'd been unmasked. Events conspired to reveal what lurked in the heart of this man.

The console, the instrument panel—whatever one called the dashboard of a boat—was crowded with stuffed animals. Boneless lions and elephants like the ones that kids called Beanie Babies slouched on the radar screen and peeked from beneath charts. Anna recognized Nola from *The Lion King* and a crustacean in red velveteen that might have been from *The Little Mermaid*. Bears were well represented, as were dinosaurs. The keeper of this menagerie was the frail, intellectual-looking child of eight or nine who had been hidden behind Dwight's considerable self.

"What's all the excitement on Liberty?" Dwight asked. "The radio's been jammed with emergency chatter."

Anna looked at the man's son. "Jumper,"

she said, and left it at that. Dwight whistled long and low; then he too shelved the subject till little pitchers took their big ears elsewhere.

"My son, Dwight junior," the captain said proudly. Anna and the little boy murmured "Howdoyoudo" in unison. "We call him Digby," Dwight said.

"That's so people can tell us apart," Digby volunteered.

"Two peas in a pod, right, son?"

"Two peas."

Cal cast off and Dwight turned his attention to conning the *Liberty IV* away from the dock and clear of the dredging barge that toiled most hours of every day keeping the boat channel from silting in. Various creatures, animated by Digby, assisted in the process. A turquoise burro rode the top of the wheel, and a grape-colored, forked-tongued beast that more closely resembled a slug than a snake insinuated itself into the crook of Dwight's elbow.

"How come you're not in school?" Anna asked, and was startled at how like her maternal grandmother she sounded.

At the querulous tone, Digby looked injured. "It's summer," he said.

"Monday, Wednesday, Friday Dig usually has piano, but his teacher's sister's having her baby today. C-section. So Dig's come to work with me. Dig's a musician. A regular Liberace."

Digby rolled his eyes and Anna laughed. "Harry Connick Junior?" she offered.

"Maybe..." Clearly Digby didn't want to be pigeonholed this early in his career.

As Manhattan, already formidable, grew to fill the windscreen, Anna watched Digby's zoo wander across Dwight's bridge and felt better than she had since she'd arrived in New York the previous Thursday.

The boat became part of the balletic weave of ships in the harbor. Out the starboard side of the cabin, Anna could see the statue. A helicopter chopped the air over the plaza. No doubt retrieving the dead child. Ahead was the distinctive geometric shape of Ellis Island.

"I was one of the last immigrants through there, did you know that?" Dwight said.

Anna didn't know whether to believe him or not. He liked to string her along to see how long it would take her to get a joke. The past few days it had been quite a while. Not feeling mentally acute, she just nodded.

"No kidding. I was a little shaver, not more than four years old. I came over from Czechoslovakia with my mom. She was an old widow lady of twenty-two. That was in 1951. We were just about the last folks through."

"I was born here," Digby said proudly. "Right there." Using the tail of an armadillo as a pointer, he indicated most of Brooklyn.

In need of harmless conversation, Anna asked: "Do you remember any of it?"

Dwight shook his head. "Not much. But when I started working here, it was like that baseball guy said, déjà vu all over again. I'd remember stuff I'd never thought of before.

Just little scenes and things. Mom remembers, though. She had to stay out there close to a week. Some kind of paperwork snafu. My grandmother, or the lady that would be my grandmother soon as her son and my mom got married, came out and got me, so I was only there maybe overnight.

"They must have known they were closing up shop soon. The people Mom spent her time with were these old geezers who'd worked Ellis since day one—"

"That'd be fifty-nine years, Daddy. They'd be too old," Digby said.

"Hey, tell it to your gramma. This is her story."

"You tell Gramma," Digby said in a tiny voice only he, Anna and a brown plush turtle heard. Anna gathered that Gramma was a formidable woman.

"Ma came home from that week on Ellis with enough stories to last a lifetime. People born, people hanging 'emselves rather than be sent back to the old country, ghosts and royalty, a lady in the loony bin found dead wearing nothing but her knickers, operas, ball games, this shock treatment machine they rolled from ward to ward, guys falling in love with gals who didn't speak a word of their language, folks with money stuffed in their shoes. Good stuff. There's tapes from lots of immigrants in the library. They got Ma to make one.

"Never make it, Cal," he hollered out the window as the deckhand tossed the rope expertly over a piling. "Cal missed his calling,"

Dwight said as he cut power and let the *Liberty IV* drift gently dockside at the Marine Inspection Office in Manhattan. "He should have been a bronc roper."

For Anna's money, the boat trip had been too short. The hospital, the ICU, Molly on tubes and drugs, exercised an uncomfortable polarization. Anna could not bear to be away and couldn't stand being there. Once in either place—at Molly's side or tucked in the city exclosure of Ellis or Liberty—she was okay. In transit, both ends of the journey attracted and repulsed her simultaneously. Time went out of whack, either passing with mind-bending rapidity or creeping by so slowly she could hear her bones shrinking with the onset of old age.

True to expected perversity, the subway ride to the Upper West Side ate up several years of her life. At twelve-thirty she was eating pizza at a stand-up table in a sidewalk restaurant on 168th Street. At twelve forty-five she presented herself in the intensive care unit on the fifth floor.

"Please wait. The doctor will be right with you." This was pronounced in indifferent tones by a distracted woman in white. It was said after she'd looked at a clipboard. That meant something; it meant she didn't say the same thing to everybody, that there was some special reason Anna had to wait, a reason articulated on that board.

The two slices of pizza congealed in Anna's stomach and sent a geyser of what felt like quick-drying cement up her esophagus. In the eternity, she continued to stand before the counter trying to say, "Is there a problem?" The opaque pebbled glass of the sliding window closed.

For a moment she hesitated, wondering whether to tap on the glass, but in the end she was too afraid of what she might hear. Knowing herself for a craven, she retreated across the waiting room to a blue plastic armchair flanked by angular wood-look tables covered with magazines. A woman in her early forties sat on a sofa of the same blue leatherette along the opposite wall. She was heavyset, with big hips and thighs. Her face was overly made up but open, with an eager friendly expression. The woman wanted to talk. Anna hid behind a magazine, raising the top edge till it screened not only her eyes but the whole of her face. Without being aware of it, she tucked her elbows close to her body as if she could protect all of her person with the glossy pages.

In the next twenty minutes half a dozen people came and went. Each time, Anna jerked her head up and watched with the frightened expectant eyes that must come to haunt the sleep of medical professionals. Never was it for her. Thirty-seven minutes had creaked by before Dr. Madison finally came into the room.

Anna didn't move. She couldn't. *Don't sit, Doc,* she thought. *Sitting is bad.* Good news was delivered standing, shouted from the door: "It's a girl!" "He's alive!" Bad news called for chairs and exaggerated eye contact.

Madison stepped across the small area, smoothed his lab coat over his behind, sat in the chair next to Anna's and crossed his legs, plucking the seam of his trousers straight. Anna didn't utter a sound. She thought of Shakespeare, of his writing that someone's tongue clove to the roof of his mouth, and that this, then, was what he had been talking about.

"Molly's about the same as yesterday," Dr. Madison said.

Anna eyed him coldly. "For that you had to sit down?"

"My feet hurt," he defended himself.

"Wear sneakers." To her surprise, he laughed. It wasn't so much pleasant as infectious, high-pitched—almost girlish—but utterly unself-conscious. Anna liked him better for it.

"Sorry," he said, and pulling off his bifocals, he scrubbed his eyes on the sleeve of his lab coat. "I get it. I sat. Scared you. I'm so sorry." He was still chuckling. It was beginning to lose its charm.

"I've been sorry since your dye fucked up my sister's kidneys."

Madison looked as if he'd been slapped. Before the words had passed her front teeth, Anna regretted them. Out of a primitive need to do battle she might have stood by her statement. Two things stopped her: The doctor looked more hurt than angry, and in this imperfect world, her bad manners might be taken out on her sister.

37

"Sorry." The word was hollow, feeble. "Really sorry." Somewhat better but still lame. "Abjectly, grovelingly, idiotically sorry. I would abase myself, throw myself at your feet, pluck out the offending member, but I'm afraid it would embarrass us both. I'm..." Her mind shut down with sudden fatigue. "Sorry," she finished.

Several seconds ticked by while Dr. Madison looked at her, disdain or concern rumpling his high forehead, creasing the skin to a hairline that had retreated four inches since he was a young man. "That," he said finally, "was the finest apology I've ever received. The groveling, the abasing, the plucking—it was positively eighteenth-century in its humility. Drawn from the days when humility and gratitude were considered good things. I accept. I would, however, enjoy a little groveling when Molly's better. I think a laugh would do her a world of good."

"It's a promise," Anna said.

Dr. Madison put his bifocals back on and brought his watery, slightly protuberant blue eyes into focus. "Molly is not improving. Yesterday afternoon we tried taking her off the respirator. Her lungs didn't fail completely, but she was only taking five or six breaths a minute. Barely enough to sustain life. Not enough to recover from major surgery. We had to put her back on. She's been fighting it and she's pulled out her feeding tube twice. I'm telling you this because we've had to sedate her and we've strapped her wrists to the bed.

It looks a whole lot worse than it is. Much of these tube-pulling actions are sub- or semi-conscious, like swatting a fly in your sleep. But I wanted you to be prepared."

"I'm prepared." Anna stood.

Madison blinked up at her with his mild blue stare till she sat down again.

"Sorry, Dr. Madison." Anna gave him the short version.

"David."

"Good name. David and Goliath. Davy Crockett. Go ahead." Anna knew she babbled, but felt the need to make human noises and couldn't manage to fix her mind as to content.

"I think it's not only wrong but dangerous to assume Molly can't hear or understand you. She's very ill, desperately ill. She has the body of a woman of seventy."

"The wages of sin," Anna said.

"All too common among my fellow physicians," Madison said. "Often, after a major illness like the one your sister is going through, particularly in cases where the patient is physically helpless—where she is hooked up to life support machines and so forth—and mentally helpless in the sense that she's in and out of consciousness, unable to speak, possibly unclear as to what she hears and sees and what she only dreams—in cases like this the patient can feel overwhelmed, lost, as if they've failed somehow. It's not unusual for them to give up."

"And?"

"They die," Madison said simply.

"Not Molly."

"Ah. That's it. That's where you come in. Not Molly. You need to talk to her, keep her interested in living. Don't let her forget she has to come back, wants to come back."

"I'll stay here. I'll talk around the clock."

Again the merry girlish laugh. "Molly hasn't a chance. You'll probably drag her into her nineties. Round the clock won't be necessary. Your sister has to rest. To mend. Three to five hours a day will suffice. And closer to three for a while." He squeezed Anna's hand reassuringly.

Resenting it, she curled her fingers around the chair arm, the closest thing to forming a fist she would allow herself.

"Do you want to see your sister now?"

"Is that a rhetorical question?"

Dr. Madison—David—appeared to give up. The kindly bedside manner disappeared and weariness—or professional distance—took its place. With an effort he levered himself out of the chair. The chairs were too low for a man of his stature. He was six foot five or six, stooped, no doubt from having banged his head on numerous objects in his youth, lanky, myopic and bald. Quite like some sort of benevolent insect, Anna thought, a walking stick or a praying mantis.

She followed him through the door. Away from the pseudo homeyness of the waiting area was the high-tech bustle of the ICU. In his wake, she drifted down a hall of windows and flashed on the long brick walkway on Ellis. Through

40

these windows was not the dripping green of Mother Nature in a frenzy of vengeance, ripping back her world, but pathetic and heroic pictures of frail broken human beings battling death with their little machines. In the third cubicle on the left was Anna's only sister.

David Madison left her at the door.

A straight-backed chair with red plastic cushions, the kind Anna had seen in a hundred roadside cafés in the West, sat beside the bed. Looking shrunken and old amid the tubes lay her sister, arms pinioned to her sides by soft white-fabric restraints.

Anna sat down. She'd boasted she could talk the clock around. Now she wondered what she should say.

4

It's me, Anna." She began as she had begun hundreds of phone calls over the years. For the first time in her life there was no response. Molly lay as one dead. Not dead, missing. Her humanity, her soul some might call it, was hidden from mortal eyes. The hospital had made her but a component part of their system, a flesh-and-bone cog in the machinery, the cheapest, weakest, most easily replaced link in the chain of medical technology. A translucent tube taped in her mouth forced her lungs to rise and fall precisely the same distance exactly twelve times a minute. No room for sighs or sobs or laughter. Another—the feeding tube, Anna guessed—hung from an intravenous fluid sack on a metal pole, the end needling into Molly's inner elbow and secured with surgical tape. A catheter for urine snaked out from between sheets untroubled by human wrigglings. Palms up, Molly's hands lay pinioned at her sides. Visions of the Virgin Mary flickered behind Anna's eyes. Serene in blue plaster robes, she watched countless students pass through the halls at Mercy High School in Red Bluff, California.

Delighting in her irreverence, Anna had called the statue Our Lady of the Lobotomy. The pose, the dearth of inner life, was echoed now on her sister's face, as was the grainy pallor of plaster. Only Molly's hair remained untamed by intensive care. Deep russet, once strawberry blond but coarsened now by age and the incursion of rebellious wiry silver hairs, a tangle of curls ran riot over the pillow. She wore it longer than Anna remembered. Combed, it would reach her jawbone.

Anna wanted to touch it but didn't. She wanted to touch the imprisoned hand but didn't. She wanted to speak but couldn't. Words formed in her mind much as thunderheads form on a summer afternoon. One would float in, others cluster around, mass and weight would build. Before a storm of conversation could ensue, they dissipated into mist. Molly was too sick to tell her troubles to,

42

too frail to be cried over. So many of their exchanges over the years had been about Anna: Anna's love life, her work, her fears, her feelings. It hurt to realize that though Molly knew every kink of her psyche, Anna knew very little about *her*. Molly's opinions she knew on everything from thong panties to Israeli politics, but of Molly herself, very little. When their conversations weren't centered on the health and well-being of little Anna Pigeon, they'd been a rapid-fire exchange of ideas, metaphors and jokes. It wasn't a one-woman show; without her partner giving her cues, Anna couldn't remember her lines.

Digging deep in a well dry as dust, Anna dredged up topics. She told Molly of her flight out from Colorado. She told her of Hatch and the statue at night. It was on the tip of her tongue to tell her of the child crushed against the pavement, but Molly had blamed herself for a patient's suicide several years before and Anna stopped herself lest she send Molly farther in the direction of darkness. She talked of Patsy and Kevin, Digby and Dwight, of the pizza she'd eaten for lunch and not yet digested. Even to her own ears she sounded like a parody of the boring party guest. When she finally droned to a halt, the clock above the bed had chipped away only seventeen minutes from the hour. For three more Anna sat without speaking, her mind an empty place surrounded by shadows.

"I guess I'll go check out your apartment," she said at last. "Water the plants or whatever.

I haven't had a chance to get up there yet. Can I bring you anything?"

Twelve lifeless breaths hissed by.

"Cigarettes? Scotch?"

And twelve more.

"I won't be gone more than an hour or so." Anna backed out of the room, half believing at any moment Molly would sit up, call to her, be alive.

Molly's apartment was on Ninety-third Street between West End Avenue and Broadway, apartment 14D. Built before the war, it was a forbidding gray box punctured with symmetrical windows. The key would be with the doorman. This had been arranged before Molly went in for bypass surgery, before Anna flew out from Mesa Verde. Anna was to have stayed there. From the airport she'd gone to the hospital and from the hospital to the narrow rolling cot in Patsy's spare room on Liberty. With her sister lying in the ICU, her lungs unwilling to take in enough air to sustain life, Anna couldn't bear to be incarcerated in a box surrounded by hundreds of thousands of like boxes. The thought made her own lungs begin to shut down. She'd wear out her welcome with Patsy before she'd spend a night in the city.

At 125th Street she got off the subway, then walked the last thirty blocks between the hospital and Molly's building. Killing time, lulling her mind as she often did with the lifting and laying down of her feet. Block passed like block, a spatter of shops in tawdry hues, odors that would transport a discerning nose from the slums of Somalia to the Champs Élysées. Noise was constant, mingling, blurring till it became as white noise: meaningless.

The doorman, dressed even on a warm summer day in the maroon and gold livery that enhanced doormen all over the city, was polite and helpful. A key was pressed into Anna's hand and she was pointed into the opulent gloom of the late 1920s. There, flanked by mirrors in bronze and wood black with polish and age, Anna took an elevator to the fourteenth floor.

Leaving the hospital, she'd had no plan but the feeble one she offered Molly: to water the plants. By the time she turned the key and heard the dead bolt slide free, she'd devised one slightly less tinged with self-interest. She would search through Molly's things. Not snooping precisely—diaries and personal letters she would leave alone lest she uncover her sister's secrets or, even less appealing, inadvertently stumble across some criticism of herself. Digging, then, gently, the way an archaeologist would dig uncovering a lost civilization, Anna would find the things that tied Molly most firmly to the surface of the planet. These she would take with her to the hospital and talk of them till Molly came to join her. Or to tell her to leave her stuff alone.

Anna laid the key on a table designed nose. Because it was the city, she aranoia and threw the bolt and

45

engaged the chain lock. She'd not been to Molly's apartment often, once every few years, maybe three times in all. With both money and good taste, Molly had created a home for body and spirit. By West Coast standards the apartment was spacious. By New York standards it was palatial. A wide entry hall led to a dining room made airy by an enormous wall mirror and interesting by an intricate Persian rug in cobalt, red and ocher. A large window with a deep uncushioned seat and pale gold diaphanous curtains suggested a grand vista. Architecture suggested an air shaft.

The hall, like all of the apartment but kitchen and baths, was floored in oak finished to a deep honey glow. It opened into a living room with two windows overlooking a building across Broadway six lanes and two sidewalks away. Molly had mixed Art Deco and Far Eastern design elements with the twenties hardwood and plasterboard. The effect was stimulatingly exotic and at the same time homey, with a color scheme Anna would not have tried to duplicate on her most fashionable days. A wine couch, long and low, in leather so soft it felt and looked like old velvet, was angled beneath the windows. It was the original piece around which everything el had been fit. Molly had bought it for office with what then had amounte month's pay. Clients had a tenden asleep in its feathery embrace. Th undoubtedly been relaxing for the she'd begun to develop a complex and had traded it in for the sterner version that now graced her clinic.

Everything was tidy, neat. A cleaning lady of course; Tuesday and Friday mornings, Anna remembered. No dust, no litter of magazines, not even the smell of stale cigarette smoke. Knickknacks were few and told a lot about Molly's sense of style and travels but little else.

A stealthy sound slipped from the hallway and stopped Anna on the edge of a thick Persian carpet. *Cat,* she thought, but Molly didn't own a cat. Her excuse was that she traveled too much, but lots of cat owners traveled, none more than Anna. This trip, Mesa Verde's new dispatcher, a fey and charming young man fresh from the IRS, had agreed to take on her family obligations: Piedmont—her orange tiger cat—and a dog named Taco, whom she'd inherited. Taco was a golden retriever. A good enough dog, but a dog for all that. Thinking of him, Anna felt an unpleasant twinge. All dogs were Catholic at heart. It was in their eyes, liquid brown accusation. Taco had watched her pack her suitcase as if she were digging a doggie-sized grave.

Not yet alarmed, Anna listened. This was New York. A cat was not necessary for the promulgation of sneaky noises. There were rats for that, mice and large aggressive cockroaches.

The creak of a floorboard brought the frisson of fear to her vertebrae. Even Manhattan

47

had yet to breed rodent or roach sizable enough to make the timbers groan. Someone was in Molly's apartment, either in the study or in the bedroom. It not being Tuesday or Friday, it wasn't the cleaning lady.

Anna drifted noiselessly back toward the front door. With her sister missing in action, there was nothing in the apartment she was willing to wrestle with some idiot drug addict to preserve. This was an excellent time to practice one of the earliest American battle strategies: run away and live to fight another day.

Keeping her eyes on the hallway, she backed as far as the entrance to the foyer. Footsteps, definite and purposeful, came from the direction of the bedroom. The intruder was coming out. Anna turned and fled to the front door. Chain lock and bolt secured, it would take precious seconds to unlock—seconds she didn't have. Ducking into the dining room, she pressed herself against the wall. The footfalls came across the hardwood, then, striking the runner, were muffled. The chain was released with a characteristic clatter. Then there was nothing; the intruder was remembering he had not chained the door behind him when he came in. As she crushed herself tightly against the wall, Anna's shoulder brushed a picture frame. In the tense silence of a supposedly deserted apartment, the screech of wood on plaster hit her eardrum like a stifled scream.

The intruder heard it as well. He would have had to. His shoes made tiny sounds as

48

he shifted on the carpet. The shush of something, probably whatever he'd come to steal, brushed against his trouser leg. He was turning.

Quick as the thought, Anna snatched a pewter candlestick off the polished surface of the credenza, spun through the arch and, before he could face her, jammed the end of the candlestick against the base of his spine.

"Don't move. Don't move. Don't."

He was Caucasian, tall, badly dressed and in need of a haircut. All this Anna took in in the two seconds it took him to absorb the unexpected turn of events. In his left hand was an old leather briefcase, badly battered. Anna had bought it for Molly when she graduated from medical school. At the time, it had represented two weeks' salary. Seeing it in a stranger's hand while her sister lay in intensive care brought on a rage so sudden and white-hot Anna forgot she held the thief at bay with only a chunk of pewter.

"I would very much like to shoot you," she said, and her voice was devoid of any humanity. "Think twice before you give me an excuse."

"Anna?"

For a moment the word held no meaning. When she realized the thief had spoken her name, still she said nothing. Rage had welded shut her brain and jaws.

"Is that you, Anna? It's illegal to carry a gun in New York. Didn't Molly tell you that?"

The glare receded. Anna's brain was returned to her management. Familiar names, the

49

familiar voice, banished fear but not the adrenaline high. She took the candlestick from the man's back.

"What are you packing these days? That felt like the bore of an elephant gun," the intruder said as he turned. Then he saw the candlestick and laughed. "You made me a believer. I'll send you the laundry bill."

"Frederick," Anna said stiffly. Frederick Stanton was an FBI agent, an ex-boyfriend; ex because he'd fallen for Anna's sister when he came to New York to help her with a stalker two years before. Came at Anna's request. Shock, relief—some strong emotion Anna couldn't identify—wiped her mind clear. She remembered the rudiments of the English language, but just barely.

"You wonder what I'm doing here," Frederick said helpfully.

"I do." Anna put the candlestick down carefully, as if unsure of her own strength.

"I got some of Molly's things." Frederick held up the satchel. "Music, pictures, things that might help—you know."

"I know," Anna said. Suddenly her legs were shaking too much to allow her to remain standing. She lowered herself into one of the cherry dining chairs and let her breath out slowly. "You and Molly have been in contact, then?" The words shamed her twice: once that she could be so weak as to feel petty betrayal when her sister was so ill, and twice that she could be so weak as to let Frederick see it.

Stanton didn't sit down. All elbows and knees like an awkward schoolboy, he stood in the archway, the briefcase clutched in both hands. He'd aged since Anna had seen him last. Features always comically too large for his face loomed even larger now that some of the flesh had melted away. Stick-straight thick hair still fell over his forehead like black straw, but now threads of silver showed. "Molly's not been in contact with me," he said. "I haven't called...I haven't talked to her. I don't even know if she knows I'm here. I went to the hospital this morning and they let me see her. Maybe she woke up once, but she didn't nod or anything."

The pain in his voice, and the knowledge that Molly had been true to her, picked up Anna's spirits considerably. "Sit down," she said, more sharply than she intended. "You're making me nervous."

Obediently, Frederick sat. Bony knees, bare and hairy, poked out from madras shorts worn too long. Sandals and socks finished the costume. Anna knew him too well to write it off as simple bad taste. Frederick enjoyed being underestimated, traded on it. "How did you get in?" she asked, just to have something to say.

Frederick looked sheepish. Another highly effective technique he'd mastered.

"You flashed your badge," Anna said flatly. "You are unethical scum, you know that, don't you?"

"Unethical scum," he agreed.

51

Suspicion returned to blight Anna's heart. "If you weren't in contact with Molly, how did you know she was sick?"

"NYPD," Frederick said. "After the threatening-letter stuff, I had a friend sort of keep tabs on her. Make sure she was okay."

"You had my sister under police surveillance for two years?"

"Part of the service, ma'am." When Anna didn't smile, he defended himself. "Not so fancy. Not official. Emmett would just call her office every couple of months, chat up the doorman now and then. It was the doorman who told him she'd been sick. I had annual leave built up. I'm vacationing in New York on Emmett's living room sofa."

Anna let his words sink in. Two years was a long time to sustain a crush.

"What have you got in the bag?" she asked abruptly.

"Boy, I'd sure like your take on this," he said as he opened the briefcase and began fishing things out. "I was lost, lemme tellya, *lost.* The woman hasn't got anything. Just rich tasteful stuff that's worthless, if you know what I mean." He babbled as he unpacked, talking as though he and Anna were old friends. In a way, they were.

There were three snapshots, each in its own frame: Anna in college in her shorty nightie, a scarf tied buccaneer style over long hair. Molly on the back of an elephant in Thailand. And a small photo in a frame no more than an inch and a half square of a gray cat.

"Rajah." Anna picked the name out of a catechism of Fluffys, Bootsys and Tippys that had walked through their childhood on little cat feet. Frederick had packed a small boom box, a handful of CDs and a large silk scarf fringed in mossy green.

"I thought we could, well, drape it around the way women do. Color," Frederick said of the scarf. "And this perfume spritzer was on the dresser. She wore it. I can't forget the smell." Apparently remembering the circumstances, he stopped enthusing. "We could maybe sprinkle it on the pillow so she can smell something besides the hospital. Smell's supposed to be a primal kind of conductor." He was looking at Anna, seemingly genuinely in need of her approval. Unsure of how much she trusted him and miffed that he'd stolen her plan, she wasn't generous.

"Can't hurt," she said.

For a minute they sat without talking. Exhausted by the roller-coaster emotions of the day, Anna was content just to be a lump. Frederick's fidgeting brought her out of her trance. "What?" she asked irritably.

"I'd like to get back to the hospital."

"Yeah," Anna said. "I guess." She didn't move till he was up and unchaining the door.

Anna returned the key to the doorman and stepped back into summer in New York. East Coast weather, seemingly more capricious because she was unused to it, had gone from raining and fifty to steaming and eighty-five. Frederick hailed a cab and they rode uptown.

She let him pay the fare and they entered Columbia-Presbyterian together.

The watch on Stanton's wrist let her know she'd managed to kill two hours. *And a painful and ugly death it was,* she thought sourly as she followed the FBI agent into the elevator. Before the doors could close, a woman in a wheelchair was rolled in. She was bent double under a dowager's hump, her hands gnarled with arthritis and grown to the chair's arms like gingerroot. Cottony hair was permed, a froth so thin scalp showed through. She smelled of talcum powder, like an infant. Anna quashed an urge to move away, separate herself from sickness, age and death.

Because she didn't know where else to look, she looked at Frederick. Whistling tunelessly, he was peeking into the leather satchel as though he had a treasure tucked away there. Oddly, that helped. She was able to meet the old woman's eyes, smile at her.

"We brought you stuff," Frederick said cheerfully as the nurse closed them in Molly's cubicle.

"Beware of geeks bearing gifts," Anna said.

"Your own stuff," Frederick told Molly's silent self. "That makes me a thief, but paradoxically trustworthy since they cannot be considered true gifts."

Anna plugged in the CD player and put on the first CD from the pile Frederick had brought. Dark notes, swelling with nostalgia, filled the room. Music that made Anna ache without knowing why, the score to a long sad movie she'd never seen. Picking up the jewel case, she read aloud: " 'Enya, *The Memory of Trees.*' Jesus, Frederick, couldn't you find some Guy Clark, some Etta James, something visceral? Enya would spirit away a beer-drinking good ol' boy." She turned down the transporting strains as Stanton arranged the pictures on a metal table near Molly's head. After he'd finished fussing, he sat in what Anna had come to think of in caps as The Red Chair. He took Molly's hand in his—a comfort Anna had dared not offer. "I'm here for the duration," he told her sister. "Should you wish to get rid of me, all you need do is open your eyes and say three times, 'Get thee behind me, Stanton.' You can dispense with swinging a dead cat around your head in the graveyard at midnight."

A faint scratching arrested their attention: Molly scratching at the sheet with clipped unpolished nails. As they watched, she opened her eyes, a flash of hazel between papery lids.

"Hi," Anna said. "We're here." Again the nails made their mute protest. "What?"

"Undo her hand," Frederick whispered.

Anna hurried to unfetter the hand away from Frederick. Mesmerized, they watched as it lifted. Hope turned to alarm as it strayed toward the feeding tube. As the fingers were closing around the plastic, Anna caught her sister's hand.

"No you don't."

The arm went back into its restraints. There was no resistance, and more alarming, not so much as a flicker of annoyance crossed Molly's face. Her eyes closed again.

"Damn." Tired to the point of weeping, Anna slid to the floor, stretched out legs traumatized from too much concrete and leaned back against the bed. From where she sat she could see Frederick's face, but he didn't seem aware she was watching him. Molly was older than Frederick by five or six years. Lying in the hospital bed, she appeared older still, sixty or seventy. Molly looked bad, frail and worn and colorless.

And Anna could see that to Frederick it didn't matter a damn.

5

New York City was farther north than Anna had pictured it in her mind. This close to solstice, its latitude was manifest in the twilight. Light lingered in the western sky long after sundown. The timelessness of a summer evening was the only taste of immortality most humans ever got, and as Anna cherished the soft golden forever, she wished she could capture it, carry it across the harbor to Molly's windowless world.

Dr. Madison had put Anna and Frederick out of the ICU at ten minutes past four. He'd walked with them as far as the elevator, making reassuring noises regarding Molly's progress. Anna had been grateful for his optimism and the extra attention, and for being rescued from three minutes alone with Frederick. She and Stanton parted ways at the hospital door, he seemingly as glad to be on his own as she.

Anna had grabbed a deli sandwich and caught a boat to Ellis Island. Central Park, the city's one green space of any size, crossed her mind as a possible picnic spot, but the park had always depressed her. Many times, when she lived in Manhattan, Anna had gone there seeking the solace of nature only to be revolted by the mass of humanity swarming over its rocks and meadows. It put her in mind of the wedding feast in *Great Expectations,* a fine and wonderful thing spoiled by crawling vermin. Probably because she was in no particular hurry now, had no appointments to keep, the connections of trains and boats had been perfect. Just after five she was ensconced on the sunset side of Island III with a Coke and her cheese and tomato sandwich. Island III was on the southern shore of Ellis, separated from the Island II buildings by a wide grassy field that had been an outdoor recreation area in the old days, used for baseball, picnics and physical therapy. On this last "island" were housed the morgue, a kitchen, a lab, the infectious disease wards and the living quarters for the nurses and the island's Immigration Commissioner. Laid out in a line, the buildings paralleled those of Islands I and II. The Island III buildings were connected by a long walkway sheltered by walls of glass gridded by rotting mullions. At the entrance to many of the wards and in the nooks and crannies between the buildings had been gardens, places for respite and healing. These ancient gardens had become overgrown; they were as teeth of the jungle devouring the historic structures. Most were dense with greenery and impenetrable by anything more substantial than a chipmunk.

Anna had carried her soda and sandwich out through the old kitchen located halfway down Island III and sat on the crumbling steps of its rear door. Each of the structures had a stoop, much like those in neighboring Brooklyn. Ellis was largely man-made and thus expensive and labor-intensive. Land was not wasted. The concrete steps were mere yards from a stony breakwater that dropped into the harbor. Between the buildings and the sea was a strip of weedy earth. Broken rock, sharp and gray-white, formed a steep, unwelcoming beach. From her stoop, Anna had a wonderful view of Ms. Liberty's backside. The morgue kindly cropped most of the Jersey shore from the picture.

Having finished her supper, she pocketed the refuse and set out to explore the infectious disease wards. At eight-fifteen the last NPS boat would leave Ellis for Liberty. Patsy was staying late to finish up her part of the report on the carrying capacity of the monument; Anna would ride back to Liberty on the last boat with her. Till then she'd declared a holiday. Molly, Frederick, all of that, was shelved in a cupboard deep in the recesses of her mind, to be taken out tomorrow when she again braved the metropolis. The next three hours were hers.

Following the glassed-in passage toward the "front" of Ellis, the easterly shore facing Manhattan, Anna was caught up in the twin mysteries of water and time. Leaves pressed close against the ten thousand windowpanes. In places they forced their way in, tendrils that would, over the years, destroy the world of man. Westerly light, rich burnt umber from sun through the New Jersey smog, shone behind the green blood and bone of the foliage, streaked red-gold through the gaps. The hall, twelve hundred feet long, shimmered like a wormhole through a watery universe. Savoring the surreal nature of reality, Anna walked slowly, stopping every few yards to watch a changing pattern or see pictures in the debris on the floor or the rust and mildew on the window frames.

Offset one to the right, then one to the left, infectious disease wards thrust out perpendicular to the walkway. She peered down darkened corridors, noted squares of dusty light, sensed the heavy presence of stairwells and metal doors. The last three of the seven wards had different floor plans. Glassed-in walkways forked off from the one Anna followed, then divided into a wishbone shape providing a glass hallway that curved to either side of a tiny half-circle of what had once been garden. The prongs of these wishbones let into buildings wider and higher than the previous wards and sufficiently intriguing to lure Anna from the sun-green path.

These structures had suffered more from the elements than those she'd wandered through on Island II. Island III took the brunt of the wind and storms. Windows in the seaward walls were broken and the walls themselves beginning to crumble. She walked with care, avoiding flooring that looked particularly green or soft.

In these decrepit spaces the flotsam of many bureaucracies—Immigration, the Coast Guard, the NPS—was squirreled away. One upstairs ward, once sunny with sash windows from the chair rail to the fifteen-foot ceiling, now as muted and murky as any greenhouse from the encroachment of trees, was chock-full, wall-to-wall with rotting cardboard filing cabinets.

Rooms with screen doors opened into wide, dark inner hallways. Indoor screens struck her as odd till she realized it was the only way to provide internal ventilation and bug control simultaneously.

The last ward, at the end of the glass passage, had been battered from two fronts. On the southeast corner of Ellis, its windows looked out on both Liberty and Manhattan. This, Anna decided, would be where she would have her city abode. Two or three hundred grand and the place could be made livable.

The sun had sunk into the blood-red miasma over the western horizon. Shadows lost their edges and migrated out from closets and corners to cloak the passages and pool in the middle of the rooms.

It was time to get back to the world of the living. Even in the broad light of day these ruins were hazardous, and Anna hadn't thought to bring a flashlight. Prosaic physical danger, real as it was, wasn't the only thing that spurred her to finish her explorations. With coming darkness, the place was beginning to feel creepy. Like any self-respecting ruin, Ellis Island had its ghost stories. The first day Anna had lunched in the employee break room, the actors hired for the summer to portray immigrants filled her in on the paranormal wildlife. At noon she'd been polite but skeptical. Now, close to nightfall, in the confusing, disintegrating maze that was Island III, stories of women in white, strange cries and flickering candles in abandoned attics were no longer amusing. With the willies came a preternatural sense of hearing. Shuffles and whispers, creaks and skritches that had been inaudible when sunlight was streaming in began to take on a sinister orchestration.

"Nerves are shot," Anna said. Her voice startled her and she wished she hadn't spoken aloud, called attention to herself.

Across the harbor the city would be donning its evening dress; she decided she would find her way above stairs, take in the view, then come back down and return to Island I by the outdoor path that ran along the eastern side of the island to the slip where the ferries docked.

Leaving the open area of the ward for the stairs, she realized how much of the day was gone. For a moment she had to wait in near darkness for her eyes to adjust. The stairs were in bad shape. Risers were missing. Plaster, moss and mold covered others so it was impossible to guess at their condition. The rail, but for the upper third, had fallen away from the wall and lay partway down the stairwell. In the black recess beneath the steps, between a rotting upright and a door to another room or closet, was a small storage cache long abandoned like the rest of the islands. A rank smell both sweet and nasty permeated the air. The wise choice was to wait till daylight returned, but then the view would be lost. Taking pains to stay near the wall where the support would be strongest, and never to put all her weight in any one place, Anna eased up the staircase.

Manhattan's lights seen from the high windows of the upstairs ward were worth the climb. The harbor sparkled with its own brand of industrial fireflies and the bridges were strung with necklaces whiter than diamonds and bisected by the ruby and gold of auto running lights. All this against a sky of pale sea green. Enjoying the show, breathing the soft air of a June evening, Anna stayed longer than she had intended.

When she finally turned to go, darkness had crept closer. As had the ghosts. Mocking herself even as she listened for clanking chains and spectral footsteps, she made her way back through the inner twistings of the building, darkened by empty cupboards and closed doors, to where she remembered the stairs being.

Shut away from dusk's ambient light, she felt her way along, trailing her fingers against one wall and straining her eyes for the gleam from a polished drawer handle, any scrap of light to focus on. Flapping, sudden and loud, stopped her heart for an instant. *Pigeon,* she reminded herself. The old hospital was haunted by roosting pigeons.

The head of the stairs brought some small relief. Though the bottom opened into an unlighted hallway, to her night-wide irises the faintest tinge of gray was discernible where the hall angled into the downstairs ward room with its generous windows. Wishing she'd been born with more sense—or more rods on her retina—Anna trod gingerly on the top step, her foot close to the wall, some of her weight suspended on the remnant of handrail. The tread gave slightly, not through structural failure but because a woodland soil of dust and moss had taken root there.

Ghouls and wraiths continued to scuttle to and fro just out of sight. Below her, floors settled and creaked as if the dead walked there. Above, suspicious whispering suggested starched aprons from the turn of the century and long skirts of wool. The skin on the top of her head tightened and she felt the chill that came into her veins when she was truly afraid. *Nerves,* she said again but this time to herself. The situation called for care, not fear. She was overreacting, but it was nothing daylight and open air would not set right. The next step groaned alarmingly but held. *Of course it held*, Anna growled mentally. *You don't weigh any more going down than you did coming up.* Three more stairs and she was out of handrail. Willing herself as weightless as pigeon-down, she took the next step. A shriek: old wood ripping from older metal. Most of her weight was on the lower step, and with a suddenness that took her breath away, it was gone. Gravity would pitch her face-forward. With a spine-wrenching twist, she threw herself back onto the stairs she knew had recently been able to carry her. Arms flung wide, she tried to spread her tonnage over the most territory possible. Her left hand smacked painfully into the edge of something solid and vicious. Her right hit the railing behind her head.

Her fingers closed around the smooth hardwood. Searing pain in her shoulder, as it took the brunt of her weight when her body dropped, let her know the remainder of the stairs had fallen away. Without the lower steps in place, their own inertia dragged them down. Twisting, she felt every pound of her crack into the ball-and-socket joint in her right shoulder. Numbness wanted to travel up her arm, loose her fingers, but she willed her grip to tighten instead. Screaming timber, the muffled crash of time-softened wood, then mold-ridden dust billowed up in a choking cloud that clogged her throat and nose. The racket of her coughing and retching drowned out all else. By the time she had it under control, all that remained of the shattering was a liquid-sounding trickle of dirt and plaster.

Held aloft by the fingers of her right hand, Anna dangled over the ruined stairwell. Between dust and night there was no way of knowing what lay beneath. Soon either her fingers would uncurl from the rail or the rail would pull out from the wall. Faint protests of aging screws in softening plaster foretold the collapse. No superhuman feats of strength struck Anna as doable. What fragment of energy remained in her arm was fast burning away on the pain. With a kick and a twist, she managed to grab hold of the rail with her other hand as well. Much of the pressure was taken off her shoulder, but she was left face to the wall. There was the vague possibility that she could scoot one hand width at a time up the railing, then swing her legs onto what might or might not be stable footing at the top of the stairs. Two shuffles nixed that plan. Old stairwells didn't fall away all in a heap like guillotined heads. Between her and the upper floor were the ragged remains, shards of wood and rusted metal. In the black dark she envisioned the route upward with the same jaundice a hay bale might view a pitchfork with.

What the hell, she thought. *How far can it be?* And she let go.

With no visual reference, the fall, though in reality not more than five or six feet, jarred every bone in her body. Unaided by eyes and brain, her legs had no way of compensating. Knees buckled on impact and her chin smacked into them as her forehead met some immovable object. The good news was, the whole thing was over in the blink of a blind eye and she didn't think she'd sustained any lasting damage.

Wisdom dictated she lie still, take stock of her body and surroundings, but this decaying dark was so filthy she couldn't bear the thought of it. Stink rose from the litter: pigeon shit, damp and rot. Though she'd seen none, it was easy to imagine spiders of evil temperament and immoderate size. Easing up on feet and hands, she picked her way over rubble she could not see, heading for the faint smudge of gray that would lead her to the out-of-doors.

Free of the damage she'd wreaked, Anna quickly found her way out of the tangle of inner passages and escaped Island III through the back door of the ward. The sun had set. The world was bathed in gentle peach-colored light. A breeze, damp but cooling with the coming night, blew off the water. Sucking it in, she coughed another colony of spores from her lungs. With safety, the delayed reaction hit. Wobbly, she sat down on the steps and put her head between her knees.

Because she'd been messing around where she probably shouldn't have been in the first place, she'd been instrumental in the destruction of an irreplaceable historic structure. Sitting on the stoop, smeared with dirt and reeking of bygone pigeons, she contemplated whether to report the disaster or just slink away and let the monument's curators write it off to natural causes. She was within a heartbeat of deciding to do the honorable thing when the decision was taken from her.

The sound of boots on hard-packed earth, followed by a voice saying, "Patsy thought it might be you," brought her head up. A lovely young man, resplendent in the uniform of the Park Police, was walking down the row of buildings toward her.

"Why?" Anna asked stupidly.

"One of the boat captains radioed that somebody was over here." The policeman sat down next to her. He was no more than twenty-two or -three, fit and handsome and oozing boyish charm. "Have you been crawling around or what?"

Anna took a look at herself. Her khaki shorts were streaked with black, her red tank top untucked and smeared with vile-smelling mixtures. A gash ran along her thigh from the hem of her shorts to her kneecap. It was bleeding, but not profusely. Given the amount of rust and offal in this adventure, she would have to clean it thoroughly and it wouldn't hurt to check when she'd last had a tetanus shot.

"Sort of," she said, and told him about the stairs. "Should we check it out? Surely we'll have to make a report. You'll have to write a report," she amended. "I'm just a hapless tourist."

The policeman looked over his shoulder. The doorway behind them was cloaked in early night. "Maybe in the morning," he said, and Anna could have sworn he was afraid. There was something in this strong man's voice that told her, were it a hundred years earlier, he would have made a sign against the evil eye.

6

Dwight was on time. Dwight was always on time. Effortlessly, Cal lassoed the piling, and in the seedy back lot of Ellis Island's showcase museum, between the old powerhouse and a rickety-looking bridge that tied the island to New Jersey, Anna and Patsy boarded the Liberty IV.

"Was it you who got me busted?" Anna asked the captain good-naturedly as she slid onto her favorite seat on the high bench.

"Serves her right, doesn't it, Patsy?" Dwight pretended to be shocked, keeping his back to Anna. "Creeping around closed areas like a middle-aged mutant ninja ranger."

Patsy laughed and Anna assumed they had a private joke. She smiled to be part of the gang but didn't participate in the conversation. She was as tired as if she'd done something all day, and was content to sit in the sweet wash of air that came off the bow through the open window, to be part of the night life of stars floating on the water.

"Who's the cute boy policeman?" she asked, after the drone of the boat engine and the cheerful murmur of Patsy and Dwight's chatter had soothed her into a sociable mood. Patsy laughed again. Patsy Silva laughed a lot, smiled a lot and resolutely saw the good in life. Anna had known her for a long time, since she'd started as a secretary in Mesa Verde. Now she was moving up the ladder, running with the bigger dogs. Anna had no doubt she'd be a superintendent within ten years. Though she seemed a threat to no one, Patsy had a good mind and a genius for organization. Like most professional women, she was a bit of a Jekyll and Hyde—or perhaps a Margaret Thatcher and Cinderella. On the job, she was a study in efficiency and put in more hours than anybody on staff. Off work, she was subject to the myriad romantic fantasies that plague single girls between the ages of thirteen and dead.

"Billy Bonham's a cutie pie," Patsy said. "Do I detect a hint of Mrs. Robinson?"

"Sometimes I forget," Anna admitted.

"Me too, till I look in the mirror. Billy's as sweet as he looks. Fresh off some farm in North Carolina by way of Boston University. Our Park Police guys are all cute. I don't think they hire them like they do regular rangers. I think they cast them like Disney casts young blue-eyed blondes to run the Alice in Wonderland ride. Maybe they have Park

Police pageants." Patsy laughed again, a genuine peal, the kind described in old books. "God, but I'd love to see the bathing suit competition."

"Cut that out," Dwight said mildly. "I'm feeling sexually harassed."

Patsy winked at Anna and smoothed her short blond hair back with both palms.

"Billy didn't seem too anxious to assess the damage," Anna said, remembering the fear in his eyes.

Dwight docked neatly at the end of the covered pier where the Circle Line brought visitors. They disembarked and he motored away, the wake of the *Liberty IV* catching the day's final hurrah, glowing iridescent green against the oily night harbor.

As Patsy and Anna walked down the planks, a figure disappeared into the darkness under the wooden roof at the far end of the pier. With the wattage of Miss Liberty, two cities and a basin full of boats, there was little true night on Liberty Island. Anna's eyes had adjusted before they met the man in the middle of the dock.

"Andrew, this is Anna. Andrew's another of our Park Police. Usually he works days. Anna's staying with me for a while." Patsy's introduction served two purposes: common courtesy and letting law enforcement know who was on the island. Andrew was over six feet tall with a body out of a muscle magazine, hair shaved so close he looked bald and skin as black and polished as his shoes. Anna shook the proffered hand. His grip was firm but gentle. If Andrew had any unresolved issues about his masculinity, bone crushing wasn't one of his compensations.

"What did I tell you?" Patsy tittered like a teenager as they left him. "Central Casting. Who else could find guys like that?"

Completing the picture of their regression to adolescence, Anna giggled. Briefly, she hoped Andrew hadn't noticed; then she dismissed it. Odds were slim he was unaware of the effect he had on women.

"Where's Hatch?" she asked.

Patsy opened the kitchen door. It was never locked—almost unheard of in these environs. "My God, didn't you hear? Where have you been, girl?"

The moment she spoke, it came back: the cry, the crumpled child, the crowds, Hatch staring down, the adenoidal voice whining, "Naw, man, he was pushed. That cop shoved him off." Anna's own concerns had effectively blocked it from her mind.

"I heard," she said, and told Patsy she'd seen the dead boy.

"Girl," Patsy contradicted her. She dumped the pack she used as a briefcase beside the refrigerator. "Beer?" Anna accepted a Bud Light, not because she particularly liked the stuff but because it did contain alcohol and she'd forgotten to buy wine. When Molly was well, she promised herself as she popped the top, she'd go back to AA for a few meetings.

"Girl. It was a girl," Patsy repeated. "The

71

medical examiner thinks she was fourteen or fifteen. Thin and flat-chested but definitely a girl. She had brown hair down to here." Patsy had led the way into the living room, and indicated the length of the child's hair by a chopping motion in the vicinity of her butt as she flopped into a comfortless government-issue armchair, not unlike those in the ICU at Columbia-Presbyterian.

"There's talk of suspending Hatch. The Chief Ranger was in the Super's office half the afternoon."

Anna eased down on the sofa and put her feet up on a coffee table that looked as if it had been custom-made for George Jetson, a sixties version of the future. The gash on her thigh had clotted and the torn flesh was pulling tight. Each place she'd banged in her fall was reasserting its need for sympathy. She took another pull on her beer. "Why? What happened?" If nobody else heard the kid saying Hatch had pushed the girl, Anna wasn't going to volunteer the information without talking with him first. He didn't strike her as the type who went around chucking strange children off parapets.

"This is all second- and thirdhand," Patsy said. "But according to Hatch, this kid had been acting strange. Somebody'd reported her or something. Hatch got to watching her and thought maybe she was picking pockets. We get our share of that. Tourists. Crowds. The pickings can be pretty good. For the price of one ticket a thief can work the boats and monuments all day. She—Hatch thought it was a boy too—evidently started acting really peculiar on the top of the pedestal where you can go outside. Hatch thought she was stuffing things in her backpack. He was going to talk to her and—again according to him—she just took off out the doors. He ran after her. The way he tells it, he was trying to catch hold of her to stop her from jumping, was a second too late—and *splat.*

"Hi, Mandy, we're talking about Hatch." Patsy broke off as her housemate came in. Mandy was young and round of face, eyes and tummy— everywhere but where a woman might choose to be round. Her hair was baby-fine and cut in a bowl shape, like most depictions of Joan of Arc. Anna had found no call to either like or dislike her. But she was about to.

"Hatch should be fired," Mandy said, as if what she thought mattered. "This Keystone Kop routine. Chasing a kid! This is an island, for chrissake. Where did he think she was going to go?" The condemnation was delivered with scathing finality.

Anna was tired, and somewhere between 1975 and the present, she'd ceased caring what the Mandys of the world thought, but out of loyalty to Hatch and the brotherhood, she roused herself. "You've got to chase 'em," she said. "You don't know why they're running. Maybe they'll hurt somebody. Hurt themselves. You let 'em go, it turns out you knew, you'd been told they were acting fishy. You tried to talk to them. They ran and you just

73

said, 'Oh well, win some lose some,' then
they pull out a forty-five and start shooting visitors—or worse, damage the resource. Try
explaining that to the Chief Ranger. Not to
mention John Q. Public. That's the luxury of
not being in law enforcement. You don't have
to engage. Hatch did. He had point two seconds to figure out what to do."

"Okay. Sure. Whatever." Mandy looked
around the room, vaguely peeved, then pushed
her stubby bangs off her forehead with the edge
of her hand. "Anybody want the bathroom?
I'm going to have a soak." Finding no takers,
she stumped off down the hall.

"My junior year in college I took third
place in the state finals for persuasive speaking,"
Anna said. "Evidently I've lost my touch."

"Mandy suffers from arrested development," Patsy whispered after checking to see
that the bathroom door had closed. "She
views the world from a training bra."

Patsy's own form was a fifties wet dream,
movie stars before anorexia and gym mem-
berships became fashionable. Anna laughed.
"Another beer?" Patsy offered, further
endearing herself.

"There was no backpack," Anna remembered
suddenly as Patsy came back with two more
Bud Lights. "Hatch said she was stuffing
something in her backpack? When I checked
the boy—the girl—after she fell, she didn't have
a pack, not a purse, nothing."

"Maybe one of the EMTs picked it up for
her."

"I was there before the EMTs." They sipped their insipid brew in silence for a moment.

"God," Patsy said. "Somebody *stole* it? Can you believe somebody would steal a back-pack off a broken little kid like that?"

Having a fairly dismal view of her fellow humans, Anna found it easy to believe. Certainly easier than believing Hatch had made up a nonsensical lie about picking pockets, then purposely pursued a child through a hundred witnesses for the sole purpose of shoving him—her—to her death. Even evil had to conform to some twisted sense of logic.

"Who was she?" Anna asked.

"Who knows. A kid. No ID. Nobody has claimed her as far as I know. Maybe she was a runaway."

"Her picture will go out," Anna said. "Somebody will recognize her. The world's not that big anymore."

Patsy went to bed. Anna poured the last of her beer down the sink. If she drank enough to drop the veil over her mind she'd be up all night running to the bathroom. Without sufficient alcohol to slow the spinning of her thoughts, sleep would be a while in coming. A hot bath might have been the next best thing, but Mandy had drained the tank dry and, given the age of the equipment, it would take it longer to recover than Anna cared to wait.

Pulling on her Levi jacket against the breeze off the ocean, she let herself out. A walk around the island to clear her mind; then she would read herself to sleep with something familiar. Knowing Molly might be in the hospital some time, Anna had packed several comfort books: *Great Expectations, The Moonstone, The Small House at Allington.* Stories she'd read before and would read again, finding reassurance in the formal language and happy endings.

For reasons of professional interest or a natural morbidity, she made her way to the base of the pedestal where the girl had fallen, jumped or been pushed to her death. Bright scraps of pink littered the granite. Azalea blossoms had been scattered, a tribute to the dead. Squatting on the unnaturally clean stone—scrubbed by an NPS that didn't like blood shed any later than the Civil War to become part of the attraction at their historic monuments—Anna closed her eyes and conjured up what memories she had of the incident.

The child's face and her injuries were paramount, coming into focus with unpleasant clarity. Anna let them sit, waiting for them to lose their shock value. It was not brain and bone she hoped to recall. Gore, like loud noise and bright light, had a way of blinding one to pertinent detail. Inexperienced EMTs had been known to lose patients because they wasted precious time dealing with a spectacular but non-life-threatening injury while the patient quietly ceased breathing from an unrelated problem.

Graphic images faded. Bits of the child came clear. The ball cap hiding her hair had a funky decoration on it, a football or a rock. Her skin was good—no acne—and pale, as if she spent little time in the sun. Some of her teeth had been broken in the fall, but Anna could see the bottom row. They were crooked but white and without fillings. She wore a white T-shirt and green trousers. Army fatigues maybe; they were a couple sizes too large and frayed at the cuffs where they dragged the ground. New, expensive sneakers—Reeboks. If the child was a runaway, she'd either bolted recently or done well by herself.

Without opening her eyes, Anna tilted her head back, looking around at an imaginary crowd. Backpacks: there was nothing on the ground near the dead child. Her mind's eye saw only shoes, feet and shins. From the knees down people were a tacky lot, Anna thought, as the grubby, hirsute parade passed through her mind: running shoes that looked as if they'd been used as third base for a season, hammer toes, army boots under unhemmed Levi's, ridged and yellowed nails poking from strappy sandals.

Mentally, she raised her sights. Backpacks: the people she could recall pushing closest had all been carrying something. A minute's concentration brought out a camera, two waist packs—one in purple, one in green—and two backpacks. The boy nearest—the one in the huge shorts—had carried one. Behind him she'd seen a part of another, as if someone held it by a single strap.

She opened her eyes. It was no use. She

couldn't recall anyone's face clearly. She was unsure of the color of the packs or who, precisely, carried them. Even in cities packs were ubiquitous, and there was no reason to believe the person who stole it would have hung around. From her conversation with Patsy, Anna got the idea that the missing pack had only been missed later, after the crowd had dispersed. Not too great a loss from an interviewer's point of view. When people ran in herds their senses became dulled. One good witness in twenty was a small miracle.

The happy growl of a small motorboat caught her attention. It was the *Liberty IV* making its last trip back from Manhattan. Any Liberty Islander who missed the ten-fifteen boat was marooned in the city for the night. The roar of the diesel engine reminded Anna she had a question for Dwight. When she tried to get to her feet, the cut on her thigh raised such a fuss that she had to push off the stone with both hands.

At a limping trot she managed to reach the end of the pier just as Cal was reeling the *Liberty IV* dockside. Ever the gentleman, he handed her on board with a grace and dignity rare in modern times.

"Hey, Dwight," she called up the narrow steps to the bridge. "Got a minute?"

"One," he returned.

It was the end of his shift. Dwight was a family man and not one to dawdle when his working day was done. Pulling herself up in a vain attempt to spare her leg, Anna was annoyed to find she was breathing hard. Physical stamina after forty wasn't a given, it had to be earned.

"What time did you see me on Island Three and radio it in?" she asked.

"You're not mad, are you?" he asked with surprise.

"Nope. Just curious."

"I don't know. Maybe eight or so."

"Where was I?"

Dwight laughed nervously. "This an IQ test?"

Anna waited.

"Sort of in the trees there between the buildings."

"Earlier you said something to Patsy about my being a middle-aged mutant ninja ranger. What was that about?"

Dwight looked pained. "No offense meant," he said.

"No, no," she reassured him. "None taken. Just curious about the image."

Dwight was still uncertain whether or not he was being taken to task in some arcane manner. "You know those turtle things from a while back? That's all."

"Teenage Mutant Ninja Turtles?" Anna asked.

"Yeah. Just trying to be funny. We got any comers, Cal?" he hollered out the window to let Anna know it was time to leave. The dock was obviously deserted.

"The rhythm. I get it," Anna said hurriedly. "Teenage/middle-aged, turtle/ranger. What put the picture in your head?"

Dwight was suddenly absorbed in fiddling with his radar.

"Other than me being middle-aged?"

"You said it, not me." Then: "You know, just those ninja men all dressed in black. Got a stowaway, Cal," he called to the deckhand in hopes of getting rid of Anna.

"That's it?" she asked. "The person you saw was dressed in black?"

"That's it," Dwight said.

"Terrific." Anna backed down the stairs. "Thanks a heap. Regards to Digby. Good night." Cal handed her off the boat and for another brief moment she was allowed to feel like a lady.

Around eight o'clock, Dwight said. She'd been inside the wards from five-thirty till she'd stumbled out to be caught by Billy Bonham. Black, Dwight had said, a ninja. She'd been dressed in khaki shorts and a red shirt. Whoever Dwight saw, it wasn't her. Whoever he saw hadn't been authorized to be there. And whoever it was had been leaving the area immediately after the stairs fell from under her.

It had to be coincidence. Surely even she couldn't make a mortal enemy in only three days.

7

Anna caught an early boat for Manhattan, the Liberty IV captained this morning by Kevin. He wasn't alone on the bridge. A slender, handsome man of indeterminate age sat in Anna's spot drinking coffee from a fat-bottomed plastic mug. Trey Claypool. Anna remembered a hurried introduction in the hall when she'd first come to Ellis. Claypool was the Assistant Superintendent, an often thankless job. Not unlike vice president but without the entertainment factor of going to galas. Assistant superintendent was a way station for the upwardly mobile or a parking place for burnouts and black sheep that the Park Service couldn't get rid of and never intended to grant the power of a superintendency. Anna had no idea whether Claypool was on the fast track or had been shunted off onto a siding. There was something off-putting about the man. Lack of facial expression: either he was brain-dead or so adept at hiding his emotions that not so much as a twinkle showed through. Eyes like a carp, Anna thought as she backed unseen down the stairs from the bridge.

In the open area on the stern Billy Bonham, riding home after the night shift on Ellis, stood under the Stars and Stripes gazing back at Lady Liberty. Both of them looked fine in the morning sun: healthy, vibrant and forever young. Pleased with the picture, Anna joined the policeman.

"Good morning," she said, just to watch him smile. She was disappointed. Billy looked at her and his face was drawn, pale under the beginnings of a summer tan. His thick honey-colored hair was greasy, as if he'd been running his hands through it. There was no smile to alleviate his gray cast, just a pained expression tinged with doubt and sadness.

"You look like shit," Anna said kindly. Maybe it was the wind off the water, but she could have sworn his eyes teared up in the moment before he turned away. It seemed rude to just run off and leave him but that was her plan. Who knew what to do with weepy men? He was too young to sleep with and too old to hold on her lap. "Looks like it's going to be another nice day," she murmured, preparatory to sidling away and scuttling to the far end of the boat.

"I've got to find another line of work," Billy said, aborting her escape. His voice was heavy with the unself-conscious melodrama of youth.

"There's lots of things to do," Anna said, not yet giving up hope of retaining her God-given right to indifference.

"I've never wanted to be anything else. Never will," Bonham said stubbornly.

Anna capitulated, leaning both elbows on the rail beside him. "A drag," she agreed.

"Do you ever see things?" he asked suddenly.

Anna had braced herself for a tale of star-crossed love or boss-crossed ambition. The question caught her off guard and she answered truthfully: "Sometimes." Immediately she wished she hadn't. Public servants entrusted with deadly weapons were strongly discouraged from admitting any symptoms of mental instability.

"What sort of things?" Billy pressed.

"Why?"

The policeman hadn't faced her since his eyes filled with tears, and he didn't now, but let his words blow over the stern to be carried away on the wake of the *Liberty IV*. "I need to know."

Anna watched him, the profile still rounded from his teens, a square forehead free of lines and cheeks more suited to down than whiskers. He really did seem to need to know. Hoping she wasn't opening the door to some unwelcome and eminently reportable revelation, she told him.

"Cats, mostly. When I'm tired or distracted I sometimes see cats out of the corner of my eye. Then they aren't there. It used to scare me," she said, in case that was what he was worried about, that he was going nuts. "Now I'm used to it. They keep down the hallucinatory mice."

"Cats? Is that it?" He sounded so disappointed she half wished she had a more impressive delusion to relate.

"Just cats," she admitted, feeling she'd let him down. He slid back into morose silence. "Why?" she asked again. "What do you see?"

"Who said I see anything?" Abruptly, he left her with the cracking of the flag. Through the windows of the passenger cabin she saw him slide onto a bench and slump against the wall as if instantly asleep.

Set up, then snubbed, Anna chose to spend the rest of the short trip without the dubious pleasure of human companionship.

Frederick was already at the hospital. "Your sister's beau has been here since the cock crowed," she was informed by a plump and kindly woman in white pants and tunic as she made her way down the all too familiar hallway in the ICU.

Creepy butterflies stirred in the region of her duodenum. Anna stopped at the water fountain to examine the infestation of lepidoptera before exposing herself to the FBI guy and the shadow of her only sibling.

Was she still in love with Frederick? That one was easy. She'd never been in love with him; not like she'd loved Zach, not like she knew love could be. A memory of love that, on the Romeo and Juliet Principle, grew more perfect with the untimely demise of one of the participants. And, Molly had told her more than once, a memory that tolled the death knell for any relationship she might attempt with a man not perfect enough to be dead.

Possessiveness then: Frederick had been hers. Now he was "her sister's beau." Though Molly was too ill to take note of the fact.

Closer, Anna thought, and pinned one of her inner butterflies to the corkboard. *Hers.* That was the key. Not that Frederick Stanton was in any way hers. That illusion had died with nary a whimper two years before. *Molly* was hers. Hers to rescue, to bring back to life, to repay, to save, to be a hero for.

And Frederick was the usurper.

"Do you load up camel-like and then go without drinking for weeks in the desert?" A voice so low it came to her almost as a thought murmured behind her.

"Dr. Madison," Anna said.

"David."

A tiny qualm twisted amongst Anna's butterfly collection. "Can I call you Doctor?" she asked, knowing she sounded mildly pathetic. "A doctor is better than a David, given the givens."

"Feel free to call me Captain America if it helps." He smiled and, despite the graying beard, bifocals and balding head, looked boyish. "Can I get you a canteen or anything?"

Anna realized she still had her thumb on the button, letting the stream sparkle by. "Sorry," she said. "I was thinking."

"What about?" Pushing his glasses up on his head and holding his stethoscope back the way a woman would her hair, he bent over the drinking fountain. Beside him it looked too small, like the chairs in a nursery school.

"I was thinking about Molly," Anna said, wondering what chemical imbalance rendered her so honest and forthcoming this morning. "I want to do whatever she needs. Even if it's not me."

"You will," Dr. Madison replied, just as if she'd made sense. "Who's the boyfriend?"

He sounded as protective of Molly as she felt and Anna began to actually like the man. They walked together toward Molly's room. Madison hunched over to hear as Anna gave him a brief and highly edited version of Frederick Stanton's *raison d'être*. One of two beepers clipped to his belt summoned him away and she traversed the last twenty feet of linoleum alone.

Two feet shy of Molly's door, she stopped. His back to the window opening into the hall, Frederick sat in the red chair, a worm-eaten guitar resting on his bony lap. Soundlessly, Anna turned the knob and eased open the door. He was singing and not too badly. A light, sure tenor voice accompanied by rusty fingering of half-remembered chords: "I do love to breathe, I do love to breathe, like a whale too long under, I do love to breathe."

The words were ludicrous, but the sense of having heard the song before nagged at Anna. Recognition came. Frederick had stolen the tune from the old spiritual "I Will Not Be Moved."

"Hey," Anna said, to announce her presence.

"Hey your ownself," he returned, and: "Look who's breathing just as if she was born to it."

Molly had been taken off the respirator

86

and Anna watched the miraculous rise and fall of her chest unaided by Columbia-Presbyterian's machines. "So slow," Anna whispered.

"Evidently—"

"Shhh." Anna pulled a pocket watch from her jeans and timed the breaths for sixty seconds. "Eleven," she said. "Not bad. Not *bad,*" she repeated, and laughed. "It's fucking great. Move over." She butted her way half onto the red chair with a shove of her hip and stared down at her sister. "I think she's pinking up some. Do you? I think so," she said, without waiting for him to reply. A great geyser of optimism was bubbling up within her. "I'm undoing her hands," she said. "Play something that will make her remember. Something locked into our collective psyches."

Dimly, Anna was aware of Frederick, his thigh pressed against hers, fumbling with the guitar and humming pieces of music as he tried to remember. "It's been a while," he said.

"We don't care." Molly's hands were free of the restraints and Anna watched her fingers curl. She knew Molly was close, she could feel it.

"Used to be I could sing 'Kumbaya' with the best of them."

"Do it," Anna demanded. "Anything."

Softly, but hitting each note with precision, Frederick began singing the Beatles' "Here Comes the Sun."

"It's been a long time since you've been here."

87

Anna whispered words she'd not known she remembered.

Molly opened her eyes. It wasn't just a reflex, Molly was there.

"Did we wake you?" Anna asked, and was horrified to hear her voice break. Molly's hand moved and Anna started, but she wasn't reaching for the feeding tube, only to reassure herself the breathing tube was gone. "It's out," Anna said. "You can talk." Then, lest she be pushing too hard, she added: "If you want to."

"Anna," came out, a dry creak.

"Yes. Yes. It's me," Anna responded, as if Molly had answered a complex trigonometry question correctly. She was rewarded by a look of irritation. Anna laughed and the tears boiled up underneath. Lest Molly sense them, she clamped her jaws shut till they drained away.

"I thought..." Molly's eyes drifted from Anna. They clouded suddenly with alarm. "Frederick—" Molly said, and closed her eyes. Retreating.

Anna grabbed her hand. "Frederick Stanton," she said firmly. "I asked him to come."

Molly's eyes fluttered but stayed closed.

"What are we going to do?" Anna heard an edge of hysteria in her voice and forced herself to take several deep, slow breaths through her nose.

"We're not going to do anything, Anna," Frederick said. "Molly knows we are here. She knows we love her. She knows the two of us—you and me—are going to hang around singing old songs off key till she's strong enough to walk out of here."

"Right," Anna said to Frederick. "Right," she repeated to her sister. Molly was still breathing eleven beautiful self-initiated breaths per minute. Anna watched and counted and felt the panic receding.

By noon Anna had had all she could take of the sickroom. Molly had awakened once more, and though she'd not spoken, she seemed comfortable and, indeed, comforted by the presence of both Anna and Frederick. With only a mild sense of a rat abandoning ship, Anna left the confines of the hospital for the livelier confines of the city.

For an hour or so she rattled around midtown killing time by looking at clothes she not only couldn't afford but had no place to wear. Shopgirls working on commission hounded her out of the smaller boutiques and she made her way to the cathedrals of fashion on Fifth Avenue. Lord & Taylor. Saks. She remembered actually purchasing clothing at Saks occasionally when she lived in New York in the 1980s. Now it seemed merely a museum for clothes too ugly even for rich people to wear. Two o'clock came and Anna had had all of city life she needed for one day. Not willing to take time for lunch, she headed for the nearest subway and the three-fifteen staff boat to Ellis and Liberty. Anna had cab fare. She'd been a GS-9 for a few years. The money wasn't princely but it was a fair wage. Having simple tastes and no responsibilities, she'd managed a tidy savings program. But somewhere in the years after Henry Ford invented the automobile and the first one went out for hire in New York, an adversarial relationship had sprung up between cabbies and the human race. The noise, smell and congestion of the subway was less abrasive than even a brief incarceration with these unilaterally hostile strangers. Anna carried a pocketful of subway tokens, talismans against the potentially necessary evil of cab warfare.

Assistant Superintendent Trey Claypool was at the MIO dock when Anna arrived just after three. The sun was hot, the air close and humid. He waited hatless near the water, away from any hope of shade as if he, like Anna, was anxious to turn his back on the city. She wandered out to where he sat on a piling and squatted in the meager shade his body provided. "We seem to be on the same schedule today," she said, just to have something to say.

Claypool looked down at her. His hair was cropped close, a mixture of brown and gray. In the harsh light the white bristles glittered like hoarfrost and the planes of his face were without shadows.

"I'm Anna Pigeon," she offered.

"I know. Staying with Patsy Silva." He looked out over the water again. Not lack of recognition; lack of interest.

Anna could live with that. She too let her eyes be drawn over the glitter of broken water ever troubled by the passage of ships and the currents where the Atlantic met the Hudson.

"You're bleeding," Claypool said after a minute, and Anna wondered if he had eyes in the back of his head. "Your leg," he added.

He was right. Blood from the gash on her thigh was oozing through, discoloring the faded denim of her trousers. "It's only a flesh wound," she said, because she'd always wanted to. Claypool grunted. As close as he ever came to a laugh, she guessed.

Heartened by the grunt, she told him how she'd come by the injury. Finishing her tale, she was gratified at last to see a semblance of interest in those guarded green eyes.

"Where did you say it happened?" he asked.

Anna had been up and down and around and through so many deteriorating passages and rooms that she wasn't precisely sure, but she gave it her best. "Island Three," she told him. "Out near the end. Those stairs with that pile of stuff under them. Covered with an old tarp. Pipe maybe."

The interest sharpened and with it some other emotion she couldn't read, pride or aggravation. Neither fit the situation. "No," he said after a pause. "There's no dump, no boneyard where you're talking about. I know every inch of that island."

A certain bitterness of tone suggested he had little else to do but acquaint himself intimately with a resource he would never manage. "You must have been farther over. The Immigration Commissioner's house. There is some old electrical equipment left behind by the Coast Guard there."

"It wasn't that far over," Anna said, but even as she spoke she was uncertain. Without a detailed, up-to-date floor plan, the magnificent old hospital was a confusing maze.

With her failure to be more specific, Claypool lost interest. They sat without speaking, Anna watching the slow spread of blood ruining one of two pairs of pants she'd brought with her, till the *Liberty IV* motored up.

At her request, Kevin dropped her off on Ellis before completing his run to Liberty, where the Assistant Superintendent lived in bachelor splendor in a charming two-story brick house across a sliver of lawn from Patsy's kitchen door. Shortly after disembarking, Anna wished she'd gone on to Liberty with him. Her leg was beginning to bother her, but more than that, fatigue slammed down and she had no energy either to hike far enough to hide out from people, or to endure further socializing. Patsy's miserable excuse for a sofa and a few chapters of Wilkie Collins suddenly glowed with all the tragic promise of paradise lost.

Feeling pitiful, she limped to the elevator in the old power station behind the museum to wait out the hour till the next boat made a run from Ellis to Liberty.

Much of the inside of the building had been renovated to provide working space for the Ellis Island staff. Walls were white-painted cement block, the floors covered in new green and white linoleum. Despite the job going to the lowest bidder, touches of history remained in wooden doors with clear-paned glass, etched windows and an ornate wrought-iron staircase painted brick red. On the second floor Anna snaked down a hallway twisted by structural necessity to the clean sunny room that had been set aside as an employee break room. It had two refrigerators, three microwave ovens and a sink, but its chief allure came from its location. Near as Anna could tell, it was the break room farthest from headquarters, and being on the second floor, it wasn't handy to a smoking area. People tended not to use it. Anna was counting on that to provide her with the needed respite till the boat returned.

Today the quiet room had become a vortex for past and present. Anna opened the door to see a wraithlike woman, delicate and pale almost to translucence. She was clad in a brown cotton dress that swept the top of high-buttoned boots; a colored shawl was draped over her shoulders. Her hair was in a severe knot at the back of her head. She was engaged in earnest conversation with a middle-aged man in knickers, woolen stockings and a tweed cap.

Actors; Anna had forgotten about them. Naturally cliquish, they eschewed the common haunts and claimed this small isolated space for their own. On break before the last show of the day, three of them had scattered themselves around one of two tables. They glanced up briefly when she entered, but had no reason to spare a greeting. The conversation was the same as those Anna recalled from a distant past with her actor husband, Zachary: agents, roles, pictures, résumés, the blind idiocy of directors and the sublime possibilities of the next audition.

Anna borrowed a Coke from the stash Patsy kept in one of the refrigerators and took her place at the remaining table. Some kind soul had left a newspaper. She had no interest in reading it, but it was a place for a lone female to rest her eyes in this semipublic place.

Desultory leafing turned up two decent political cartoons and, to her surprise, an article of interest. Buried on page 29 was a short report of the death by falling from the Statue of Liberty. The facts were in line with the scuttlebutt: a girl, early adolescence, not yet identified, dead of massive head trauma. Hatch was mentioned by name. There was a quote from the Superintendent about sorrow, tragedy and ongoing investigation. Without any overt altering of the known facts, the piece was cunningly yellowed with loaded words and slanted connotations. A source who asked not to be identified was relied on for much of this. The park and especially the Park Police were being put in an unflattering light. Though never stating it outright, the author left the reader with a sense that the child's death was a direct result of jackbooted insensitivity.

Distancing herself from its sly ignorance, Anna pushed the paper away. She'd heard that cant before and suspected Patsy's roommate, Mandy, of being the anonymous source.

Retaining the newspaper for protective coloration, Anna allowed her attention to be diverted to the table where the actors congregated. For a change they'd stopped talking shop. The man in knickers, hired probably because he resembled the archetypal Irish immigrant—craggy, handsome, thick reddish hair, square face crosshatched with weathered lines—was holding forth in disappointingly American tones.

"I guess the night watchman—"

"Park Police," the frail blonde interjected.

"—has been talking. He told Andrew he'd seen candlelight in the windows high on Island Two and once he said he heard music. Some kind of fife-and-steel-drum Irish thing." The man laughed, a big theatrical laugh become his own with use. "He should get history straight. I don't think steel drums in Irish music have been around all that long."

"I hate anachronisms in my ectoplasm," said the third actor of the troupe, a stocky black woman tied up in bright pseudo-Jamaican rags. "Still, there is something. I've felt it a couple times when I was rehearsing. I went over to the other islands to sort of get the sense of time. That old laundry room is way colder than the rest of the rooms."

"Method acting," the man said, and winked.

The black actress took umbrage. Her back was turned, but Anna could read anger in the stiffening of the wide shoulders and the backward tip of the turbaned head. "It's there if you're not too tied up in middle-class banality to feel it."

Low blow. Accusing an artist of being normal. In the old days them had been fightin' words. The thought raised Anna's flagging spirits, reminding her of how magnificently young and ardent she had once been.

"Billy Bonham?" said the fragile blonde. "Baby-blue-eyed Billy?" The speaker was probably in her late twenties but her features were as delicate as a child's, the bones fine and light, her skin poreless and without freckle or line. Her hair, naturally blond as near as Anna could tell, had the gossamer texture of a very little girl's.

"Who?" the faux Irishman asked, eyebrows raised.

A faint pink crept up the actress's neck and Anna wondered if a romance was in the offing. Bonham was younger than she, but pretty enough to bridge a gap of a few years.

The black woman caught it instantly. "Oooh. I smell gossip. Billy who, Corinne? Is this somebody we should know about?" Corinne, the blonde, looked genuinely flustered and began shaking her head much too quickly in denial. "Uh-oh," said the other actress. "Is this somebody Macho Bozo should *not* know about?"

"No," Corinne said, her composure regained, the flush all but gone from her porcelain neck. "He's the Park Policeman who has the night shift, the one that said he saw the lights, heard The Chieftains' dead ancestors jamming."

"And just how did you come to know Park Policeman Billy Bonham?" the other woman

96

pried. "He leaves before we get here mornings and comes nights after we've gone. Oho! I thought you took an earlier boat in than we did and a later one home because you were so dedicated to your craft. It's *l'amour!*"

Again the flush. It was utterly charming, the more so because Anna didn't think it could be feigned. Lord knew she'd tried often enough when she was in high school.

"Baby-blue-eyed Billy?" the man put in. "What kind of a name is *Billy?* Are we doing a bit of cradle robbing?"

"He's old enough to be your son," Corinne said wickedly.

"Touché." He went back to a bag of Doritos. "So, tell us about *Billy.*"

Corinne flopped down, her graceful neck bowed, her head resting on crossed arms. "You two are impossible," she moaned. "I don't know *Billy.* I don't care to know *Billy.* My point was—Oh, fuck," she laughed. "Now I don't remember what my point was."

"Ghosts."

"God. Thank you, Toya. You cost me more brain cells over break than I'd lose in ten years of happy hours. Ghosts. Bill—Officer Bonham is not crazy. I wouldn't stay the night here for an audition at the Public Theatre. I know for a fact it's haunted."

"Hah!" This from Toya, who "sensed things."

Anna was totally engrossed at this point, forgetting to pretend to read the paper, but even in this small diversion she was to be thwarted.

"Time to return to reality, ladies," the man said, his accent now befitting a son of Erin.

"Like the theater is reality," Corinne said, and the three of them left in a flurry of nineteenth-century skirts and twentieth-century profanity.

Billy had been seeing ghosts. That must have been what the morning's fragmented conversation aboard the *Liberty IV* had been about. All alone on Ellis nights, he was spooking himself.

Anna could understand that. There'd been nights patrolling the Anasazi ruins on Mesa Verde when the weight of a dead people pricked at her nerve ends and she wished she'd not listened to the Navajo trail crews' stories of corpses turning into wolves and loping after the living. If there was anything to the "science" of the paranormal, Ellis Island had the prerequisites for a hotbed of ghostly manifestations. Dreams had ended here, most happily but some at the end of a rope slung over the rafters. Families were separated, mothers from children and husbands from wives. Young women were turned away from the promised land because they traveled alone. With no one to meet them, they could not enter the country. The regulation was based on humane principles. An unprotected woman in New York was vulnerable to a number of evils. But who knew what terrors had induced her to cross oceans in the first place?

Still and all, despite late nights and scary

98

stories, Anna had never actually seen apparitions. Getting the willies was one thing. Hallucinating was another.

Middle-aged mutant ninja rangers. Dwight's description of the interloper on Island III crossed Anna's mind. Perhaps Billy was not delusional. She glanced at the clock. Time to catch her boat.

Riding down in the elevator, she reassessed Bonham. Park Police: trained, educated, professional. That didn't rule out superstition, but it did render it highly unlikely that a man trained to watch for intruders would, when faced with a classic black-clad skulker, chalk it up to an otherworldly visitation. Anna would pass the gossip on to Patsy. It was her park; she could decide if the boy needed therapy, drug intervention or a spanking.

Mandy not yet back from her interpretive duties at the Registry Hall on Ellis, Anna drew every drop of hot water from the aging water heater and soaked till her muscles grew loose and her skin turned rosy and began to shrivel. A bar of hand soap and vigorous scrubbing removed the bloodstains from her trousers. With a fresh dressing over her scratch and clean sweat clothes on, she felt renewed.

Five o'clock came and went without producing either Patsy or her roommate. Anna was grateful for the prolonged solitude. Six o'clock, then seven were marked off by the wall clock in the kitchen before she began to tire of her own company. Having yet again forgotten her duties to Bacchus, she helped herself to a Bud Light and munched on French bread and salmon pâté left over from the day before. By eight o'clock she was feeling abandoned and telling herself she was not a guest but a friend in need and Patsy had every right to a night on the town without asking her along—or asking her permission. Besides, she would have turned down an invitation. She had had her fill of Manhattan for one day. Pacing the living room, she stared out at the coming evening, then the perverse dawn of electric lights on the horizon. For the first time since arriving on Liberty, she noticed Patsy didn't have a television. Positively un-American. On nights such as this, reruns would be just the thing: the mental equivalent of giving a feather to a baby with sticky fingers. Synapses could be kept busy plucking the treacle of sitcoms off of one another. A brief peek into Mandy's lair located a small TV squashed in amongst alternative press newspapers and a framed picture of brother or boyfriend with his army unit grinning out from a spiky forest of rifles. Kids and dogs crowded around, wanting to play war. Desperate as she was, Anna closed the door. The room was a wreck, clothes knee-deep on the floor and a refuse of papers, cosmetics and underwear skidding off every elevated surface.

Back in the living room, the telephone tempted her but there was no one to call. Not even Frederick. She hadn't bothered to ask for his friend Emmett's last name or phone number. Tomorrow she would rectify that. Fate had made them partners in Molly's recovery. Life would be easier if they became friends.

Should Frederick stick around—and apparently it would take an act of Congress to get him out of the ICU—he might take up where Molly had brutally left off two years before. With Anna's blessing, Molly might give in to his siege of affections. How weird would it be to have slept with your brother-in-law?

Jump off that bridge when you come to it, Anna told herself. Molly was not yet out of intensive care. It was presumptuous to be marrying her off to an ex-boyfriend.

Nine o'clock brought no relief in the form of mental distraction. Anna decided to take her evening constitutional around Liberty Island, then try for an early bedtime.

The expected blessedness of the outdoors failed to soothe. Either the eternal hum of the city grew louder or Anna's filtering mechanism grew weaker. The harbor had lost its ability to buffer Liberty from the surrounding congestion. Indeed, the black water seemed but a different kind of pavement bringing the flotsam of noise and tension to the shore. Anna longed for the simple call of a night bird, the sweet cacophony of cicadas in the pines, for a night that was truly dark, pricked only by stars, and those confined to the purer shades of white. Urban nights were garish, without rest. Fervently, she hoped Molly would get well soon. Much longer in New

York City and Anna knew she would be in need of a good psychiatrist.

Narrow wheels rattling on brick brought her out of her black study. Cleaning crew had finished the lady's ablutions and were putting away their equipment for the night. That meant the staff boat would be coming in an hour or so. Cleaning crew rode back to Manhattan on the last boat of the day. If Patsy and Mandy didn't arrive on it, Anna would have the house to herself till morning.

Men in groups made her leery and she faded into the shrubbery as they clattered near. Three of them were dark-skinned, two African-Americans and one Puerto Rican or Mexican. The fourth was almost painfully white, big and oafish with a neck nearly as thick as his head, which was either shaved or naturally bald from the edge of his green ball cap down. There was something tantalizingly familiar about him, but Anna knew she'd never seen him before. The type was familiar.

Alongside the smaller, wiry men, chitchatting in East Coast accents both Brooklyn and Bronx, he looked out of place. A big, dumb farm boy out to see the world. As they passed Anna's hiding place, he spoke. No accent, none. Like Anna, he wasn't from around here.

The four men wheeled their cart under a light and she noticed that the white boy had an unpleasantly large spider crawling beneath his collar. She was considering whether or not to warn him, when he turned his head and she realized it was something infinitely more poi-

102

sonous than a spider. Two inches below his right ear a swastika the size of a nickel was tattooed. *That must endear him to his co-workers,* she thought.

Enjoying as she always did—as she had since she was a child—the simple act of hiding and watching, she let the men rattle and babble to a nearby building that was kind enough to swallow them from sight. Stepping from the concealing branches of the bushes, she continued her walk across the plaza and up the foreshortened mall. For three nights she had walked the island. Anna had seen Lady Liberty from inside and out, from sea, land and air, yet the statue never failed to make her feel, in some indefinable way, proud.

Tonight an invisible stage manager was calling the cues to Anna's personal show. As she walked up the center of the paved area, the two great bronze doors in Liberty's base swung open and a shaft of gold spotlighted her.

"I wish I could sing," Anna said.

"Give it a go," Hatch invited. "Who knows? Maybe Broadway's been waiting for youse all these years."

Hatch was smiling, standing in his usual laid-back stance, but Anna could see the pull of nerves around his dark eyes, hear it in his lapse into the neighborhood "youse," a habit he'd kept out of his conversation the last time they met.

"Broadway'll have to go on waiting," she said. "My husband was an actor," she told him, in an unusual moment of confidence. "Zach was dying to get on Broadway."

"I didn't know you was married," Hatch said. He held open the inner security door to the statue and Anna joined him as if it had been prearranged. "He still dying to get on Broadway?"

Zach had died trying to get across Ninth Avenue, hit by a cab, but Anna didn't want to get that personal. "He went on to better things," she said.

Hearing what he must have thought was the flippancy of a slightly bitter divorcée, Hatch dropped the subject. "You come to help me with the sweep?"

Merely thinking of those 354 steps made Anna's thigh hurt, but there was such hope in his voice, and she had to admit, it wasn't like she had anything better to do. She gave in gracefully and followed him into the orgasmatron.

"How do you use this for medical emergencies?" she asked as they squeezed in, sardine fashion. "No room for a backboard, wheelchair, nothing."

"It's to get us to them. Then we carry them or whatever."

"How often does it happen?"

"Not often. Hasn't while I been here."

A miracle in itself. With the high-density traffic and no way to clear a path from level S-1 to the crown, it was a wonder there had not been at least a handful of heart attacks and strokes. "What a mess," Anna said, picturing the situation.

"You got it," Hatch replied. "If some old guy croaks up high, you got all of PS 191's third-grade class steppin' over the corpse to get down the stairs. We been lucky."

Anna followed him up the spiral staircase, through the light-drenched frontal lobe of the lady and back down to the orgasmatron. The climb had tweaked at her gash and she could tell it was bleeding again, but it was well dressed and the seepage wouldn't amount to much.

Keeping to a pattern too predictable to be desirable in a law enforcement officer, Hatch stopped at the top of the pedestal and went out to the same place he had the first time Anna had accompanied him. "Time to do drugs," he said.

There was a faint breeze. Anna welcomed its tickle in her hair. Hatch, ahead of her on the high balcony, turned when he reached the parapet. Indicating the crenel facing Manhattan, he said: "You want to sit? You being company, I don't want to hog the best spot."

Self-preservation, dragged from dormancy by the gang of cleaning men, reasserted itself. Backlit, faceless, Hatch no longer seemed utterly harmless. Alone, sixty feet above an unforgiving surface, it was not unthinkable that he had pushed a girl to her death.

"No thanks. Afraid of heights," Anna lied, and planted her back firmly against the wall beneath Liberty's big toe.

Hatch was quiet for a moment and still. For the latter Anna was grateful. With his face in darkness and his uncharacteristic failure to speak, if he'd started toward her she might have embarrassed them both by making a run for it. Was this how the little girl felt? Confronted by a nameless threat? Or *was* he nameless? The child was not identified. Nothing existed to prove she hadn't known Hatch, or he her.

"You're afraid of heights?" Hatch said after too long a silence. "You was okay in the elevator and it's all glass. That gets to most—what do you call 'em? Acrophobes? Agoraphobes?"

"Acrophobes."

"I get it," he said, and there was a change in his voice that made her uncomfortable, an undercurrent of anger. "It's okay." He turned away, swinging himself up onto the chest-high parapet.

Anna sucked in her breath, took two steps toward him, thinking for an instant he meant to jump.

He settled himself, legs dangling, and fished the foil packet with its Gauloises from his shirt pocket. "You're thinking of that little girl. I've about thought of nothing else." He seemed himself again. His anger was at the child's death; nothing to do with Anna. Prickling subsided from the back of her neck and she walked over to lean on the wall, close enough to be companionable but not so close she could be grabbed had she misguessed his intentions.

Hatch smoothed out his cigarette and lit it, cupping the match against an imaginary windstorm. "She didn't go off here. It was over on that side." He waved smoke in the general direction of Wyoming. "I been over there maybe a hundred times tonight. The cleaning crew probably thinks I'm dingy. I been trying to figure it. Why she ran. And jumped. Jeez, she was just a kid. I thought she was a boy, maybe ten years old." He looked at Anna. She managed not to flinch at the sudden movement. "They don't know who she was, you know that? This beautiful little girl and nobody claims her. I don't get it."

Anna had no response and no way to help with whatever demons he was exorcising but to let him talk.

He took a drag, tapped the ash and leaned out, watching it fall through the beams of light trained on the lady from the ground. "Long way," he said.

"Long way," Anna agreed.

He smoked and she shifted her weight, trying to ease the ache in her thigh.

"This punky pimple-faced kid said I pushed her. You hear that?" he asked, his eyes still on the ground.

Several lies occurred to her, but she could think of no reason to employ them. "I heard," she said, and told him she'd been the first to get to the body—first in a semiofficial capacity. A hundred others had milled around before she arrived.

"Did you see her go over—jump? Her or me?" Hatch asked. Hope, or alarm, tightened his throat and Anna felt the little hairs on her nape stir again.

"I didn't," she said truthfully, and waited for him to believe her. "I came when I heard the crowd beginning to stampede."

"Nobody claimed her." Hatch took another lungful of smoke.

"So you said."

"Did you hear anybody has ID'd her?"

"I haven't," Anna replied.

"It bothers me, her layin' in a morgue some-where all naked and cold and nobody to take her home. Know what I mean?"

Anna didn't. Dead was dead. What differ-ence did it make how the body was dressed or where it lay? To be polite, she made a friendly noise.

"Not even a name to put on a headstone. You hear a name at all?"

Anna shook her head.

"You'd tell me if you heard?"

"Sure. I'd tell you."

"Not even knowing who she was, it's kind of got to me."

Anna could see that it had. Hatch's hands trembled, palsied like a very old man's, as he smothered his cigarette butt in the tin of Wal-dorf sand and buttoned it back into his breast pocket. He had all the symptoms of a deeply troubled soul. Anna ran her hand down over the back of her neck, but the little hairs wouldn't lie all the way down. This fixation of his, the child's identity—Anna couldn't tell if he was genuinely obsessed with finding out who the dead girl was or desperate to ascertain that others had not.

Either way, she didn't much want to be alone with him in the dark any longer.

8

Patsy was waiting when Anna got back to the house. Either by choice or circumstance, Mandy was marooned on Manhattan Island for the night. Both developments suited Anna. She was glad not to be alone, but in no mood for Patsy's roommate. Patsy brought some excellent rigatoni left over from her supper at the Supreme Macaroni Company on Ninth Avenue and a summons from above. Trey Claypool requested Anna's presence in his office on Ellis Island "at her convenience no later than eight-thirty" the following morning.

Sleep kindly stopped by for Anna shortly after midnight, and such was the wimpiness of the Bud Lights that she slept undisturbed by alcohol jitters. Curious what transgression had gotten her called on the Assistant Superintendent's carpet, she rode over to Ellis on the eight a.m. staff boat with Patsy.

Because of the recent and beautifully executed renovation and restoration of the building housing the Registry Hall, the work spaces were nice enough by normal standards and positively lavish by NPS standards. Offices were situated on either side of a wide, high-ceilinged hall that led from the old powerhouse, through the nonpublic areas, to open onto the famous "kissing post." The kissing post was a pillar at the bottom of an open staircase connecting the second-floor Registry Hall with the first-floor business section where train and boat connections to a new life were made. Families meeting immigrants weren't allowed into the registry area. The first time they saw their loved ones was descending those stairs. The first chance they had to lay hands—or lips—on them was the pillar at the bottom. Hence, the "kissing post."

Two sets of double doors, like the air lock in a submarine—or, according to the noise-bedeviled interpreters who worked in the museum, a noise lock cutting off the din of excited voices echoing in the enormous tiled room—separated the pragmatic infrastructure of the island's management from the drama and romance of its past.

The official parts of the building were carpeted in a surprisingly unbureaucratic peach color. Walls were off-white, rooms well lighted, desks modern and made of metal.

Feet up on his desk, coffee mug in hand, Trey was waiting in his office. He was speaking in a low monotone and at first Anna thought he was dictating into a tape recorder. When he broke off and waved her in, she saw he was not alone. Looking ashen and impossibly young, Officer Bonham sat in the visitor's chair, hunched over, his forearms resting on his knees.

"Glad you could make it, Anna," Trey said, generously pretending she'd had a choice. "Billy here has offered to stay an hour over and help us find your stairwell." Anna suspected the "offered" was another illusion of freedom granted by the Assistant Superintendent. Billy, for all his youth and honey-brown hair, was haggard. Either night shift or personal worries were sapping his energy.

Claypool swung his feet down. "No time like the present. This thing's been driving me crazy. Yesterday I went all the places we've got boneyards, and no wrecked stairs."

Anna was getting the unpleasant feeling that a black mark was going on her record, that she would forever be known as the ranger who destroyed examples of our precious national heritage on Ellis Island. This dismal future must have showed in her face. Claypool said, "Not that we care about the ruined structure—I mean we care, of course we care, but once it's that far gone there's no salvaging it. A lot of Islands Two and Three is beyond hope of stabilizing. It's been let go too long."

Letting her off the hook was an act of kindness. Someday Anna might have to reassess her opinion of Trey as a cold fish. Not today. He'd made her get up too early.

A spring in his step, a man of action now that the smallest of goals was in the offing, Claypool led the way down the hall and into the brick and glass passage connecting Islands I, II and III. Liquid green light and weathered brick embraced them, the curve of the passage destroying perspective so there was no beginning and no end. The hypnotic timelessness of Ellis closed around Anna and she drifted along in Trey's wake, her mind in neutral.

At a T-shaped intersection the passage joined the hall that formed the spinal cord for the ward buildings on Island III. Unlike the rest of the covered walkways, here it was open at the sides as in warmer climates. To the left, over the brick wall edging the walk, tucked in a tiny jungle of its own, was a square building: small, one room, one story, very different from the interconnected functioning units of the hospital.

"The jail?" Anna asked, unable to think of any other use for the stalwart structure.

"Who knows?" The Assistant Superintendent walked back to where she stood. Resting his elbows on the wall after a careful removal of the ubiquitous glass shards, he stared at the square of brick, though he must have seen it a hundred times before.

This was a different man from the one Anna had met her first day, crossed paths with on shipboard. In the backcountry of his urban wilderness a keen intelligence shone out of his carp eyes. Anna could almost see the images his mind must be forming: reconstructing, restoring, ferreting out the secrets of the past.

"It's called the Animal House," Trey said. "Could have been used for storage or office space. The name and some of the stories suggest it was used to house research animals for the medical facility."

"I've heard—" Bonham said.

Anna had forgotten he was with them. He'd been so withdrawn his very corporeal self had faded from view.

"What?" Trey prompted.

Fear skittered across Billy's weary face. "Just the stories. Same old," he said, and Anna wondered why he was lying.

"Are you okay, boy?" Trey asked.

If the term "boy" offended the Park Policeman, he didn't let it show.

"No sir. I mean, yes sir, I'm fine. Tired. Night shift and all." North Carolina, Patsy had said. Anna could hear the faint drawl under the words. She hadn't noticed it before. Maybe, like Hatch, he hid the sounds of home for fear he would seem a bumpkin to the sophisticated ears of the Big Apple.

Claypool eyed him narrowly, came to some conclusion he didn't intend to share and brought his attention back to Anna. "Want to see the morgue? It's right here."

Unable to resist the inducement of a genuine turn-of-the-century New York City morgue, Anna followed him, picking her way over the litter of glass and plaster.

"A little something for the spelunker," Trey said, apparently apropos of nothing. Then Anna's eyes lit on a fringe of stalactites creeping like icicles from the roof of the walkway. Leaves, ocean storms, mineral deposits, pigeons: all the forces of nature—earth, water, land and air—vied for the privilege of being the first to wrest back the island from the clutches of man.

Claypool led them around an immense incinerator and back into the bowels of the building. The last door on the left opened into the morgue. Anna and Trey enjoyed it with the ghoulish delight of children. Billy Bonham stood in the doorway, bored or trying to look that way. The facility was as grim and Victorian as any fan of Dickens could wish. A row of concrete steps descended to a tiled floor eight feet below. Beside them, three concrete terraces the width of the room: the gallery where medical students once gathered to watch autopsies.

At the bottom of the room, over the staging area, a rectangular lamp two by three feet in size was suspended on a long metal arm. Directly below was a deep porcelain sink. With very little imagination Anna could see blood dripping down the white sides, hear the rasp of saw through bone.

"This is the best part," Claypool said. In the classic pose of a circus ringmaster, he stood before an immense cupboard built into the wall to the left of the sink. Eight square wooden doors were stacked in double rows. The bottom doors were at floor level, the top two a foot shy of the ceiling.

Trey opened the one on the bottom right and pulled out a wooden rack made of slats, the sort of thing used to dry jerked meat. "The cooler," Trey said. "They could keep up to eight corpses at a time for research."

"Ever get in one?" Anna asked.

"Sure. You want to try it?"

114

She did, just because it was one of those opportunities that seldom knock and she hated to miss anything. But her clothes were clean and Columbia-Presbyterian was her next stop. "I'll take a rain check," she said regretfully.

Crossing broken gray tiles fitted with floor drains to carry away splattered effluvia, she opened another of the cupboards and peeked in. "A much more amiable place to lie than the steel filing drawers of a modern morgue."

"I'd think so," Claypool said.

Anna opened the door next to it. "Jesus Christ." She slammed the door.

"A mouse?"

"Not a mouse." Recovered from the initial shock, she opened the cupboard again. The image burned into the back of her eyes was that of a child as shriveled and desiccated as a body mummified by the New Mexico desert.

Claypool was at her shoulder. "One of the little people, a Ratner. I'll have to have a talk—another talk—with the head of Interpretation and that woman in charge of our troupe of theatrical immigrants. That little blond snippet is the practical joker of the bunch." Reaching past Anna, he said, "Give me a hand. These little buggers are heavy. Solid bronze."

Dragged into the light, Anna's child mummy turned into a sculpture of an immigrant. Age, race, country of origin, were glossed over with a generic motif of bonnet and ankle-length dress.

"Why is she two and a half feet tall?" Anna asked.

"Beats me. There are dozens of these around. They were done by an artist named Ratner. Everybody calls them 'the Ratners.' A race apart. The interpreters swear they breed in the dark, and I'm beginning to believe them. Most of them are stored in the old recreation hall on Island Two. For reasons that are a mystery to me, the seasonals have taken against them. We find them in the strangest places."

"The morgue?"

"This is the first here, but it's not an original idea. This is a popular place. We've found mannequins dressed in NPS uniforms, unpopular SOP manuals. Once—before my time—two curators were caught in flagrante.

"Billy," Trey barked. "Was this Ratner here when you did rounds last night?"

There was a hesitation just long enough so Anna guessed Billy didn't check the morgue.

"I don't think so," Bonham said, and Claypool let it go. The Park Police had no directive to check the buildings room by room. Not only would such an expedition take all night, but after dark it would be foolish from a safety standpoint, too much to trip over and fall into.

They left the midget immigrant at the intersection of hallways to be retrieved on the return trip, and continued on to the infectious disease wards on the southeast corner of the island.

After three false leads and an increasing

116

feeling of unreality, Anna found the ruined stairwell. It was as she remembered, with the exception of size. She would have sworn the one she'd dangled from was three times as high and the splintered wood and metal far more piercing in aspect.

"I didn't think to look here," Claypool said accusingly. "There's never been anything stored in this part of the building. What there is is upstairs in what used to be the nurses' quarters."

"I could have—" Anna stepped gingerly over the debris, having no desire to skewer herself on a nineteenth-century nail steeped in fifty years of bird shit. Beneath what remained of the upper landing she picked through the fragments of plaster, what looked like wax shavings, nails, pieces of rusted metal and mouse droppings. There was nothing under the mess but interlocking circles where paint cans or nail kegs had once been. "It could have been somewhere else, I guess," she said, but she didn't think so. "Could it have been moved? Dwight saw somebody here at about the same time I was."

"That was you," Billy said, the first words he'd spoken since they made their unscheduled stop at the morgue.

"Not me. Dwight saw somebody dressed in black. I wasn't. And I wasn't outside."

"Why didn't you report it?" Trey asked.

Professional guilt stabbed at Anna's middle. "I thought Dwight...I guess I had other things on my mind," she finished lamely.

"A sister in ICU? Are you two close?" the Assistant Superintendent asked.

"Very. Very close."

"With stress like that it's hard to keep things in perspective. You might not want to poke around back here by yourself for a while. One minute's inattention and..." He gestured meaningfully at the collapsed stairs.

Anna was being treated like an overwrought tourist. Though she'd done it to others more than once, she didn't like being on the receiving end. "Could the stuff I saw under the stairs have been moved, is what I was getting at. Moved by whoever it was Dwight saw?" she went on doggedly.

"Nothing is impossible," Trey said, and she knew she was being brushed off. Proving himself once again more sensitive than she'd given him credit for, when he saw her face turn to stone the Assistant Superintendent changed tactics. "Black is big in New York. It's a city in mourning. Everybody wears black winter and summer. Probably Dwight saw a straggler or an adventurer. We get them over here fairly regularly. We're not so much concerned about them damaging the resource as hurting themselves. Uncle Sam's deep pockets. It's a litigious man's dream come true back here. I know what you're thinking, though. I've worked the western parks. Could be somebody stealing artifacts, poaching, drug-dealing. We just don't have that. Things worth stealing— appliances, plumbing, copper pipe—were mined out long before we got it. There's nothing to poach but pigeons and no reason for anybody to rendezvous here to deal drugs. You can do it anywhere in the city and call less attention to yourself than you would here."

The speech had Anna convinced. Billy was pointedly looking at his watch, loath to miss the next staff boat. "I was thinking more along the lines of the little people. A joke." She tried saving face.

"Could be," Trey said, letting her. "But those things are awful heavy."

"Right." Suddenly Anna was as anxious as Billy to be away. There was that about the forgotten islands of Ellis that made one doubt oneself and yet resent the voices of sanity trying to explain away the discrepancies. When Molly was well, Anna would ask her if stress could be manifested in confusion and imagining things.

Even as the thought crossed her mind, Anna caught the "when." A beautiful word. Now it was "when" Molly got well, not "if." Shadows vanished. Anna was reborn in sunshine.

With a convenient attack of executive urgency, Trey left to walk back on the straight and sunlit path by the water. Anna and Billy were to go back via the Animal House to pick up the displaced little person and return her to the old recreation hall where the rest of her clan awaited.

Bonham was in a hurry and walked rapidly

down the light-riddled passageway. Leaf litter, deposited patiently one leaf at a time through cracked panes and broken mullions, was imbued with false life only to die again the moment after his gusting passage.

Shorter of leg, Anna trotted along behind. The unnecessary pace—they had twenty-five minutes to catch the boat—irked her thigh, but she didn't want to lose Billy. It was a dull morning. She wanted to tease stories from him. Years of campfire programs righteously elevated to educational tools to assist the public in appreciating the natural world left her nostalgic for good old-fashioned ghost stories. And it would give her something to talk about in the ICU. If nothing else, she could bring Molly interesting case studies. Molly was not a believer in the paranormal, but was fascinated by the quirks of the human mind.

The pint-sized immigrant was at the junction. Billy lifted the sculpture with a grunt. He was strong enough but without bulk, and so retained grace of movement. Anna enjoyed the play of muscles along his forearms and biceps as he adjusted his burden.

"What did you hear?" she asked. "You started to tell us you heard something here, by the Animal House. What was it?"

Billy didn't want to answer—that was clear in the crimp of his mouth and the fact his eyes wouldn't meet hers. Anna knew she'd win. He was a southern boy. She was a lady and old enough to be his mother. An irresistible force south of the Mason-Dixon Line. "Come on," she cajoled. "I told you about my psycho-cats."

Billy looked sheepish, but he smiled. "Psycho-dogs," he admitted. "One night when I used to patrol here I heard a dog barking, high and yappy, like a dog in pain."

"Did you check it out?"

"Not right away. I had some things to do," the officer defended himself. "But I came back at the end of shift—the next morning—and couldn't find anything."

"You think it was a real dog?"

"What do you think?"

"Could a dog get on the island?" Anna asked.

"Sure. All it would have to do is walk across the bridge from New Jersey."

He didn't sound convinced. A ghostly manifestation of a long-dead animal used in medical experimentation struck Anna as unlikely. But then so did a dog trekking over the water for no apparent reason, never seen by an island daily overrun with people.

Bonham opened the padlock to the recreation hall and Anna followed him into the dusty recesses of an enormous room filled with metal racks that reached nearly to the high ceiling and were cluttered with historical refuse: chairs, desks, lamps, boxes. At the far end of the room was a raised stage crowded with, among other things, a community of midget immigrants who appeared to be roughly formed with hammer and chisel. Caps, satchels and babes-in-arms were well represented. Bonham bumped the lady down among her peers. "These things give me the creeps," he said. "This whole island gives me the creeps. I don't want to get branded a flake but I do want to get off of here. I signed on to fight flesh-and-blood bad guys."

"What do you see?" Anna pressed since he was in the mood to talk.

"It's not like I go around looking for things," Billy said. "I'm not one of those guys who are always communing with crystals. Before coming here I'd only ever seen one ghost in my life and I was so snockered at the time, it was probably a pink elephant kind of thing."

He relocked the theater and the two of them abandoned the brick passage for the less imaginative path in back of the buildings. Anna resisted the temptation to quiz him, knowing the pressure of silence would be more effective.

"Here, cripes! It's one thing and another. Candles flickering in attic windows. Music I barely hear that stops when I really listen. That dog. A pale face behind a dirty window. Up high where you can't get to it without risking your neck. I don't much care whether I'm nuts or haunted. I just want off the island."

The dock behind the museum was empty, but a hundred yards out they could see the *Liberty IV*.

"Keep this to yourself," Billy warned. The boy was gone. Looking out of the baby-blue eyes was an angry man.

"Mum's the word," Anna said, and watched for the boy to return. He didn't.

9

A nna and Billy shared a boat back to Liberty, then across the harbor to MIO, but he was no longer speaking to her. Not surprising; confessions, not hedged neatly about with incense and holy water, were unsettling things. People seemed driven by twin devils: the need to unburden themselves and the fear of being undone by their secrets. If past experience was anything to judge by, Billy Bonham would avoid her for a good long time. Should his ego be slightly deformed, he might even go so far as to hate her for knowing him too well.

He'd taken the passenger cabin. That left the stern or the bridge to Anna. She chose wind and sun and sea over Kevin's jovial company. The harbor, the boat captains had told her, was on the mend, recovering from the days when a city's pollution was a testament to its economic well-being. Dwight said he'd seen seals and Kevin had sighted a school of silver-scaled fishes close to four feet long. Good news. Anna tried to dwell on it, and for a minute or two, actually succeeded. Then the fog of Billy Bonham's tired gray anger began to creep back. A dull ache started in the base of her skull where the weight of her head balanced precariously on the tip of her spine.

Without the splendors of nature to ameliorate it, the tawdriness of humanity loomed large.

All the tacky, needy, sordid, whiny, frightened, peevish citizens grasping for their daily dose of happiness began to gather in her mind-scape, peopling what should have been an arresting view of the Jersey shore.

A bony forest of iron and steel scratched against the blue of the sky. Machines engineered to lift or to pump, to load or to move, etched out an industrial "park" west of the Verrazano Narrows. Between this spiky horizon and the graceful drape of the bridge was an apartment complex. *Location, location, location,* the three most important things in real estate. Idly, Anna wondered if the word "Folly" had been added to the developer's name yet.

At the dock on Liberty Island Kevin took on two more passengers, neither of whom Anna recognized, then churned back into open water for the short trip to Manhattan. Billy still slept—or feigned it—in the cabin. The others joined him. Anna lost herself in the roar of the *Liberty IV*'s engines.

Before she saw Molly she wanted to shake the sense of unease that had settled around her, shrug off the venom of Billy's last words. No threats had been made. "Keep this to your-self" scarcely constituted verbal abuse. *Pre-monitions, signs and portents,* Anna realized. She had a bad feeling. Modern law enforcement techniques hardly recommended reading the entrails of chickens or calling 1-800-PSY-CHIC for clues, but no cops—at least no old cops—recommended ignoring what they called their "gut." Women, being less encumbered

124

with the need to link feelings to bodily urges, knew it as intuition.

The eye saw and the mind stored more than the conscious brain could readily assimilate or immediately articulate. A hundred tiny things—the way a person stood, something missing or added, a smell, a shift of the eyes, things done and undone—that were too minute to take focus, but when recorded by eye and mind, coalesced into a feeling. This morning Anna felt all was not right with the world. She was not safe. This was a dangerous and angry place. And it had nothing to do with the reputed horrors of New York City. New York had never frightened her. Annoyed her, yes. Pissed her off, occasionally. Disgusted and amazed her on a regular basis. But never scared her. This had to do with the little islands. Or, she admitted as the *Liberty IV* docked and she joined the short queue disembarking at MIO, maybe more to do with Molly, alcohol, too little sleep and—who knew?—maybe perimenopause. Anna had always been precocious.

The subway conspired to add to the pervasive sense of unease. From the 125th Street station on, a scrofulous young man in leather and chains, with various parts of his anatomy shaved, pierced or tattooed, sat across the aisle staring through her. The fact that he scurried after her at the 168th Street stop shouting, "Pardon me, ma'am, but you forgot your backpack," lightened her mood somewhat, but not so much that Molly, wits sharpened by being the firstborn and a psychiatrist, wouldn't note her gloom. On the short and sunny walk from the subway to the hospital, Anna whistled a happy tune to see if the prescription worked anywhere but musical comedy.

She needn't have worried. Something occurred that she'd not foreseen. Molly was, for once, too wrapped up in herself to pay much attention to her little sister. Anna was both relieved and, though she'd never have admitted it regardless of red-hot pokers and bamboo shoots under the fingernails, just a wee bit miffed.

This miniature snit was blown away by the stunningly beautiful sight of her sister's smile. Weak, watery, lips dry and cracked, it lit up the room, put a glow over Manhattan beside which the bright lights of the Great White Way paled.

The breathing tube was still out and, Anna noted with vicious satisfaction, the apparatus had been banished from the bedside. Gone too was the dialysis machine. As Dr. Madison had promised, her kidneys had recovered on their own.

Molly wasn't sitting, precisely, but she was propped up on three pillows. Her hair was combed and she had a touch of color in her cheeks. Makeup, Anna could tell, but for a woman like Molly the act of applying cosmetics was a slap in the face of death. The gauntlet of rouge had been thrown down; Molly had entered the fray.

"Looks like you've had quite a night," Anna

said, and laughed with delight so pure it threatened to melt into tears. "Good thing I got here early before you left to play golf or something."

"Maybe tomorrow. Today I'm just hoping to get out of the ICU."

"Blastoff is thirteen hundred hours according to Dr. Madison," Frederick Stanton added. "After lunch, if Molly doesn't screw things up for me. Downstairs they have real chairs for visitors." Frederick did look awkward with his bones sprinkled haphazardly over the narrow straight-backed chair. Today he was without props. The guitar had been left behind; no new inspirational items had been imported from Molly's apartment. A paperback copy of Robert Frost's poems and a shoebox rested on the floor by his chair.

Robert Frost. He's come a-courtin', went through Anna's mind, surprising her because the realization was so devoid of personal rancor. She found herself liking this unforeseen aspect of the FBI guy. Should he perform a hundred more acts of sensitivity and commitment, she might consider entrusting her sister to his care. With that thought came the not entirely welcome knowledge that she did have that power. One word from her and Molly would again slam the iron door of her heart.

"Hey, Frederick," Anna said, making a mental note to be very careful what she said around the two of them lest she inadvertently slam any iron. Having unfolded a plastic chair

127

some kind soul had left in the room, she scooted it near Molly, occupying the space where the hated respirator had been. Fifteen, twenty seconds ticked by. Nobody said anything. Molly and Frederick exchanged a look Anna could not fathom.

"What?" she demanded. Another look passed between them. A thready little cry leaked out from nowhere.

"Stop that, Anna," Molly said. Though still whispery, authority had returned to her voice.

"What?" Anna said again, beginning to lose her hard-won good cheer. Again the creaky little noise. Molly was making it or Frederick was. A game of some kind. Anna was not amused. She regressed: "You stop," she snapped.

Molly laughed. Out loud. The old good whiskey laugh, and it all fell in place. Back in the days when it meant a week in a darkened room, Anna had had the measles. Because she was a giving little beast, she'd infected her sister. At twelve, Molly had somehow missed the disease. As a special treat, their mother had let the two feverish children spend the day in her and Dad's double bed. By two o'clock the sisters had worn out one another's patience. Around quarter past, their mother had poked her head in. After she left, Molly started making weird sounds and blaming them on Anna. They'd nearly come to blows before they discovered the gift their mother had left to help them pass the dark, dull hours.

"A kitten!" Anna exclaimed. "You've got a

kitten." A half-smile playing around her mouth, Molly reached beneath the sterile white sheets. In that instant she looked twelve years old again.

"Frederick brought her," Molly said. Cupped in her hands was a small gray Persian kitten, a kitten like the one in the picture Stanton had brought from her apartment. Anna couldn't even guess how many pet stores he'd have had to canvass to find such a perfect match. *Ninety-nine more acts of sensitivity and commitment.*

"Rajah," she said stupidly.

"Rani."

"Right. You don't want a cat," Anna said, wondering why she wasn't entering into the spirit of the thing.

"It's my cat," Frederick said. "At least until Molly falls hopelessly in love and decides to keep us."

The "us" wasn't lost on either of the Pigeon sisters. Molly looked uncomfortable and Anna stomped in to make things right. "She will. We will. Molly likes cats. It's a fine cat." She was floundering, but her sister seemed to understand she meant well. Molly relaxed, holding the gray puffball to her drawn cheek and closing her eyes.

Molly's love life was an enigma Anna had spent quite a bit of time fantasizing about when she was younger. Molly never talked much about it, thus adding an irresistible aura of mystery. As Anna grew up she'd come to believe there were no great secrets, just little interest.

Molly was made for the cliché "married to her work." Psychiatry and ambition filled the places in her life where other women stashed husbands and children.

She had been married once, for eighteen months, when she was an intern. If the dissolution of that union left any scars, Molly had never let Anna see them. It wasn't that Molly lived a celibate life. For eight years or so in her forties, she'd carried on a desultory long-distance affair with a neurosurgeon in Laguna Beach, California. The romance died from neglect. Frederick was the first man Anna had seen really spark something more than desire in Molly's eyes. Anna wasn't sure how she felt about that, but there was a faint stench of the Wicked Stepsister about it, of not wanting something until it proved of value to someone else.

The short morning's visit had exhausted Molly. When lunch came, her visitors left—Anna, Frederick and, hidden away from the vigilant eyes of the hospital staff in its shoebox, the kitten.

"What do Emmett and his family think about Rani?" Anna asked when the silence in the elevator began to prickle.

"We're staying in Molly's apartment," Frederick said. His voice was oh so carefully neutral. He was scared. Anna toyed with the idea of throwing her weight around, abusing her power just because she could, but in the end, she couldn't drum up the energy required to be spiteful.

130

"I'm okay with this, you know," she said. "You and I were what we were, had what we had, but that's blood under the bridge. You make Molly happy, you make me happy."

A silence followed, long enough for the elevator doors to open and the two of them to walk through the aching, injured aura of the hospital halls to the bustling sunshine outside.

"And if I don't make her happy?" Frederick asked at last.

"I will devise a slow and Machiavellian torture comprising three parts Spanish Inquisition and two parts Nazi war crimes," Anna said. She laughed and Frederick tried to.

"Why don't I think you're kidding?"

Anna didn't reply, but she suspected it was because the man had good instincts.

Seated on the cool, slick plastic of the subway car benches, he spoke again, leaning into her to be heard over the clatter of metal on metal. "It's not just me who needs to know you're okay with this."

Anna waited while nasty retorts cleared off her tongue. Her tender feelings hadn't been consulted in Frederick's pursuit of Molly two years before or two days before. Her being "okay" with the romance hadn't mattered a damn from the moment he laid eyes on her sister.

It was Molly who cared.

Anger born of injured pride spewed vile thoughts into her brain and acid remarks into her mouth. Jaws locked, eyes ahead, she sat till the eruption passed.

131

It was Molly who mattered.

"I'll tell her," she said, and was pleased at the very nearly friendly tone of her voice. "Give me the kitten."

With the air of a man sealing a bargain, Frederick passed the ventilated shoebox to her lap and Anna squeezed her fingers under the lid to be rewarded by the velvet pats and needle pricks of tiny paws.

The A train bashed on. Unlikely worlds flickered through the windows. Hitchcockian views of strangers on a train, startling Christie images of the four-fifty from Paddington, shattered by a disorienting strobe of shadow and light. Anna played with the cat. Frederick stared at his feet, long and biblical in leather sandals. He had hair on the tops of his toes, like a hobbit. Anna had never noticed that before. In the grumbling bowels of Manhattan, she found the touch of whimsy endearing.

"Do me a favor?" she asked suddenly.

Frederick shot her a glance that was an interesting mixture of hope and trepidation. Again, Anna realized her power. In this bizarre circumstance, she held, as the nineteenth-century romanticists might have expressed it, the key to his future happiness in the palm of her little hand. The hope, she guessed, was that he could win her over with favors. The trepidation, no doubt, over just what those favors might be. Slaying dragons and ogres was the standard going rate for the hand of any self-respecting princess. Psychiatrists with a profitable practice might go for considerably more.

A moment passed and Frederick said: "Name it."

Anna's mind had been turning on James Hatchett. She liked him, pitied him his predicament. The body of the fallen child had been plowed into New York's considerable justice system. In a city of over seven million people the identification of a dead child, probably a runaway nobody wanted, would of necessity take a backseat to more pressing matters. A Park Policeman, particularly one suspected of possible involvement, would have a tough time sorting through jurisdictions and cutting red tape to get information.

"I need a corpse identified," Anna said, and smiled at the relief on the FBI guy's face. Dead people, Frederick was comfortable with. The dead, and those who assisted them into that state, were a goodly part of his job and, as he'd said more than once, some of his best friends were dead people.

Briefly, Anna told him of the jumping death at the statue, of Hatch, the child, the accusation, the missing backpack. "I thought maybe you could lean on your buddy Emmett. Turn over a few rocks for me."

"Consider it done." Frederick shook her hand, then dropped it as if it had suddenly morphed into a suckery tentacle.

He rode with her to the Seventy-second Street station. There they both detrained to spend an exceedingly agreeable hour at the pet shop where he had purchased Rani. The cage housing Rani's two sisters was marked: "Pure-bred Persians—$499.95." Anna whistled appreciatively as she passed. "You've got it bad."

"Bad," he agreed, in the tone of a man diagnosed with an inoperable tumor.

Anna didn't laugh. He was still scared. And well he should be. He'd already gone through two wives, three kids and Anna. The time had come for him to wake up and be seriously frightened before he dove into another relationship.

After Rani had been outfitted with food, litter box, toys, a tiny purple harness with "diamond" accents and a matching lead, Anna and Frederick repaired to Central Park across the avenue from the subway entrance. While Rani tried her Houdini impersonation in an attempt to wriggle out of her new finery, Anna and Frederick enjoyed ice cream and a rare perfect day in early summer when the park was still fresh with new green, leaves and grass not yet having taken on that soiled, trampled aspect of tired carnival grounds.

Neither of them talked of Molly, though Anna wanted to and, from the way he jumped from topic to topic and gusted forth half-sentences, she suspected Stanton was bursting with the need. She remembered and was jealous. Not of Molly but of Frederick, of that wild ride of new love. Or, in his case, old love aflame with new possibilities.

By mutual unspoken agreement they did not

speak of the past, their affair or its limping conclusion.

Areas of conversation thus limited, all that remained was the day, the park, the cat and Anna's island gossip. For her it felt good to have a death and a small mystery to discuss. She and Frederick had met over murder and worked two cases together before their first date. To dwell again on crime turned the clock back to the days before sex and muttered reticent declarations of love had complicated their friendship.

By the time they again wormed their way under the spiny surface of Manhattan, rush hour had commenced. Frederick left her to the downtown side of the tracks and took the uptown.

The subway platform was crowded. Trains and commuters complained. Elbows jostled, bags and hips nudged. Anna sweated, claustrophobia climbing up her esophagus to dump foul-tasting bile behind her teeth. Coping mechanisms were pulled from memory and she dug Wilkie Collins out of her daypack and retreated gratefully to the previous century.

People continued to pour down the stairs, an unending flood of humanity. No train came. Anna was pushed closer to the tracks. Around her, New Yorkers indulged in the fruitless pastime of leaning out over the six-foot drop where the tracks were recessed to stare into the sweltering tunnels as if they could create trains with sheer willpower. The crush intensified. Anna shifted her weight to

135

her heels to keep from being squeezed off the platform. Shoulders hunched, she reduced her world to the freedom of the printed page. Dimly she was aware the air around her was being breathed in by ever more pairs of lungs. Mere sips were left for her. She read on doggedly.

When it seemed the station must spontaneously combust from the fetid friction of so many bodies, the roar of an oncoming train stirred the crowd the way wind stirs a field of grain. People began jockeying for position, semisentient roulette balls guessing where the doors would stop.

Anna marked her place in the book with her finger and looked up, ready to do battle for a space in the nearest car. Air was pushed from the canyon housing the rails, bringing up the scent of metal and electricity. A picture of bumper car rides at the county fair flashed behind Anna's eyes. Image triggered action. As the train thundered into the station, someone bumped her, hard, in the small of her back. Wilkie Collins flew from her grasp and she watched, helpless, as the paperback was sucked down onto the rails.

Unbalanced by the shove, she began to tumble after, her moccasined feet slipping from the edge of the platform. A scream—an aborted bark of sound—was drowned by the approaching wreck of noise. Her arms windmilled as she tried to regain control. Her hand smacked something remotely fleshlike and another cry was added to the din. Still she fell. The world kaleidoscoped, mismatched pieces forced together as brain and body flailed for equilibrium. The train smashed into her peripheral vision, filling the station with bone-crushing force. Below, the rails glimmered faintly, scraps of litter swirling between them. In the cropped edges of her vision the feet of those still firmly rooted to the platform flickered: crimson high heels; battered sneakers; army boots, the leather scuffed and torn.

The instant of her death was frozen in time and space. The straps of her daypack jerked her back. Loose-jointed as a puppet, she flopped into the man behind her. He was big of belly, shoulders and head. An immense black man in a tailor-made gray silk suit had grabbed her pack in one meaty fist and lifted her to safety.

"Watch yourself," he growled when she tried to thank him. "You fall under a train it ties things up for hours."

The train stopped, doors opened and he was gone. A flock of lesser beings hurried along in his wake as he cleared a path onto the downtown A train. Anna made it on just as the doors closed. Knees still weak from her brush with disaster, she turned her back on the human meat packaged with her and stared out the window. Halfway down the now sparsely populated platform she glimpsed a tall, dark-haired man. Spectral fingers tapped out the theme from *The Twilight Zone* on the xylophone of her spine.

"Get a grip," she whispered. "Cut out the alcohol. Start exercising. Get more sleep. Eat less sugar." People under stress were more accident-prone. That was fact. The stairs on Ellis. Now the subway.

The train lurched. The window blanked with tunnel wall.

Under the tall dark-haired man's arm was what Anna could have sworn was a shoebox. Just the size for transporting a five-hundred-dollar cat.

10

Several stops came and went. Anna was aware of them only in the sense that an increasingly odious press of bodies was injected into the car, edging her from her place by the doors. So tightly was she hemmed in by pliant walls of flesh, through the insult of stops and starts, she didn't need to hold on to remain upright.

Despite the duress of forced camaraderie, she didn't miss the companionship of Wilkie Collins or feel the suffocating nearness of her extemporaneous neighbors. Preoccupation closed around her, rock ramparts intact. The debilitating weakness that flooded her in the wake of her near miss had passed. Once again her knees were sufficient to hold her.

Her heart no longer pounded high in her throat.

Manhattan was undoubtedly home to thousands of tall dark-haired men blessed with the physique of pencil-necked geeks. It wasn't even unlikely that a handful of them might be passing through a subway station shortly after she'd received a fright. But the odds of any one of them carrying a white perforated shoebox of a size and shape suitable for the incarceration of kittens were some excessively large number to one.

Frederick Stanton had been fleeing up the stairs of the downtown side of the tracks moments after her silk-clad angel of mercy snatched her from the proverbial jaws.

That didn't mean Frederick had pushed her.

Under her breastbone Anna felt a gnawing: tiny teeth, sharp and vicious, like the fox the Spartan boy hid in his coat. Like the boy of legend, Anna didn't let the bite show on her face, hid her pain. The gnaw wasn't the fear that Frederick had pushed her but the unpleasant evil that she almost wished he had. A reason to hate him, to lash out, to keep her sister from him. An assertion he'd been a low and scaly creature bent on hurting more than her ego, trifling with more than her affections. A defensible place to dump the anger and frustration she'd felt for the past days. Scenes ran behind her eyes, fragmented film clips of telling Molly, of the righteous indignation and tears of sympathy.

At Fifty-ninth Street Anna moved with the herd, changing to the Number 1 train. When the doors opened under Christopher Street she detrained and climbed above ground to settle her mind in the relative peace of the twisting European streets of Greenwich Village. One of the ubiquitous sidewalk eateries, cloned from some immigrant's vague memory of a bistro, beckoned. A jolly young man rehearsing an Irish brogue brought her a sauvignon blanc. In the strengthening sun of early summer she organized her thoughts and sipped 12.5 percent in glassed courage.

Thus fortified, she searched out a pay phone tough enough to have survived the neighborhood vandals, and punched out the number of the phone in Molly's apartment. Frederick answered on the third ring, the familiar "Hello" of a man at home. "I think 'Dr. Pigeon's residence' would be more appropriate," she said. Frederick made no reply and she wished she'd kept her venom to herself. "I just called with a couple of questions," she pushed on.

Across the street, at another in the array of alfresco cafés, a giant rainbow-hued tricycle, the seat a dozen feet from the sidewalk—piloted by a person in a clown suit and trailing a French poodle in a purple tutu—rolled to a gentle halt. The clown began to play an accordion. The little dog danced. Anna stuffed a finger in her free ear and nosed into the half-shell of metal and plastic that housed the phone. Like much of the city, it smelled of stale

140

urine. "Did you come over to the downtown side of the A platform?" she asked.

A beat of silence dulled her ear. Then: "Sorry. Rani was climbing up my leg. What did you say?"

Frederick was going to lie. Anna repeated the question and waited for the inevitable. He didn't disappoint her. "Why would I do that?" he said, as if he were having a problem rec-ollecting any subway station in his recent past.

Even people trained to detect lies, to note the signals—vagueness, evasion, answering questions with questions—fell into the same patterns of deceit. Anna chose to cut through the fog. "I saw you. You were walking up the exit stairs with the cat under your arm just as my train was pulling out."

Another silence. Anna watched the tricyclist. The clown had stopped playing. The dog ran from table to table with a hat in his mouth.

"Why the elaborate trap?" Frederick said finally.

"Not elaborate."

"I was on the downtown side. I won't deny it." Resentment laced through his words.

He'd already denied it, but Anna let that pass. "Why?"

"What difference does it make?"

He was in full defensive posture now. It made Anna tired. Too tired for games. "Somebody tried to push me in front of the train," she said.

The dog was trotting back to his master, still perched on the seat above the crowd. The clown lowered a butterfly net mounted on a long pole and the dog placed the hat in it to the desultory applause of the onlookers.

"Anna, you don't think I pushed you, do you?"

Frederick's mix of hurt and affront sounded genuine, but Anna had been lied to by experts. Mostly she'd believed them. At least for a while.

"No, I don't," she said truthfully.

"Why would I?" Frederick demanded.

She'd already given that considerable thought. The only reason she could scrape up was his fear that she would come between him and Molly. A motive for murder only if the murderer was insane and did not truly love. Frederick was not and Anna believed he wouldn't intentionally hurt Molly. Her death would hurt Molly; ergo, Frederick was off the hook.

"No reason," she said. "Why did you lie to me?"

A sigh, pregnant with all the toxins of a man found out, blew through the wires. "I was embarrassed," he admitted.

"Why?"

"Anna, you're beginning to sound like a broken record. Or a three-year-old."

"Why were you there?"

"Oh, Jesus. Okay, Sherlock, I came to ask *when* you were going to tell Molly it was okay...you know...for her and me."

"Yup. That's embarrassing all right."

"You never thought I pushed you."

"Not with any conviction."

"So who did?"

"An accident," she replied wearily. "It happens."

"You don't believe that."

She didn't but couldn't say why.

"You want to come stay with me?" Frederick offered.

"I would rather embrace the third rail." To her relief and annoyance, he laughed.

"See you tomorrow?" he asked.

"Yes. Work on that ID for me?"

"I'm on it."

Anna hung up the phone but stayed where she was, looking through the scratched plastic at the tricycle as it lumbered, dog in tow, down the street. Not something one saw every day in Cortez, Colorado.

"You making a call or what?" came an executive whine.

She pushed herself from the phone and left it to a prosperous-looking man in spandex and a helmet, a fifteen-speed bicycle balanced on his shoulder.

Accidents waiting to happen; Anna had read statistics on that somewhere. A dollop of stress, a family tragedy, a lost job. Mind skittered, reflexes slowed and the chances of having an accident skyrocketed. Making a poor decision. Climbing rickety stairs in the dark. Standing too close to the tracks on a crowded platform at rush hour.

For a minute she stood on the sidewalk, half a dozen feet from the phone, and pondered another sauvignon blanc. Pedestrians eddied around her, taking no more notice of her than they would of a tree or a fire hydrant or—in New York City—a hippopotamus smoking hashish. Greenwich Village was a place of dogs, she noted idly. Big dogs on leashes. Labs and Dobermans and huskies that lived in tiny apartments, out twice a day to "do their business." Allowed to run only on weekends and then only when their owners weren't otherwise engaged. A city of happy prisoners.

Wine evaporated from her wish list. Two glasses would not be enough. More than two would be overkill. Condemned to moderate sobriety, she began to walk. Though there was much to be said for it, urban hiking didn't work the way a walk in the wilderness did. The seedier parts of town west of the burgeoning gentrification on Hudson Street more closely suited her taste. The stained warehouses, the wildlife in the doorways, the occasional predator glimpsed through a shadeless window, the myriad smaller fry decked out in camouflaging plumage, strutting in hopes of so closely aping the killers as to avoid being killed. These streets sharpened her senses. The need to remain alert and aware took her outside of herself. As evening came, and with it the chill off the Atlantic and the changing of day people for night people, she felt alive and clearheaded.

Before descending to Manhattan's end, where the NPS boat docked, she indulged in a pleasure not available in small towns. She

144

foraged for food: crisp lettuce at a vegetable stand, fresh bread from a bakery, pasta and coffee and wine, each item from its own store. Each lovingly selected and anticipated. The convenience of supermarkets, the tossing of packaged goods into a rolling metal cart, saved time but did little to fill a woman's primal urge to hunt and gather.

By the time the *Liberty IV*'s pale wake cut a ragged line through the lights reflected on the harbor, Anna had come to a resting place: Frederick Stanton wasn't a psychopathic killer and Molly was on the mend. Sometimes one had to simply take the bad with the good.

11

Party boats plied their trade till Anna dreamed of rearming Fort Wood, now serving as Lady Liberty's step stool, and smashing them into the sea with cannonballs. When silence came, sleep followed, deep and dreamless. She awoke to an empty house and a clock that insisted it was ten-fifteen. She'd not slept that late since she was a teenager. Middle age seemed bent on thwarting this adolescent pleasure. She felt more groggy than refreshed.

Coffee and a shower drove away the cobwebs

and she discovered the day was worth venturing into: clear with the promise of intense heat. Years in the high deserts had turned her into a bit of an exotherm. Bright baking days of true summer recharged batteries drained by long nights and cold winds.

If all went according to plan, Molly would be in transit today, moving from the ICU to the less threatening climes of a private room on a regular ward. The move—no doubt with Frederick in panting attendance—would take up a chunk of the morning. Anna wouldn't visit till afternoon. Realizing she felt let off the hook, she accepted a small pang of guilt, but it was short-lived. Given New York City, threats to life and limb and the turning over of a slightly used but still serviceable boyfriend, she'd been a veritable saint. She deserved a morning off. She would spend it lost in the badlands of Ellis Island.

Having packed a lunch gleaned from the gourmet forage of the previous day—raspberry truffles, blue corn chips, smoked catfish pâté, sweet pickles and some peachy-colored muffinlike item that looked determined to keep one regular, Anna pushed open the kitchen door. Pinched between screen and frame was a legal envelope with the statue's NPS address in the upper left corner. An official, if unofficially delivered, communiqué for Patsy. Plucking it out to keep it from falling, she saw her own name scrawled across the front.

To the right of the door, beneath the spare and beautiful branches of an old plane tree, was a bench. The only use Anna had ever seen it put to was as a lounge for Mandy's sporadic cigarette smoking. Not willing to go back indoors even for the brief time it would take to read the note, she plopped herself and her goods on the wooden slats.

The missive was written in the same round childish hand as her name.

*"Dear Ms. Pigeon (Anna)," * it read. *"I thought about banging on your door but as it was only 7:30 and early, I was afraid you'd still be in bed. That's where I'd be if I had any sense which I don't. What I was wondering was if you'd found out anything about that little girl, who she was. I went to the morgue in the city. It's not that they wasn't helpful exactly but they didn't seem much interested. Can't say as I blame them. There's a lot of dead people in New York. One more didn't exactly put them into a frenzy or anything. I think it's maybe up to me to find out who she belongs to. I feel responsible anyway.*

"They wouldn't let me see the body which was okay by me. Once was plenty, let me tell you. I've seen dead bodies—you know, car crashes and froze climbers and the like, even a vagrant or two when I worked in D.C.—but kids is different. You don't get used to kids. They let me look at her stuff, her 'affects.' There wasn't much but maybe I got an idea but not much of one.

"If you come up with anything I could sure use the help. This has got me pretty down. One of the interpreters kind of laid into me last night. Not saying I pushed the little girl, but maybe as how I'd scared her and more or less chased her off that

balcony. *That maybe is true. I guess I'll never know. I sure didn't mean to but 'mean to' is pretty sorry at this point.*

"I know I'll feel a whole lot better if I could at least get her home and buried properly. I didn't ask where they put unclaimed bodies but I know it's a kind of lonely and nameless place. Not right for a little girl.

"I'll be on tonight, midnight to eight like regular. Come and see me if you don't have nothing better to do."

It was signed, *"Yours truly, James Hatchett (Hatch)."*

Leaving her backpack on the bench and delighting in the knowledge that she was in one of the privileged few places in New York City where one could do that with a fair expectation of finding it there on one's return, Anna went back into the house.

There was no answer at Molly's apartment. She'd expected none; she was just covering her bases. Columbia-Presbyterian politely routed her to various helpful souls before they tracked down Molly's new room number.

"Hi," Anna said when her sister picked up. "Is Frederick there?"

"What, no small talk?" Molly asked, and Anna mentally kicked herself for failing to at least pretend she occasionally thought of someone other than herself.

"One-track mind," she apologized. "Remember that guy Hatch I was telling you about? The Park Policeman with the jumper?" Molly didn't. Anna had related the tale when drugs and tubes were taking up most of her sister's attention. She began to give a shortened version, when Molly cut her off.

"Oh, right, the little girl Frederick is investigating."

Anna quashed a surge of irritation. It was one thing to preempt a sibling, but taking over a case—even one not technically hers—was a serious breach of etiquette.

Out of courtesy and guilt, she managed to stifle her impatience and ask Molly a few polite questions: "How are you? How's the new room?" But she didn't hear the answers. Molly, sensing Anna was to conversing what empty calories are to dieting, handed the phone over to Frederick Stanton.

"Hey there, what's up?"

He was too jolly by half but he was at Molly's sickbed and Anna was truant, so she let it slide. "Did you find out anything about that unidentified corpse?"

"Molly, your little sister is playing with dead children again." Frederick's voice veered from the phone. Anna heard Molly laugh and imagined she heard the faintest of snicking sounds, the FBI guy winking at her sister. Molly's laughter paid for any annoyance incurred and she waited with moderate good cheer till Frederick refocused on the matter at hand.

"I did get to it," he said. The caution in his tone let her know not to expect too much. "There's not a whole lot to go on. They figure she's thirteen or fourteen years old. No dental work—none. She's missing a couple teeth. The report said it looked as if they'd been pulled or knocked out. Nothing recent—maybe two to four years ago. No fillings but three cavities, the kind a kid getting regular checkups would have had filled."

"That tallies with the runaway theory," Anna said.

"Except for the pulled teeth."

"Knocked out? Family abuse?"

"Maybe. There was evidence of an old break to her left ulna, but no other signs of physical abuse. No bruising not caused by the fall. No scars. No injuries in various stages of healing. She was small for her age but not from malnourishment. Skin, hair, teeth, bone development, were all consistent with a child who's been well fed and well cared for, with the exception of the teeth and scarring on her right eardrum, probably from an ear infection untreated and causing the drum to burst."

"Sexual activity?"

"Hymen intact."

"That doesn't go with making a good living on the street, enough to feed and care for herself well."

"Your buddy the Park Policeman thought she was a thief, a pickpocket," Frederick offered.

"Crime doesn't pay like it used to, not at fourteen, not in the city. Somebody was looking after her. Or she ran off recently. So recently she hadn't time to lose weight or virginity."

"No match with missing persons reports,"

Frederick went on. "It'll take a while. She could be from anywhere in the country. New York's a magnet for runaways."

"And actors," Anna said, apropos of nothing but a fleeting image of Zachary.

"Like I said," Frederick teased.

While he related this feeble witticism to Molly, Anna let the information he'd given her settle in her mind. "Did you see the body?" she asked.

"How's that?"

Dutifully Anna repeated the question. Love was making Frederick Stanton goofy. "No," he replied. "I did look at her effects. The girl traveled light."

"Whatever she had would have been in the pack that was stolen," Anna reminded him.

"What they've got are her pants—either hand-me-downs or thrift-shop, but probably not hers originally. A size too big and the cuffs cut and hemmed by hand. No help there. A boy's shirt. Ralph Lauren, long-sleeved, a hundred percent cotton, oxford style. Expensive but also probably hand-me-down or secondhand. No belt, no brassiere. Cotton underpants, new, white with blue flowers, Wal-Mart. Socks and shoes no longer new but in good shape. The wear patterns suggest they were bought new for the girl. All the clothes were clean but not ironed."

"That's it?" Anna asked.

"All I got."

"Thanks," she said absently, and: "See you guys this afternoon."

151

She hung up Patsy's cordless and wandered back out to the bench under the plane tree. The little girl was cared for insofar as she was fed and clothed and no one had apparently sexually or physically abused her. Yet her teeth had been pulled or knocked out, the cavities left unfilled, and an ear infection, which Anna remembered from childhood as being very painful, left untreated, resulting in a burst eardrum and possible loss of hearing in one ear.

Several possibilities suggested themselves. The child's parents or caregivers could be poor. That might account for the second-hand clothing and the lack of medical attention. They could be ignorant and/or poor and so let the child's health suffer. They could hold religious convictions that forbade the interference of modern medicine in the healing process. None of these explanations fit with the body going unclaimed.

A vague sense of something forgotten weaseled around in Anna's skull as she walked the "back alleys" of Liberty Island—a short concrete work area between the building used by park personnel and a line of maintenance storage areas. Mentally she went over Stanton's oral report and could find nothing missing. Except any real comfort in the form of hard information to offer Hatch when next she saw him.

Once she was clear of the tourist-choked quay, all that glittered was gold to Anna. Sunlight, splintered into mirror shards by a choppy wind teasing the harbor, sparkled from below. Sailboats were out in force, triangles of winged color blowing across the water. The occasional fisherman, lines cast from his boat, hoping for edible fish. Ferries, one from Staten Island and two from the Circle Line, churned unstoppably through the lesser fry.

Stepping off the *Liberty IV*, Anna realized the something missing that had been plaguing her had nothing to do with Frederick's report on the girl. It was a beverage. In her lunch-filled knapsack, she'd neglected to pack anything to drink.

Knowing where Patsy kept her stash, she rode the elevator to the second floor of the powerhouse behind the registry building on Island I and made her way down the kinked corridor to the employee break room.

Minutes after the noon hour, it was inhabited by the park's acting troupe. The faux Jamaican and the faux Irishman sat at one table lunching in what struck Anna as sullen silence. At the second table, alone at the far end of the room, sat a third character clad in the garments of a nineteenth-century western European immigrant. The familiar brown dress was a couple sizes too small for the woman wearing it and, to Anna's surprise, the hair wasn't the pale yellow of the fragile blonde who'd professed such an interest in Billy Bonham and his pet ghosts, but flaming-red hair cut in a modern ear-length bob.

"Hey, Mandy," Anna said as she took a

Coke from the refrigerator. "Nice uniform."

"Hah!" Mandy returned. She actually said "Hah!" just like Anna imagined it when she came across the expression in books. "That size-one bitch—"

A spoon was clacked forcefully down on the Formica at the actors' table. "Poor little Miss Mandy." A warm Irish burr cut into the interpreter's words. "Havin' to squeeze her considerable 'talents' into Corinne's costume has ruined her temper."

The woman portraying the Jamaican finished the insult. "Tight clothing constricts the lymph flow. Throws the bodily humors out of balance. Hence Miss Mandy is out of humor."

"It's that or bad acting," Brooklyn Irish muttered, a stage whisper meant to be audible at a distance.

A flush crept up Mandy's pale cheeks. Baiting her would be child's play, Anna thought. "I've had about enough of you," Mandy said, and stood to gather up her lunch things.

"Right you are, lass, right you are," the actor said, still using his character accent. "It was ungentlemanly of me to enter into a battle of wits with an unarmed woman."

The black actress laughed. Mandy knew she was being insulted, but Anna was willing to bet she didn't know exactly how. At a loss for a sharper retort, she said: "At least I show up." With a snitty-sounding click of heels on the linoleum, she stomped out of the lunch-room.

"Where is Corinne?" Anna asked.

"Maybe she got a real acting job," the man in knee britches replied.

"Fighting with Macho Bozo," the actress suggested.

"Ran off with sweet Billy Bonham," the man added.

"More power to her," said the actress. "Wish she'd called in sick or dead, though. Working with the Mandy beast is what I believe they refer to as suffering for one's art."

"She is most definitely a black hole on stage into which all talent vanishes," the actor agreed.

From this rattled exchange, which was not directed at Anna but meant only to amuse the two theater people, she surmised Corinne had gone AWOL and left them holding a Mandy-sized bag.

Having little interest in taking on the role of audience in this comedy, she wished them luck, tucked her soda in her daypack and followed the pitter-patter of Mandy's feet down the corridor toward the elevator. Avoiding human interaction on Island I, she slunk down the bricked walkway and through the decaying laundry room with its rusting mangle and shredded ceiling. Ascending floor after floor, each more decrepit than the last, each housing its own biosphere dictated by how much of the natural world had penetrated the old hospital's man-made defenses, Anna felt the cares of the peopled world dropping away much as they did when she stepped off trail and hiked into the wilderness on the mesas of southern Colorado.

She'd not been into the labyrinth of rooms and hallways of Island II since the first days of rain. Golden light poked warm fingers through broken windows, down skylights and into the chinks in mortar and wood. As she climbed into the final stairwell leading to the fourth floor, the one sans stairs that could only be ascended by clinging to an aging rail and finding footholds on the stubs of long-gone risers, each patch of light was verdant with tiny green mosses. Above, on the landing beneath a skylight, were the familiar branches of the little oak glowing yellow-green with new foliage, its roots sunk in the verdure of rot and bird droppings, its leaves reaching for the glory of an obscured sky.

Anna muscled up the last yard and stepped away from the crumbling hole that once housed five stories of stairs. For a moment she stood tasting the peculiar brand of urban silence. Across the inlet, on Island I, was the mutter of thousands of voices, the growl of ferryboat motors. Muted by thick stone walls and the knowledge that the babbling hoi polloi could not reach her, it deepened the quiet of the ancient building for Anna. She listened until the small voices of the gods began to make themselves heard. In a nearby attic a pigeon murmured. A rat, a mouse, a small bird or a very large spider scratched through dead leaves. Quietly, like the ringing of tiny bells, the previous week's rain dripped unseen behind the walls, beneath the floorboards. Breathing deeply, as if iron bands had fallen from around her chest, Anna skirted the captive sapling and entered the second door on the left; her aerie, her hiding place.

Remnants of the Coast Guard's mess were scattered across the floor, covered now with several inches of dust and debris. Moss, green and thick, carpeted the floor in oblongs beneath each window where air, light and moisture had made their way inside. Treading with great care lest she prove the Assistant Superintendent right about her ability to take care of herself in this derelict backcountry, she crossed toward the sun-dappled balcony. Planting her rump on the granite sill, she prepared to swing through to freedom. *Self-defenestration.* "Defenestrate," she said, and smiled, wondering if it was a verb.

This idle amusement was aborted. Between her feet, inside the window, clearly marked in the new-made loam of the fourth floor, were two clear prints of human feet, bare feet.

A jolt, possibly as deep as that of Robinson Crusoe on seeing Friday's track in the sand, wiped Anna's mind clear. For no reason she could put her finger on, she felt afraid. Though difficult to reach, the top floor of the Island II buildings could hardly be called inaccessible. And she could scarcely be the only explorer lured into the twisting heart of the old hospital. How did the law put it? The words surfaced: she had no "reasonable expectation of privacy" in this place.

A bootprint, she decided, would not have shaken her. It was the mark of little bare feet. A small woman or a child pattering about without shoes in a place that only a lunatic would attempt to traverse unshod. Islands II and III were a mecca for lockjaw germs— or whatever microorganism caused the condition.

Ghosts, Anna thought, Billy Bonham's stories coming to mind, the pallor of his lips and the twitch of his lower eyelid as he told them. A tremor ran through her, a sensation her grandmother would have attributed to the unexplained phenomenon of a goose walking across one's grave.

"Ghosts don't leave tracks," she said aloud, and laughed because she was absurdly relieved by that piece of paranormal wisdom.

She slid from the sill, crouching down for a closer look. Moss covered half the area where this creature had stood. The springing nature of the plant obliterated most of the print of the left foot and a quarter of the right. Choosing a patch of virgin territory, Anna pressed the heel of her hand into the moss, putting her weight behind it. Miniature fronds were crushed, releasing a pleasant forest smell. They stayed crushed. How long the plants would remain that way, she could only guess, but judging by the recovery of the plant material that had been stepped on, the prints were probably eighteen to twenty-four hours old. They were approximately the size of her own feet. In her distraction over Molly's illness the last time she'd fled to this hideout, could she have kicked off her shoes without thinking? That would be like her were she at home, or even in a camp she'd policed. Not so in a crumbling wreck of nail and brick and glass. She'd hiked too many miles not to have learned to take care of her feet.

This little creature, then, was not a ranger—or not a very bright or very experienced ranger. "Hah!" Anna echoed Mandy as she suffered nostalgia for the good old days when National Park Rangers were generalists. They knew the flora, the fauna, enforced the laws, picked up garbage, deported hostile raccoons and, when called upon, played the guitar around the campfire. No more. Specialization had taken over. It was not unusual to find a law enforcement ranger who was merely a cop in green pants, who didn't give a damn for the resource, just liked carrying a gun and the excitement of the chase. Or an administrative ranger who didn't know a bighorn from a bobcat and worked only for salary, retirement and medical insurance.

A ranger could have made the footprints. A ranger who'd never walked the wilderness, depended on her boots and muscles to carry her that last twenty miles out to a cold beer and a hot bath. Anna huffed, a noise very like the "Harumph!" found in England's comedies. The sound made her smile at her own snobbery. Still and all, she doubted the tracks were made by a ranger.

Since the footprints were the size of her

own feet, it was a safe bet the owner of the feet that made them had a stride about equal to hers. Without moving, she searched the floor in a two-foot radius from the marks. Her scrutiny was rewarded by a portion of a heel print toward the center of the room. Painstaking searching led her to three more. The barefoot intruder had come in by the same door as Anna.

In the hallway Anna lost the trail. Away from the windows, the rubble was of larger chunks and a harder consistency. Not a good medium for tracking.

A glance at her watch told her it was one-thirty. She had to abandon the hunt or give up her picnic lunch. Since she didn't know why she was so intent on tracking a person she had no pressing need to find, hunger won out.

Molly was regaining her health with a rapidity that warmed Anna's heart. That she could take no credit for it pinched a little in the vicinity of her ego, but not so much that she couldn't keep it from showing. Frederick too was looking better with every passing day. He'd gotten a haircut that wasn't half bad and was dressing like a man in love: shirt pressed, trousers with a crease and a good fit through the butt and crotch. The Jesus sandals were gone, replaced by a pair that looked vaguely Italian.

Sartorially speaking, Anna was definitely outclassed. Ensconced in a private room, free of tubes and machines, Molly was sitting up and wearing a new bed jacket. Not the cliché of peachy quilted pseudo satin and feathery weirdness that Anna might have expected from a man not accustomed to shopping—for it was obvious from the joy with which Molly wore it and the proprietary pride on Frederick's face that he'd bought it for her—but a buttery-soft stonewashed Levi jacket embroidered with a colorful riot of jungle birds and tropical blooms.

Rani was not in evidence and Anna missed her. And Molly and Frederick were bending over backward to make her feel included. So much so that she strongly suspected they had discussed "the problem of Anna" in advance of her arrival. It would have been nice to have a playmate, even one with claws and a tail.

As she began to cast about for an excuse to escape, she was rescued by the timely appearance of Dr. Madison. Long-necked, balding pate, his head preceded him into the doorway like a cartoonist's depiction of a balloon.

He blinked several times, his pale blue eyes looking unfocused and rabbity behind the bifocal lenses of his spectacles.

"Good afternoon, David," Molly said.

Anna noted with pride that Molly's power was flowing back. The sheer force of her wolfish personality cloaked in the sheepskin of good manners instantly relegated Dr. Madison to the role of guest in his own hospital.

The doctor seemed to sense it too. He

smiled, a sweet guileless grin that ruffled his short beard and showed a row of very white but singularly crooked bottom teeth. "Looks like you don't need me," he said, and came into the room checking charts and feeling pulses in a routine made so familiar by medical dramas on television that Anna couldn't help feeling it was an act.

That done, there was some tepid doctor banter he and Molly dredged up to fill time. It petered out and still the doctor loomed around the room, his six-foot-five-inch gaunt frame teetering like an unbalanced question mark. Surely if he needed a private word with his patient, he would exhibit the professional wherewithal to say so outright.

"Earning your visit fee?" Molly joked. Madison laughed but made no move to leave. Armed with the short-lived but potent telepathy of new love, Molly and Frederick exchanged glances. Anna edged toward the door.

"Well," she said. "I guess I'd better be getting back to..." Since she had no job, no family, no life to be getting back to at the moment, the sentence faded out.

"Would you like a tour of the facility?" Dr. Madison asked.

"Facility?" Anna echoed.

"The hospital." He seemed very close to animated and Anna realized that till this second he'd moved with the slow grace of a man seen through thick fog.

"No. God no," she said. "I've seen way too much of it as it is."

"Do it," Molly commanded. She and Frederick exchanged another psychic glance and Anna realized it wasn't Molly Dr. Madison wanted a word alone with. It was her. A hollow place opened up and she felt the sickening adrenaline rush one gets when Death rears his ugly head unexpectedly. Madison was going to tell her that Molly was dying, that this apparent recovery was a false dawn.

"Okay," she managed, and walked woodenly from the room. A warmth was on her lower back, Madison's propelling hand, but she felt it distantly, as if it happened in a dream.

"Let's see." Madison's voice floated above her head. "I can offer you the morgue, the newborns' nursery, the operating theater and the cafeteria. What suits your fancy?"

Anna stopped abruptly and he plowed into her. Stepping back so she didn't have to look so far up to meet his eyes, she said: "I don't need to see anything. Just tell me."

An irritating blankness smoothed his face. "Tell you?"

"What you dragged me out here to tell me. Tell me."

Shoving his hands into the pockets of his ill-fitting lab coat, he looked down the hall in the direction from which they'd just come. Maybe he hoped for rescue. An image of grabbing that long slender neck and wringing information from it flickered violently through Anna's mind. "Tell me," she repeated.

"I was hoping to ease into it a little more naturally, but I'd thought now Molly's out of

163

danger, and I can't be considered to be black-mailing you into being nice to me, we could go out to dinner or something. Drinks. Coffee," he finished when Anna failed to respond to his first offer.

She still wanted to strangle him—for frightening her if for no other reason—but she knew she was out of line. The mistake had been hers. Frederick had known. Molly had known. Hence the command: "Do it."

"I don't think so," she said, and walked toward the elevators.

David Madison drifted along at her left shoulder, a wayward cloud between her and Columbia-Presbyterian's fluorescent suns.

"I was married for twenty-three years. I've been divorced for two and a half. Since the divorce I've been on three dates and one of them doesn't count because it was my cousin. What I am saying is, if it's not me personally you find unacceptable, then there's the chance that my admitted lack of experience has caused me to ask all the wrong questions the wrong way. In the last quarter of a century it's possible 'dinner, drinks and coffee' might have become slang for some unspeakable practice. I'll never know unless you help me out."

Anna poked the elevator button several times in hopes of hurrying it along.

"We could go to the zoo," he suggested. "Or an art museum. I'm pretty worthless at art museums. I'm the kind of person they could rent a bicycle to at the front desk. I'd enjoy the ride but no stopping and studying the masters or anything. Especially at the Guggenheim. Wouldn't you love to ride a bike down the Guggenheim?"

Anna was being charmed. It wasn't an altogether unpleasant sensation. "I thought you were going to give me bad news about my sister," she admitted.

"What! But I was so careful. I never sat down once and I made a point not to appear benevolent or caring."

It felt good to laugh and to see the pleasure her laughter brought him. The elevator doors opened and Dr. Madison took Anna's elbow protectively. A nurse in her sixties and most kindly described as "Rubenesque" stepped out. Her name tag identified her as Sonya Twining. In a glance she took in Anna and Madison. "Forty-five?" she asked the doctor, and smiled so sweetly Anna suspected an underlying dislike.

Ignoring her, David Madison said, "After you," ushered Anna into the elevator and rode to the lobby with her. By the time he walked her out to the sidewalk she'd agreed to drinks at the Rainbow Room and dinner at a Chinese restaurant she'd never heard of but he assured her was "the finest in the city."

She was halfway to the subway before it occurred to her that she had only Levi's to wear. Times might have altered considerably since she'd lived in New York, but there were anchors of sanity in the ever-changing sea of culture. She had a sinking feeling that the

165

Rainbow Room was such an anchor. It had been a jacket-and-tie kind of place. Scruffy specimens such as herself were turned away at the door. Usually by an impeccably dressed male who took few pains to disguise his abhorrence for peasants who had the unmitigated gall to storm the castle gate.

Suffering the teenage angst that only menopause can cure, she was afraid to go back to the hospital lest she run into Dr. Madison. She called Molly's room from a pay phone in the back of a bar two streets from the hospital.

With the annoying need of all lovers to have others catch their dread disease, Molly and Frederick fell in enthusiastically with her plan. By four-thirty, Anna and Frederick were on the Upper West Side. He sat on the sofa and sipped Scotch. Anna and Rani repaired to Molly's bedroom to effect the magical makeover so beloved in romances: rags to riches, pauper to princess, ranger to femme fatale.

Once the process was under way, Anna found herself having terrifically good fun. For the fashion-deprived, Molly's closet was the mother lode. And accessible to the style-handicapped. Clothing was arranged by type— evening, work, casual—and then by color. Tidy racks held shoes of every shade and heel height. Plastic hanging bags, cut into tiny windows, showed off the hosiery and scarves to accessorize each variation on the ensemble theme. Cosmetics, jewelry, bath luxuries all received the same anal-retentive devotion.

For nearly an hour she played dress-up. As a psychiatrist, Molly wasn't a great proponent of inner-child reparenting. Anna made a mental note to give her this anecdotal evidence next time they talked. When she was a little girl she'd loved playing in Molly's things. They were deliciously grown-up. Sitting in her sister's expensive satin slip on a padded bench before a mirrored vanity of inlaid wood from the height of the Art Deco craze, Anna felt the same tingling sense of forbidden fruit and endless possibilities.

When she emerged in a dusty-rose sleeveless summer dress, low at the neck and flaring over the hips, her labors were rewarded by a brotherly wolf whistle. Because the dress was Molly's, it was made not of rayon but of silk. Sweat would probably discolor the armpits before Anna got anywhere near Rockefeller Center, but she was in a mood to live on the edge.

"The good doctor hasn't got a chance," Frederick said.

"You don't have to make sure I get a new puppy," Anna grumbled. "I told you I'm okay with you and Molly." She hadn't meant it unkindly—at least she didn't think she had. God and Molly only knew what her subconscious was up to at any given moment. Still Frederick looked hurt.

Unable to think of words that would undo any damage, she said, "Wish me luck," and left.

Her date was neither a smashing success nor a crashing bore. Food was good, talk was easy, compliments satisfying, but by the end of dinner she found herself envying Molly and Frederick's love-at-first-sight scenario, and wondering if she still had the capacity to be swept off her feet. If she did, would the experience exhilarate or terrify?

By nine-thirty she was glad to have the Liberty Islander's Cinderella excuse. One didn't turn into a pumpkin at ten o'clock, but that's when the last boat left MIO. Stragglers were marooned on Manhattan for the night.

Her clothes were at her sister's, but she'd not left herself time to change and so rode the subway in Molly's silk dress and Louis Vuitton shoes. Theoretically she should have felt like a target; a lone woman in the subway at night wearing what probably amounted to a month's wages for half the city's denizens. She didn't. Other travelers looked at her not with envy or malice but with the polite disregard one bestows on those who arrive at wienie roasts in Chanel suits.

Because she was cutting it close, trains came with aggravating infrequency. After twenty minutes, she lucked into an express. She would have to switch to a local for South Ferry farther downtown. As the train shrieked through the next station, Anna saw Mandy, Patsy's roommate, waiting for the local. It was comforting to know somebody was cutting it even closer than she. By South Ferry, Anna had made her way from car to car and stood in front of the doors nearest the conductor, the portion of the train closest to the stairs to the street. When the doors opened, she broke through. Molly's evening clutch tucked under her arm like a football, she took the stairs two at a time, then ran across the street to the chain-link fence and guardhouse that protected the dock.

The guard was a man Anna had met twice before, a genial fellow in his early thirties with velvety brown skin and wide-set eyes under sparse black brows. Revealing a mouth full of braces, he smiled as she skidded to a stop before his booth. "Your ship done sailed," he said. "Time and Dwight wait for no man. Speaking of which, you comb your hair and mop the sweat off your face and you'd be purely worth waiting for. How come I never seen you in a dress before?"

Inane as the question was, it brought Anna up short. Somehow it seemed important that she recall how long it had been since she'd worn a dress. The answer eluded her. Children born the last night she'd disguised herself as a girl were riding tricycles by now.

"You got a place you can stay?" the guard asked kindly.

There was always Molly's apartment, but the train ride back to the Upper West Side and facing Frederick in his new avuncular persona were too vile to contemplate.

She must have looked as forlorn as she felt. "Tell you what," the guard said. "Sometimes we let castaways bunk in the Coast Guard's conference room. It's not swank but it beats sitting on the pier all night."

Gratefully, Anna followed him through the door of the building opposite the security kiosk and up a narrow flight of stairs. He flipped on the overhead lights in a room housing a sizable wooden table surrounded by chairs. "I never tried it myself, but I hear you can make yourself a pretty decent bed if you stack up a bunch of seat cushions. I'm on all night. Holler if you need anything."

With those comforting words, he left her alone.

Having located a phone, she punched in Patsy's home number. A peal of laughter met the story of her predicament. "I've spent a few nights on that conference table," Patsy assured her. "Slept like a baby. Just be sure you put all the cushions back. I don't know if the Coast Guard brass know they're running a flop-house for homeless park rangers."

Anna promised she would bring to bear her considerable experience with minimum-impact camping.

"Be sure you catch the early boat," Patsy told her. "I've got a treat for you, but you've got to get here early. Remember Charlie?"

Anna cast about in a mind overloaded with new people and unexpected situations. "The Keeper of the Flame?" she asked when she'd made a match.

"That's him. I've got an in with Charlie. He's promised to take you up into the torch if you get with him first thing. Be properly appreciative. Charlie doesn't just let anybody go up there."

Tired as she was, Anna made the effort to sound as pleased as she felt. Going into the torch: the sort of perk that rangers sometimes got.

"Don't let the bedbugs bite," Patsy finished, and Anna hung up the phone. The disgruntled rumble of a gasoline combustion engine took her to the window of the Marine Inspection Office. At the end of the dock a figure in dark sweats, the hood up though the night was mild, threw off the moorings from a boat so low in the water Anna could see nothing of it. "Hey!" she yelled, and pounded the flat of her hand on the glass. The sound must have carried. The dark hood turned toward the high window. With no light to catch the face, it looked like the costume customarily given to Death. For a long moment the dark oval stared at Anna with unseen eyes. Then turned away. In seconds the boat was motoring away, its wake a silver-blue V. On the stern was painted *Puddle Jumper II*.

Nobody but NPS and Coast Guard used the MIO dock. That boat was Liberty-bound.

Having no idea what the phone number of the guard shack was, Anna padded down the steps in Molly's soon-to-be-ruined panty hose. The guard met her near the door. By the way he was fiddling with his belt, she guessed he was just back from the john.

"Who owns a boat called *Puddle Jumper Two?*" she asked.

"Guy named Claypool, the Assistant Superintendent. You want to catch a ride home?"

"Too late. He's gone." Anna sounded accusing.

"Hey, I had to take a leak," he defended himself.

"Not your fault," she said. Her apology was curt and not accepted. The guard didn't say anything but she knew goodwill was lost, at least for the moment. He went back to his post. She retraced her steps to the conference room.

Since arriving in New York she'd had the disconcerting sensation of being on the fringes of life, a spirit wandering unseen, unheard and unnecessary in the world of the living. Molly and Frederick, Hatch and his dead visitor, bare footprints where none should be, aborted falls from subway platforms, collapsed stairs, grouchy actors and Park Policemen who saw ghosts, now Claypool leaving her in the lurch—all seemed to be happening in a realm she was not a part of and yet was not free to leave. Perhaps, like an unsettled wraith, she had to find answers before she would be set free.

Exhausted by the need to interact with members of her own species, Anna found the lonely expanse of the conference table inviting. On a nest of cushions, clad in designer silk and covered by an army blanket smelling faintly of mildew, she slept.

12

At eight the next morning, when Kevin docked the Liberty IV, Anna was waiting. Staggering into morning in rumpled evening clothes, shoes in hand, she looked a classic wastrel. Perversely, she didn't mind the knowing winks and sly comments. If one couldn't actually have had a wild night on the town, it was pleasant to know others still believed one had the stamina for it.

The water was smooth, the *Liberty IV*'s engines loud. She isolated herself in the worst of the noise at the stern under the flag and enjoyed the view of Manhattan on a golden June morning. Most of the ferry's other passengers disembarked at Ellis. When they had pulled out again into the harbor, Anna made her way to the bridge to visit with Kevin for the short leg from Ellis to Liberty.

Kevin, as ever, seemed delighted at the company. He politely refrained from noticing Anna's state of dress, his very delicacy suggesting a racier time than she'd enjoyed in years. Hoisting herself up on the high shelf behind the wheel, she watched the water divide over the captain's shoulder.

"Anybody on Liberty commute in their own boats?" she asked, thinking of the defection the previous night.

"Not as much as you'd think," Kevin answered, a touch of the mariner's disdain for landlubbers seeping through. "This isn't a water park—you know, like Voyageurs or St. John or even Fire Island," he said, referring to the National Park scattered in pieces along a sandbar-become-island off the coast of Long Island. "Though the monument is set on these two dots in the harbor, it doesn't attract seafaring types. Law enforcement doesn't mess with boat patrol. Nothing like that. On Liberty one house is a secretary's. Then Pats and Mandy. They're more your talk-and-push-paper kind of people. They're happy to let someone else do the driving."

"Nobody keeps a boat?" Anna pressed.

"Trey's got one, I guess. I see it moored there at the dock, but he doesn't use it much. He prefers to ride with me and Dwight. Truth is, I think he's scared of the water. That boat used to belong to the old superintendent. He retired someplace in Arizona. Didn't need a boat there and let it go for cheap. I think Trey picked it up not because he couldn't resist boats but because he couldn't resist a bargain. Me? I'd sure have a boat if I lived here."

Scared of the water but heading out alone at night on a busy commercial harbor. Claypool must have had compelling reasons to come and go at odd hours.

Not my problem, Anna thought as she caught sight of Charlie on the dock. Charlie DeLeo wasn't a national treasure—at least not officially—but he was in the hearts and minds of some. Unprepossessing in the green and gray of the NPS maintenance uniform, a cap looking as big and balloon-topped as a conductor's on his head, he sat on a piling waiting for the boat to dock.

He couldn't have been much taller than Anna and she doubted he weighed as much. As Cal looped the *Liberty IV*'s line to the pier and Charlie stood, Anna could see his trousers bag straight from prominent pelvic bones. His shirt looked as if it were still on its wire hanger. She had no idea how old he was—around fifty at a guess—and over half his life had been dedicated to keeping Liberty's flame burning bright and ministering to the health and dignity of the lady herself. Charlie was arguably the most celebrated maintenance person in the service. And NPS maintenance workers had countless jobs, from cleaning toilets to clipping the bushes from President Roosevelt's nostrils at Mount Rushmore.

Periodically the press rediscovered Charlie DeLeo and an article would be run on him. He'd designed and rigged climbing gear and routes. With a heavy vacuum on his back, he'd scaled each and every inch of the statue's infrastructure, keeping clean the girders of her skirts, the crooks of her elbows, her rivets and folds. Outside, he'd climbed to the tip of the torch to make repairs. The flame, he'd said, was pockmarked from lightning strikes. As far as Anna knew, Lady Liberty was the only woman in his life.

An ember of childlike excitement was fanned within her as Cal handed her ashore. Seeing the statue with Charlie DeLeo was akin to river-rafting with the Archdruid or bird-watching with James Audubon.

Charlie smiled and shook hands formally. His hand looked too large for wrist and forearm, the knuckles swollen into knots by years of physical labor and, perhaps, the beginning twinges of arthritis. A tooth or two had gone missing over the years and never been tended to. Self evidently wasn't as important to Mr. DeLeo as service.

"You're going to want to change your shoes," he said matter-of-factly, and they walked together in companionable silence to Patsy's house. In Liberty's one alley, Patsy Silva passed them at a run, catching the boat to work.

Charlie was walking stiffly, his back bent. "I'm stove up," he said when Anna remarked on it. "Hurt my back pretty bad yesterday. One of the boys does the cleaning was trying to be funny. He threw one of those five-gallon detergent cans and yelled 'Catch!' "

Charlie was more generous than Anna. It didn't sound like the idiot was trying to be funny, just plain mean.

"You'll be on your own a little. I won't be climbing ladders or anything else for a few weeks."

He waited on the bench under the London plane tree while Anna changed back into her real self: Levi's, moccasins and a black Jockey tank top. In her middling years, and with brassieres back in style, she'd considered abandoning thin clingy tops worn sans foundation garment but decided there were few enough perks for the small-breasted. Freedom was one. If somebody's eye was offended, they could damn well pluck it out.

The transformation from uptown to down-home took considerably less time than the reverse. In a matter of minutes she was back with Charlie DeLeo.

"Needn't have hurried," he said, and she realized the patience a man might develop who spent a quarter of a century waiting on a woman who neither moved nor breathed but stirred souls by her mere existence.

Burying her hands in her trouser pockets, Anna unintentionally aped him as they walked the wide plaza to Miss Liberty's doors. Charlie talked and Anna listened. He spoke of God, His calling him to tend the statue. It was said with such simplicity and unassuming faith that it didn't grate on her nerves. The torch, Charlie said, was like a chapel, so high, close to God, with a humbling view of His world. Anna murmured politely and made a mental note to mind her manners. Charlie talked of not being as young as he once was, of feeling his age in the aches in his joints. He'd trained a handful of others to wait on his lady, but they hadn't the calling and had moved on to other parks. There was concern in his voice and Anna allowed herself the fancy that the statue would shed a tear the day Charlie DeLeo died.

Could be a while, she thought, forced to abandon her maudlin romance as Charlie, accustomed to climbing the sixteen stories from the elevator's last stop to the torch, moved right along. Without his back injury, Anna doubted she could have kept up.

A ways below the crown he stopped and stepped through an opening in the waist-high iron wall hemming in the corkscrew stairs. A metal platform, just big enough for the two of them to stand, was closed off by a gate of heavy iron mesh. A chain lock secured it.

"Nobody can go into the torch," Charlie said. "Just me and God. Today you."

"I'm lucky," Anna said.

"Me too. This is some job for a poor kid from Brooklyn. I been admiring her all my life and here I am. You got to be grateful for that." He unlocked the gate and Anna stepped back as he swung it open. "A guy got under here once." Charlie pointed to the space between the bottom of the gate and the flooring. "Lay down and scooched under."

Before Anna had been forced into the world of caving by a call for help from a friend, she wouldn't have believed it possible. Cavers—and so, maybe mere mortals—could squeeze through ridiculously tight places.

"Did he just want to see the torch?" she asked as Charlie ushered her into a dark rounded chamber with a metal ladder affixed to the wall.

"Nope. Wanted to bungee-jump. *Bungee-jump!*" Charlie repeated, still amazed at the irreverence of the would-be perpetrator.

"I'll wait here, if you don't mind," he said, and she knew his back was hurting. Forty-two feet up inside Lady Liberty's right arm, Anna ascended in a circular twilight of copper, false stars created by pinprick holes in the lady's skin. She imagined herself a bizarre corpuscle in the brachial artery of a giantess.

Splendid reality banished feeble fantasy as she emerged onto the torch itself. Anna had been higher, had seen farther, yet she felt as if she'd come to the top of the world. The torch swayed slightly in a stiff breeze off the harbor. Behind and above, the gold flame burned in the clear light of morning. Below were the spikes of the crown, Liberty's nose, the pages of the book she held. The harbor, Staten Island, Brooklyn, were spread out as if in tribute. Anna felt the hush of Charlie's chapel and the nearness of Charlie's God.

When she left, she was touched by sadness, the intensity of which caught her off guard. In the normal scheme of things, she would never again visit the torch. She comforted herself with the thought that she'd never lived much in the normal scheme of things.

At the top of the pedestal, where the elevator waited to take them down, she and Charlie stopped for a moment to look at Manhattan from the balcony.

"Uh-oh. Door's unlocked. Hatch must have forgot," Charlie said after a brief fumble with keys. His tone was neutral, but Anna suspected this careless attention to the lady's security would not go uncorrected. He held the door and she slipped by. At Hatch's favorite spot, she leaned her elbows on the parapet, the granite still cold from the night, and took in the view.

Charlie DeLeo came up beside her. After a moment, he hooked his gnarled fingers over the far side of the stone wall, weight on his forearms, and peered straight down. He crossed himself and made a small ugly sound in his throat. "If this is a joke it's not funny."

She pulled herself over the ledge to look down the side of the pedestal where he was looking.

"Not funny," she agreed.

Turning, they left the sunshine for the elevator. Charlie hurried, but neither ran. Halfway down, the floors flicking by at a glacial pace, DeLeo said: "You got medical training?"

"Emergency medical technician is all," Anna replied.

"You go check. I'll get whoever's on to start the calls. Somebody'll be back with you fast as anything. You won't be left too long," he promised.

Anna nodded. Charlie couldn't know she didn't much mind being left alone with the dead—at least not in the light of day when she was sure they were really and truly dead. There was little doubt on that score.

The elevator stopped at the level that opened onto the gracious Star of David–shaped rooftop of old Fort Wood, the base of the pedestal. Anna got off. Charlie punched a button and rode on down. Free now to run, she did. Not because she thought response time was a factor—the platinum fifteen minutes, even the golden hour EMTs referred to were long gone—but because she needed to burn off the wild feeling bad news and disaster bred within her.

The sprint was short. She knew better than to barrel headlong into an accident scene regardless of how straightforward it appeared.

Hatch lay ten or fifteen feet from the base of the pedestal. His right arm was folded beneath the thickness of his chest, the left outflung, twisted, palm up, elbow bent backward as if he'd tried to break his fall with his hands. His legs were splayed in a neat V, one toe turned out, the other in. What had been his face was toward Anna.

There's a graphic depiction of taking it on the chin, she thought, grim humor serving not to amuse but merely to allay horror till a more opportune time. Watching where she stepped lest she damage any trace that might prove of importance later, she moved to kneel beside him.

No pulse. No breath. No surprise.

The skin of his neck was cold and his joints stiff with rigor. Maybe it was beginning to pass off the jaw, but there was no way to tell. The bottom half of his face was smashed to bone fragments and pulped flesh. His hair and clothes were damp, not from rain but from dew. At a guess, he'd been dead eight to twelve hours. The deduction didn't make Anna feel particularly bright. His ten-hour shift had ended less than thirty minutes earlier. It didn't take a forensic pathologist to figure out he was probably alive when he reported in for work.

Voices and the sound of feet pounding preceded Anna's being swallowed up in a cloud of green and gray. Radios crackled, orders were issued. She removed herself from the epicenter of the quake.

Above her, nearly lost in the glare of a sun already high, was the shallow crenel in the balustrade where Hatch had smoked his nightly tribute to Lady Liberty's sister in Paris. Sixty feet. The pedestal tapered, became narrower near the top. The girl—Hatch's jumper—had bounced off on the way down. Anna searched the stone blocks to see if there was any indication Hatch had done the same. If he'd hit, she couldn't see where.

Photographs were taken. More people than she had imagined were on the island found reason to come up and were duly shooed away by the Park Policeman. The Superintendent was called. Trey Claypool was on his way over from his office on Ellis. A helicopter had been dispatched from NYPD. The mess would be gone before the first tourists arrived at ten o'clock.

A second jump in a week. The park would be heavy into damage control. Like anything else, suicide was prone to fads and trends. The last thing any park wanted was to become a destination for people seeking their own final solution.

Second jump: Anna realized, from the scraps of conversation she was overhearing and the natural bent of her own thoughts, that everyone was assuming Hatch had jumped. There'd be a search for a note, but notes weren't as key as people liked to think. Lots of suicides didn't think their life of enough value to bother explaining why they'd chosen to cut it short.

Hatch was a man alone: no wife, no kids. Friends maybe, family—Anna didn't know. What she did know was that he'd felt responsible for the death of a fourteen-year-old girl, that he'd become obsessed with it, that an interpreter—probably Patsy's roommate, Mandy—had exacerbated his feelings of guilt and responsibility not twenty-four hours before. Even on short acquaintance, Anna knew James Hatchett to be sensitive, sentimental, ritualistic and romantic. The sort who might jump into a balmy summer night if he felt a need to atone. Maybe it went deeper. Maybe there was a genuine need to atone. Maybe he had murdered the child and could no longer live with what he had done.

The monument's EMTs, helped by Charlie and the handsome black Park Policeman, were stuffing the last of James Hatchett into a body bag. Rigor locking joints, the corpse was uncooperative. One of the men ended up putting a knee on Hatch's chest, the way Anna did when her suitcase was jammed too full to close properly.

Eventually a compromise was struck. Right arm, torso and legs were bagged. Head and out-thrust left arm were draped with a blanket. The package was ludicrous. It bothered Anna that a man of such innate dignity must be carted off in scarecrow attitude.

Two men lifted the unwieldy bundle onto a gurney and rolled it away. Presumably to

183

wherever the helicopter was slated to land. That done, the Park Policeman and the Assistant Superintendent asked Anna and Charlie all the questions they could think of. There weren't many. Hatch was dead. They saw him. Nothing enlightening about that. Anna told them of the letter she'd had from Hatch and promised to deliver it to Trey Claypool's office.

Talking of the letter hurt. It hadn't been on her mind till the questioning started. Now she was plagued with the meaningless swarm of "ifs" that suicides leave behind to torment the living. If she'd met Hatch last night like he'd asked. If she'd tried a little harder to ID the dead child. If she'd bothered to call him at the law enforcement office from the phone at MIO. This barrage of guilt, and its attendant grandiosity, surprised her. As a park ranger, she'd been in emergency medicine for a dozen years or more. There'd been plenty of people who didn't make it, who died because she hadn't been there, hadn't gotten to them quickly enough. That was part of the charm of the backcountry, the wilderness: there wasn't anybody there. Like most people who lasted any length of time in the rescue professions, she'd worn out the "if" factor pretty quickly. You were where you were. You went where you went. You did what you could. Mostly, people were better off after you showed up than before. Most people lived. As long as you didn't actually screw up and push a wheelchair off a cliff or administer cardiac shock to a perfectly sound specimen, you were home free. "If" and "should" were self-indulgent.

Suicide was different. It denied everybody a chance. Suicide was a violent act against the living. Anger at Hatch would have helped, but as she watched them take him across the plaza, she couldn't dredge up any. But he deserved it. If he left relatives behind, he'd get it too. Suicides tore families apart the way even murder couldn't. Suicide was somebody's fault and blaming the dead was intrinsically unsatisfying.

Charlie DeLeo left and Anna wondered if he was going to have a word with the Almighty about the care and feeding of one James Hatchett. It crossed her mind to ask if she could tag along, but being alone was better than being with God, even one as benevolent and believable as Charlie's.

Out into the harbor, left of the sun, a Circle Line ferry pushed around Liberty from Ellis. Behind Anna, doing a do-si-do with the departing corpse of the dead policeman, two National Park Service interpreters were approaching the statue. Within minutes it would be open for business. In a quarter of an hour the first of the twenty or thirty thousand feet that daily trod the monument would be shuffling up the stairs, scuffing over brick and granite. Sweaty hands would rub the parapet where Hatch had last seen life. What, if anything, spiritual or corporeal, Hatch might have left behind when he shucked off the mortal coil would be obliterated.

A need to beat the crowd, look again from Hatch's balcony, overwhelmed Anna and she returned to the elevator at a trot and pushed the button for the top of the pedestal. The urgency that drove her up the pedestal turned into helplessness as she stepped out onto the balcony. What in hell she'd hoped to find, to see, she wasn't sure. The granite block where Hatch had sat and smoked each night, if it had any secrets, did not choose to give them up. Perhaps if she were Sherlock Holmes, a microfiber of blue fabric from the seat of the Park Policeman's pants would have manifested. She wasn't and it didn't. Not that it would have proved anything. Judging from the place Hatch landed, there was little question this was where he'd jumped off. No scuff marks or scratch marks were left to indicate he'd made any attempt to save himself. Not that there would be. Fingernails had little effect on granite.

Because she could not yet bring herself to give up, she made a minute search of the floor beneath the crenel he'd launched from. Crawling on hands and knees, she was aware of the cold and the age of the stones; they smelled faintly of night, old earth and Pine-Sol. A bobby pin and the guts of a ballpoint pen crushed into the crack between wall and floor were all that turned up. Both looked as if they'd been exposed to the elements for a while. Simply because she needed to keep doing though there was no more to be done, she searched the entirety of the balcony, all four sides. A handful of tourist detritus showed up: gum, a 1959 penny, a cardboard stick with the residue of red-colored candy on one end.

Unable to think of anything else to fill her time and her mind, she wandered back to Hatch's perch, hooked her hands over and stared down. What would it feel like to fall that far? What would one think in that last moment as the weight shifted from wall to empty space? Would it be done on a sudden rush of courage or despair? There was a time, after Zach was killed, when she'd thought a lot about death. Alcohol and weeping shrouded the memories. Mostly what she recalled was fatigue. Was that what Hatch felt? That he was too tired to do anything but give in to gravity and oblivion?

Sixty feet below, the mark of his blood on the stone was barely visible. Skin was a remarkably tough organ. Often, all within could be smashed to jelly, and if a sharp bone end didn't pierce it, the carnage was contained. Hatch had bled some from the mouth. A brown-black mark the size of a handprint was all that was left.

Not quite all. Anna pulled herself over the high wall, squashing her breasts against the granite, till her head poked over the edge. Three or four yards from where he had hit was a small round object. It had been in shadow, unnoticed, but the sun had moved and now struck a bright splinter of gold from its side.

A swell of sound brought Anna's head up. They were coming: the first of the shuffling feet, the grubby hands, voices mixed, robbing language of meaning.

Anna slammed back through the door to the inside of the pedestal. The hum of machinery let her know the first elevator of sightseers was on the way up. Unable to bear the wait for a ride to the bottom, she ran for the stairs that snaked down, steps hugging the pedestal walls.

Out on the star-shaped plaza, a stain of tourists was beginning to spread. She darted past a maintenance man armed with mop and bucket, sent no doubt to cleanse the last of James Hatchett from the face of the world. No one had yet gone near the corner where Hatch died. Anna caught her breath and, shading her eyes from the glare off the water, got her bearings. The maintenance worker began mopping. She drew a mental line from where he worked to four yards out. The sun no longer reflected from the metal, but the small round container Hatch had carried in his pocket was still where she'd spotted it from the balcony.

She sat on her heels and stared without touching. One side was scratched and slightly dented, but otherwise it had survived the fall in good condition. When Hatch was airborne, or perhaps just as he struck the ground, it must have been dislodged from his pocket and rolled the twelve or so feet to where it presently rested on its side, like a coin toss that ended on edge and remained there.

Fingerprints were probably not an issue; still, Anna couldn't bring herself to pick it up without protection. Having neither gloves nor handkerchief, she pulled off her socks and, one hand looking like Shari Lewis's Lamb Chop eating a rice cake, lifted the container and gently loosened the lid.

Inside was nothing but clean white sand.

Didn't the condemned, even the self-condemned, have a right to a last smoke? It wasn't like Hatch had to worry about the Gauloises shortening his life. Maybe he jumped earlier—before his accustomed smoke break. A man of strong habits, he probably would not have moved up his nicotine ritual even for the Grim Reaper.

On a hunch, Anna went back to the base of the pedestal and, eyes focused on the ground, began a tight zigzag-pattern search. Knowing that what she sought, if it existed at all, could be destroyed by one tourist in flip-flops, she moved as quickly as she dared. Three feet out from the wall, she found it: a worm made of silver-gray ash, the granite beneath discolored from the heat.

Hatch had sat facing Manhattan; he had started to smoke that ritual Gauloise. He had not finished it.

Anna didn't believe for a second that a man who carried a tin of Waldorf-Astoria sand in his shirt pocket had flipped the butt over the wall. It had fallen from his fingers when his fanny left the balustrade.

Surely such a fastidious man would not intentionally go to meet his maker with a lit cigarette in hand.

13

Tourists swarmed. Anna marked the ash and the place she'd found the tin of sand the only way she had at hand. With the leather punch on her Swiss Army knife, she scratched the stone of the plaza. Defacing a National Monument. At the moment, the number of the Code of Federal Regulations she was breaking slipped her mind, but it was a classic.

That done, she ran a serpentine pattern through the throng, down the mall and to the headquarters building across from Liberty's gift shop and restaurant. Not a soul was in attendance. There was no dispatcher for the monument. Doors were locked.

The chopping cadence of rotor blades took her to the wide lawn area behind Patsy's cottage. As she arrived the helicopter was lifting off. Claypool was gone with the corpse. Standing in the prop wash was the Park Policeman, Andrew—Anna forced herself to recall his name. Thinking of him only as "that handsome black guy" was as tacky as the boys remembering only "the blonde with the great ass." "Andrew," she said, to reassure herself she wasn't a sexist pig.

He turned; sunlight caught the sweat on his high cheekbones. He smiled—good strong teeth, straight and square, the best of Burt Lancaster and the Masai.

Maybe she *was* a sexist pig.

"I've got something to show you," she told him. "Nothing probably. But your headache, not mine."

"If food can be worked in, you're on." He fell into step beside her. At headquarters, he took possession of the tin of sand, bagged it and wrote the appropriate information before sealing the evidence bag. Whether or not he actually viewed this relic as evidence, Anna couldn't tell, but he treated both her and Hatch's memory with respect. She appreciated that.

Andrew then got the park's 35mm camera from its cupboard and the two of them returned to the top of Fort Wood where Hatch had fallen. Wind or feet had taken the ash. Even the scratch marks were hard to find, searching as they had to through the aimless wandering herd. Anna found where Hatch's idiosyncratic ashtray had lain and where what she claimed was the ash of his cigarette was located. Andrew photographed the places indicated and entered time, date and other pertinent data into his log to be filed along with the photographs. They spoke little during this exercise, and as Andrew went through the motions, Anna couldn't help but feel it was just that: an exercise. So Hatch jumped before he smoked? So this once he threw caution to the winds and flipped his cigarette butt instead of smothering it neatly in his pocket tin? Could be it wasn't even his cigarette. Anna didn't know French Gauloises' ashes from those of a Camel. She didn't even know if there was a test for it, and since she hadn't collected the ash when she had the chance, the point was moot. A maintenance man, one of the janitorial staff, anybody who smoked nonfilter cigarettes, might have dropped the burning fag end and walked on. By some freak it could have remained intact overnight.

Anna didn't believe it. But since her flight back to Colorado wasn't booked yet and her convalescent nursing duties had been usurped by the Federal Bureau of Investigation, she'd nose around, see who, if anybody, smoked nonfilters. It wasn't that common. She'd only known two: her sister Molly with her Camel straights and John LeFleur, a crew boss she'd fought fire with in Northern California. Pall Malls were his drug of choice.

Over hot dogs and Cokes bought at a vendor's wagon on the esplanade, Anna told Andrew her idea that Hatch had been pushed or had fallen accidentally, and how the ash and tin figured into the theory. He listened in silence, his jaw muscles rippling with each bite. When she'd finished he waited a minute before speaking. Either he was a man who gave all information due consideration, or somewhere along the line he'd learned to look as if he did. He'd be a natural at interviewing witnesses.

At length he sucked his teeth clean, neatly wiped his mouth with a napkin, then proceeded to roll it into a tight ball between meaty palms.

"Pretty hard to fall off there by accident,"

he said. "The sill is wide, not sloped or slippery or anything. Maybe he could have been leaning out to see something?"

Since the wall around the parapet was nearly chest-high, that sort of tumble wouldn't be plausible unless Hatch already had his legs on the downhill side. "Him sitting, smoking, something happens down below, he leans out for a better look?" Anna suggested.

"Could be."

They both thought about that, their eyes on the towering pedestal, the visitors dwarfed to ant size in its shadow. Even Hatch, come through familiarity to be comfortable on the parapet, wouldn't treat the sixty-foot drop with the casual disregard it would take to merely lean too far, lose one's balance and fall.

"Probably not," Anna said, discarding her own suggestion.

"I wouldn't think so," Andrew agreed. He tossed the rolled napkin at a trash barrel and missed by three feet. "Underprivileged youth," he excused himself as he retrieved his litter. "No inner-city midnight basketball for this child. I'm from Wyoming. Green River."

A cowboy. Anna had always had a weak spot for cowboys.

"That leaves murder and suicide," she said.

"It's early yet. There'll maybe be a note."

Tourists, girls of about twelve or thirteen, descended upon them like a flock of starlings, all racket and flutter. Andrew patiently answered the vacuous questions they'd dreamed up to get the pretty cop to pay attention to them.

193

Anna waited. It was one of the things she liked about the Park Service—liked about America, when one thought about it in the grand scheme of things. Policemen were still the good guys. They were still the ones people turned to in times of trouble, the ones lost children sought out in crowds. People in the United States didn't scurry indoors and hide when a uniform appeared. Watching this microdrama unfold within shouting distance of Lady Liberty's elephantine ear pleased Anna's sense of symmetry.

"Let's walk," Andrew said as the girls giggled away. "Moving targets are harder to hit." Taking the initiative, Anna sauntered down the walk circling old Fort Wood. "Where were we?" Andrew asked, then answered his own question. "Suicide note. Right. I didn't know Hatch that well. Working alone, day shift, night shift, you only see each other in passing. I heard he was upset about the kid that jumped. I also heard he was under investigation. Good reasons to check out if your mind works that way. Mine doesn't. Suicide makes no sense. Why crash a party you're going to be invited to sooner or later anyway?"

Anna had nothing to say to that. Andrew was apparently too well adjusted to realize that by the time one is suicidal not only does the word "party" carry no cheery connotations but real-world logic has gone by the wayside.

⭐   ⭐   ⭐

Anna's pilgrimage to Molly's shrine was short. When she arrived Frederick, half-glasses with magnifying lenses of the sort one might purchase at Wal-Mart perched near the end of his beaky proboscis, was reading a sonnet aloud. Sonnet 29 if Anna wasn't mistaken. She left before his heart did the "lark at break of day arising" part, and though she exited amid a storm of protest, she seriously doubted she'd be much missed. As an excuse for her early departure she said she wanted to look up Dr. Madison before he went off shift. This brought her those gee-there's-hope-for-Anna-yet smiles that she would never learn to appreciate.

Knowing full well Molly would check up on her to see how the "romance" was going, Anna asked a passing nurse how to find David Madison. The woman verbally mapped out the way to his office. TV would suggest doctors do not have these havens of sanity but dash about from patient to patient, eternally free of paperwork. Anna had to either give up on television as even a distorted mirror of reality or believe Dr. Madison was highly placed in this particular organization.

The doctor was not in, but his door was ajar and, having carried the charade thus far, Anna decided she'd stay long enough to leave him a note—quick thanks, door open for future possibilities sort of thing. She edged inside, feeling out of place and mildly sneaky though her motives were no more under-handed than usual.

His office was utilitarian but by no means sterile. Evidently the man never threw anything away. Or filed it. Medical journals were piled along the walls. Out of knee-jerk snoopiness, she glanced at a couple dates. The old-timers had graced his floor since June of 1988. Manila folders in various colors and states of disrepair were packed into a bookcase behind a desk lost beneath more of the same, loose papers and what looked to be Mardi Gras trophies—cheap beads and plastic cups.

Madison might have one of those minds gifted with a Gestalt location system. Anna had had an aunt like that, Aunt Margaret. Margaret could dive into any of the many rat's nests in her study and within moments produce whatever yellowed newspaper clipping or antiquated recipe she had in mind. Researchers were just beginning to uncover evidence that the female brain was built for big-picture thinking and the male for categorization and separation.

That or Madison was just a slob. Since Anna had matriculated into middle age, it took very little to knock a man off her "possible" list. A slob was borderline. She tucked this away without even being aware she did so, and moved to the desk to find paper and pen for the intended note.

This seemingly simple task was thwarted by the plethora of documents. A Post-it note, a Bic pen, the necessities of life, were lost in the debris. She circled around the desk and sat in a maroon leatherette ergonomically correct and, because it was designed for a man six foot five, uniquely uncomfortable chair. Her feet barely touched the floor. For an unsettling moment she felt like a very little girl playing where she shouldn't be playing.

Then, in essence, that's what she became. Before her eyes were two dreadfully tantalizing folders awash in the sea of pulped trees. One, a corner protruding, was labeled "Dr. Pigeon, Molly, Mary, Margaret." Thinking there might be but one daughter, Anna's parents had taken the precaution of naming their firstborn after every female relative still living on either side of the family. Seven years later, when Anna made her appearance, there was no one left. Fortunately her mother had been reading *Anna Karenina,* or she might have ended up being named Tiger or Coco or Potkins or Skeeter after a favorite family pet. The other, less obvious but equally enticing folder was labeled "Consultant—NYC Med Ex." A connection with the person who had autopsied Hatch's Jane Doe and, perhaps, would do Hatchett himself.

Giving in to her baser instincts after a moral struggle lasting a nanosecond or two, Anna pulled Molly's file from the heap after noting precisely where it had been so her deviltry might leave no traces. There were several sheets of medical gobbledygook which she scanned without much understanding. Then two tag lines written by hand, the penmanship as appalling as tradition could have hoped. The first read: "Molly P: looking good. Recovery astonishing. Boyfriend?" and the second, the one that, despite herself, pleased Anna: "Sister (married?)."

A glance at the door: nothing, nobody. She carefully replaced Molly's folder and extracted the one labeled "Consultant." Another folder slid out and she kept it rather than screw up the order of the pile—a deviation from the chaos-as-usual that mightn't go unnoticed. The consultant file was regarding the details of the death of one Josh Redkin. Nothing of interest there.

Before she could restore it to its place, the door opened and her heart leapt as if she'd been nailed making off with the monthly payroll. Madison stood, shoulders stooped, as if he had never come to believe doorways were built for men with a six-foot-six-inch frame and he had an inch to spare.

When unavoidable, confession is good for the soul. Anna said, "Red-handed," and held up the file.

Dr. Madison blinked twice, his exophthalmia giving him an aspect of perpetual confusion. Anna expected disgust, anger, outrage, irritation, those good emotions so enjoyed when an opportunity for righteous wrath presents itself, but he seemed more embarrassed than anything and, for an instant so fleeting she wasn't sure she'd seen it, afraid. Not big fear—life, death, large spiders—but a cringing that rippled down from the rounded shoulders. This passed in the time it took him to step over the clutter and take the folders from her hands. No snatching—he merely took them and opened the top one as if interested in any questions she might have. The bottom file, the unmarked folder she had scooped up incidentally to the medical examiner's file, he slid into a side drawer and nudged it closed with his thigh. Furtive, Anna thought, but he was so calm she figured the past week had given her, if not a full-blown case of paranoia, then certainly one of hypervigilance.

"Are you interested in Redkin, Josh?" the doctor was asking.

Anna made herself focus. "No. Nosy on another account. Do you remember the jumper I told you about?"

Madison nodded and folded himself into the chair she had vacated on his arrival. He finished closing the desk drawer into which he'd secreted the file with a casual push of tapered fingertips. Such was the man's length that sitting, he and she were eye to eye. Despite his gesture toward a chair, she chose to remain standing. "Hatch, James Hatchett, was found this morning. He went off the pedestal at the Statue of Liberty. A sixty-foot fall. Suicide is what they're saying."

"He's the man who chased that little girl you told me about?" Anna nodded. "Now he jumps because of the girl jumper—guilt?" Madison's beautiful hands were folded on a neatly trousered knee, well-defined lips crinkling his beard in a look of concern that would have melted the reserve of Freud himself.

Bumping the pile on the corner of the desk, she rested her hip on it. The desktop was high. She'd not noticed it from David's over-sized chair, but it had been raised by the expedient of putting the base on two lengths of four-by-fours painted black to blend with the soulless storage-unit decor. "So it would seem," she said.

"But you don't think so." Behind the bifocals and the blue eyes Anna saw a glimmer of mockery or just good-natured teasing. As a potential paranoid, she wasn't willing to decide which.

"Nothing to say it wasn't." She backed down, feeling childish, not knowing why but not liking the sensation.

"Redkin, Josh?" Madison brought the matter back to the folder she'd been prying into.

"I just saw 'consultant to the medical examiner' and couldn't resist seeing if it had anything to do with the little girl, Hatch's Jane Doe." The desire to escape to a realm where she was again a grown-up was strong within her. She lifted herself off his desk.

"I don't get those. Nothing straightforward: blunt trauma, car versus pedestrian, gunshots. They call me when there's some kind of an anomaly and they need a cardiothoracic expert."

Anna should have known that.

"But I know people who know people," Madison said. "Would you like to visit your Ms. Doe? Talk with the forensic types?"

Bait Anna could not but rise to.

He made two calls and wrote her a note. She was to be treated as an honored guest of the dead in New York City. On leaving, she found herself accepting a theater date for that evening. It wasn't till she was on the elevator, one floor down, that she remembered the file hidden in the desk drawer. For three more floors she lectured herself on physician-patient privilege, breaking and entering, and the just deserts of generally being a Nosy Parker. Nothing availed. At the second floor, she stepped off and, bored with standing and waiting, took the stairs two at a time up six flights.

The coast, as the dime novelists would have it, was clear. Walking purposefully down the hall, spine straight, head high, she still felt like Pantalone sneaking through an Italian comedy. Dr. Madison's office door was again ajar. Feeling the rush of adrenaline that hooked burglars so viscerally into their chosen profession, she slipped inside.

The top right drawer of his desk, the drawer into which he'd put the unlabeled file, was locked. The good doctor had taken the time and trouble to secure it. There was something about a secret, any secret, that brought out the cop in her. For a brief moment she considered searching for the key, but decided she lacked the motivation—or the foolhardiness—to do it. She left without being seen and again took the stairs, mercifully deserted by a sedentary population.

Brought on by New York City or Frederick and his sonnets—or maybe the nearness of the ghost of Zachary—theatrical allusions continued to haunt her. "All the world's a stage, and all the men and women merely players"—the much-quoted line from *As You Like It* came to mind. If she didn't get a grip, she was going to slide those immortal words into a modern Bellevue bastardization: "All the world's a plot, and all the men and women merely suspects."

She needed occupation for her fevered brain: first the morgue, then the wilds of Ellis. Entertainment, distraction, and in ten days or less, she'd be back on Delta to Denver and then a puddle jumper to Durango; to reality as she had chosen to know it.

As usual, the subway got her within walking distance of her goal. Dr. Madison's note in hand, she presented herself at the New York City morgue like a tardy third-grader. With the impersonal brusqueness out-of-towners often mistake for unfriendliness, a bespectacled man with one eye that didn't track—giving the impression he kept one eye on the visitor and one on the security cameras—led her to an autopsy room, where Gentry, the doctor who had autopsied Liberty's Jane Doe, was working. As Anna pushed open the door, she cast down a quick prayer to the gods of this underworld that Gentry wasn't in the process of hacking up James Hatchett.

The room wasn't as gloomy as Anna deemed suitable for its purpose. With its cracked and moldering concrete, body cabinets and dirt-encrusted windows, the morgue on Ellis was more in tune with imagination. This one was brightly lit. The rocking cadence of Jerry Jeff Walker singing "Navajo Rug" made the place downright chipper. At one of several spotless tables, Dr. Gentry, draped, gloved and goggled against giving or receiving contamination, raised a welcoming instrument. "One of David's friends?" she asked.

Anna nodded and the doctor waved her in with whatever shiny implement of dissection she was holding. It looked bloody but it could have been Anna's imagination. She took a step inside. The swinging door gave her a gentle smack on the behind. Thus encouraged, she moved toward the doctor. A glimpse at the operating table—if tables for dead people went by the same name as those for the living—reassured her it wasn't Hatch. Whoever was under the knife had long wavy brown hair.

"Dr. Gentry?" Anna asked, keeping her eyes well above cadaver level.

"Call me Colette," the woman said, and dug into some portion of the body. Colette had a soft southern accent, more song than drawl. Louisiana, Anna guessed. "Forgive me if I don't shake hands. Unsanitary practice. How do you know David?"

"He's my sister's doctor," Anna said, glad of the small talk. Chatting over the rotting dead took a little getting used to. "Does he work with you?"

"Has. Off and on." She laughed for no

apparent reason. "As needed. Good doctor. Great backdoor man." Colette Gentry reached deep and pulled out a bit of red and slippery stuff that forced itself into Anna's peripheral vision. Anna was not a regular in morgues: it was not a duty rangers often performed. Another good reason to work for the National Park Service. Morbid curiosity urged Anna to peek, but her mental library was already sufficiently stocked with grisly images. She kept her eyes on Dr. Gentry. Or the parts of her that showed. Colette had brown hair, cropped at earlobe level. She was short, stocky, and looked strong. Her hands were blunt and her eyes, above mask and behind goggles, a very attractive brownish gray.

"Did you do the girl from the Statue of Liberty?" Anna asked.

"That I did. Poor little bugger. Basic. Except she lit nearly square on her head. I guess she dove rather than jumped. Her legs weren't broken. Skull, neck, upper spine, all suffered serious damage. Wrists and forearms shattered. Unless they're unconscious, most people, even though they think they want to die, try and stop themselves when it comes down to it. I don't see many going headfirst like that."

The doctor laid aside the instrument with which she'd ushered Anna in, said, "Excuse the racket," and began working with a power tool. The sound conjured up graphic pictures of bone being sawed. Spatters of dull red, blood without oxygen, flecked the front of the pathologist's plastic apron. Anna stepped away and feigned interest in the floor, a predictable washable tile, white crosshatched in gray.

Little Miss Doe didn't jump, she dove. That went better with the flight theory than the suicide theory. Flight from what? Was the child mentally unbalanced or was her reaction sane, at least to the adolescent mind? Did she willingly sacrifice her life to keep a secret, to avoid a discovery that would cause her or someone else pain? Heroics came more easily to the young. If anyone would bite down on a cyanide capsule, choose death rather than betray a cause, it was a good bet that person was under thirty. If Miss Doe was a runaway, was death preferable to what she would be sent back to? There was no sign of sexual or physical abuse. Emotional abuse? Maybe.

Anna would lean on Frederick again, get him to see if there had been any escapees from mental institutions or juvenile detention facilities who fit the time frame and the physical description of the girl.

It crossed her mind that she was intentionally overlooking the obvious: that the girl had fled from exactly what it looked like she was fleeing from—James Hatchett. Was there something between them that made a sixty-foot plunge onto granite more acceptable than letting him lay hands on her? Having talked with Hatch, it didn't seem likely, but Anna knew her perception to be worthless in this area. Everybody's was.

When she was in college in San Luis Obispo, California, she'd gone out to the Atascadero prison for sexual offenders. The inmates were child molesters, rapists, perverts from every walk of life. The reason she, along with other students, visited Atascadero was to socialize with the "white-card holders," men soon to be released. The idea was that it would be helpful for these men to have some practice with regular (and preferably female) citizens before they were thrust into society.

For a semester of Thursday nights, Anna played board games with the white-card holders. They wore no mark of Cain. They were ordinary—grocery clerks, computer programmers, carpenters, schoolteachers, bus drivers, engineers. They were nice, sometimes funny, warm, often kind. Nobody leered. Nobody drooled. Nobody played pocket pool. And eighty percent of them would be back in prison within a few years for the same offenses.

James Hatchett could be one. There would be no outward signs. A wife might suspect, or a friend close enough to notice when answers didn't fit questions, when times were vague or unaccounted for.

The wretched grinding stopped abruptly. "Well, I'm glad that's over," Colette said, and laughed. "This lady was one tough old bird. Can I tell you anything else about your girl?"

"Did anything strike you as odd?" Anna asked, for lack of a better question.

"Other than the headfirst attitude, not a thing."

"Can you determine mental illness in an autopsy?" Anna asked, knowing the answer was no.

"No," Colette said. "Brain tumor et cetera, sure. There was nothing like that. Did the usual blood work. No drugs—Thorazine, lithium, Paxil, Depakote, not even Prozac or Zoloft. Nothing that might suggest she was being treated for mental illness. But then, not everybody gets treated."

"Thanks," Anna said.

"Anytime." Colette fired up the saw and Anna let herself back out into the hall. Mental institutions dropped to a lower priority on her list. Had the girl escaped from one recently enough to be in as good shape as she was, there would probably still be some sign of psychotropic drugs. Anyone sick enough to be committed to a mental institution required medical intervention. Talk therapy only worked on garden-variety neurotics. She'd have to ask Molly how long those drugs stayed in the system.

The building was bustling. Full of businesslike people in nice clothes. Her preconception of empty gray halls echoing with spooky footsteps was suffering a severe onslaught of reality. After a few wrong turns and asking directions once, she found her way to the property room, a large, well-organized place of drawers. Since there was no crime reported, Jane Doe's worldly goods were not evidence and so had not been taken into the chain of custody by the New York

Police Department. An exceedingly disinterested young man, a hardcover book on higher math reluctantly abandoned at Anna's intrusion, checked a computer. Anna's name was on it.

She reminded herself to thank David Madison when they met for their date. Anna was *dating*. The thought made her uncomfortable.

The young man vanished to reappear with a box precisely sized and marked with Ms. Doe's particulars. He opened it and Anna was allowed to look without touching. Sneakers, socks, shirt, trousers, underpants: all the items Frederick had mentioned. Again she had the feeling something was missing. This time she couldn't write it off to an incomplete picnic lunch. Seeing the child's clothes brought to mind the girl crumpled on the granite.

This collection was incomplete.

"Do you have a list of all items turned in?" Anna asked.

Affronted, the young man silently tapped information into his keyboard, then turned the monitor so she could read it. She was right. The ball cap. The girl was wearing it when Anna saw her and she was wearing it when her body was delivered to the morgue. Now it had gone missing.

"Do you keep a list of everybody who has access to this?" she asked.

"We do."

"Can I see it?"

"You can't."

Anna had no idea whether it was policy or

personal, but since she was officially a nobody, she didn't contest the decree.

It was possible one of the people working in the morgue had stolen or lost the cap, but from all appearances this was a well-run, security-conscious organization. Anybody could be tempted to theft if the prize was worth enough. The employees here struck her as high-end moralists. They might steal diamonds and make for Rio, but probably none would stoop to pinching a baseball cap.

"Can I see the effects of a James Hatchett?" she asked on impulse. The young man fetched another shoebox but was not gracious about it. Anna was treated to sighs and eye rolling. He pulled off the lid. Out of habit, she took the 35mm from her bag and began photographing the box.

"You can't do that," the young man said, but she already had.

"Sorry."

"Yeah, well..."

The day had been long and it was just past two o'clock. She was to meet Dr. Madison at the Oyster Bar in Grand Central at seven. Drinks, the theater, dinner late, overnight at Molly's apartment. The thought of all that fun to be had was exhausting. Killing five hours on the pavement of Manhattan was too tiring to contemplate. Anna decided to return to Ellis, hide in the quiet greening ruins. Embraced by the illusion of nature, she would regenerate, decide whether to come back for the proposed gala evening or weasel out on one pretext or another.

The harbor, the Circle Line, Ellis's Registry Hall, were in full hue and cry. From the NPS dock on the Jersey side of the island, Anna could hear the gabble. Turning left, she entered the back doors of the registry building, the part the NPS used for administrative purposes. The hall was wide and quiet and cool, the way only old buildings with thick walls and deep-rooted foundations can be.

Patsy wasn't in her office and Anna left a note to be personable. On her way back out she passed the law enforcement offices. The door was open. Curiosity lured her within. The office struck her as phony, a stage set. It was so clean and light and tidy. At Guadalupe, Isle Royale, Mesa Verde—all the parks where she'd worked—law enforcement could be counted on to bring a cozy clutter of incomplete paperwork, malfunctioning weapons, confiscated booze and boxes of unidentifiable objects that were essential to some project, very possibly that of a ranger already moved on to a new park. On Ellis the cubicles were neat, desks uncluttered, walls free of bizarre humor and postings so old they threatened to become historical artifacts if not attended to. This unnatural order gave her a Stepford ranger sort of feeling. She suspected, if there was a refrigerator, it would contain no moldy half-eaten sandwiches, the freezer no strange animal parts tagged and ready for court.

"Trey in?" she asked a Park Policeman who was not Billy Bonham and, to her surprise, wasn't handsome. Possibly in these politically correct times, even the elite Park Police had quotas to fill and were required to hire a token ugly guy every few years.

Unsuspecting of this harsh assessment, the policeman smiled politely and pointed to a half-open door. "Always," he said. Anna detected a note of censure. As the Assistant Superintendent wasn't law enforcement, it might be a real estate issue. By rights, his office should have been down the hall in Administration.

Claypool hollered, "Come in," before she knocked. Nothing wrong with the man's hearing. Her moccasins on the new carpet made but a whisper of sound. Feet on the desk, hands folded behind his head, he looked quite at home.

"Am I interrupting anything?" she asked.

"Nothing that can't wait," he replied, unperturbed by the sarcasm. "What can I do for you? Lost? Damaging historic buildings?"

"Not today." Uninvited, she dropped into the chair by the door and let her daypack fall at her feet. "Just wanted to see how it went with Hatch."

The Assistant Superintendent took his feet from the desk and sat up straight; a show of respect for James Hatchett. It pleased Anna. "Bad news, that," Claypool said, and she thought she heard genuine regret in his voice. "I worked with Hatch once before, out at the Presidio in San Francisco. I was one of several acting chief rangers they rotated through before they filled the position. A good man. Solid. Did his work."

Anna let the eulogy stand for a moment. It took most people two or three minutes before they were willing to speak ill of the dead. Then she said: "Can you tell me what there is to tell? I spent some time on the statue with Hatch. He was easy to like, easy to talk to."

Claypool shot her a hard look, wondering, no doubt, if there'd been a budding romance. Anna allowed her face to soften, her eyes to mist. Maybe he'd tell her more if he thought her closer to the deceased than, in truth, she was.

"No big secrets," he said, and she knew the calf's eyes had been overkill. He wanted to talk. Claypool was isolated for a man so high in the bureaucracy. The walls of his office held framed posters of other parks—presumably parks in which he'd worked—but there were no pictures of people: no wives, children, not even the ubiquitous group shot of grinning hikers against a backdrop of breathtaking scenery.

"Dead on impact. No signs of a struggle. The toxicology report isn't in but drugs are unlikely. Not Hatch's style. Massive bruising from the fall and faint bruising above the kidneys that could have happened if he struck the wall on the way down. Knees broken, arms, hands, one femur, pelvis, neck. What you'd expect."

"Time of death?" Anna asked.

"Between one and two a.m. Seven or eight hours before you and Charlie found him."

"Cigarette break," Anna said, remembering Hatch's ritual smoke.

"Andrew told me of your ash and sand observations," Claypool said. "It will be taken into consideration, but I wouldn't make too much of it. Don't start stirring up the idea there was foul play. That kind of thing doesn't do much for morale."

Anna nodded. He was right. She had no desire to play the role of what the mother of a dear friend aptly called a "shit disturber." Hatch could have pitched his cigarette butt for any of a hundred reasons, including anger, despair or momentary disrespect or resentment. It might not even be Hatch's cigarette.

"Anything on the body?" she asked, to see if his list tallied with the box at the morgue.

"Just the usual pocket flotsam. Forty-five cents in change. His wallet with his law enforcement commission. Half a roll of Life Savers—"

"I guess they don't really work."

Claypool laughed, then stopped suddenly as if she'd tricked him. "A square of tinfoil in his shirt. That was odd, I thought."

Anna told him about the packaging of the nightly Gauloise. "He did smoke it," she finished. "The ash I found was his ash."

"One anomaly explained. In his pants pocket he had a lighter. A carabiner, brand-new from the look of it, was hooked through a belt loop."

Carabiners were lightweight, sometimes locking oval links climbers used in many facets of their rope and harness gear. It was not totally unrealistic that Hatch might have had one. They floated around the Park Service like paper clips in an office, put to all sorts of uses, from key chains to holding one's pants up. In some parts of the country they were an affectation, left about to suggest one was a cool and groovy member of the climbing community.

Hatch didn't fit that profile. Anna had not seen the carabiner on him before, and she knew from experience it was not particularly comfortable to clip something lumpy between trouser belt and duty belt. Worth a question or two. Charlie would know. He climbed the lady. He might have dropped a 'biner.

"No note?"

"Not a suicide note," Claypool replied. "In his shirt with the tinfoil he'd scribbled a few words on the back of a gum wrapper, the way you do when you have a sudden thought you're afraid you'll lose and haven't got any real paper." Anna had seen a note with Hatch's belongings, but it was folded shut.

"What was on it?"

"I wrote it down just because it was unusual. Hang on a sec." He opened the shallow middle drawer of his desk. From where she sat, Anna couldn't see in, but she imagined it as Spartan and impersonal as the rest of his office. Without hesitation, he plucked out a small ledger, opened it to a page marked with a blue plastic tab and read aloud: "Little girl. Spud. Call Caroline."

"That's it?"

"That's it. Not much more than a grocery list."

Anna committed it to memory in case she found a hole this piece fit in at some later date. "Little girl" was probably the dead Jane Doe. "Spud" could be anything, a nickname, a potato. A firefighter Anna had worked with on Cumberland Island had an alligator in a pond behind his house his wife had dubbed Spud. "Call Caroline" was intriguing but could be anyone from an aging aunt to an auto insurance agent. Without a last name the search could prove time-consuming and fruitless.

"How long are you here for?" the Assistant Superintendent asked.

His question was well modulated and pleasantly spoken, but Anna detected a subtle reminder she was a guest of the park and her welcome could be worn out.

"Till my sister is better," she replied.

"Your sister still need you pretty bad?"

Not so's you'd notice, Anna thought. "She's not out of the woods yet," she said, and changed the subject: "You worked with Hatch in San Francisco?"

Claypool looked mildly alarmed. "Not with, exactly. He was one of the Park Police there when I was."

"Anything noteworthy?" Anna was just casting about, no bait, no hook and no idea what, if anything, she might catch.

"Do you mean was he a homosexual?"

The question struck her as a non sequitur until she put together "San Francisco" and "noteworthy." She laughed. She'd been fishing for a pedophile angle: Hatch and little girls. Gay didn't work. Pedophilia was no respecter of gender. Grown men, convicted abusers of young boys, weren't gay. They were pedophiles. It was about power, about control, about twisted minds and mutilated souls. Sexual orientation didn't enter into it.

"Not that," she said. "Just anything that caught your attention at the time."

Claypool shook his head. "Hard worker. Open. Friendly. Not a party boy. Not a prig." He was quiet a minute and Anna waited on the off chance he was thinking.

"Hatch had his moods," Claypool said finally. "Golden Gate Bridge is big with jumpers. While I was there we had one who sort of misguessed. She didn't land in the bay but splattered her fool brains all over Fort Point."

Anna had toured that fort once by candlelight. Another perk that helped to make up for the fact that the NPS went with the lowest bidder on uniforms and women could not get pants that fit. Fort Point, like Fort Wood built to withstand cannon fire, was a fortress in beautifully intricate brickwork. Within the walls was an open plaza. Anna remembered standing there, hot wax dripping on her wrist, mesmerized by the glory of lights on the bridge above. "Landed inside the fort?" she asked.

"Nope. People used to. One day a leaper was bound to land on a ranger or a visitor, so in the seventies we built a fence on the bridge above. This one walked to the end of the fence and jumped. She landed between the fort and the bay."

"A kid?"

"A middle-aged lady. Just divorced. Walked out around eleven o'clock one morning in September. Put her wedding band and her shoes on the rail and over she went."

"Hatch found her?"

"No. That's why it stuck in my mind. He came on duty later. The body was gone. Maintenance was mopping up. Yet he got, not hysterical—Park Policemen don't—but withdrawn. He talked about it a lot, like somebody who'd seen it would. After his shift there were wildflowers tossed on the place she hit. Didn't have to be Hatch. The lady's friends or a relative could have come and done it. But it was on Hatch's shift."

The Park Service, without being stiff-necked or hard-hearted about it, quietly discouraged private memorials on public lands. Not always easy in the southern and southwestern parks, where it was common practice for the locals to put a great Styrofoam cross bedecked with plastic roses at the site where the dearly had departed. Roads in New Mexico were strewn with these makeshift shrines.

"Interesting." Anna filed the information away with other fragments. "I'm off to the wilds," she said. "Thanks for talking."

"As long as it's just curiosity," Trey said, his feet going back up on the desk. "We've got people here to look into these things, just like you do in the 'real' parks out west."

From the derision in his voice, Anna guessed his heart was set on a western assignment but his hopes weren't high. The western parks were a little on the snobby side, as Anna thought only right and fitting.

"See you," she said by way of farewell.

"Be careful."

Anna wondered if he meant in her poking around on Islands II and III or poking around in James Hatchett's business.

As she stepped out of the registry building into the breezeway between it and the old powerhouse, the small company of actors was chattering back to the hall for the last performance of the day. Mandy was still with them, squished sausagelike into Corinne's costume, a sour look on her moon face. The ethereal blonde was evidently still AWOL.

"Macho Bozo was here again asking for Corinne," the black actress said.

"I wish he'd ask *me* for her. I'd give him a piece of more than my mind," Knickers and Cap replied.

"Yeah, except he's big and mean and fast."

"Good point," the actor conceded.

Not wanting to hear any more than she had to, Anna fled down the bricked corridor into the hypnotic mix of death-in-life that was the ruins of Ellis Island.

She had much to think about and needed

space and silence in which to do it. Who was on Liberty when Hatch died? What was it about suicide that seduced or repelled the Park Policeman? Was Caroline important? Spud? How hard—how illegal—was it going to be to get a look into James Hatchett's personal locker in the law enforcement office's basement on Liberty?

And more to the moment, could she stand another honest-to-God put-on-your-panty-hose date so soon on the heels of the last?

14

During the boat trip from Ellis to Liberty the date lost out. Or at least was postponed a couple days. Anna wasn't sure why the idea was so off-putting. She'd had a nice enough time on their first date. Madison wasn't a firebrand when it came to conversation and he wasn't glamorous—at least not visually. To women who found power and prestige alluring, a cardiothoracic specialist at Columbia-Presbyterian would be considered a knockout. He wasn't sexually aggressive, which she appreciated. Slap and tickle was unsettling at sixteen when a girl didn't yet know she had a choice. Thirty years later it was likely to get somebody's arm broken. He did do a bit of what Molly, in her homemade psychiatric jargon, referred to as "leaning." A leaner was a man who stood too close, loomed in one's airspace, always seemed to be between his date and any convenient escape hatch. Despite his drawbacks Anna had to admit Madison was kind and attentive and oh-so-pleasant. Like Elwood P. Dowd, she thought. But some ingredient was lacking in Madison that Jimmy Stewart had in abundance.

Maybe she'd been out of circulation too long. He'd said he was newer to the game than she, but he seemed totally at ease. Anna hadn't the least excuse for turning down a night on the town. Except the way he slid that unmarked folder into his desk. Then locked the drawer.

Could be anything: politically sensitive patient, movie star in for cosmetic surgery, an abortion...

"Stop it," Anna ordered herself.

"I didn't mean nothin'," came a mumbled response, and she realized she'd been talking out loud. Not an uncommon practice in New York City.

Dragged from self-absorption, she saw that the guys from the cleaning crew had come to the stern for the short trip from island to island. The speaker was the oversized white boy with the offensive tattoo. Anna wondered what he was apologizing for. He looked like one of those habitual screwups who either bow and scrape or stab and punch, and both with equal lack of provocation.

"No problem," she said, stepping away

from his bulk. Clouds of smoke suggested the janitors had come out not to enjoy the late-evening air but to have a cigarette. Three had lit up. The fourth chewed. A quick survey: everybody smoked filter cigarettes. The observation was knee-jerk; Anna didn't doubt her ephemeral ash was from Hatch's Gauloise.

"Hey, Idaho, you bidding for S-six again tonight?" This from a wiry Hispanic man. Smoke came out with every word. At the end of the sentence he took a deep drag lest any moderately unpolluted air should make its way into his lungs.

Anna sneaked a look at his chest. "Jason" was embroidered over his pocket, proving fashion could be thicker than culture.

"Yeah. S-six," mumbled the lunk they called Idaho.

"White guys," Jason said with disgust. "Boobs is everything. Latinos know the power's in the boot. The bigger the cushion, the better the pushin'."

Anna let this sexual shorthand rattle around in her head till she made sense of it. S-6: the sixth level in the statue. That would be about where the lady's bosoms would be located, if she had bosoms. Anna moved away. She didn't want to get to know these guys that well. If she thought her obvious aversion might offend, she was mistaken. Nobody noticed. To a clot of twenty-year-old males, a middle-aged woman was only slightly more interesting than a stray cat.

Having drifted toward the bow, she joined

Dwight in the cabin. "Fine night," she said, because it was.

"It's always a fine night on this harbor. Fog's fine. Gales are fine. The sea never makes a mistake. Of course she's not very understanding when we do," he said, and laughed. "But that's part of her charm. Sailors who get bored aren't paying attention. Everything's always changing."

Anna attained her accustomed perch and let her legs swing with childlike freedom, her heels bumping the wood gently. She asked after Dwight's son, Digby, and found, as she'd expected, that the boy was perfect, had done and said any number of funny, dear or genius things. Letting Dwight ramble on about this scrawny child who had taken over his heart, Anna basked in his contentment, his love and his pride. Without hearing each and every word, she let the essence of happiness wash over her, removing the sting from the paper cuts life had left on her psyche.

When he'd finished and silence, made isolating by the guttural roar of the engines, had slipped between them, Dwight said, "I hear you got marooned the other night."

"Yes," Anna replied in sepulchral tones. "You abandoned me and I wandered the streets in the rain fending off gang-bangers and stepping on drunken homeless people."

"Terrance said you sacked out on the Coast Guard table."

"God, I hate small towns," Anna said mildly. "Nobody can get away with anything."

"I couldn't wait." Dwight was explaining, not apologizing. "At eleven-thirty when I get home, I tippy-toe in to give Digby his good-night kiss. If I'm late he don't sleep so good."

Anna doubted much would disturb the rest of a boy Digby's age, but Dwight's reasoning delighted her just the same. "Did Mandy make the boat?" she asked, remembering her flashing by, framed in the window of the subway train.

"Nope. She got left behind too. You party girls have got to pay for your sins."

"She didn't stay at MIO," Anna said.

"She might not even have been headed to the boat. She's got a boyfriend stashed away somewhere. She's tucked up in her own little bed tonight, though. I took her on the four forty-five from Ellis."

Anna laughed. "Fishbowls have got nothing on islands when it comes to lack of privacy."

"You got that right," Dwight said amiably. "Somebody knows everything. Maybe not a single somebody, but all the somebodies added up. Right down to how much toilet paper you use."

Patsy was home, and despite Dwight's assurance to the contrary, Mandy was not "tucked up in her own little bed." She was nowhere to be found. An ideal situation, from Anna's point of view. She left an apologetic message on Dr. Madison's phone machine, changed into her bear cub pajamas, accepted a glass of her own wine and folded down on the sofa with a heaping plate of spaghetti left over from Patsy's dinner. A far superior evening to dining at Windows on the World with the double burden of having to be pleasant and attractive simultaneously.

As Anna twirled pasta and wiped sauce from her chin, Patsy talked on the cordless, her lush and compact body draped over a chair only a woman as loose-limbed and well upholstered as Patsy could make look comfortable.

The conversation was centered on the disposition of a Honda and a battered old pickup truck she had left behind in Cortez when she abandoned Mesa Verde for the fast track. Anna remembered Patsy's daughters, both blond and as sumptuously constructed as their mother. They'd be in high school now, one maybe off to college. Both had opted to stay the year out with Grandma in the Southwest when Patsy moved. From the one-sided conversation, Anna figured the younger had just been divested of the Honda in honor of the elder's pilgrimage to the university and was arguing the damage her deep and abiding shame at being demoted to the pickup truck would cause her. Not to mention the end of her social life for all time.

Anna enjoyed the byplay. A year younger than Anna, Patsy sounded like a "modern" mom, the kind that read the books and knew it was important to be firm yet validate feelings, compassionate yet authoritative. A thin and faded line between mother and friend.

Not for the first time, Anna was glad she was childless. It was traumatic enough to deal with the emotional needs of a dog. Children were probably worse. At least dogs couldn't call you on the phone. The guilt trip had to be laid on as one left, and by the time one returned, the silly buggers were so overjoyed, all sins were forgiven. Dogs were eternally optimistic. They seemed to believe each abandonment was the last and each homecoming eternal. They were Catholic not only in their ability to inspire guilt but in their unwavering faith.

"So," Anna said as Patsy hung up, "were you on the island the night Hatch tried to learn to fly?"

Patsy laughed her wonderful laugh and said, "Shouldn't you be on Prozac or something? Or did you come visit because not enough people were dropping dead in Mesa Verde?"

Anna spun up another forkful of pasta. There *was* a touch of the compulsive about her. Maybe when her mother was pregnant with her she'd been frightened by a bloodhound. Anna had been sniffing out the truth most of her life, one way or another. Usually it wasn't worth knowing. Still, she had to search. Prozac could perhaps save her—if salvation was what she needed.

A folk art exhibit she'd seen once in New Orleans bloomed in memory. Fabulous stuff done by strange fundamentalist people with unique visions executed on old barn siding, corrugated metal, pipe, rocks, weathered pickets from decayed fences. Much of it was inspired by the Bible. There were many depictions of heaven and hell. Anna's favorite was made in an old potbellied stove. Heaven was on top, slathered with sky-blue house paint, clouds and hand-carved angels with wings hefty enough to keep a B-52 aloft. Inside, where the wood had once burned, lurked hell. It dripped in red paint, was floored in cracked black rocks and housed devils holding pitchforks, each sporting an erection a third his body size.

Prozac was going to wipe out an entire art form, Anna was sure of it.

"I'm used to being me," she said. "If I were nicer, I'd annoy myself."

"Yeah, me too. Mellow is too weird to contemplate. So. What? You think Hatch was pushed?"

"He could have fallen by accident, I guess, but suicide doesn't sit right with me." She told Patsy about the cigarette and was gratified to see her take it seriously. It was a first for that particular string of revelations.

"I used to go up with him sometimes. Night shift's a bore and I tend to stay up late anyway. He did his cigarette ritual a couple of times," Patsy volunteered.

"What time?"

"Eleven forty-five on the dot," Patsy said with a laugh. "Irregularity was not Hatch's problem."

In law enforcement, however, regularity

was a problem. It made the officer predictable and therefore vulnerable. Bad guys—assuming there were bad guys involved—could watch and know precisely when one was at one's weakest.

"I can't see him dropping his cigarette butt either," Patsy continued. "Hatch cared, I mean *cared,* about almost everything. Too much. He was a softie with everybody else but hard on himself. He'd never litter. Maybe he accidentally dropped the cigarette, was totally appalled and dove off to retrieve it."

They both laughed, albeit a little shrilly.

"God, we're awful," Patsy said. "I really liked Hatch."

"Funny image, though." An undercurrent of giggles rippled the surface of the silence for the next several seconds.

"Hatch was moody," Patsy said after a while. "I can't imagine him littering, but I can sort of see him killing himself if I squint and try real hard. I've been here—what? Eight months. You get to know people quick on an island."

Patsy would get to know people in a trailer park in Yazoo, Mississippi, in the Sahara or in downtown Hong Kong without being able to speak a word of Chinese, but Anna didn't interrupt the flow with this irrelevancy.

"Hatch knows everything about me: kids, exes, favorite color, Mom's death, Dad's new Land Rover. All this time I thought we were having two-way conversations, but you know what? I don't know anything about Hatch. God. I feel awful. I just talked and talked and didn't notice. I don't know if he has family, friends. I don't even know if he's got a wife, where he goes on vacations—nothing."

Letting a sip of red wine roll around on her tongue, Anna mentally reviewed her conversations with the deceased Park Policeman. The talk had been fairly unstrained, open and honest but, she reflected, it was not personal. Hatch didn't talk about himself. He spoke of the statue, of the jobs he'd had; enjoyable but, when analyzed, fairly free of content of the kind that could give a peek into the man's heart.

"Moody," you said. The word echoed those of the Assistant Superintendent.

"Yes. He was always good as gold, polite, friendly, all that, but he'd kind of go on autopilot once in a while. You've seen the look: hiding the pain."

Anna had seen. EMTs learned to love brave patients—they weren't nearly such a pain in the ass as the whiners—but not to trust them. In the name of courage, they would hide symptoms, not ask for help when there was help hovering around anxious to give succor—or just anxious to stick an IV in. Less than four sticks a month and an EMT-IV lost her license. "Like they're seeing you through a thick piece of cheesecloth and your voice is distant and so tiny they can barely make out what you're saying."

"Yes. That."

"I take it he never did any classic suicide things: previous attempts, references to being

228

'too tired,' suddenly going from morose to peaceful, giving things away?"

"None of that. At least not around me."

Anna told her the story of the leaper at Golden Gate National Recreation Area while Hatch was serving a tour of duty there, of his being deeply affected by the death of a stranger and a death he, personally, did not witness. She told Patsy of the wildflowers strewn over the death site. In the telling she recalled a detail she'd put out of her mind. "There were flower petals at the base of the statue where the girl hit. I went out late that night because I am a morbid, blood-sucking voyeur, and someone had scattered azalea blossoms."

"Hatch?"

"Looks that way."

"Does it mean anything?"

"That Hatch was a nice guy?"

They sipped a moment. Patsy had moved on to chamomile tea. Anna was sticking with wine.

"Okay, so maybe he could have jumped," Anna said finally. "But for the sake of argument let's say he didn't. Who was on this island that night?"

Patsy threw her head back and howled like a hound after a fox. "You are incorrigible, Anna!"

"I have never been corriged," Anna admitted. "Or if I was, it was so insignificant I never even felt it."

"You were sacked out on the conference table, so that lets you out," Patsy said. "I was here. Hatch trusts me. I didn't see anybody and nobody saw me and I wasn't on the phone or anything nifty during the—what shall we call it? The window of opportunity. I was curled up in bed, dreaming of Sean Connery or, if I was feeling particularly depraved, Leonardo DiCaprio. *Such* a pretty boy. Charlene—she's the Chief Ranger's secretary—was home. I saw her lights on next door. And her kids, fourteen and seventeen, both boys, were home. I heard the pounding bass of something totally witless. Those boys could teach the party boats a thing or two about rude noises."

"Maintenance?" Anna tried.

"Let's see. What time are we talking about? When he smoked? Eleven forty-five to midnight or thereabouts?"

"Thereabouts."

"They could have been, but if the earliest Hatch could have died is eleven forty-five they would have been minutes from catching the boat and, as you have reason to know, Dwight does not wait for stragglers."

"How about Dwight?" Anna suggested.

"You're serious?"

"Why not. Can't stoop to prejudice. Dwight is big and strong and wears a diamond stud in his ear. What more could you ask for in a murderer?"

"Well, I guess he could have come in a few minutes early, jumped ship, sprinted to the top of the pedestal, done the deed and hoofed it back. Why not Cal? He was probably deckhand that night."

It was Anna's turn to be surprised.

"See. You're prejudiced too. Because he's genteel and treats you like a lady, you think he's above murder."

"He's old—" Anna thought aloud.

"Ageism. Illegal. Cal is strong and, since he's sixtyish, I guess the word would be spry. Think about how strong his hands must be, handling and throwing line thick as your wrist all day."

"Okay. Cal, Dwight, Charlene, her boys, you, cleaning crew. How about Trey Claypool?" He'd marooned Anna at MIO shortly after ten. He could have been home in plenty of time.

"He was here," Patsy said. "Well, his lights were on and I heard his door. So I assume he was here. I suppose it could have been a housebreaker without any sense of sneakiness."

"What time did you notice the lights, the door?" Anna demanded.

"God, girl, can I get you another glass of wine? Some Xanax?"

"Sorry. What time?" she asked again, careful to keep her voice meek and kindly.

"Better," Patsy commended her. "Beats me. I went to bed around eleven, so it must have been before then. If pressed I couldn't even swear to it. It's kind of background music, you know. You remember it but it's so unimportant and everyday it could even have been another night I'm thinking of. Repetitious events sort of acquire a timelessness. Did the sun come up August fifteenth, 1965? It must have but I don't remember it."

231

"True." Big events stood out—deaths, marriages, births, divorces—landmarks between the miles of sameness. Not that sameness was bad. Anna recalled the Chinese curse "May you live in interesting times." "I'll find out."

"You do that," Patsy said.

Even Patsy Silva had her limits. Anna let the subject drop.

"Bedtime," Patsy said, looking at her watch. "I wonder where Mandy is."

"I thought she was off island."

"Nope. She's here. Went out jogging. Evidently you can get a decent workout if you run around this rock enough times. I, personally, would not know. Unless Dobermans or Nazis are after me, I'm your basic stroller."

Mandy struck Anna as a stroller too, but she didn't want to draw unflattering comparisons. Not ruled by justice, she was perfectly at ease with liking Patsy's soft silhouette and finding Mandy's offensive.

In accordance with the ancient warning "Speak of the devil and up he jumps," the front door banged and Mandy stomped into the living room. Her jogging suit, lavender with narrow piping in lime green, gave her the look of an overripe kiwi. The suit was rumpled but spotlessly clean, no sweat stains. The woman's hair was disheveled and she was breathing hard, so Anna had to accept the fact that maybe she did run.

"You look rode hard and put away wet," Patsy said cheerfully.

Mandy, who'd apparently intended to go to her room—or the bathroom—without so much as a by-your-leave, stopped in the hallway and turned to face them.

"What's that supposed to mean?" Her voice was edged, her fists balled as if she was looking for a fight. Instinctively, Anna eased her feet from the coffee table and centered her weight in case some evasive maneuver might be required.

"Oh, sweetie, what happened?" Patsy asked, with such sudden sympathy that Mandy's fingers uncurled and her eyes teared up. Her hair fell back from her face and Anna saw what had triggered Patsy's maternal concern. Mandy's right eye was swollen shut, the lid as round and purple as a grape. The lower lid puffed out, revealing the thin blood-red line of inner lid. The right cheekbone was burning with an angry raised welt half an inch wide and two inches long.

One plump white hand fluttered up, exploring the damage. "I fell," Mandy said, and her voice broke like a child's. "I was running and I slipped and fell."

"Ouch," Patsy said. "You got a real shiner. Let me get you some ice to put on it." She scrambled up from the low chair and bustled out to the kitchen. Mothers bustle. Anna couldn't put her finger on the precise mechanism of locomotion that transmuted a walk to a bustle, but she'd never seen Patsy do it except when she was tending to a sick or wounded child.

Comforted by the role Patsy took on so effortlessly, Mandy followed toward the kitchen. Walking past the couch, her left profile was to Anna, the undamaged half of her face. Below her ear, halfway between lobe and esophagus, was a vicious-looking bruise about the size of a quarter.

"What did you do to your neck?" Anna asked. She thought she sounded perfectly kindly—not like Patsy, but close enough to pass muster. Evidently not. One of Mandy's pasty little paws flew up and she clapped it over the mark with the vehemence of a woman swatting a biting horsefly. Tears dried, burned away with the heat of returning anger. She glared at Anna.

Seconds ticked by and Anna watched in fascination. From the kitchen came the sound of ice breaking from trays and chatter, as Patsy talked to an audience that had lost interest in her. Hand still glommed over the bruise, Mandy was frozen in place by some strong emotion. Hate, confusion, fear, flickered over the round face with such rapidity it was as disorienting as being caught in a strobe light.

"There was this thing," she said, searching for words. "A thing that stuck out..." Her voice trailed off and the one eye Anna could see took on a vague unfocused look. She wondered if Mandy had suffered a slight concussion.

Anna started to rise from the sofa. The movement snapped that one blue eye back into white-hot focus.

"Like I've got to explain anything to *you*," Mandy sneered. "It's none of your goddamn business. Nothing here is any of your business. This house is as much mine as it is Patsy's, though you wouldn't know it from the parade of losers she's got coming through. But I pay the same rent as she does, and for my money, you're not welcome. Go back to Colorado and bugger a moose."

"Elk," Anna said automatically. "No moose in Colorado."

For a heartbeat, Mandy was at a loss for words. She fell back on the classics: "Fuck you," she said, and stomped down the hall. The end of the journey was punctuated by the violent slamming of her bedroom door.

Patsy appeared from the kitchen, ice cubes in a plastic bag, the bag wrapped in a soft terry cloth towel. "What happened?" she asked.

"I don't know," Anna replied honestly. "I asked her about another bruise she was sporting, and boom, meltdown. Just like that. Zero to sixty in sixty seconds. She finished up with 'Fuck you' and stormed off."

"Were you horrible?" Patsy asked, having known Anna many years. "Mean or poking or anything?"

"I don't think I was horrible. I asked as nice as I know how."

"Your nice isn't too bad. It shouldn't set any-body off like that. You're sure you were nice?"

"Intentionally, premeditatedly nice," Anna assured her.

"Then whatever it is is her problem," Patsy

said philosophically. "Want ice for anything?"

Anna didn't. Patsy dumped it into the sink, then followed Mandy's example, if less histrionically, and took herself off to bed.

Anna turned out the lights, carried the remnants of her wine to the dining table and stared out over the water to the fairy lights of the murder capital of the world. Unless Los Angeles or Hong Kong had usurped the title in recent decades. Eyes on this wonder of generated electricity, she played back Mandy's scene from captivating entrance to dramatic exit. Mandy was what Anna's mother-in-law would have referred to as "a pill," hard to take under any circumstances, so it wasn't the woman's general peevishness that struck a wrong note. Anna slowed her mental projector down, clicking frame to frame: Mandy in the doorway; turning to the hall; facing back toward the living room, anger on her face; Patsy's kind words; Mandy softening, tearing up; Patsy to the kitchen; lamblike, Mandy following; Anna seeing the bruise on the left side of her neck; mentioning it; Mandy hiding the mark; half-sentences; anger; exit.

Clearly Anna's mention of the bruise triggered a strong reaction—of fear, the need to hide something. Hence the anger.

Damage on the right side of the face.

Two-bit-sized bruise on the left side of the neck.

Mandy had said what? Anna closed her eyes and leaned her head back to listen for the past. "There was this thing. A thing that stuck out." When she'd spoken, her eyes wandered to the northwest corner of the ceiling. Her voice became a monotone.

Mandy was lying and Anna knew why. She hadn't hurt her neck in a fall. The bruise configuration wasn't new to Anna, just forgotten; she'd seen dozens like it. But not for over twenty-five years. It was a hickey. Mandy had a big fat old-fashioned hickey on her neck.

Anna laughed. Time she too should be going to bed.

She did go to bed but not to sleep. Though the wine called her into its own dark version of rest, her mind would not let go of the puzzle.

Mandy could have gotten her hickey on the mainland from the apocryphal boyfriend Dwight alluded to. But had she had the thing on her neck for twenty-four hours, not only would it have lost its vampire bloom but Mandy would have covered it with makeup, a Band-Aid or a scarf, tricks all high school girls learned. Or she wouldn't have been alarmed when Anna remarked on it. Given Mandy's usual attitude, Anna would have expected her to wear her hickey with pride, a red badge of love, a puerile desire to shock. Though if Mandy thought Manhattan found hickeys shocking, she wasn't from around here.

None of that had transpired. When Anna

noticed the hickey, Mandy's instinct was to hide it. Then to explain it away with lies. And last, to confuse the issue with a personal attack on Anna.

Mandy didn't want them to know she'd gotten the hickey that night and on Liberty Island. The only logical explanation was that she wanted to keep the giver of the hickey a secret.

This was beginning to get interesting. Anna sat up in bed and crossed her legs under her, enjoying the cool ocean air on her skin as the sheet fell away.

Who would be harmed by the knowledge that they had bestowed a hickey on the thick white neck of a GS-7 National Park Service interpreter? As far as Anna knew, nobody living on the island was married, so that angle didn't work. Andrew? Because he was black? That didn't feel right either. Andrew was so good-looking anybody but a dyed-in-the-wool racist would brag about getting his attention. From a few comments Mandy let drop in unguarded moments, Anna suspected she just might be that dyed-in-the-wool racist. In which case Andrew would not be her type. *And a good thing for Andrew*, Anna couldn't help thinking. Cleaning crew? Maybe, but there was little cross-pollination between day interpreters on Ellis and night janitors on Liberty. Odds were good Mandy didn't even know them.

Charlene, the secretary next door, might account for a hidden lesbian hickey. Two kids didn't mean a thing. Half the lesbians Anna

knew had children from previous hetero-
sexual marriages, or had borrowed sperm
from a gay male friend. Usually via turkey baster
since neither party was interested in anything but procreation. Sex at its purest form,
if one decided to take the conservative fundamentalist interpretation. Either of Charlene's
sons could be the culprit. They were of proper
hickey-bestowing age. Mandy might be embarrassed about robbing the cradle next door.
Embarrassed, yes, but afraid? Anna didn't
think so. Not the kind of fear that makes it
impossible to move or speak.

Trey Claypool.

That made sense. Assistant superinten-
dents are severely frowned upon if they go about
sucking upon the necks of their inferiors—
sucking upon any portion of the anatomy of
their inferiors for that matter.

Another detail niggled into the mind picture
Anna was painting. The kiwi-colored jogging
suit. It was rumpled—as would befit a bout
of heavy necking, or being left on the floor in
a heap had the deal been consummated—but
spotlessly clean and sans sweat stains. No
running. No falling down.

Mandy had been given a hickey and a black
eye. Probably by the same person and around
the same time. A scenario common enough in
law enforcement that it wasn't remarkable. Sex
and violence were so linked in the American
subconscious that movie theaters on Forty-
second Street alternated XXX shows with
slasher films.

Anna had no proof anything had happened the way she pictured it, but the pieces fit, and perfect fit was often a sign of the truth.

Mandy could have been both ashamed of being beaten and protective of whoever had beaten her. That was the usual pattern. Absolutely none of this was Anna's business. However, at the moment, she had no business but other people's. Thirty years from now, she'd probably sit on her porch and watch her neighbors' comings and going so she could piece together their secret lives.

She smiled at the image and slid back between the sheets. It wasn't everybody who was lucky enough to be born with an avocation.

15

Sorry, Anna. Wake up. You've got a phone call." Anna opened her eyes. Patsy, wrapped in a blue brocade kimono with rich purple edging, bent over the bed.

"I'm awake," Anna said, and was. Patsy's demeanor called for instant and total consciousness.

Patsy handed Anna the cordless. "I'll make coffee." Even in nonbirthing emergencies humans felt compelled to boil water.

Sitting up, back against the bookcase that

served as a headboard, Anna said: "Anna Pigeon speaking."

"This is Paulette Mallory at Columbia-Presbyterian. You are Dr. Molly Pigeon's sister?"

"That's right." Anna felt things visceral shifting, teetering on a precipice over a bottomless world.

"Your sister has been moved back into ICU. I'm sorry. She's stable. That's about all I can tell you."

"What happened?" Anna asked, ignoring the disclaimer.

"Pneumonia."

"She had pneumonia? Again?"

"It happens. The immune system gets weakened. Dr. Madison said to have him paged as soon as you get here."

"Thanks," Anna said automatically, and punched the off button. Setting worry aside with frenzy, she began pulling on clothes. A look at the travel alarm on the bookcase robbed her of her hurry. It was seven-fifteen. She couldn't catch a staff boat to Manhattan till eight. Trey Claypool's boat was probably moored at the dock and Anna would have no trouble piloting it—it wasn't anything but an eight- or ten-foot runabout with an outboard motor—but by the time she looked up Claypool, got clearance and drove the slower boat across a busy morning harbor, she'd save only minutes. If that.

She joined Patsy in the kitchen, watching coffee trickle from the filter into the pot.

241

"Molly?" Patsy asked.

"Pneumonia."

"Bad?"

"Stable. Whatever that means."

Each imprisoned in the ivory tower of her own cranium, they waited until enough liquid gathered to fill a mug. "First one's yours," Patsy said gallantly.

Anna gentled the brew with heavy cream and left Patsy watching a second cup trickle through the grounds. She took her cup out the back door and sat on the picnic table, her feet on the bench. Manhattan was hard shadows and harsh edges in the glare of the rising sun. Not a breath of air stirred, not a cloud touched the sky, no mist rose from a harbor so still it mirrored the rocks edging Liberty and the high ruin of hospitals on Ellis.

A ferry, canary yellow and navy, plowed from Staten Island toward Manhattan, leaving a perfect white wake. The scene lacked reality. Even the moving boat appeared only a model moving along a track in front of a painted backdrop.

Anna wondered how Molly could survive, indeed thrive, in a place so removed from that which was eternal, that which was real. That which grew and carried within itself the seeds of rejuvenation. *Not thriving now, Molly,* Anna thought, and took a gulp of coffee.

Unfiltered cigarettes were very bad karma and no karmic debt goes unpaid. After thirty years of Camel straights, Molly's lungs probably rivaled the La Brea Tar Pits. God knew what might be dredged up out of the bubbling ooze. The most pathetic excuse for a germ could take down one of the finest minds and greatest hearts Anna had ever known.

Tears boiled hot and Anna blinked them back. Molly didn't deserve homage. If she hadn't been so fucking stupid, so fucking pigheaded, so fucking *addicted*…Anna's anger was no match for the salt water. Fury poured down her cheeks. For years Molly had lectured her for putting herself at risk: climbing mountains, fighting fires, rappelling into caves. And all the while she—an M.D. with an IQ about the same as the top NASCAR speed—all the while she'd been sucking down poison. "God damn you!" Anna muttered. "Do anything for me? Live for me." Having set the coffee cup down, she pulled the tail of her shirt free of her jeans and mopped her face. She stopped short of blowing her nose and smiled at the sound of her mother-in-law Edith's words in her head: "Really, Anna, is such crudity *necessary?*"

"Edith, somebody should tell you you're dead," Anna said to the exquisite blue of the sky. But she felt better. Another sip of coffee and she was able to think of somebody besides herself: Frederick Stanton.

A quick trip into the house, then back on the picnic table, coffee mug refilled, Patsy's cordless in hand, Anna dialed the number she'd called so many times she could recite it in her sleep or punch the buttons in total darkness: the number of her sister's Upper West Side apartment.

"Hello," Frederick answered, and Anna begrudged him the good cheer in his voice yet was sorry to be the one to destroy it.

"Molly's back in ICU," she said without preamble. "Pneumonia. She's stable, that's all they could tell me."

"That's it?"

"That's it."

"Shit. See you there."

Frederick hung up while Anna still held the receiver to her ear. "Shit" was the strongest expletive she could remember him ever uttering. "See you there," she said to the dial tone.

As always, the Liberty IV was on time. Anna was waiting at the end of the dock, blessedly free of tourists at this time of the morning: the sweeter sounds of gulls and lapping water could be heard. A young black deckhand who was not Cal handed her aboard, not with grace but with a perfunctory eye to safety. Anna didn't bother to see who the captain was. Kevin probably, given the time of day. She went to the stern to hide in the engine noise beneath the Stars and Stripes.

An interloper had usurped her spot. A Park Policeman in blue and bluer—*like a Smurf,* Anna thought uncharitably—stood watching her, a half-smile on his face. Not as if he was smirking, but as if, though tired from night shift, he was still willing to meet friendliness halfway.

Anna let her crabbiness go, and like a kid's kite carried away on the wind, it was gone. Of course he was pretty. She'd already met the token ugly policeman. Stocky, Asian and something else, this one had a coal-black crew cut that sparkled in minute waxed spikes, black single-lidded eyes, a nose from a plastic surgeon's stud muffin menu and a crooked mouth just to prove he was a regular guy. His name badge read "Joshua Hoang." Another trendy name. The melting pot was melting the minds of young mothers.

"Where's Billy?" Anna asked to make conversation. "Lieu day?"

"Billy's working days now," Joshua said, and rotated his compact muscular form to ape her pose, forearms on the gunwale, eyes on the churning water as the *Liberty IV* eased from the dock.

"Since when?"

"Since they dragged me here from D.C.," Joshua replied. His voice was light. Not a good voice for bullhorns or barking orders, but a great voice for eliciting confidences. "I came in yesterday and went on duty," he elaborated. "Are my dogs barkin'."

For half a minute Anna was stymied; then her stint in the Midwest—or Upper Midwest, on Isle Royale—came to her rescue. "Dogs barking" somehow equaled "feet tired" in Minnesotan.

"Hmong?" she asked. Hmong refugees from Laos made up the latest in the waves of immigrants to hit the Upper Midwest.

Joshua looked pleased and surprised. "St. Cloud, Minnesota," he said. "Second-generation. How'd you guess? You buy a quilt cheap or something?"

"Something like that." Anna was too distracted to map out the tortuous route of her thoughts. "Tell me about Billy."

"I don't know the man," Joshua said, but he sounded as if he'd already met, accused, tried, judged and sentenced young Billy. Weakness was not a trait that went unforgiven in blue and gold circles. "But I hear he's got some problems. Said he wouldn't listen to 'them' moaning and groaning. 'Them' being *'them,'* I take it. As in paranormal manifestations. So. He's days. He's happy. I'm nights. I'm still employed. Who can complain?" He flashed her a smile of such perfect orthodonture the sun practically glinted off his incisors.

"Not me," Anna said.

Molly was back on the respirator, Frederick back in the red plastic chair.

"Dr. Madison will be along in a few minutes," Anna said, and shook her head as Frederick offered her the one chair. "The duty nurse said she would page him." Bumping Frederick over, she perched on the chair next to him as they'd done the first day.

"Good thing I've got a skinny behind," Frederick said.

"It's how Molly and I always pick our men," Anna returned. "The bonier the better."

Fifteen breaths a minute, Anna counted.

Molly had slid a very long way backward in a very short time. Her skin was drawn and gray, the purple beneath her eyes giving her a battered look. *Not battered,* Anna thought, remembering the rich, life-filled anger of Mandy's bruises. *Cadaverous.* The purple not of living blood but the foreshadowing of death.

"Talk to me," she demanded as a wave of panic ran up her spine, making the flesh tight and cold.

"Oh gosh, Anna," Frederick said wearily.

"Anything. Anything at all." Neither looked at the other; both kept their eyes fixed on the fragile form in the bed as if, by will, they would tether her to earth.

"Anything? Okay, let's see. Today's supposed to be partly cloudy, a high of eighty-five, chance of showers in the afternoon. Rani is learning to sharpen her little claws on Molly's leather couch. She sleeps on my throat. I keep waking up with paws in my mouth."

"Litter box paws," Anna said.

"Thank you for pointing that out."

"Keep talking. You're doing good."

"Lordy. Hey, there is something. This"— he waved a hand over Molly's inert body—"put everything else out of my mind. They've ID'd your Jane Doe."

Anna perked up a little, but with Hatch no longer around to tell, the victory was hollow.

"Remember the fractured ulna? It was an ugly and old break—a pin had been inserted, a special kind that they use on kids so they can grow with it. It's not common. They traced the pin back to a Dr. Crosby in Mill Valley, California. The doctor still had the files and actually remembered the kid. I take it it was an extremely delicate operation and there was no follow-up care."

"Who was Jane?" Anna asked.

"Agnes Abigail Tucker of Turlock, California, survived by her mother, Pearl Tucker, and a half brother, John Tucker."

"How old was she when she broke her arm?"

"Seven. Just started second grade. She fell off the horizontal ladder on the playground at school."

"You've been thorough," Anna said.

"Visiting hours are short."

She noticed his hand had crept out and, with his index finger, he stroked the back of Molly's wrist feather-gently, as if he were soothing a baby duckling.

"How old was she when she died? Fourteen?" Anna asked.

"Almost. Fourteen in August. Here." Reluctantly, he relinquished his tenuous contact with Molly and fished a notebook out of his shirt pocket. In crisis he reverted to type. Gone were the neatly creased Dockers and ironed button-down collars. An aged olive T-shirt with a faded design on the back and wrinkled madras shorts had reclaimed him.

Having opened the notebook, he tore out a page and gave it to her. She scanned it: names, dates and addresses of both the doctor and Agnes Abigail Tucker's mother.

A real little girl from a real town with a

mom and a grade school and a horizontal ladder. Anna felt a wave of melancholy well up for Agnes Tucker that Jane Doe had not evoked. She folded the paper and put it in her pocket. Maybe she'd call the mom, see if there was a connection with James Hatchett. He'd been in San Francisco at the Presidio, she remembered. They could have crossed paths then.

Frederick's finger went back to Molly's hand. Anna let her mind turn on the California Bay Area just because it was beautiful and she and Zach had once spent a glorious weekend in Sausalito, a ritzy tourist town across the Golden Gate Bridge from San Francisco. A map of the coastline unfurled in her brain, full color with the green cliffs of Point Reyes and the white froth of waves breaking. Sea lions barked and an otter, belly to the sun, an abalone lunch in his paws, floated placidly in the swells of her memory.

"Mill Valley," she said suddenly. "That's just north of Sausalito."

"Sounds right."

"Serious real estate. Money."

Frederick ignored her, which was fine, she was just vocalizing thoughts as they followed their path. "The doctor must be a big dog. High-end pediatrician, or he wouldn't be practicing in Mill Valley."

"She."

"She. So. Mrs. Tucker cares enough to buy her daughter the very best and then no follow-up care?"

Frederick's soul slowly came back into his body. He unglued his eyes from the death mask that had settled over Molly's features and turned to look at Anna. "I'm sorry. Didn't I tell you? The girl was kidnapped two days after she got out of the hospital. She was a staple on milk cartons for two years, but nobody found hide nor hair of her till she jumped off your statue. So Mom Tucker gets her back and loses her again in the same phone call. Glad it wasn't me who had to make it."

A seven-year-old kidnapping case. Anna let her mind wrap around that for a minute. A second-grader is snatched, never found, to reappear years later dead at the base of the Statue of Liberty. It made a creepy kind of sense if Hatch had kidnapped her. There was no sign of physical or sexual abuse, but he could have been some other kind of psycho, kept her in the basement like a beloved pet. She was very pale. Or maybe he just liked to watch her, touch her. Anna shuddered convulsively. Frederick didn't notice. She continued with her story. The girl escapes. A couple days later—not too many or Agnes might have been in worse shape, a week or two at most—she comes out to the statue all by herself. Why?

She could see it from the basement window.

Hatch told her about it and she thought she'd be safe because he only worked nights.

Whatever.

Out she comes, up she goes, and either she sees Hatch and kills herself to evade capture or Hatch gives her an extra nudge over the wall

250

lest she start blabbing to all and sundry about his basement peccadilloes. Later, Hatch, bereft because he's lost or murdered his little pal, whom in his own berserker way he loved, slides into a suicidal depression and kills himself the same way she was killed.

The only flaw in that was the cigarette. Rituals die hard. And to Anna's mind, had that been the case, he would have jumped over the parapet exactly where Agnes had gone over—poetic justice—not from his smoking perch. Even flawed, the theory answered the most questions; Anna decided to file it away rather than trash it.

"Can I show you something?" Frederick asked suddenly. His words were so out of sync with the fiction she had been spinning that she was jolted, as if plucked up from sleep by the ringing of a phone.

"Sure," she said.

"You won't think I'm an idiot?"

"I already think you're an idiot."

"Fair enough. Looky here." Out of the right-hand pocket of his dilapidated shorts he pulled a black velvet box, the kind with a spring hinge and a rounded top; the absolute Tiffany-to-Target, movie-classic box.

"You're kidding," Anna said. "You've only known her a week or so. And most of that she was unconscious."

"I've known her two years, ten months and a week or so. I could tell you how many hours, but my preoccupation with my love life might strike you as juvenile."

Anna snorted.

"Wanna see?"

She did and he so obviously wanted to show her that she nodded. With care, as if what dwelt within could take fright and fly away, he turned the box toward her and opened it.

Not a diamond. Frederick did things his own way. The ring was deep gold—probably twenty-two karats—not filigreed but delicately patterned in a bas-relief of vines and swirls. The stone was set flat in the band, a clear, dark green, liquid emerald, the edges beveled.

"It's perfect," Anna admitted. "Absolutely perfect for Molly in every way. She will marry you just to get that ring."

"And I will marry her."

"You'd better hurry," Anna said, the hissing of the breathing tube ominously loud in her ears and the stark smell of sterile sickness threatening to clog her throat.

Whether she swooned or just really pissed Frederick off, she was never sure, but all of a sudden his hands were clamped painfully over her upper arms and he was shaking her with a strength his scrawny body belied.

"Molly will live," he said. "Don't you for a single second doubt that. She will live to be an old, old woman. She will bury you. She will bury me."

Oddly, Anna was comforted by the outburst: the pain, the anger, the vehemence. Because she believed him, she began to cry. The FBI man wrapped his long arms around her and, awkward on their shared seat, he rocked her.

"Okay. Okay. Enough. I'm fine," Anna said when she could stop the unwanted outpouring of emotion. She struggled free and escaped to the end of the bed. "Jesus." She grabbed a handful of paper towels from beside a sink attached to the wall and scrubbed her face. "Fuck."

Frederick laughed. "Anna, why do you always have to be such a dink? This was supposed to be a special bonding moment between us where I humbly request your permission to ask for your sister's hand in marriage, and you screwed it up."

"Sorry." Anna blew her nose.

"Can I?"

"Sure."

"Will you be my best man?"

"If you rent the tux."

"Done." Frederick stood up, reached over Molly's feet and shook Anna's hand. The moment, as highly emotional moments tend to do, became embarrassing because there was no place else for it to go.

"Yes. Well. It's settled, then," Frederick mumbled, and backed ungracefully into his chair.

Anna remained standing at the foot of the bed, watching her sister's chest rise and fall to the unpleasant mechanical sounds.

"She's got to say yes," Anna warned.

"There's that," Frederick admitted. "I know her better than you think I do."

Anna started to get the cold feeling around her sternum that impending news of betrayal brings on, but Frederick dispelled it with his next words.

"She never knew, but I've read every article she's ever written. Your sister's brilliant, did you know that?"

"It crossed my mind a time or two," she said dryly.

"Whenever I was in a city where she was lecturing, I'd go—sit way back like the skulking Tom I am." He smiled crookedly and Anna could see the relief on his face when she smiled back.

"How often did you 'happen' to be in a city where Molly was speaking?" she asked.

He had the grace to look sheepish. "Quite often, actually. And I've read every article about her."

"Even the one in the *Sentinel* responding to her speech that suggested Gulf War, chronic fatigue and a handful of other syndromes might be based on cultural stress rather than organic causes?"

"Somebody should have slapped that bozo upside the head. He screwed it all around and attacked her for his own ends. The toad even admitted he'd 'never heard Ms.'—*Ms.*, mind you, not Dr.—'Pigeon's speech but...' "

Frederick was protective. Anna liked that. Molly was not so tough as she liked everyone to believe. She deserved someone to lift heavy objects for her: couches, suitcases, the death of friends, the loss of years.

"I want a silk tux," Anna said. "Peach with a matching cummerbund."

"Fan club meeting?" Dr. Madison asked as he came in and closed the door behind him.

Neither answered. They wanted the news. "Molly's not so bad as it might look," he said, sensing their potential hostility if he didn't cut to the chase. "The respirator is as much a precaution as a necessity, given Molly's recent history. She's responding well to the antibiotics. I expect tomorrow we'll try her off the respirator, and a day or two after that she can probably move out of the ICU. We don't want to get premature. The sedatives are helping her with the natural anxiety and discomfort of her situation, but she's remained fully conscious and alert."

"She has?" Frederick and Anna's alarm confused David Madison.

"That's a good thing," he reassured them.

Anna looked back at the bed to see Molly's clear hazel eyes watching her. Molly signaled for a pen by miming writing, and Frederick scrambled to fulfill her request.

For a moment she wrote, then handed the pad back to the FBI agent.

He read it aloud to Anna: "I was asleep right up to the part about the silk tux. I swear it."

16

Anna took the Number 3 train to Brooklyn. A call from Dr. Madison's office to Patsy had gotten her Hatch's address and that of his nearest kin, James Hatchett, Sr. The addresses were only differentiated by a letter. Anna guessed they had upstairs/downstairs apartments in the same building.

In the middle of the day the train was sparsely populated and she had the car to herself. Stations clacked by to the accompanying sound of train car doors opening and closing and announcements so highly intelligible and gratingly cheerful that Anna wondered how the conductor had managed to get into the union.

Thinking of David Madison's office pleased her. He'd asked her to wait for him there, first making it perfectly clear it was a personal request and not a professional one, lest she worry. Knowing he was going to ask to reschedule their date, Anna had been gearing up to turn him down. Not for any specific reason, simply because of the vague feeling of wrongness that seemed to emanate from him. Or her. Probably her. While she was waiting she underwent a change of heart. Sitting in the oversized chair behind his high desk, she had, naturally, checked the drawer where the slippery file had vanished: locked. Looking around for other amusement, she hit one of the keys on his computer screen just to see what would come up. The screensaver vanished to be replaced by the doctor's AOL bookmarks. Under "favorite places" was *Persian Kittens*.

Madison must have known about Rani, chosen not to rat them out to the nurses and even gone so far as to read up on the breed. Anna was touched. When the doctor arrived, she accepted a date for Saturday, July 4. It being only Tuesday, that wasn't too threatening.

Persian Kittens. Maybe the man had depths of soul she'd not suspected.

At the Clark Street stop, Anna detrained and emerged into the sunshine. The Hatchetts, Junior and Senior, lived in a nice neighborhood. Pricey now, but James Senior may have bought and paid for his home in the fifties when it could still be done by regular people. With that thought, it occurred to Anna that she had assumed Hatch was from a blue-collar background. As she looked for 364 President Street, she realized why: his accent and his usually successful attempts to correct it. Speech patterns learned from a workingman who wants his son to have better.

By Colorado standards President Street was narrow and, with cars parked down both sides, almost choked, but the trees were mature. Late June found them in the fullness of their splendor, not yet tinged by smog or drought. The brownstones lining the street were simply designed, with square fronts and wide stoops. Unlike the Upper West Side's deep canyons, here buildings were on a more human scale, four stories mostly. That small concession changed the light, allowing the street a dappled neighborhood quality.

Number 364 was halfway down the block on the left. It had only two stories, quaint and cottagelike between its taller neighbors. The stoop was swept and two potted geraniums stood sentinel on either side of a formidable wooden door. Beside the door were two bell pushes. A: James Hatchett, Sr. B: James Hatchett, Jr.

Anna pushed A and waited for the buzz. When it came it engendered in her, as always, a sense of urgency, as if the person within would let go of the buzzer before she could yank open the door. She made it with seconds to spare and stepped into the gloom of the hallway. The house was laid out like many she'd been in in New York City: apartments to the left, stairs to the right zigzagging up to the floor above. Flooring and stairs were of dark wood, worn but cared for. The inevitable nicks and scuffs had recently been restained and the whole had a new coat of varnish. A rug cascaded down the steps like a tongue in a Disney cartoon. It was held in place at the back of each riser by a brass bar. The same blue paisley configuration continued on a runner over the hardwood to the door to apartment A.

As her eyes adjusted, she saw a man standing at the far end of the hall. There was a light above him, but either it had burned out or he'd decided not to turn it on.

"Excuse me, are you Mr. Hatchett?" she asked.

"The same." The voice was strong but had the coarsened quality of age. Walking into the darkness, she could see he was well into his sixties and leaned on a walker. His upper body was heavy, barrel-chested and short-waisted, with thick ropy arms. In his youth he must have been immensely strong.

"What can I do you for?" The offer was spoken in a friendly manner but it stopped Anna. This was territorial. This was a city. One did not accept strangers into one's home unexplained. Not even small female strangers.

She put her hands where he could see them and shifted her weight so the light through the high window in the front door reached him. He was square-headed, his hair black and white, in a grizzled old-fashioned crew cut. High and hooked, his nose jutted out from between thick black brows. Beneath, his eyes were gray and sharp. Even old and crippled, he wasn't a man Anna wanted to mess with.

She'd spent some time concocting a story to feed the old guy, but under his steady gaze she abandoned it. Either he'd help her or he wouldn't, but that nose looked as if it could sniff out a lie at fifty paces. "I met Hatch at the statue," she said. "We spent a little time together, not much. I was helping him identify the girl that died. I don't think Hatch jumped. I wanted to talk to you. If it's too painful, I'll go. I know I'm intruding on what must be an unendurable grief."

The old man pulled a large white hand-kerchief out of the pocket of the blue jump-suit he wore—the unstructured kind that doesn't bind when one is sedentary. As the hankie was released, she noticed a silver sliver disappear into a leather case snapped to a belt loop. It was long and narrow-bladed, like the knives used to gut fish. She'd been right to respect the man's space.

Mr. Hatchett blew his nose with a honking sound, then pushed his glasses up onto his fore-head and unashamedly wiped the tears out of his eyes. "Nothing's unendurable. But damn near. Damn near. Come on in." He pushed the door open with his hip and held it for her with one foot of his walker. "Lou Gehrig's dis-ease," he explained as she passed him. "When it gets to your lungs, they say it kills you. We'll see."

Anna's dad had died of Lou Gehrig's dis-ease; cheated her and Molly out of another twenty years of having a father. "That's what got my dad," she told Mr. Hatchett, "but it took fourteen years to do it."

"I got two left then. Sit down." He pointed to a rocking chair beside a fireplace filled with a dried-flower arrangement. Anna sat and James Hatchett Senior swung himself and the walker to a sideboard beside the door. "Scotch?" he offered.

It was eleven-thirty in the morning. "Don't mind if I do," Anna said, surprising herself. The Scotch was in honor of old Mr. Hatchett, Molly and her own father.

"A man's a damn fool to drink before he's forty and a damn fool not to afterward," Mr. Hatchett said. She heard the sound of liquid pouring into a glass; then he said: "I'll let you do the honors. Mine's the one with the straw."

Anna thought he was joking, but his was in a single-serving apple juice jar with a straw. She remembered then how stiff her dad's back and neck had gotten at the end. Stiff and terribly weak. It had been hard for him to put a glass to his lips, then tip his head back. That was soon before he died. Mr. Hatchett might not have two years left. She hoped she was wrong.

"Here you go, sir." She put the jar on the wide arm of the La-Z-Boy he'd settled into.

"Jim."

"Jim," she said, and took her seat. Recalling Hatch's accent, she said, "You don't sound like you're from Brooklyn."

"Seattle," he said. "Originally. Then all over. Then here. Stevedore for thirty-one years down on the docks. Here's mud in your eye." They toasted solemnly and sipped their drinks.

The apartment—or what she could see of it—was built in railroad style. They called it "shotgun" in the South. Each room was connected to the others in a line, like railroad cars. The living room, where they sat, was at the rear of the building. Two windows, uncurtained and opened to catch the breeze, looked out on a tiny garden fenced off from a dozen other gardens, equally tiny, behind the buildings that

261

lined this street and the next. Hatchett's garden was well kept, roses in beds and potted plants around a square of brick paving. His apartment was equally well tended, if totally masculine. The few knickknacks looked to be souvenirs from around the world: a plaster Leaning Tower of Pisa, a wooden pagoda, a metal Eiffel Tower about six inches high, seashells and a plastic hula dancer in a faded grass skirt. There were lots of books, one floor-to-ceiling bookcase of paperbacks. At a glance, the complete works of Louis L'Amour and Edgar Rice Burroughs. Two black-and-white pictures in old frames—one of a woman, one of a ship—graced the mantel. Faded prints of heavily forested mountains framed the chimney. The only feminine touch was the dried flowers in the fireplace. Anna must have looked at them, because Jim said, "The housekeeper does that. She puts 'em in every June and lets 'em collect dust till September. I don't see the point but it keeps the old bat happy. Look out. We got company."

Anna turned in time to see a big tiger cat jumping from the windowsill to the arm of her chair. He paused, showed her his rear end long enough for her to pay her respects, then leapt to the arm of Jim's lounger. There he flopped down, legs hanging limp, chin on the upholstery in the same pose Anna had seen his larger cousins take when draped over tree limbs in the Serengeti.

"Hey, Crumbum," Jim said, and rubbed the cat's head with scarred knuckles. The cat's left ear was a ragged stub and one of his eyes was missing.

"Used up a few lives?" Anna asked politely.

"A few. He used to be quite the ladies' man. A real fighter. Till we got him fixed and he forgot what it was he was fighting for."

Silence settled between them. Anna could feel the sun warm on her shoulder, the Scotch warm in her stomach, and hear the uneven rattle of the tiger cat purring.

"You want to talk about Jimmy," Mr. Hatchett said after a fortifying sip from the straw.

"If you don't mind."

"Nah. I want to talk. Memory's all that keeps 'em alive. Jimmy, his mom, my folks, all alive and well in here." He tapped his temple. "A piss-poor excuse for the real thing, but you take what you can get." He pulled out the handkerchief and whisked it under his nose. Crumbum lazily batted at the cotton as it brushed by.

"Do you think he killed himself?" Anna asked bluntly.

Jim didn't answer and he didn't meet her eye. After half a minute she wondered if he'd heard her. "I like to think he didn't," he said finally.

"Sounds like you might think he did."

Again the silence. For a man who said he wanted to talk, words were coming hard. "Get that picture off the mantel, would you?" he asked at length.

Anna got up to do as he requested.

"The one on the end there in the black wood frame. Careful. That frame's falling apart. I keep meaning to get around to regluing it but never seem to quite make it."

Holding it securely together, Anna lifted down a photograph of a sweet-faced woman in the fitted coat and wide collar fashionable in the forties. She was leaning against the rounded fender of a car, her hand shading her eyes from the sun. No. Anna looked closer and smiled. She was saluting. The clothes looked about right for World War II. She appeared to be Italian, great dark eyes with straight black brows and shoulder-length waves of lush dark hair.

"Hatch's mother," Anna said. There was no mistaking the eyes.

"Hatch...Right, that's what they called Jimmy at work. Jimmy's mom, Angela. I took that the first day I met her. She was seventeen. It was wartime. I was in the Navy and we got married a week later. Two days after that I shipped out and was gone three years. We were so hot for each other you could see the sparks. And in those days, if you cared about a girl, you married her first. You can't tell at that age what's hormones and what's love, but Angie and I were a couple of the lucky ones. We fell in love writing letters. All those three years. Hundreds of letters. I'd still know Angie's hand-writing if I saw it tomorrow on a flyer in the gutter. Spiky little backhand. She was a southpaw. I got home and we got right to the business of being married like no time had passed at all."

Jim sucked up some Scotch and scratched the cat's head, flattening what was left of his ears out at right angles to his skull. Anna waited. She knew the beginning of a story when she heard one.

"What Angie'd managed to hide in her letters—not on purpose, she didn't have a dishonest bone, but because she'd hid it her whole life—was she had some kind of problem just being happy. She had dark times when she'd go off, walk by herself for hours. I was pretty worthless. Looking back, maybe there's something I could have done, but we didn't know much in those days. Only crazy people saw head doctors. I knew she wanted a family. I did too. I didn't become Catholic like they wanted, but I signed papers saying the kids would be raised Catholic. Church isn't all that bad for kids if you don't take it too seriously. There weren't any kids, though. We didn't run around testing ourselves like people do now. It was just the woman's fault. 'Barren' was the word Angie used to beat herself with."

Never having had much interest in children except from a scientific viewpoint, Anna found it hard to imagine the emptiness a woman like Angela Hatchett must have experienced when she was unable to bear. On two occasions she'd watched friends go through a frustrating fertility quest in their late thirties; seen it take over their lives, nearly destroy their marriages. Both cases had ended in not one but two successful pregnancies. She'd celebrated for them but known, deep down, she did not understand. As she did not truly understand now.

"To make a long story short," Jim went on after a minute, "the dark times got longer and darker. That woman must have walked a thousand miles. Hell, maybe she sat. I wasn't allowed to go with her. At thirty-nine she got pregnant. Everything went well, even the delivery. Angie had that baby laughing. Just like that's what she'd been born for."

"Hatch," Anna said.

"Jimmy. He was the best baby I ever saw. Sweet-tempered. Almost never cried. Laughed before he could sit up. A cat's tail and an empty box were all the toys he ever needed, though you can bet we bought him everything that wasn't nailed down.

"I thought that'd do it. A baby. For a while she was so happy, my Angie. Like the sun had finally come out. But whatever it was came back. When Jimmy was about five, she started walking again."

Anna had thought this fairy tale was going to have a happy ending, that the old man had forgotten the original question and was enjoying his reminiscences. Now she got a bad feeling Jim was just answering her in horrid detail.

"When Jimmy was eight, Angie jumped off the Brooklyn Bridge. It was more than a month before we knew. The body had to wash up and then it wasn't like it looked like Angie anymore."

"No note?" Anna asked.

"No note."

"No threats?"

"Never. I suppose I should have seen it coming, but I didn't. I always thought if I had it to do all over again...Then I did have it to do all over again, with Jimmy this time, and I didn't see it coming. Son of a bitch."

Out came the handkerchief.

Crumbum abandoned his master and, tail switching, stalked off through French doors that Anna guessed, from having frequented apartments like this in her younger days, opened into the dining room.

His mother's suicide explained a lot: Why Hatch reacted so badly to the lady who jumped off the Golden Gate Bridge, the flowers, his distress at the death of the girl at the statue, the azalea blossoms. Why he had needed so desperately to find out her ID, remembering, maybe, the weeks he and his dad had waited, not knowing. Anna waited till Jim had done with crying for the moment; then, briefly, she told him the story of the woman at the Presidio.

"That sounds like Jimmy," he said when she'd finished. "They say kids who had a parent commit suicide are more likely to do the same than kids that didn't. Jimmy never had dark times like his mother. He was a sunny little guy from the day he was born. I figured he'd be okay. Maybe there was something I wasn't seeing. He was brooding about that little girl killed at the statue, I know that. He never said outright, but he blamed himself. I think he blamed himself for his mom too. Hell, we both did. But I was a grown man and he was just a boy. I see these things on TV about little kids harboring these awful thoughts for years and then something triggers it and they go haywire. It was on Oprah."

"I don't think he killed himself," Anna said. Psychologically the facts might fit, but viscerally it didn't feel right.

Jim looked up from his apple juice bottle. "I don't want to think he did, but I'm an old man and Jimmy's father. Do you have anything or are you just wishing too?"

Anna gave him her best stuff: the ash and the tin. Spoken aloud, it sounded pretty feeble.

"That little meathead." Jim laughed. "He told me he'd quit smoking. Though I don't suppose one cigarette a day would kill anybody."

Given the situation, the words rang hollow and the two of them waited out the ensuing silence.

"Can I see Hatch's apartment?" Anna asked abruptly.

"Now, why would you want to do that?" Jim asked amiably, but suddenly Anna was acutely aware of the fish-gutting knife on his hip.

"I don't know." She wasn't being entirely honest. Hatchett's gray eyes hardened as if he sensed it. "I was hoping to find something that could go toward explaining things. Just looking," she admitted. "Not looking to find."

He said nothing and her nerves began to tingle. Had Hatch kept a child for seven years, the old man would have known it, been a party to it. "The police have already looked for a note," Jim said finally. "I haven't been up there in a couple years." Tapping his walker with the back of his hand, his wedding band ringing dully against the aluminum tubing, he watched her as if guessing the weight of her soul.

"Sure. Why not. The key is on that hook by the door. Come on back when you're done. I'll leave my door open."

"Thanks." Knowing a burden of trust had been laid upon her, and hoping she'd find nothing more sinister than dirty socks, she took the key and left. Jim didn't ask her if she knew where she was going. He knew she'd already figured that out. Whether he suspected why depended on how much he had to hide, either on his own behalf or that of his son.

Clearly the "old bat" who cleaned for Mr. Hatchett Senior did not perform the same services for his son. Had Anna not seen many bachelor apartments in her life, she might have thought the place had been searched, ransacked by slovenly amateurs. The floor plan was the same as downstairs. Windows were closed and blinds drawn. The air was hot and smelled of garbage and unwashed laundry. Anna's mind flashed back to a sickening sweet-sour smell. Where? The infectious disease wards on Island III. No, this was different—homely, stale odors of a life lived. Obviously, Mr. Hatchett Senior had not had the heart to have his boy's place cleaned yet. Anna understood that. The bizarre permutations of grief were not unknown to her. After she was widowed—and she'd never told anyone this, not even her sister—she had slept on the same sheets for eighteen months, never washed them, because they were the last sheets she'd ever slept on with Zach.

The blinds were old-style paper rolls and the light through them cast a sepia tone over the piles of clothes and newspapers, the relics of a short and solitary life. Anna opened the blinds and surveyed the wreckage. Clearing her mind to sharpen her senses, she walked slowly through the clutter: Lacrosse clothes and sticks—Hatch either played or coached. *Police Marksman* magazines, a *TV Guide*. Anna flipped through it. Hatch had circled in red everything he wanted to watch that week. He was hooked on the afternoon soaps and old westerns: *Rawhide, Gunsmoke* and a handful of others in syndication that aired during the day.

The living room held little of interest. The dining room was a nest of old newspapers, but nothing stood out, no clippings of special interest: kidnappings, suicides, runaways. His personal mementos, and they were few, were in the bedroom. A photograph of his mother and him as a boy of six or eight. Maybe the last shot of the two of them before she took her life. A cross on the wall. A statue of the Virgin Mary on the dresser. Catholic. James Senior had mentioned that, but Anna had not quite realized the import. To a Catholic, suicide was one of the worst sins a person could commit, a betrayal not only of life but of faith.

She riffled through a closet, which regurgitated Park Police uniforms and little else. A row of tractor caps were the only pieces of apparel treated with respect. A collection of nine hung across one door, each on its own hook. They were standard tourist fare. Hatch had probably picked them up in the parks he'd worked in or visited. As she was closing the doors, giving up the search as pointless, one of the caps caught her attention. Having removed it from its hook, she turned it in her hands. The cap was dirty white canvas with an adjustable back. On the front, where the logo is usually displayed, was a brown lumpy shape. A potato, Anna realized, and knew she'd seen it before on the dead child. She'd remembered it as a rock or a football, but this was a potato. A spud.

Was this what was referred to on the cryptic list found on Hatch's body? And what did it mean? That he'd known the child, that the hat had special significance? Or was this the clue to her identity he'd hinted at in the letter he left Anna? Identity was moot. Little Agnes Abigail Tucker once was lost but now was found.

Anna closed her eyes, the better to bring the list Trey had read to mind. "Little girl. Spud. Call Caroline."

Back in the living room, she cleared a stack of old pay stubs and assorted bills off the desk. It was an antique secretary rich with cubbyholes and compartments. Anna found what she was looking for in a recess under the pigeonholes: a Rolodex. One by one she flipped through the cards. He had the numbers and addresses of two Carolines: Caroline Rogers in Queens and Caroline Colter at Craters of the Moon National Monument. Having pulled the two cards out, Anna stuffed them in her hip pocket.

A rapping on the floor let her know her company was missed below stairs. Taking the cap with her, she let herself out and locked the door.

Jim was waiting for her in his chair. Crumbum was back, squashed over the arm as before.

"So, did it look like a cyclone hit it?" Hatch's father asked.

"Pretty much." Anna took her seat in the rocker and watched Jim Hatchett's eyes dull as he looked back through the years.

"He's always been like that. Angie threatened, cajoled and prayed but he never changed. Everywhere he went he left a trail—sweaters, socks, books. I always figured he'd grow out of it."

Jim was digging down by his hip again. Anna trusted he was looking for the handkerchief and not the knife. To give him a semblance of privacy, she stared out the window. Three little sparrows hopped along the brick in search of seeds.

"Did you find what you were looking for?" Jim asked when he'd recovered himself.

"I don't know," Anna replied. "Have you seen this before?" She took the ball cap out of the back of her waistband, handed it to him and watched closely. No glint of recognition or alarm.

"Jimmy collected these things but I never paid much attention. They all look alike to me. What's this supposed to be? A potato?"

"I guess," Anna said.

"Looks more like a turd."

There was nothing wrong with Jim's eyes or his sense of art.

Instead of handing it back, he put the cap on and asked: "Why did you take it?"

She answered with another question. "Does the name Tucker mean anything to you? Agnes Abigail Tucker or Pearl Tucker?"

Jim's face altered almost imperceptibly, a tightening of the skin around the eyes. Anna didn't know whether the names triggered some response or the man just didn't like being questioned. "Not offhand," he said evenly. "Why?"

"Do you have a basement?"

He looked at her long and hard. "What is it you're getting at? It's not just Jimmy jumping. Square with me or stop wasting my time."

Anna thought about it for a minute, then decided to tell him. If he and his son had collaborated in kidnapping and perversion, she could probably get to the door before the old guy got the knife out from between the cushion and the cat.

"I was trying to find a connection between Hatch and the dead girl. Her name was Tucker. She was kidnapped in California seven years ago."

"What...Wait." He thought. "That would've been about '92 or '93."

"Thereabouts."

"Jimmy was working at that big park they got in San Francisco, down on the bay."

"The Presidio."

"And nobody found the little girl—found who kidnapped her—and then she was killed?"

"Right."

"A basement?" The pieces were falling into place behind the gray eyes, creating a picture Jim Hatchett did not like. "You thought maybe Jimmy stole this kid, brought her home like a stray kitten and kept her in the basement for seven years?"

"I didn't really think it," Anna hedged. "It just sort of crossed my mind as one remote possibility."

"Remote, hell. I've got half a mind to throw you out on your ear. What kind of mind sits around dreaming up psycho stories like that?"

"Somebody stole her. Somebody kept her for seven years."

"Jesus. What a world. Get us both another Scotch if you will."

Anna did as she was bade, making hers a short one. As she sat with her drink she considered asking again about the basement, but Jim was looking dangerous and she felt she'd pushed him about as far as he was going to be pushed.

He slurped up a snort of whiskey, his head heavy on the weakened neck. Anna saw her own father, his last days, skin loose, body failing him, but still able to tell a good joke and generous enough to laugh at ones he'd already heard.

"You never thought Jimmy'd do a thing like that," Jim stated. His voice was flat and strong. This was as close to pleading as he ever got, Anna would have bet her life on it.

"No. I never did," she said. And she never did, not really. It was just a lead, and like a hound dog that knows nothing else, she had to follow it to the end. "And I don't think he jumped."

Jim grunted his satisfaction.

"Can I take the cap?" Anna asked as she stood to go.

"Nope."

"Can I come back?"

"You damn well better."

The door to the building's basement was under the front stoop, as were many in the old brownstones. Anna hadn't noticed it before— she was too busy looking for the address. On the leaving-no-stone-unturned principle, she slipped around and down the stairway. In the basement door, a monolith of solid oak and nail studs, was a barred window. Standing on tiptoe, she looked inside. From the thin light leaking through ground-level windows, she could see a clean open space. To the right were a utility sink, a washer and a dryer. Down the middle ran a clothesline. Against the left wall were two cubicles, storage units for the apartments.

The odds of keeping a child captive in secret under these conditions were all but impossible. Still, she climbed the steps and walked into the narrow alley of grass and shrubs between Hatchett's building and the next. Dropping to hands and knees, she peered in the dusty windows. Both cubicles were filled with boxes, bicycles and other household paraphernalia. It all looked as if it hadn't been disturbed for a good long while.

Having brushed the evidence of her inquiries from her trousers, she regained the sidewalk.

"Hey."

Anna suppressed a guilty twitch. Jim Hatchett stood on the stoop above, leaning on his walker. "I brought you the key to the basement," he said. "You still want to see it?"

"Nah," Anna said. "I trust you."

He laughed, a deep chest laugh that was infectious. "Like one old fox trusts another. Here." He tossed her the baseball cap with the potato on it. "I don't know what good it will do you."

Anna didn't either, but since Hatch thought it was important enough to pinch from the New York City morgue, it had to mean something.

17

By the time Anna landed on Ellis Island and plopped herself down in the visitor's chair in Patsy's office, it was after four. Phone clamped between ear and shoulder, Patsy was furiously scribbling, punctuating her sentences with "Got it" and "Okay, go ahead."

"Whew!" she sighed when she was done. "What a mess." She tipped her chair back and demanded: "Did you bring me candy? I require gobs of chocolate at this moment."

"I have quarters," Anna countered. "We can get Hershey bars from the machine."

"Let's do it," Patsy responded, with the air of a naughty adventuress off to heist the family silver.

"What's the mess?" Anna asked as they made their way to the basement and the candy machine.

"Not a mess, really. In fact it's beautifully organized, but there's just a lot of it. Do you know of Mrs. Weinstein?" Anna didn't. "She's a terrifically rich philanthropist type. For the past couple years she's been romancing senators, congressmen, lobbyists and the press, trying to get a bill through Congress. You know how they're required to teach environmental ed in some states? Well, the Spice Bill—as in 'variety is the spice of life'—will require federally funded grade schools to teach multicultural appreciation. She hopes to get it passed this year so it'll go into effect in 2003. She'll do it too. She's something else. She's throwing a Fourth of July bash on Liberty. The guest list is a Who's Who in Technicolor: Asian-American, African-American, Native American, Mexican-American. You name it. And all of them the biggest of wigs. She'll woo them and the press. Fitting, don't you think, here at the 'golden door' where all these mix-and-match Americans began? This bash will be very high-tone. You know that wall around the plaza at the beginning of the mall to the statue?"

Anna nodded obediently.

"She's hired Ralph Lauren—*Ralph Lauren,* mind you—to design cushions to go along the whole thing so those horrifically important heinies won't get numb watching the fireworks."

Anna began pumping quarters into the machine while Patsy picked out the appropriate letter/number combination to convince it to dispense Hershey bars with almonds.

"I didn't know people could have parties on Liberty," Anna said.

"You betcha. Very important people and lowly little rangers. It's a prime spot, especially on the Fourth of July. The view of the city, the boats in the harbor, the fireworks: you can't beat it with a stick. You'll still be here, won't you? We'll crash. It'll be a hoot."

278

*　　*　　*

Patsy was too busy to play, so Anna followed her back to her office, watched her work for a few minutes, then wandered off to find a phone that wasn't in use.

Only one of Hatch's Carolines was home, Caroline Rogers in Queens. In her single-minded quest for information, it had slipped Anna's mind that she could be the hated messenger, that these women might not yet know of Hatch's demise. Probably wouldn't, unless they were family or Park Service, where news of this kind would appear on the Ranger Reports on every computer in every park in the country.

Caroline Rogers was neither. She'd been dating Hatch for eight months, and from what Anna could gather, was set on marrying him whether he liked it or not. Small children could be heard shrieking in the background. When Anna broke the news of Hatch's death, there was more anger and disappointment in Ms. Rogers's tears than grief of the deep and abiding kind that drew the handkerchief from Jim Hatchett's pocket. Anna sat out the storm for what she figured was a polite amount of time, then wedged her questions in between fresh outbursts.

No, Caroline Rogers knew nothing about Agnes Tucker, nothing about a potato hat, nothing about a child who had committed suicide on Hatch's shift. Clearly, Caroline was not Hatch's confidante, much as she might have wanted to be.

Anna spent another seven minutes trying to extricate herself gently from the one-sided conversation before she gave it up as a lost cause, said, "Got to go, thanks," and hung up abruptly, cutting the other woman off in the middle of another "So anyway..."

Virtuously using her AT&T card to avoid misappropriating taxpayers' funds, Anna dialed long-distance information. There was no Pearl Tucker listed in Turlock, California, but there was a P. Tucker on Weatheral Street, would she like that number? Anna copied it down. If she were a male predator looking for lone women, she'd visit addresses in the phone book where the first name was replaced by an initial. It was a dead giveaway.

This time around Anna was acutely aware that she might be treading on sacred ground. Before calling the number, she sat for a moment letting the mental dust settle until she could see what information she sought and choose an avenue of inquiry that a woman suffering again the loss of a child—probably as acutely as she had seven years earlier—might be responsive to.

When she was ready, she punched in the numbers. It was ten past five New York time, ten past two in California. Anna hoped Mrs. Tucker was home. It would be a shame to have wasted all that energy gearing up to face a distraught mother only to get a machine.

The phone rang seven times. Anna decided

to give it fifteen. On nine it was answered with a "Hello" so dull she waited for the beep. "Hello," came again, a little stronger, and Anna responded.

"I'm calling for Pearl Tucker. Is she in?"

"This is Pearl." The voice was on a sliding scale, the last word hitting the lowest note and giving the short, empty sentence the ring of finality.

"My name is Anna Pigeon." Anna picked up what was going to be a very heavy conversational ball and forged ahead. "I'm a park ranger. I'm at the Statue of Liberty." If one stuck to the letter of the law, this was true. "I was there when your daughter died."

"And you think I'd like to know the details." Again the descending scale, "details" landing like a rock at the bottom of the basement stairs.

"No, ma'am," Anna said quickly. "I was the first emergency medical technician on the scene"—again strictly true and totally misleading—"and there was something about your daughter that captured me. It was I who brought in the FBI through a friend of mine. They identified your daughter."

"And you want me to thank you." Basement stairs. *Thud.*

Anna had thought finding out who the girl was, though not done by her in the flesh, might be the key to the mother's heart. Another, less fortuitous possibility was that, in the mother's mind, her child was alive till the New York City morgue marked her dead. This put Anna in only slightly better odor than the actual killer. From the drop of Pearl Tucker's voice, she found it impossible to guess what the woman was feeling and even harder to think any of it was good.

"No, ma'am. I've been trying to figure out how she came to be on the Statue of Liberty and why such a beautiful young girl would have jumped. The police told me she'd been kidnapped but no one had ever been able to find out who did it—"

"Oh, I know who did it," Mrs. Tucker interrupted.

That got Anna's attention.

"A low-life scum named A.J. Tucker took her. Her father took her."

At last Anna identified the strange cadence of Mrs. Tucker's voice. It was anger grown cold and weary. The kind that could squash you like a cockroach and never bother to look back to see if you were dead or just maimed. Anger without hope, remorse or fear of consequences. Anna was in total sympathy with it. "What a son of a bitch," she said kindly. "Never a word to you? Dead or alive?"

"Not a word in seven years."

She might as well have said seven thousand years.

"You remarried?" Anna asked, remembering Frederick mentioning Agnes was survived by a mother and younger half brother.

"And redivorced. I got a son out of the deal, and the house. He got the truck and thirteen stitches in his scalp." The woman laughed, no humor, just a small triumph.

"Yet you kept your first husband's name," Anna said.

"If Aggie ever got away, got near a phone, I wanted her to be able to find me. She was only seven but she knew her mama's name was Pearl Tucker. I didn't leave the house, not once, for over a year. Not to take out the garbage. Nothing. Welfare ladies came and did for me. I didn't go to the toilet but I dragged the phone in with me. Every time I'd fall asleep I'd dream the phone was ringing, but it never was. Then I began to dream she was hurt, sick, calling for her mama. Then I gave up sleeping. I'm still not good at it, but I don't dream. Not of anything."

This was said without a hint of self-pity. She spoke as if she told a story that she didn't believe about a woman she didn't like.

At first Anna had expected Mrs. Tucker might hang up on her. Now she knew she wouldn't. Talking, shoveling horse manure, seeing the Bolshoi Ballet—it was all the same to Pearl. Anna had been in that place. She sent up a quick prayer of thanks to Molly and whatever gods were tuned in over New York Harbor that she hadn't had to live there for seven years.

"According to the medical reports your daughter was well taken care of." Anna was glad to have some fragment of solace to offer. "She'd eaten well and was clean and healthy. There was nothing to show anybody had ever hurt her or...interfered with her in any way."

"He took her to hurt me. I guess that was enough. He didn't need to hurt her." That was it, no expression of relief or joy in the child's care. Anna thought of Jane Fonda in *They Shoot Horses, Don't They?* Despair so impotent, anger so tired there's no life to sustain the emotions.

"Where was he from?" Agnes Abigail's clothes had held no clue. Jeans and ball caps could have been acquired in any state in the union.

"He wasn't from anywhere," Pearl said unhelpfully. "He was an army brat who went in the Army himself right out of high school. He made big veteran noises, but he wasn't a veteran of anything but bar fights. He never got anywhere near Vietnam or anywhere else. He liked to tell people he'd volunteered for 'Nam, but he never did. Then he got to telling people he'd been there, fought, but he never had. A real loser."

"Do you have any idea where he might have gone with her?" Anna asked, cutting into the monotone.

"Anywhere. He could have gone anywhere. Mexico. Canada. He liked camping. Roughing it. He was big into hunting and fishing, killing things. Trapping. Building what he called tepees but were just sticks and blankets in the woods. The police knew he'd taken her. I told them and they believed me. But nobody ever could find him. He had another wife from before and a half-grown kid in Redding—kid was a real piece of work. Last I heard, he was in jail. He and three of his boyfriends beat a little Negro boy nearly to death. His ex said she hadn't seen him and didn't want to. The cops said he'd probably set up a new identity for himself somewhere, new name, maybe even driver's license and credit cards. Though he never could get any credit when I knew him and he'd lost his license on a DUI. Never got another one. Just drove without it. He liked that. The government made him paranoid, thinking they traced everybody through their Social Security numbers and things. That was a laugh. He hates the government, when the only jobs he and his old man could ever get were in the Army."

"Did he have any favorite places he liked to camp?" Anna tried. She knew that seven years ago the police would have asked these questions. She also knew that after the heat died down and people began to feel safe again, they tended to drift back to their old ways.

"Oh, God, let me think." A series of noises followed that Anna recognized from her many phone conversations with her sister. Pearl was lighting a cigarette. "Montana," came out on a lung-deep sigh. "Colorado. Idaho was big. Northern California till they put in that prison up there near Susanville. He said it brought in too many niggers, wetbacks, wops—his words, not mine."

"He sounds like a dream come true," Anna said.

"Oh, yeah. If I hadn't been born stupid, I never would have married him. If I hadn't grown up even stupider, I'd've killed him when I had the chance."

Anna had a pretty good picture in her head of Tucker's insides. She wondered if his outsides were as unappealing. "Do you have any photos of him?"

"I burned every goddamn one."

"Can't say as I blame you," Anna said. She'd learned all she was going to from Mrs. Tucker and was wanting to hang up. The woman's voice could have been used as audiological warfare. Twenty minutes on the phone with her and Anna was ready to stick her head in an oven.

"Thanks for your time," she said. "I'm sorry about your little girl."

"Okay. You too," Pearl returned, her words as empty as an abandoned house.

Anna put down the receiver and rubbed her ear. Too long on telephones was disorienting. Images the conversation called to mind didn't match images before the eyes. Over time it was anxiety-producing.

And it wasn't as if Caroline Rogers and Pearl Tucker had been a barrel of laughs.

18

Exhaustion swept over Anna in enervating waves; the grief of others coalescing into an internal darkness. She escaped to Island II, made the perilous climb up the fallen stairwells and through the window to her fourth-floor balcony. The sky above New Jersey had claimed the sun. The glow of a smog-born sunset dyed the light. Shadows diffused. The air was warm, humid, smelling of earth and ocean and the faint intangible scent leaves make when they rub against one another in the wind.

Her daypack her pillow, she stretched out on the stone floor of the balcony and fell into sleep.

When she awoke it was full dark. For an instant she thought she was back in the high country and someone had stolen all but a handful of stars. Memory returned. She dug through her pack for her wristwatch, a Timex that lit up. It must have been designed with the aging eyes of baby boomers in mind. One could actually read it in the dark. Ten past nine. She had napped for over three hours.

Allowing consciousness to bloom fully in its own time, she stayed supine on her night balcony. Cloaked in darkness, the world was utterly changed. A supreme gentleness personified eastern summer nights that, living so long in the West, she'd forgotten. A kindly, dreamlike quality that the sharp dry air of Colorado could not emulate. Two floating sparks caught her attention and she laughed in delight. Ellis Island had fireflies. Fireflies put her in mind of Tinkerbell and she wanted to clap because she believed.

At length, fully alert and wonderfully refreshed, she rose, stretched out the kinks to the accompaniment of the cracking of ankle and knee joints. The older one got, the more difficult it became to move stealthily. Old bones had a litany of their own, reciting past injuries to any who would listen.

Having been caught by nightfall on Ellis once before, Anna had taken to carrying a Mag-Lite in her daypack. Now she congratulated herself on her foresight. There was no hurry. In fact, she had all night; the last boat to Liberty had left some time ago. Island commuting was not designed for someone who had come to view time much as the Navajo. The prospect of a sleepover on Ellis was not daunting. There was a Park Policeman, probably Joshua, on duty. He would have the keys to the kingdom: drinking fountains, flush toilets, carpeted floors to sleep on. But she wasn't feeling the least tired or in need of company.

Enjoying the luxury of time, she sat in the window, her back to the out-of-doors, letting her eyes adjust. She played her light over the floor where she'd seen the footprint in the moss. The faintest of signs remained. There were no new tracks.

Tired of that small amusement, she walked into the pitch-dark innards of the crumbling hospital. Not daunting but certainly challenging was egress from her fourth-floor aerie. The ruined stairwell was not something she would tackle in the inky darkness of the building's gullet. Island II was immense, the buildings linked by hallways, wide tunnels running nearly a quarter of a mile, one on each floor and one in the basement. There would be other stairways in better repair.

As she stepped into the central hall of the fourth floor, darkness flowed around her. Not too long ago she would have found this black absolute, but last winter she'd been in one of the deepest caves in the world, Lechuguilla in Carlsbad Caverns National Park. Caves were a world so utterly without light that dark was a palpable thing pressing on eardrums and eyelids. Here, when Anna clicked off her Mag-Lite and waited, light did appear: a faint spark through a skylight, the pastel glow from a window facing the city; not the elemental dark of the underground.

At one time the vast hall had been rectangular. Nature, abhorring a straight line, had muted the angles, distorted the planes. Plaster crumbled and dust from brick and mortar settled till drifts formed between wall and floor. Paper peeled from walls, lending a ragged, leafy effect. A ruined light fixture, a globe in a ball of filigreed metal, hung from a cord. Doors, some closed, some open, some cemented halfway by the residue of decay, molded the line of the walls into a landscape Escher would have loved.

Anna's feeble light did not reveal this all at once but showed her irregular slices cut into ribbons of illumination. Without the cheery sun and tourist buzz, the hospital looked as dangerous as it was, but in time, all things were possible. Due consideration could be given each step and in an hour, probably less, she would emerge from one of the ground-floor rooms none the worse for wear. She headed east. Her balcony was nearest that end of the complex.

Billy Bonham and his ghosts crossed her mind, but either they were not in attendance in this part of the hospital or she was not in the mood. Regardless of the cause, there was no pricking of the thumbs and she moved easily down the rotting passage, feeling changes in firmness underfoot, noting odors as she drifted by, listening for the secret whisper of aging stone.

After thirty carefully traveled feet, a narrow stair, deliciously black and gothic, opened to her left. Up it, she knew, was an attic lit only by two hexagonal windows, one of which perfectly framed the southernmost turret of the registry building. She was tempted to climb the stairs to see the effect of that turret illuminated by night and New York City.

Good sense overcame temptation. The floor of the attic was not to be trusted in the light of day, and a twinge from her torn thigh reminded her she had no wish to re-create the drama of the stairs on Island III.

The end of the passage brought her to an intersection, wide healthy-looking stairs to her left and a large, windowed ward room with a view of Manhattan to her right. Feeling virtuous, she eschewed the windowed room and, staying next to the wall though the stairs seemed to be in good repair, walked uneventfully down four flights to find herself at a door leading out to a stoop.

There she stopped a moment and took in the view she had denied herself earlier. A three-quarter moon hung fat and subdued over the Verrazano Narrows Bridge. Manhattan was made of light and New Jersey glowed as if radioactive. Boats cruised the harbor. The urban jungle beat of nuevo disco—elevator music on crystal meth—polluted the air. Natives were restless, party boats out in force.

Across the inlet, where the Circle Line docked, was the registry building, bright and civilized next to the untamed parts of Ellis brooding magnificently in uncertain light. Raw and mysterious, history, not yet sanitized by the National Park Service.

Anna deliberated which world to visit. Joshua, if he was the policeman on duty, would probably be in the registry building doing paperwork. His company would be welcome. Especially if he had an extra sandwich or two. But not yet. Anna felt the spirit of the cat stirring. She wanted to prowl the dark leafy edges of the rotting monolith, listen to the lap of waves on the breakwater and the rustle of night things in the undergrowth.

Slipping the Mag-Lite in her pocket, she sauntered along a path worn deep in the grass between the buildings and the harbor. To amuse herself she searched the high windows for ghostly manifestations or floating candle flames. Imagination managed to create a pleasant frisson of the creeps, but she saw nothing but the occasional firefly, the moon reflected from a roosting pigeon's wing.

On the island's southeastern corner, where the infectious disease wards thrust out nearly to the water's edge, she was treated to a look at Miss Liberty, flooded with light as if awaiting with open arms the next wave of immigrants.

Having absorbed as much grandeur as she could on an empty stomach, she was contemplating going begging to the night security person or, failing that, the candy machine, when Billy Bonham's paranormal paranoia reached out and touched her with icy fingers. In a lull in the pounding of boat music came a faint creak, a groan as ephemeral as an old board stepped on in the hours before dawn.

She turned from the statue's enduring vision of freedom and faced the bulk of masonry and wood behind her. She was near where the stairs had collapsed, where she'd felt as much as heard the rustling footsteps of the past.

Shaking herself as a dog just in out of the rain might, she cleared her mind of bogeys and listened: boats, the ubiquitous purr of Manhattan, the licking of water at her heels. Breathing evenly, completely relaxed, she shut down her thoughts and opened wide her senses, ready to wait till sunup if need be. Ten minutes passed and fifteen and twenty. Mosquitoes were dining on her ankles, and her stomach, un-Zenlike, began to add dispirited growls to the night's concert.

Half an hour slipped softly by before it came again. A groan, directionless and spine-chilling. No wonder Billy, already half scared to death, had asked for day shift. Silently, Anna crossed the grassy strip and walked up the stairs to the entrance of the old nurses' quarters, the last room on the infectious disease wing of the hospital. The door was wedged partway open, stuck there in the debris. Sideways, pack in hand, she slipped through. On the twilit edge of internal darkness, she again stilled her breathing and waited. Thick walls deadened the sound of the richness of life without. She began to feel the cold pressure of the lives lost in this mausoleum before it too began to be reclaimed by the earth.

Unsettling thoughts fluttered through her mind, tensing muscles and distracting her, but she held her ground. Curiosity was a greater force in the Pigeon sisters than fear. If an opportunity presented itself to see a bona fide ghost and she didn't take it, Anna would never forgive herself.

Next time the sound came it was fainter. The apparition was either moving away or running low on ectoplasm. Even as she held on to her mockery, the sound was frightening, containing as it did the hopelessness and pain of the years. Anna followed it deeper into the building, then out into one of the glassed-in walkways that connected the nurses' quarters with the corridor to the other wards. The moon was high. Enough light came through the leaves that she did not need her flashlight.

What glass remained was dulled with pollution, salt and dust. The moon shining through this filter created the illusion of fog lying along the floors, pouring over broken sills.

Graveyard fog, an evil voice murmured in her mind. She ignored it. She waited. The shivers passed. Moonlight turned back into moonlight. If not peace, then a truce with the building and the night was reestablished.

This time the wait was so long the soles of her feet grew numb from standing in one place.

Finally, a third moan crept through the corridors. Head held to the side the better to follow the haunting noise, Anna moved quickly down the walkway. At the intersection with the main corridor and the spur that cut around what had once been the Commissioner's garden and was now a black and silver jungle, she lost the sound.

Three moans. That was enough. If it was a ghost, let it show itself. If it was a game, she was done playing. "It's me, Anna Pigeon. I'm a park ranger," she called. "Answer me. Talk to me." She held her breath and it came: a tiny quavering cry. Near as she could tell, it originated from the overgrown mass choking the derelict garden.

At the door at the top of the steps leading into the tangle of vine and brush, she stopped again. Overhead the sky was nearly obscured by trees and vines that had intermarried, creating a canopy.

Clicking on her light, Anna poked the

narrow beam into the crush of greenery. "I'm here," she said. "Can you talk?" There was no answer this time, not even the ethereal whimper she'd been following, but she could hear something breathing—uneven, rattling breaths. Cheyne-Stokes: the breath of the dying. Squashing an impulse to turn tail and run, she forced her way down the steps, pushing at the branches reaching out to stop her. "Hang on," she said, as much to herself as to whomever—or whatever.

The last step was broken. Her foot fell into nothing and she toppled forward. Bushes broke her fall, leaving her more scared than hurt. The stumble did a good turn: she'd managed to hang on to her flashlight and, on elbows and knees, there was space to belly-crawl beneath the more forbidding shrubs.

Light from the Mag formed a tunnel of shocking green through the black of the surrounding foliage. "Hello?" She prodded the leaves and sticks with her light, inching toward the painful snoring. Ten seconds' crawling revealed a white spider the size of a hand and she shrieked. Eyes refocused. It was, indeed, a hand. A dead body wasn't nearly as alarming as a spider of uncivilized dimensions. And she didn't think the body belonging to this hand was dead. Yet. Something still breathed. Stretching on her stomach, Anna wormed her arm through what was probably poison ivy and closed her fingers around the wrist: a pulse, thin and thready.

She plowed ahead. Peripherally she was

aware of branches scratching at face and arms, but it was of too little import to register. Holding back the talons of a feral azalea, she knelt over the island's ghost. Barefoot, clad in a long pale blue nightgown, blond hair loose, skin bloodless, Corinne did look otherworldly.

Anna did a lightning assessment, found no gushing blood. Corinne was breathing on her own. Nothing could be done for her but to get her to medical care as quickly as possible. "You keep right on breathing, Corinne. You're a good strong woman. I'm going to get help. I promise you, five minutes and I'm back. Breathe for five minutes and you'll hear me coming. Got to go. Breathe."

More than five minutes elapsed before Anna made it back to the garden, but not much more. With her she brought the park's oxygen kit and the EMTs' red jump kit filled with advanced first aid supplies. What she didn't have was any way to cut through the brush. In this era of specialization, NPS maintenance didn't dabble in law enforcement and law enforcement couldn't lay hands on a pair of loppers or pruning shears to save their souls.

Joshua had given her a six-cell flashlight to replace her Mag-Lite. With its powerful assistance, she had no need to crawl through the shrubbery. Holding the oxygen kit to her chest, the red pack on her back, she waded to where Corinne was and tore open the shroud of greenery enclosing her.

The actress was dangerously dehydrated.

296

When pinched, her skin stayed tented till Anna pushed it flat. Another day and thirst would have killed her. She had also suffered severe blunt trauma to the head. Anna felt the wound. Dried blood caked Corinne's hair. She had been struck or had fallen and injured the back of her skull to the right of center. Only one of the classic signs of brain injury was extant: raccoon eyes, dark circles around the eye sockets. No cerebral spinal fluid leaked from nose or ears, though it may have done over the past days and the traces evaporated. No battle sign—dark bruiselike marks—showed behind the ears.

The garden was too soft, too choked with plant life for an accident of this type to have occurred within its walls. The concrete steps and the brick side of the ward were the two exceptions. A wound of this magnitude could hardly have been engendered by any casual slip of the foot. Tremendous force was indicated. Either a fall from a considerable height, or a blow delivered with power. Two choices presented themselves: Corinne had fallen elsewhere and, in confusion, staggered into the garden. Or she had been struck down, either in the garden or elsewhere, and then tossed into the garden to die. Anna favored the latter. If not for the groans, the corpse might never have been found. The smell of rotting flesh might even go unnoticed. Stray cats, gulls, unlucky pigeons and careless squirrels frequently added their postmortem perfume to the atmosphere. Who would fight through brush and poison ivy to view that? Here, on a small island visited by thousands of people, were some of the most isolated places Anna had ever found.

Though probably too late to save any little gray cells, Anna intubated Corinne and put her on full-flow oxygen for the head injury. For the dehydration, she started her on an IV drip of normal saline. She had no luck propping the six-cell anywhere that worked, and reverted to her tiny flash when both hands were required. Given Corinne's advanced state of dehydration, finding a vein took a while. Anna added a number of punctures to the crosshatching of scratches on the actress's left arm. By the time the needle was taped in place, Anna's chin and the end of the flashlight were covered in drool. *The glamour never stops,* she thought, and put the used needle in the sharps box. Because a blow as forceful as the one Corinne had sustained could have cracked or broken vertebrae, Anna stabilized her neck.

Joshua arrived with lights and noise and a promise of more help on the way. He'd found gardening tools and he'd brought a backboard. Between the two of them they cut enough space in the brush so they could get the board near Corinne. Before they finished packaging her—less than seventeen minutes by Anna's watch—the sound of rotor blades was heard and Joshua left them to guide the helicopter down and lead the paramedics to Corinne's secret garden.

Anna finished strapping Corinne to the backboard and immobilizing her head and neck between orange foam cubes designed for the purpose. A perfectionist when it came to emergency care, she hefted the big flashlight and methodically checked Corinne's packaging: oxygen, backboard straps snug but not too tight, neck stable, IV in place. In the powerful beam of the Park Policeman's flashlight the scratches on Corinne's arm, though smudged with dirt, ceased being a meaningless crisscross of accidental injuries. Gently, Anna rolled her patient's arm till the wrist and inner elbow were fully exposed. Corinne's assailant had carved her up. Not deep enough to bleed much or scar, but clear and intentional marks made by a knife tip, a pin or needle, something small and sharp. The scratches were almost bloodless, as fit with the depleted fluid level of the woman's body. Remembering that under certain conditions fingerprints could be lifted from human skin, Anna resisted the urge to clean away the dirt. Painstakingly, she pieced together the pattern of the scratches. Words. A message had been scraped into the flesh.

STOPMUDP4J

"Well, that sure as hell clears things up," Anna muttered.

19

Joshua and three uniformed paramedics appeared with a clatter. The backboard, with its featherweight occupant, was whisked away. Start to finish, white spider to gone, had been less than an hour.

Walking back to the registry building beside Joshua, in the now unnatural silence of early morning, Anna was left with only a whirling impression of greenery, white skin and the efficiency of New York's emergency medical response personnel.

Joshua gallantly shared his sandwiches with her, bologna and Kraft American cheese on white bread with lots of mayonnaise. Because it echoed box lunches from childhood, Anna found the meal comforting. She devoured even the bologna. Over the years her vegetarian ethic had softened—or weakened, depending on how one chose to view it—like many other staunchly held rules she'd embraced in her younger years. If she was hungry and somebody offered her meat, she ate it. Otherwise she preferred not to eat her little friends.

After the welcome repast, this being a civilized park, Anna showered. As hot water poured over tired muscles, she tried to remember whether heat and soap spread or removed the oil from poison ivy.

Food and cleanliness should have relaxed her into sleep, but both she and Joshua needed to talk, to debrief, to process what had gone by. Rejoining him in his office, she shared his coffee and they rehashed the night.

There was no sense checking the crime scene until sunrise. They would only muddy the evidence—if the rescue efforts hadn't already obliterated any signs of what had happened. Frustrated with the present, they wandered back to the past, to the day Corinne failed to show up for work. By the nightgown she wore, they assumed the incident had occurred after sundown. She must have been lying in that garden for about forty-eight hours.

How she had come to be on Ellis after sunset, barefoot, in her nightclothes was a question Joshua speculated on far more than Anna. She was pretty sure she knew, and hoped, with daylight, to prove her theory before sharing it. Much time was spent speculating upon who might have assaulted the young actress. Anna told the snippets she had overheard Corinne's co-workers drop regarding someone they called "Macho Bozo." Anna surmised he was a boyfriend-gone-bad of the little blonde. Joshua was convinced he was the culprit until he remembered a story no one had yet related to Anna.

The night policemen—the one on Liberty and the one on Ellis—being boatless, couldn't back each other up, but they could and did talk on the phone nearly every night, exchanging news or just passing the time. The previous night Andrew had told Joshua of his own adventure. Around ten p.m.—half an hour, if Anna remembered correctly, before Mandy stumbled home looking like something the cat dragged in—a chunk of flotsam in the person of one Michael Underwood had washed ashore in a small motorboat. Andrew found him in the plaza in a torn undershirt, shrieking for his beloved. Since there were no auditions for *A Streetcar Named Desire* being held on Liberty Island, Andrew promptly arrested him and charged him with drunk and disorderly, entering a park after hours and assault on a federal officer. An assault that left Mr. Underwood the worse for wear and Andrew—according to Andrew—without a mark on him.

Undermining Anna's theory that Macho Bozo had attacked the actress was the fact that Mr. Underwood had been alternately screaming threats at or weeping piteously for "Corinne." His storming the island had been the result of a good deal of Jack Daniel's and the mistaken belief that Corinne was hiding or being held against her will on Liberty—Mr. Underwood was unclear on this point.

If Anna and Joshua's math was correct, when Michael Underwood landed on Liberty crying for his lady love, the lady herself had already been in the garden for twenty-four hours.

Loath to let go of such an obvious suspect, Anna suggested he might merely have been establishing an elaborate alibi.

"Pretty fancy for a guy nicknamed Macho Bozo," Joshua pointed out. "Not to mention one that landed him in jail with what's going to amount to a shitload of fines to pay and, since he swung at Andrew, maybe some time."

Anna had to give up at that. Taking her leave, she crept into Patsy's office, saluted the woman as a Girl Scout when she found a blanket and pillow in the coat closet, and snuggled down on the carpet for a catnap.

The sun was just stretching over the roof of Manhattan when Anna returned to the abandoned garden on Island III. Joshua was already there, waist-deep in ravaged greenery, a pad and pen in hand, 35mm camera slung around his neck.

"Anything left?" Anna asked. She sat on the top of the steps leading into the enclosure.

"Not much," he admitted. "Tracks all over, yours, mine and ours. The leaf litter makes it impossible to sort it out. The stuff is half a foot deep." Anna remembered it curling up in front of her knees like fecund sea-foam as she'd crawled through it. "There's a dab of what will probably turn out to be Corinne's blood where her head was. I found this seven feet, six inches from the body. The woman," he corrected himself. She hadn't officially become a body yet. "Nearly at the wall." He pointed to the ward that formed the west side of the garden. Not much brick showed, as it had been transformed into a living monument to the tenacious power of vines. He held up a neatly bagged and tagged pewter candlestick with a handle. Of old-fashioned design, it reminded Anna of the one Wee Willie Winkie carried on his nightly rounds. A candle stub, not more than an inch or so high, was firmly waxed in place.

"It's not like flashlights haven't been invented. You couldn't see diddly with this. What in the heck was she doing out here with a candle?"

Corinne was an actress. It all fit together quite satisfactorily. Except for the attack.

"One other thing is a little odd. Maybe. Come down and take a look," Joshua invited. Anna scooched down the steps to look at the place he was indicating. To the left, where the undergrowth was thickest, in the corner between steps and wall, Joshua parted the leafy branches of a young tree. Underneath were imprints in the litter where heavy round objects had been.

"Ah," Anna said. "That explains it. She was struck down by a rogue elephant."

"They *are* the right size for elephant tracks, aren't they? Do you remember any of us setting anything down here?"

Anna didn't. Nothing they'd carried was that shape or that hard-edged. "Whatever it was, it was here recently," she observed. "In this climate and litter it wouldn't take too long for the impression to fade. Maybe a day, a couple days at most."

"What do you make of it?"

"Nothing," she admitted. "You?"

He shook his head. "I'm taking its picture

and measuring it and recording. That's as good as it gets for now." He did all he said he'd do. Watching, Anna recalled seeing a cache of something under the stairs before they'd collapsed, recalled Trey insisting there was no cache there and taking the time to visit the wreck of the stairs on Island III to prove to her it wasn't there. He was right, but there had been marks, round, like elephant tracks. A number of pointed thoughts jabbed at her: Why was Trey Claypool so anxious she see there wasn't anything under the stairs? Had he put something there, heard her story of seeing it, moved it, then dragged her back to Island III to convince her she was nuts? Suspicion sharpened her memory. Just before the stairs fell she had heard a loud, solid *crack*. At the time, she'd been thinking of other things—like how not to get skewered in the dark—and had written the sound off to wood breaking. Why, of a sudden, would an oak beam give way? That *crack* could easily have been the sound of a sturdy boot smashing into the timber supporting the top of the stairs. If that was true, someone meant her harm. If someone meant her harm, maybe the incident in the subway was not an accident either.

"Are we about done here?" she asked, too restless to sit by and do nothing. Joshua finished up in short order, and she said, "Let's go. I think I have something to show you."

"What?" he asked, falling in beside her to walk through the grassy field between Islands III and II.

"Maybe nothing."

Joshua asked another couple of questions, but Anna was intent on retaining her mystery. Possibly because she was so sure she was right, it was going to be hard to cover her disappointment if she wasn't.

At the easternmost building on Island II, she led the way up the stairs she'd located the night before when darkness forbade her the quick and dirty climb she was accustomed to when seeking the solace of her balcony.

Full-bore, the rising sun poured through every window and crevice. Even deep within the fourth-floor hallway it was easy to see. "Take it slow," Anna said. "I've only been here in the dark since I noticed them."

"Them? Aliens? Grizzlies? What are we looking for?" Impatience didn't hone his words. Joshua exhibited a rare and wonderful patience, the ability to let a story unfold to a timetable other than his own. Rare in a man, even rarer in a policeman. Anna wondered if it had anything to do with being Hmong or, perhaps, Minnesotan. Whatever caused it, she admired it and took time to stop and smile at him.

"Footprints," she said. "Little bare footprints about a woman's size six."

"Or a boy's size five," he added, and it gave her a jolt. She hadn't considered a child. A little boy, brought here by one of the employees when day care failed them, and let loose to play where he oughtn't to play, was more likely than the scenario she'd dreamed up.

"Could be," she had to admit. But it wasn't. She was sure. Mostly sure.

The only new, obvious tracks were her own, easily identifiable. Minnetonka driving moccasins, an addiction she'd picked up when she worked on Isle Royale, were soled in hard rubber pegs that made tracking a cinch. She made a mental note to keep that in mind next time she wanted to keep her travels to herself.

Anna could not match Joshua's patience. "The hell with this," she said, after peering through murky light at the uneven floor for less than a minute. "Let's just search every room. It'll be quicker. You take the right. I'll take the left." It would be on the left, overlooking the meadow between II and III—that's where Anna would have put it.

"Search for what?" Joshua asked politely.

"You'll know it when you see it." Anna realized she was being exasperatingly like Hercule Poirot in her refusal to divulge information and she wasn't quite sure why. New York City, Columbia-Presbyterian, the islands, Molly, Frederick, Dr. Madison—something in the chemistry of all or any of these things had worked in such a way that she did not completely trust her own truths, her own observations. She was reminded of college when she and her friend Ted were doing a lot of drugs and reality was a nebulous commodity. At parties they would sidle up to each other periodically and inquire, "Confidentially, am I blowing it?"

She entered the door to her left: an old operating theater with low central light and white tile on walls and floor. When this room was in use surgery had been a bloody business. Architects designed the space with an eye to cleanup. To one side were two small, windowless utility rooms fitted with unusual sinks. Nothing of interest. The next door down the hall led to a suite of rooms, possibly a doctor's living quarters. Anna opened every cupboard. Nothing. Three more rooms. Nothing. Frenzy was taking over. She forced herself to stop and breathe. Searches could not be rushed. And if she was right, the plan would have been to fool at least the casual observer. Joshua came to the door of the room where she stood. His black spiky hair was frosted with plaster dust. Cobwebs traced fine lines from epaulette to badge. He was looking enormously pleased with himself.

"You found it," she declared.

"Found it."

She followed him back one door to the right side of the hall facing the Registry Hall—there was no accounting for taste. Fallen plaster and mildew had grown up around the partly opened door, cementing it in place.

Clever. Casual—or fat—observers would be discouraged.

"After you," Joshua said.

Anna slipped through easily but the policeman, thick of shoulder and chest, gathered a few more cobwebs as he squeezed in a second time.

308

Like the others, the room appeared empty and decaying.

"It took me a minute," Joshua said generously, then ruined it by adding: "And I'm a trained observer."

A shift in perspective and Anna saw it. The floor in the corner away from the windows was not a floor. A tarp, painted in the theatrical tradition of trompe l'oeil, had been spattered and speckled to match the mildew, moss and rubble of the real floor. "It's well done," she said.

"Actors and guerrillas," Josh said. "Masters of disguise."

Anna crossed the room and peeled back the canvas.

"A squatter," Joshua said unnecessarily.

"It had to be," Anna said. Underneath the canvas were the components of a comfortable camp: stove, sleeping pallet and bag, gas lantern, candles. Anna remembered the wax she'd found under the stairs on Island III, but those had been shavings, not drips. Corinne also had had a metal chest for food storage, even a battery-powered CD player. One of the actors had remarked that Billy's paranormal phenomena were anachronistic. The Park Policeman had sworn he'd heard steel drums late at night. The Chieftains' jewel case was in Corinne's collection.

"Corinne was living here," Anna said, and told him of the gossip, how the actress came earlier and left later than the rest of the troupe. Corinne wasn't coming and going at all, she was staying and lying.

"Hiding out from the bad-ass boyfriend?" Joshua suggested.

"That or the high rents in Manhattan." Anna put the tarp back as she'd found it. This was the Park Police's problem now.

"That explains why she was on the island," Joshua said, "but why was she in the infectious disease wards in her nightie with a candle?"

"Waiting to scare the pants off Billy Bonham is my guess," Anna replied. "Not much else to do nights for a creative type. Torturing Billy probably passed the time."

"Oh gosh." Joshua came to a sudden realization. "The groaning he heard. Oh, Jesus. That was real, her in that garden. If she dies, Bonham as good as killed her."

"He gets second billing," Anna said. "Whoever bashed her over the head killed her." Then an ugly thought surfaced. It turned into pictures and they flickered behind her eyes like a silent film. Billy, making his rounds. Scared, strung tight from nights of seeing ghosts, hearing things. Corinne, waiting, trying not to laugh, planning her next performance. Billy passes in a dark hall. She steps out with the candle, wails in proper banshee fashion, and the boy, too scared to think, strikes her down with his baton. Bending over her, he realizes what he's done, can't face the music, tosses the girl in the garden and switches to day shifts.

"Not good," she echoed Joshua. "Not good at all."

20

Anna slept most of the day. Because going to bed after sunrise was too much like being sick, she sacked out on the couch in Patsy's living room.

At length, voices intruded pleasantly into her dreams and she let herself wake into the comfortable security that can come from knowing one is not alone.

"Bad juju," Patsy was saying. "Corinne, Hatch. I feel like some new age woo-woo sneaking into a kiva to meet the spirits saying this, but I swear I sensed something the night Hatch died. You must have too. In the wee hours when I got up, you were rattling around."

"Everybody says that shit after the fact," came a voice not nearly so welcome: Mandy. She shut Patsy down: "I didn't hear you 'sensing' anything at the time."

"Who knows," Patsy said, always the peacemaker. "Something's out of whack, though. Maybe it's just tourist season. Or maybe the monument slipped into a karmic warp. Sins of the past and all that."

"Sins is right," Mandy said. Anna chose to feign sleep a tad longer. Before she faced Patsy's roommate she needed to let her blood pressure creep back up to a consciousness-sustaining level. " 'Open the golden door.' Fuck. A swarm. Come here and get on welfare."

That did it. Anna's diastolic shot up.

"Hey, look who's awake," Patsy said cheerfully. "Even the dead will rise someday."

Honeyed afternoon light flooded through the windows. Neither Patsy nor Mandy was in uniform. "What time is it?" Anna asked, feeling like Rip Van Winkle.

"Five-fifteen. We've been home half an hour. You were out like a light," Patsy told her.

Elbows on knees, head between slumped shoulders, Anna let her body grasp this new semivertical reality.

"We heard about your adventures," Patsy said.

Anna grunted. Of course they had. News travels faster than the speed of light in bureaucracies. If information were disseminated at a tenth the speed of gossip, government agencies would be models of efficiency. "Any word on Corinne? She dead yet?"

"Miss Sensitivity," Mandy sniped.

The phrase "horse's patootie" slid into Anna's mind from some bygone conversation.

"Not dead," Patsy said. "And maybe not going to be. Josh called the Chief Ranger and he and the Superintendent got to the hospital about ten minutes after Corinne."

"Photo op," Mandy said.

Anna didn't argue. In general, the NPS was a more or less caring organization, but most of the brass did dearly love to see their names in the paper. Unless they were up to something the public would frown on—like killing burros or closing campgrounds.

Patsy laughed. "No press. A girl gets mugged.

This is big news in New York? Anyway, they talked to the doctors and Corinne's in bad shape, but she's alive. You saved the day, girl. Another few hours and she'd've died of thirst. And they say kids got no heroes anymore."

"If you ladies will excuse me," Mandy said politely, and rose from her chair, "I'm going to go puke."

When Mandy had shut herself behind her bedroom door, Patsy asked, "What did you do to get so far on her bad side?"

"Beats me. Looked at her funny, I guess."

"The kids had a puppy like you once. That puppy'd sit and look at our old dog in this one certain way and all of a sudden Tilly would go nuts and chase him all around the house clacking her teeth like an old lady with loose dentures. 'Pest telepathy,' the kids called it."

"Great. I get one sixth sense and it aggravates people." Anna's head was clearing. She began cracking finger joints to bring her body up to speed.

"Ugh," Patsy said. "One day you'll fall down in a heap of bones and it will serve you right. Don't feel too bad about Mandy. She's going through something. She used to be okay—not the kind that fits in, but the kind that wants to. Tries too hard. A couple months ago she changed. She got kind of aggressive. A worm turned or something. Like she decided to hate everybody who didn't like her instead of sucking up like she used to. My guess is some boy dumped her."

"Good for him," Anna said uncharitably. "Did they say what the extent of Corinne's injuries were?"

"Let me see..." Patsy laid her head back and closed her eyes. Anna appreciated it. Not everyone made the effort to remember things accurately. "Severe concussion. Hairline fracture of C-three—" She opened one eye and looked questioningly at Anna.

"Third cervical vertebra," Anna said.

"That's what I thought. From being hit on the head?"

"Unless she fell. But probably from a blow. If she'd fallen from high enough to do that much damage, chances are her neck would have been broken—more than just a hairline fracture."

"Okay." Patsy closed her eye again. "Dehydration. Insect bites. Cuts and contusions on hands and arms."

"Brain damage?" Anna asked, remembering the raccoon eyes.

"Probably."

"Did she regain consciousness at all?"

"She sort of mumbled to the Superintendent, but I gather it wasn't consciousness per se. If her condition has changed since, I haven't heard. Bless the Super's politically savvy little heart, she was all warm and smiley. Not a peep about Corinne squatting on Island Two. I tell you, that woman is on the fast track.

"And since you're bound to ask: No. I don't know if Corinne's mumbles were about who bashed her over the head."

"I'll find out."

"Of course you will. God forbid you should just kick back, mind your own business, take in a Broadway show."

"God forbid."

The Superintendent could not be reached. The Chief Ranger was being cagey. If he was in the loop at all, Trey Claypool might be more forthcoming. Anna chose to beard him in his den. She crossed the twelve feet of grass between Patsy's house and his, and banged on his front door.

Without inviting her in, he told her what he knew. No one had any idea who the attacker was. Corinne was in a coma.

Disappointed but not surprised, Anna thanked him and went "home." If Corinne did recover consciousness and still had the use of her brain, she might not be able to tell them what had happened anyway. The kind of amnesia old novels relied on so heavily, where people forgot their lives for years on end, was practically nonexistent, but blunt trauma to the head frequently caused temporary and/or partial amnesia. Corinne may not have even seen her assailant. The head wound was from behind. Either she never saw who did it or had turned and was fleeing when she was struck.

Showering, making herself presentable for Molly, the city and, she had to admit, David Madison, if he happened to be on duty, Anna contemplated the location of the actress's wound and was cheered. The scenario she'd envisioned where a freaked-out Billy Bonham bashed at a ghost and hit a girl didn't fit with a blow to the back of the skull. The side maybe, the temple or the face.

Anna had a sense that Corinne was smart, a good actress and mischievous almost to the point of mean. In keeping with the demands of the role she'd created, she would have placed herself somewhere she could vanish in true ghostly fashion. Never let the audience backstage. She would have stayed far enough from Bonham that he couldn't grab her or get a clear look at her in the light of his six-cell flashlight. Anna moved Bonham down on her list of suspects. Since the list was short to nonexistent, the pretty Park Policeman didn't gain much.

I n no mood to be dashing desperately through the bowels of Manhattan, a slave to the NPS staff boat schedule, Anna stowed a change of clothes in her backpack. A night away would be therapeutic. She had a touch of island fever, brought on mostly by Patsy's roommate. A piece of real estate a man with a good arm could throw a rock across wasn't big enough for the both of them. At Molly's, Anna would have a degree of privacy, more hot water, and unhampered use of the phone. The emerald ring and the statement of his honorable intentions made it okay for her to bunk with the FBI guy. And Frederick wouldn't mock her bloodhound tendencies. He suffered from

316

the same disease, the kind of illness that makes people take apart perfectly good clocks just to see what makes them tick.

Squashing a change of underwear between a paperback book and a banana, she thought of her two-year relationship with Frederick Stanton. Her ego suffered a pang because with her, love hadn't bloomed, a ring and death-do-us-part hadn't been offered. For an instant she was tempted to dwell in that pain, get all the drama out of being the woman scorned, but she couldn't make a go of it. She wasn't loved because she didn't want to be loved. She wasn't asked because she didn't want to be asked. Around her, buried neatly under the emotional sod, was the human equivalent of an electric fence. If a man got too close, he got a jolt in the neck. Once or twice was sufficient to train most.

Not healthy, Anna thought as she zipped the bag closed and slung it over her shoulder, *but convenient.*

Summer had taken off the kid gloves. As Anna waited for the subway train, her work with blow-dryer and mascara wand was undone. Temperature and humidity were hanging in the low nineties. When the Number 1 train came, the cars were air-conditioned and she offered up a brief prayer of gratitude to the Transit Authority. In packed commuter traffic, sweating humanity pressing on every side, heat would have been intolerable.

Hemmed in by an oversized handbag, an ample butt, three elbows and a fleshy shoulder,

Anna thought of the stifling crawl through the wormhole deep in the entrails of Lechuguilla Cave in New Mexico. She'd been scared, claustrophobic, yes, but the feeling was different. To entertain herself, she ferreted out why. By Christopher Street, it came to her. Rocks would never panic and stampede. Crushes of people were like herds of cows; a few flashes of lightning, a roll of thunder, and a woman could get trampled.

After Ninety-sixth Street, the crowd began to thin. At 125th, she got to sit down. People getting on and off above Eighty-sixth were a tonier crowd than when she'd lived in New York in the 1980s. Urban renewal had reclaimed many of the neighborhoods. Idly, she wondered where the poor people had been shunted to this time. Out of sight, out of mind.

Afternoon had dimmed to evening by the time she detrained at 168th Street, but the temperature, if anything, had increased. New York had to be one of the world's largest passive solar heaters. Asphalt, brick, granite, concrete, every inch of every surface giving back the heat of the day during the hours of darkness.

Names on the shops and restaurants that had sprung up around the twelve-block-square area of the Columbia-Presbyterian medical complex told her the neighborhood demographics were spicy: Nicaraguan, Colombian, Puerto Rican. She promised herself an adventure in dining after the hospital visit. For the nonce, the banana would be sacrificed to stay her hunger pangs.

318

Entering the complex, Anna saw a prominent sign:

NO: BALLPLAYING
SITTING
STANDING
EATING
PLAYING

Since it didn't say **NO LITTERING**, she was tempted to drop the banana peel, but it went against her personal code of ethics and she had to leave the joke unmade.

Molly looked better. "Good" and "bad" had become relative terms and Anna was stuck with the spineless "better" or "worse." The respirator was still in place, though Frederick told her Molly had been off it for a couple hours that afternoon. Dr. Madison had put her back on. Weak as she was, he didn't want to tire her.

Because of the tube in her throat, she'd been sedated, and though she knew Anna was there—responding with a wink or a nod—Anna could see she was in no mood for a prolonged exchange.

Frederick was subdued. The emerald ring was not in evidence on Molly's left hand. Content to let the day's evils be sufficient unto themselves, Anna settled on the cool linoleum, from where she could see Molly's face, watch the mechanical rise and fall of her chest. "Don't let me stop you," she said to Frederick.

When she arrived he'd been reading aloud. He turned the book over from where it lay across his knees, put on his half-glasses and, with a long forefinger, found where he'd left off.

Frederick had a nice voice and it was a lifetime since Anna had read *Tom Sawyer*. It was an inspired choice: beautiful, reassuring. Details were long forgotten, but she and Molly knew everything came out all right in the end.

Frederick would remain till the nurses threw him out. After declining his kind, if unappetizing, offer to join him in a tray of hospital cuisine, at seven-thirty Anna bade Molly goodbye with promises to water plants and kiss the kitten.

En route to the subway she stopped at a Jamaican restaurant with the unlikely name of Wet Willy's and had a meal of rice and black beans washed down with two Red Stripe lagers. Peasant food: always the most fortifying, starch and carbohydrates to draw on for endurance.

Bolstered by food and free of tiny island eyes, she walked to offset the soporific effect of the Red Stripes. Ritziness had extended north: shops were upscale, old apartment houses gone condo. Out of curiosity she stopped at a realtor's window and checked the going rates: $1.2 million, $1.7 million, $1.3 million.

Suitably impressed, she wandered on, enjoying the festive feel of neighborhoods stirring into their night personas. Before she reached her favorite part, the Gothic towers of Columbia University with its tended gardens, she pooped out and ducked into the subway. Napping on a sofa wasn't enough anymore.

Rani was welcoming. Molly's apartment wrapped around her like family and Anna was hit by a wave of homesickness so acute she had to sit down. She ached for the mountains, solitude, the smell of pine. She felt both feverish and chilled by the walls of steel and flesh that surrounded her. Even Rani appeared diseased, not a real cat but a man-made puffball with a squashed face and an excruciatingly tiny nose.

Sitting immobile, she made herself breathe deeply. Then she made herself apologize to the cat. That done, she felt better but knew her days in New York were numbered. During the homesick attack a thought, fleeting, all too human, had scared her. She'd thought: *I wish Molly would get well or die.* It didn't reflect how she felt about her sister, she knew that. It reflected the stress of holding seven million people at arm's length. Still, she was ashamed.

"Do something," she ordered herself. Dropping her pack on the sofa, she picked up the telephone. St. Vincent's Hospital, where Corinne had been taken, was steadfast in patient confidentiality. No matter how Anna warped and wove the truth, she could get no information. Not sure what to do with herself next, she sat on the edge of the sofa and tried to lure Rani into her clutches by dangling the stringy part of a cat toy. The kitten was having nothing to do with her. Two circuits of the apartment provided no relief from restlessness. Then she remembered one Caroline remained to be called. Caroline Colter at Craters of the Moon in Idaho.

Caroline was on four till midnight, her roommate said, and obligingly gave out the phone number of the ranger station.

With less than perfect honesty, Anna introduced herself as a fellow friend of the late James Hatchett. Caroline sounded easy and open. They spent several moments eulogizing the dead. The conversation moved into the funny stories and how-did-you-know-him realm. Having no wish to prevaricate more than absolutely necessary, Anna changed the subject.

She told Caroline she suspected Hatch had not suicided but been murdered. As hoped, Caroline was intrigued. Law enforcement rangers, customarily restricted to a diet of dogs off leash and camping out of bounds, were hungry for the big dramas city cops had wisely learned to detest.

"I've got no way to prove it," Anna said. "A few pieces of the puzzle are missing. Like motive, means, opportunity and anything resembling a suspect to pin them on." Caroline laughed obligingly and Anna was glad to be talking to a woman. Women were comfortable in the world of speculation, hard facts not so necessary for their thinking patterns. Perhaps they didn't feel that to entertain an idea was to publicly commit to it with the attendant danger of being proved wrong and, so, a fool.

Wanting to help, Caroline went over her relationship with Hatch. They'd met at the Presidio in San Francisco. She was a seasonal then. A friendship had sprung up between them and they'd kept in contact over the years.

"The last time we talked was last winter. We'd nailed a couple jokers poaching deer up here—get this: Andrew Jackson Thomas and Richard Head. Dick Head. Can you believe it? These guys are clichés of themselves. There was some scuttlebutt that the Park Police were going to be sent out here and Hatch thought he might be one of them."

"Park Police?" That struck Anna as odd. They usually went only to high-profile parks, but she couldn't see how she could say that without belittling Craters of the Moon.

"Turned out Dick Head and his pal were bigwigs with the local militia. There were threats against the rangers. The usual reasons were spouted: Aryan purity, government conspiracy. I think these boys' ancestors were so concerned with keeping bloodlines pure they never married out of the family."

Anna laughed.

"Nothing came of it," Caroline concluded. "So Hatch and I kind of lost touch again."

Anna tried the names Agnes Abigail and Pearl Tucker, but they didn't ring any bells with Caroline. She assured Anna she'd call if she remembered anything more, and Anna hung up feeling more restless than before. She wished Frederick would come home. Arguing with him would be a distraction. Television crossed her mind. Molly owned one—she was hooked on Leno and Letterman—but Anna didn't see it and wasn't motivated to search bedroom and study cabinets to see where it had been tastefully secreted away.

Upending her daypack, she spilled the contents on the coffee table. Rani, quicker than her round physique might suggest, hopped up, batted a Chap Stick onto the carpet and played it like a hockey puck till she was out of sight. The game continued, marked by clicking sounds, as she worried the plastic tube over the hardwood in the hall. Anna let it go. Scraps of paper were sprinkled through fruit, underpants, her 35mm tourist camera with automatic everything and Agnes Tucker's wretched hat. Never would she have allowed a pack to become such a disorganized mess in the backcountry.

Civilization is eroding my morals, she thought as she picked out the paper fragments and smoothed them on the table. The gum wrappers she stuffed in her pocket for later disposal. The Hershey bar wrapper had notes on it, as did the pieces of lined paper she'd cadged from somewhere.

She'd made a note to call the Carolines. That was done and she crossed it off. "Spud" and the potato hat were still a mystery. "Biner" was written on another piece of paper. Anna drew a blank. What in the hell was "biner"? *Precocious senility,* she thought sourly. Then the memory surfaced. 'Biner: carabiner, the locking metal links climbers use as a staple of their equipment. A carabiner had been found hooked through the belt loop on Hatch's trousers. Anna had meant to talk with Charlie about it and had forgotten. In the execution of his caretaking duties, Charlie served not only as Keeper of the Flame, but as his lady's immune system. Rigged and roped, he climbed every bit of her impressive infrastructure, dusting, vacuuming, looking for damage or wear.

Anna called Patsy and asked for Charlie's home number. Through the eternal good cheer, Anna could tell she gave it grudgingly. Her "pest telepathy" was evidently spreading to other arenas.

"Charlie's real sensitive. God-fearing," Patsy said, and Anna heard the warning behind the words: *Don't badger the man.*

In an attempt to make amends, Anna's thanks were too effusive, and she rang off feeling socially inept. But she had the number. It was past ten. Late for calling. She did it anyway and got a sleepy voice. "Did I wake you?" she asked, as does everybody who knows perfectly well they called at a rotten time.

"No, not at all, I only just got to sleep," Charlie answered with the expected lie.

Anna asked him if he used carabiners in his work.

He did.

Could he have lost one?

He could.

325

That was that. She'd wasted his time and ruined his sleep for naught. Surely behaving would take less energy than egregiousness. Too late. She tried to ring off but now that Charlie was awake, he wanted to talk. Relieved to be able to pay her social debt so quickly, Anna made encouraging noises while he rambled on about the lack of interest new maintenance people showed in learning the arduous and difficult service his lady required. Not being physically able to get up into the lady's innards and give her a good dusting so she'd be at her best for the party was bothering Charlie. He groused because the cleaning men weren't like they used to be. He'd found dirt and crud on the stairs mornings after they'd supposedly been swept. He worried aloud that when he died she'd not be properly cared for. Twenty minutes and he wound down, having talked himself and Anna almost back to sleep. She wished him goodnight. Anna had become fond of the little guy. Strength of purpose, purity of faith and greatness of heart were qualities one did not come across every day.

Crumpling up the note that listed the effects found on Hatch's person—three dead ends—gave her a modicum of satisfaction. Creating order out of chaos just to prove she could, she began replacing things in her pack. One scrap of paper had escaped her notice. Juice from her orange had slimed it to the back of *Saint's Rest,* a paperback she'd picked up at the airport. She peeled it off. No mystery, no answers: the stub for the photos she'd taken of Hatch's stuff. The lazy-opportunist part of her would have left them unclaimed, letting Kodak eat the cost of development, but there were pictures of Patsy and Charlie on the roll and more in a never-ending collection of cute pictures of her cat, Piedmont, doing absolutely nothing in various boxes and baskets.

Anna took Molly's bed in the master bedroom, where Frederick had been sleeping. Sisters had certain rights and privileges.

If Frederick minded, she didn't find out. He returned after she was asleep and departed before she woke. Only a fresh pot of coffee and a note, "Already fed the cat," evidenced he had been there at all. Hospital visiting hours didn't seem to apply to Frederick Stanton. Anna had been too distracted to notice before, but wearing his bathrobe, drinking his coffee and petting his cat, she remembered the man's devious ways. Never illegal or unethical except by the strictest application. But he did tend to get what he wanted. It was one of his charms. She was curious as to what he'd told the nurses—no, not *told*, lies were too plebeian for Stanton—what he had allowed the hospital staff to believe about him that gave him perks not granted other, lesser citizens.

Whatever the ruse, Anna was grateful for the time he could spend with Molly, grateful for the love he showed. Mostly she was grateful he was gone. Till she woke up in Molly's apartment, she hadn't known how desperately she needed to be by herself. She breathed like a woman suddenly free of corsets. Alone but for the benign presence of a cat, she felt herself expanding, each crushed, cringing unit of body and soul filling with solitude, resuming its natural contour.

Molly was back off the respirator. Throat sore from the tube, weak from battling pneumonia and hung over from sedatives, she was a feeble shadow of herself. Even her unruly red and white curls were defeated and lay close to her skull. She mustered a smile for Anna, croaked, "Can't talk," and closed her eyes. Frederick had cleaned up. Not because he felt like it, Anna guessed, nor to impress anyone, but simply because it might cheer Molly to see him that way. Anna was going to like him a whole lot better as a friend than she ever did as a lover.

Unless he annoyed or harmed her sister in any small way.

To pass the time, she told the story of Dr. Madison and the Persian kittens research on his computer. Frederick raised an eyebrow, a trick Anna had tried to master since high school without success. One perfectly arched brow and Sister Mary Vionney could subdue the multitudes.

"Did you look at these kittens?" Frederick asked.

Anna didn't know if he was trying to find out how deeply she'd invaded the doctor's privacy, or genuinely wanted a description of Rani's peers. She told him she hadn't. He watched her for a moment as if he had more to add.

"What?" she demanded.

"Nothing."

Not in a mood to pursue the topic of Dr. Madison, Anna described the disfigurement Corinne's attacker had carved on her forearm.

"S T O P M U D P four J," Frederick repeated. The bizarre clue drew him out for the first time since she'd arrived. Molly's eyes were open. Through a fog of drugs and pain her intelligence responded to a puzzle.

With Anna coaching, Frederick wrote it out on a paper towel and draped it over the footrail of the bed. The three of them stared at it.

"A message from the would-be-still-could-be killer," Frederick mused.

"That's the thinking at the moment," Anna agreed.

"Stop mud. That's enlightening. Mud slides, mudslinging, mud pies, your name is mud," he murmured.

"Mudluscious," Molly whispered, and Anna laughed.

"Maybe it's an acronym," Anna suggested. "Mothers Under Duress. Manhattanites Unsettled and Depressed."

"An acronym would make sense."

Anna looked at him.

"You want me to do something," he accused. "Something hard and boring and illegal."

"The FBI keeps a file of killers and other questionable types."

Frederick sighed. "I'll see if I can run it through somebody's computer," he promised. "See if the MO matches anything."

A side glance at Molly followed. It was not lost on Anna that he was being good to her to please her sister. Whatever worked.

"Then there's P four J," she said.

"Page four?"

"Could be. Of what?"

"J. *'J' is for Judgment?* Jane Austen?"

They gave it up. Too little to go on. After a minute's dead air, Frederick opened *Tom Sawyer* to Chapter 7 and began reading. Anna left them like that, Molly resting, Frederick folded over Mark Twain. They looked right, like an old married couple at ease with each other's frailty.

Anna finished up her errands: a little food, a little wine and the photos she'd remembered when she found the receipt the previous night. The pictures of Hatch's effects were as worthless as she'd thought they'd be, but there were a couple nice shots of Charlie. She'd give them to him by way of thanks for the tour of the statue and apology for waking him with pointless questions.

Shortly after noon, she got off the Number 1 train and sat in Battery Park to lunch on a pretzel with mustard and watch the tourists till it was time to catch the twelve forty-five staff boat back to Ellis and Liberty. The Circle Line to the islands took on passengers at the Battery. Lines were already long as visitors queued up for tickets.

Heat brought out the beast in people, abrading away the thin veneer of civilization till they snapped and snarled like ill-mannered dogs. Sticky children whined at sunburned parents and tired husbands nipped at overwrought wives. All in all an entertaining show. Deep in the shade, surrounded by aggressive pigeons hoping for her crumbs, Anna was content to observe the scrabble for food, sex and amusement that was the fate of earth's creatures.

The train disgorged passengers beneath the park and funneled them out through the doors of a stone station house with the look of a charming little old-world cottage. To see hundreds of people exiting a building that could scarcely hold a dozen was a delicious illusion. The doors, the masonry, the rumble of the world beneath, the bovine movements of the tourists, put Anna in mind of H. G. Wells's *The Time Machine*, with the carnivorous Morlocks running the subterranean machinery and the witless Eloi fattened up as cattle.

A familiar figure emerged from the pageant. Mandy. She carried a small suitcase and Anna bet she had spent the night in Manhattan with her mysterious beau.

"Aha," she breathed; not so mysterious anymore. Tonight she would have a juicy tidbit of gossip to share with Patsy over cocktails. Mandy's suitor was with her and as disreputable-looking as Anna could have hoped. A good deal older than Mandy, probably near forty, he dressed like a Fidel Castro clone right down to the beard. On a day that would reach the mid-nineties, the combat boots and long-sleeved camo shirt were ludicrous.

Deep in conversation, they passed without noticing Anna tucked back in the shade on her bench. She gave the last of her pretzel to the birds and fell into step half a block behind them. She had no interest in tailing them. It was time to catch the boat.

A block from the MIO pier, they stopped. The man handed Mandy a paper sack, then faded into the shadow of the trees on the periphery of Battery Park. Either by his choice or hers, he didn't want to be seen by the people she worked with. Anna dawdled, giving Mandy time to get ahead. Proximity might force them into conversation. A situation neither would relish.

By the time Anna meandered in, Mandy and Assistant Superintendent Trey Claypool waited at the end of the dock. Beyond, the *Liberty IV* motored deftly through a harbor crowded with boats.

The Fourth of July, Patsy promised, would bring out so many boats they would nearly cover the water. Anna looked forward to that with trepidation. The harbor was the only open space her eyes had been allowed since she deplaned at Newark.

Standing well apart and facing different

directions, Trey and Mandy were making it clear they had absolutely no interest whatsoever in each other. *Too clear?* If they had something going on, they would have had to go to extraordinary lengths to hide it on the island. Then there was Fidel. Maybe Mandy got smacked because she was two-timing Claypool with a scrap of army surplus. Anna tired of trying to see past the obvious, making meaning where none was to be made. She wanted to go home. *Soon,* she promised herself. *Soon.*

Thinking it would be silly to space herself equidistant from both the Assistant Superintendent and the interpreter, she opted for the Assistant Super. Waiting in the glare of the sun, eyes narrowed against the water, he looked almost handsome. Anna had been noticing that sort of thing a lot lately. Pretty Park Policemen must have triggered a tide of hormones. Men in uniform carrying big guns. How could a girl resist?

"Hey," she said, talking to justify coming to stand next to him. "Long night on the town?"

"Huh?" Again Claypool seemed not to recognize her. She was not going to reintroduce herself. "No. Business," he said curtly.

The *Liberty IV* chugged closer. Mandy moved to be in place, the first up the gangplank.

"You?" Claypool asked, after so long it took Anna a second to remember the drift of the conversation.

"Yes indeed," she replied. "But this time I actually got to sleep in a bed. My sister has a place on the Upper West Side. Last time, you abandoned me to a cold night on a hard conference table." She was only kidding, wanting to say something to pass the time, but he shot her such a strange look she must have struck a nerve. His head cranked around and he stared at her with eyes so blank the carp image resurfaced.

"I didn't abandon anybody," he stated.

"Well, not *abandoned*," she hedged. Somewhere along the line her social skills seemed to have atrophied. "But a lift home in your runabout would have been nice."

"I don't know what you're talking about."

The tail end of his sentence mingled with engine sounds from the staff boat. Anna let the failed tête-à-tête go. Lord knew what Trey Claypool was up to on his nocturnal visits to Manhattan. The sex shops on Forty-second Street flashed through her mind as Cal handed her aboard. She decided she didn't want to know any more secrets. If it wasn't one's birthday, secrets and surprises had a way of turning out to be nasty.

21

Crossing the water brought a few minutes' respite from what had so rapidly become an oppressive summer heat. As she disembarked on Ellis, oppression returned, both physically and psychologically. Anna wondered if she might be coming down with something: leukemia, AIDS, clinical depression. Corinne's assault, the meaningless deaths, the petty mysteries, the weird accidents that plagued her stay at the monument pounded inside her brain as the heat pounded down on her unprotected head. Most crimes had a linear quality. The root cause of this was that most criminals were not all that bright. Agatha Christie was bright. P. D. James was bright. Dick Francis was bright. Criminals were thugs. Not very creative. Not ingenious. Opportunists who'd flunked long-range planning. Hence nonfictional crimes tended to be fairly straightforward.

On these two islands a series of incidents occurred from which no one appeared to have emerged the winner. Hatch had no money, nobody wanted his job. He had no wife to covet, no wife or lover Anna could find to want him dead for personal reasons. His insurance policy was the pittance that went with the job. With no other living family, it would go to his father. Not only did Jim seem to genuinely love his only son, but he was too crippled to kill him if he'd wanted to. Agnes Tucker, the little lost girl, wasn't a missing heiress in disguise. She was lost to her mother, and given that her father hadn't claimed her, had probably run away from him. Since the man had gone underground after kidnapping her, it wasn't a stretch to picture him constantly on the move, Agnes grabbing her chance and finding herself alone in the big city. Considering the way she had fallen, accident was ruled out. That left murder at the hands of the Park Policeman or suicide. As there was no discernible connection between Hatch and the girl, murder was unrealistic. But Anna had never seen a suicide behave as Agnes was reported to have: running headlong, pack on her back, to dive to a gory end.

Then some SOB stole the pack off the little corpse.

That presented a possibility. Hatch wanted to look in her knapsack. He suspected her of being a pickpocket. The child had jumped when he chased her. Had she chosen to die rather than get caught with whatever was in the sack? What could she get caught doing that was that bad? Even if the knapsack had been chock-full of the body parts of dismembered babies, Agnes wouldn't have served any hard time. In New York State fourteen was legally a minor. She must have known that. After the media blitz that hit the country when grade school kids began shooting up playgrounds, Anna doubted there was a juvenile delinquent left who didn't know his or her rights.

What if the pack contained something that might get someone else, an adult, in trouble? The thought put enough of the pieces together that Anna stopped walking and stood in the heat-drenched shade between the registry building and the old powerhouse to focus her faculties on this idea. Fourteen was a perfect age to die for someone else. Anna didn't remember a lot before she was thirty-nine or so, but she did recollect fantasies of heroism and self-sacrifice that had entranced her in early adolescence. That was the age girls wanted to become nuns, work with lepers, die of scarlet fever nursing the man they loved. And boys wanted to kill large numbers of people with powerful guns to save the known universe. If Agnes thought what she carried was that dramatically vital, she might well have hurled herself from a sixty-foot parapet. Giving her life that others might whatever.

Then the backpack had been snatched away; immediately, before Anna got to the girl. Following the idea that the pack contained something incriminating, valuable or necessary to some plan, the disappearance suggested not the callous robbing of a still-warm corpse but that Agnes had a confederate as invested in the contents of the pack as the child herself was.

Drugs? Diamonds? Microchips containing Bill Gates's game plan? Anna resumed her walk. Why would anyone drag that sort of thing up the Statue of Liberty? It was a rotten place for a deal or an exchange. The worst place she could think of to arrange an illicit sale. The statue was crawling with federal employees and had security at the one entrance. Besides, any criminal arriving after ten a.m. would have to wait. Anna didn't picture underworld types being willing to stand in line for several hours to do a dastardly deed. Central Park was far more workable.

In another park, Anna would have considered resource theft. Miss Liberty was valuable only in wholeness, in spirit. Pieces of steel or copper that could be carted off by the strongest, most determined child would be worthless. The kid could make more money collecting aluminum cans for recycling.

If the pack contained incriminating evidence, then of what? Before Hatch's death, no crime of any magnitude had been committed in the monument for ages. Guns and knives would have shown up at the security gate. And the same things that made the statue a lousy place to sell, buy or trade contraband made it a lousy place to do so with anything that could be used for blackmail. Blackmail was the only purpose Anna could think of for toting around incriminating evidence.

If the child was unknown to Hatch and had suicided, then it made no sense that Hatch jumped out of guilt for pushing her. If the child suicided, it also took away the revenge motive for Hatch's death. If he hadn't murdered the child, why kill him? Unless whoever the kid was working with, the mysterious snatcher of packs, blamed Hatch because he'd chased the girl, caused her to sacrifice her life. That brought Anna back around to the pack. What was in it that was so important it fomented a suicide and a murder? And who had the means and opportunity to avenge themselves on Hatch? Means wasn't tough. It wouldn't take much strength to dislodge a man sitting on a wall. Anna could do it if she had a running start and the element of surprise. Opportunity was trickier. The pusher would have to get on the island after hours, get into and up the statue and know where and when Hatch would be at his most vulnerable. A number of people working on the island knew of Hatch's Gauloise habit. Any one of them could have done it. Or anybody who had been watching the statue for a time. Hatch's smoking perch was visible for miles in three directions.

Then there was Corinne: different island, mixed with different people, no known connection with Agnes, Hatch, the backpack or the statue. Anna wasn't a die-hard cop who didn't believe in coincidences. They happened all the time. In literature they were rife. Thomas Hardy made a good living writing about improbable coincidences that had an impact on many lives. But this didn't feel like one. There was a common thread tying all the incidents together: none of them made one whit of sense. That was a pattern. If none of them made sense, it indicated there was a key piece of information missing, the key that would unlock doors on both Liberty and Ellis.

The "attacks" on her? The collapse of the stairs, the push into an oncoming train? Her memory of those events had mutated. At the time, she'd felt a malicious intervention but in retrospect she wasn't sure. What connection had she, a stranger, to anything that might be festering at the monument? Maybe one, and it was a stretch, but if there had been something hidden under the stairs, the same thing that had been moved to the garden where she'd found Corinne, it was possible someone had been afraid she'd seen it and so tried to dispose of her. Seen what? The same flaws in logic that stymied her when she thought about the contents of the child's backpack applied. Ellis was almost as unlikely a place for the exchange of illegal substances as Liberty. The south side was relatively deserted, but given a choice of all the places in New York to hold a secret rendezvous, it would be near the bottom of any list.

Hypervigilance was a common symptom of people under stress. Perhaps the "attacks" were simply an overstimulated survival instinct latching onto common events with uncommon fear. Like her suspicions of Dr. Madison and his locked desk drawer. The identity of Agnes Tucker had been established. If Madison for some obscure reason had been trying to obfuscate his connection with the city morgue, he'd been wasting his time. Therefore it wasn't logical that he was hiding anything. Logic had to factor in. There was no reason to injure or kill her; therefore no one had attempted to do so. QED.

Patsy was in her office. Once again the phone was clamped to her ear. Plans for the Pot Party, as she'd deemed it, were in full swing. "Pot" was not the pot of parties Anna had frequented in her salad days but short for "melting pot." Because of the nature of the bill Mrs. Weinstein was angling for, this Fourth of July Liberty Island would represent nearly as many nationalities as it had during its heyday as a port of immigration. A fitting tribute and clever politics.

Anna eavesdropped until it became obvious that Patsy wasn't going to be any fun for an hour or more. With a waggle of her fingers to show there were no hard feelings, she left to amuse herself elsewhere.

Without a conscious choice being made, Anna's feet carried her to the tangled garden where Corinne had lain for so long. On the steps, tucked under the living shade of forty years' unchecked growth, the only movement a stirring of leaves, light muted, sun fragments sparkling through the canopy, there was a sense of isolation, if not solitude.

Like the other gardens, the Commissioner's was small, enclosed. One could enter only by descending the steps where Anna sat. Before, this garden had struck her as intimate. Today it was claustrophobic, dangerous: nature caged, a green tiger waiting, angry, resenting its captors.

Ambient fear, the raw pure kind that fuels panic, began building behind Anna's sternum. The tips of her fingers went numb and her scalp tingled. Years had passed since she'd suffered an anxiety attack—another legacy of her husband's death. Breathing deeply and evenly, she rode it out as she'd learned to do, mind and body lifted on a cresting wave of nameless terror. The wave broke in a gush of cold sweat, and panic faded, leaving her weak and very alone.

To occupy her mind, she listed options: She could go to Liberty, to Patsy's house. She could return to Manhattan. Both choices brought back the tingle of rising fear and she decided to stay where she was.

For a minute or two she stared at the fading impressions heavy round things had made in the leaf litter at the bottom of the stairs. Nothing new revealed itself. Undergrowth had been slashed and trampled during the rescue effort, a rude path cleared to where Corinne had lain. Enjoying, in a perverse way, the scratching of twigs against her bare legs, Anna pushed through. External pain distracted her from the claws of the inner demons.

By the light of day she could see the creeping tendrils of poison ivy and stopped to examine her hands and arms. No blisters. It had been over twenty-four hours. For once she'd gotten out of a physical scrape scot-free. Her lucky star must have been on the rise.

The ground was clear where they'd put down the backboard and packaged the actress. Anna picked what looked like a spider-free, ivy-free zone and sat down tailor-fashion. Cloying heat settled around her. Silence was just one more memory of Colorado. Sultry air thickened with the hoot of ferries, the growl of motors, the fetid breath of seven million scurrying souls.

Anna was in a foul and edgy mood.

She sat. She waited. She relaxed her body. She eased her mind. Oppression did not lift. Dark thoughts bubbled below the surface of forced calm. Leaf by leaf she began sifting through the debris, looking for anything Joshua might have missed. Looking for a clue, a project that would occupy her till Molly was well enough that Anna could go home to Mesa Verde and breathe.

The garden was rich in artifacts: half a wooden button, pop-tops from the days before aluminum drink cans were changed, a marble—a green cat's-eye. Anna pocketed that, not for professional reasons but because she liked it. A safety pin, shiny and new.

On all fours to facilitate her grubbing, Anna didn't touch it. Unlike the other oddments, the safety pin was recently brought into the garden. Not a smidgen of rust or dirt dulled its surface. Nose near the ground, she studied it. The closing end had a blue plastic cap, the big kind people used to use to fasten babies' diapers before those Velcro-like tabs and the incredible waste of disposables were invented. Judging by the color, it could have been used to fasten Corinne's nightgown. Near the pointed tip was a brownish discoloration. Blood, she guessed. The safety pin might have been the implement used to scrape the message into the actress's arm. Anna retrieved a piece of notepaper from her pack, folded it into an envelope and, using sticks as tweezers, pinched up the pin and dropped it into the paper container. She didn't know yet what she would do with it. Already she was guilty of disturbing evidence—if it turned out to be evidence. In New York she had no rights as a law enforcement officer. Training covered this situation explicitly: her duty was to report her findings to local authority, turn over anything she had, be available for interviewing should they deem it necessary, then butt out, be a private citizen.

Anna slipped the envelope into the pocket of her shirt and then buttoned it.

Boots scraping on concrete intruded into her thoughts. Billy Bonham stood in the door, blocking the exit.

Not blocking, Anna corrected herself to stop the sudden rush of a panic that hadn't been banished but merely held at bay. *Just standing. Not blocking. Standing.*

"Hey, Billy." She was pleased no quaver of fear tainted the words.

"What are you doing here?"

Not a very welcoming statement. "I'm crawling around," she said, and sat back down as if laying claim to her right to exist in the world.

"What did you put in your pocket?" This aggressive, confrontational Billy was not the same man who'd shared his tales of ghoulies and ghosties with her on the stern of the *Liberty IV.*

"You're sure grouchy," she countered. "The heat getting to you?" Dodging his probe, she realized she wasn't going to be a good little

344

ranger. She was going to keep the safety pin and pursue it in her own way. Billy she didn't trust to deliver it. She didn't think the Park Police would treat it with the seriousness she felt it deserved.

"I guess," he replied, sounding more like his old self, and he sat on the top step. Anna was relieved at this relaxing of attitude. Still, she was uncomfortable having a brawny, well-armed boy squatting between her and freedom. The crack to Corinne's skull had been vicious, delivered with the strength of rage. Maybe Billy had done it by mischance, mistaking her for a "haint." Maybe he had nothing to do with the woman's assault. And maybe he had an agenda Anna didn't want to be a part of.

"What are you doing here?" she asked, hoping if he talked long enough she'd get a feel for his state of mind.

Bonham blew a gust of air out through loose lips. Staring between his knees, he plucked a living shoot off an azalea and began methodically stripping the leaves. "It's that thing with that actress. Everybody thinks I heard her calling for help and was too scared to come look. That's a flat-out lie." Without looking at Anna he said overloud: "I didn't hear anything. Not a doggoned thing."

Up till then she was half inclined to believe him, but the remark smacked too much of a working denial: denying it to others, and most important, denying it to himself. Anna fervently hoped he'd leave the Park Service. Especially if Corinne died. The knowledge that he'd abandoned an injured woman to die because he was scared of the dark would unbalance him. Either he would push so hard to prove himself that he'd be a danger to everybody he worked with, or he would retreat into bitterness and self-justification. Either way, he was washed up as a good law enforcement officer.

"What happened that night?" Regardless of the wisdom of unsettling a questionable cop blocking the one exit, she couldn't resist pushing.

"Nothing! I told them that," he snapped. Anna nodded noncommittally and took up her own twig, stripped it and began tracing patterns on a small slate of earth cleared when the backboard was dragged across it. Billy had not turned and left when he first found her in the garden. Deep down he really wanted to talk or there was something he wanted to find out by getting her to talk. Anna would win any battle of silences. At twenty-two, it was a grievous burden to sit without doing, without speaking. At forty-four, it was a practice and a pleasure.

"I was on my usual rounds," Billy said after a short time.

"Ah." Anna made an interested noise to grease the wheels.

"I go two or three times a night. You know— walk the perimeter. We don't have to go into the buildings on Islands Two and Three," he said defensively.

That was true. They were too decrepit to be

safe by night. "Safety regs," Anna said helpfully.

"Yeah. These places are death traps."

An overstatement, but Anna let it pass.

"There was nothing out of the ordinary that night. Nothing. If I'd heard something, you think I wouldn't check it out? That's crazy. I'd check it out."

"What's ordinary?" she asked.

"What do you mean?" Billy was suddenly suspicious, his baby-blue eyes narrowing.

"You said 'nothing out of the ordinary.' What's ordinary for a night patrol of the island?"

"Nothing." He used the word again. "I mean nothing much happens. That's why I wanted day shift—not enough action." He laughed with a false bravado and Anna pitied him. Maybe over time the lies would come easier.

"You get boats wanting to land at night. Kids on adventures mostly. This is my first summer, but I guess it happens a lot. I've scared a couple off a time or two. You know, come by and seen them just offshore like they'd been here. Once or twice somebody's walked or ridden bikes over the bridge from Jersey there behind the registry building. I've chased a few of them off. That's about it. It's pretty boring. I mean it's real boring. I would have welcomed something to break the monotony." Again he laughed, same tone. Billy Bonham hadn't been bored nights on Ellis, he'd been scared.

"No ghostly stuff?" Anna prodded. "Music, odd sightings, strange sounds?"

"No. I never said any of that. Oh, maybe I made a joke about it and now everybody makes it into this big deal." Sullen, boyish; he'd dropped ten years before her eyes. His voice was petulant, his body posture changed. He looked and sounded like an unpleasant twelve-year-old.

"You weren't joking when you told me about it that morning on the boat," Anna said.

He took another twig and began pulling the leaves off.

"Corinne was behind all that," Anna said. "She was gaslighting you. Trying to scare you, make you think the place was haunted. Or you were nuts."

Billy didn't reply. Anna let the words lie. Half a minute ticked by, pushed along by the movement of the shadows.

"Yeah. Well. Maybe it was Corinne and maybe it wasn't," he muttered at last. "That's easy to say. Everybody wants to believe it. Big joke on Bonham. Ha ha. Very funny. Like I wouldn't know if some half-baked actress was screwing with my mind."

Anna was now sure of two things: Billy had heard Corinne's cries and would never admit it, not even to himself; and he was not Corinne's attacker. Billy wasn't ashamed of something he'd done, but of something he'd left undone, a hollower and more cowardly crime.

"Good talking to you," she said, and levered herself up out of the dirt. "I've got to be going."

Billy didn't say goodbye, just leaned to one side to let her pass.

Vile as the prospect was, Anna was headed back to the Upper West Side. She had a couple more assignments for Frederick Stanton.

She smiled to herself. *If you want to marry into the Pigeon family, there are dues and responsibilities.*

22

nna, it's not that simple. I'm an FBI agent, not the President of the United States. I can't just walk in with an unidentified safety pin and demand a fingerprint and DNA test run on it, no case number, no explanation, no nothin'. Besides, I doubt there's enough matter on your pin to get a reading. Science is still science, it's not yet magic."

"Do you still have the engagement ring?" Anna asked.

Frederick's face flashed three emotions in such rapidity that it looked as if he were morphing from Jekyll to Hyde. "Is that a threat?" he asked quietly.

Anna thought about it. "No," she admitted. Molly's happiness was not something she would bargain with. "But it could have been."

"In that case, I'll see what I can do." Frederick accepted the envelope and tucked it in his purse, a brown canvas shoulder bag he carried despite the ribbing from his peers.

"I'm in a hurry," Anna said.

"So, what else is new?"

"It's different this time. I feel..." She stopped to discern what it was she felt. "Rushed. Clock ticking. Time of the essence. That sort of thing. I can't tell you why."

"Ranger's intuition?"

"Maybe."

It was late. Visiting hours at Columbia-Presbyterian were over and even Frederick, with whatever special status he'd managed with the nurses, had been tossed out. In Molly's big and beautiful apartment, with its spacious rooms and tasteful decor, Anna and Frederick were hunched over a cramped breakfast table squeezed into one end of what Anna had heard referred to in the South as a "one-butt kitchen." In the 1920s designers of New York apartments must have counted on the residents sending out for Chinese a lot.

Anna was tired the way only a day of being bombarded by people could make her; tired of bone and spirit, not of body. Thoughts troubled her and the anxiety she'd felt in Corinne's garden threatened to return. Sleep was a ways away. In spite of the day with its crush of sweaty city bodies, she did not want to be alone.

"What with one emergency and another, we've not really had a chance to talk," she said, to prolong the evening.

"What about? Us? There is no *us*. "

350

Frederick was churlish. Anna had scared him. She took the hit with good grace. "Sorry I made that crack about the engagement ring," she said. "I was out of line."

"Way out of line," he said, but he softened and, in that moment, looked terribly old. Keeping a face of hope and good cheer for Molly was costing him.

"Are you sleeping?" Anna asked on impulse.

"That's where you close your eyes and don't think for a while?" He smiled wearily. "Not so's you'd notice."

"There's drugs. Molly—or David—could write you a prescription."

"You know me. I like to suffer."

They sat for a while, at peace with each other, sipping tea. Anna had purposely made hers weak. There were no foodstuffs in her sister's kitchen that weren't loaded with sugar, caffeine, cholesterol or fat. That, coupled with whiskey and cigarettes, constituted a true health professional's menu.

"Molly doesn't take care of herself," Anna said. "She takes care of everybody else."

"You." Frederick had not yet totally forgiven her.

"Among others."

Rani climbed Frederick's bare leg and he squealed.

"You scream like a girl," Anna commented.

"They're the best screamers."

Rani jumped from his lap to the table, settled her furry tummy on the Formica between their teacups and began to purr.

"We probably shouldn't let the cat on the table in Molly's house," Anna said.

"Probably not." Neither of them made a move to disturb the kitten.

"You say you don't sleep nights?" Anna asked again.

"Nope. But it's good of you to ask."

"What I was thinking was, if you can't sleep anyway you might as well check out the fingerprint—should we be so lucky as to get a good one—tonight."

Frederick looked at her, his face impassive. "You know, Anna, you have a heart as big as Texas."

"I've always suspected that about myself. Finish your tea and let's go."

E mmett was in his precinct house on the East Side—not the posh yuppie Upper East but way up, Harlem. DNA tests were costly, time-consuming, and required forms to be filled out, forms asking questions Anna didn't have answers for, such as who authorized the lab work. From the frown that met them, it looked as if Frederick was pushing his luck asking for it. Adroitly, he passed the blame to Anna where it belonged.

They moved on to fingerprints. Emmett relaxed. The print was easy. Every flunky cop and ranger was taught to lift prints. Most weren't any good at it. Like any precision skill, lifting fingerprints off different surfaces was easily screwed up. Fingerprint evidence was notoriously fragile. Once bungled, the print was forever lost. Emmett was not a flunky cop. In his career he'd lifted hundreds of prints, but he impressed Anna by refusing to do it himself, insisting they give the task to a man who specialized in collecting trace evidence.

Detective Mallow was working that night. There was a case pending, but as Emmett led them up worn and dingy stairs smelling of antique cigarette smoke, he told them Mallow was almost always at the precinct house. Detective Mallow had no life but police work. He wasn't hiding from alcohol or failed marriages—things that plagued a lot of police officers—he was simply a man with one overweening interest.

They found him behind piles of folders at his desk in the corner of a room housing four desks, all neater than Mallow's. Clamped over his left eye was a jeweler's lens. A gooseneck lamp spotlighted the area between the file folders.

"Don't breathe," he said out of the side of his mouth when he heard them approaching. They stopped at a safe distance while he meticulously covered what looked like dandelion fluff. Pushing the lens up on his forehead, he leaned back in his chair and folded his hands in a neat steeple. He was slight and old, wrinkled of skin and clothes, with eyes that bespoke a formidable intelligence. "Now, what can I do for you, Emmett?"

Emmett told him what Anna wanted and they waited while the detective digested the information. "Mmhmm," he said finally. "Checking out a theory before going public with it. Never a bad idea." He stood and Anna handed him the envelope. He held it aloft, pinched between two fingers more bone than flesh. "However," he said in his deliberate way, "this could put you in a quandary. Should it turn out to be nothing, all you've wasted is time. If it turns out to be something, you are then in the uncomfortable position of having to admit you went through unauthorized channels or having to withhold evidence. I, on the other hand, am merely an innocent soul, handed an item to process yet knowing nothing of its origins." His eyes twinkled. "There will be, in either case, no flies on *me*."

They followed him to a windowless room at the back of the fourth floor of the building. Unlike Mallow's desk and most of the precinct house, this room was spotlessly clean, well organized and well lighted. Since Mallow unlocked the room before entering, Anna got the impression it was his special domain.

The detective tweezed the safety pin from its paper and, while they watched, dusted the head, brushed away the excess powder with a soft brush, then with a piece of clear tape lifted the residue from the plastic and transferred it to a clean white square of cardboard. He repeated the exercise on the other side of the safety pin.

"The deed is done." He handed the card to Emmett. "One is quite a nice print. I hope it answers your questions. Now, if you'll excuse me, there's some lint waiting to tell me many things."

Emmett took over from Mallow. He scanned the prints into the computer and typed in the commands that would set it to matching with prints on file. "It's not instantaneous," he said, when it looked as if Anna intended to wait for the results. "I'll call you tomorrow."

Frederick thanked him. As they were being ushered firmly toward the door, Anna said, "May I borrow a field fingerprinting kit? I've got a hunch."

Emmett shot Frederick an annoyed look.

Stanton shrugged. "She's like this. It's a sickness."

"This is the family you want to marry into?" the policeman asked.

"I do." Frederick mocked himself and the marriage service.

"It's your funeral." Emmett found a spare kit. Before handing it to Anna, he said, "You promise you'll return it?"

"Cross my heart and hope to die."

"You will if you don't." Emmett gave her the kit. As the elevator doors were closing, he said, "I don't want to know how this turns out."

Gentrification hadn't moved much above 110th. Buildings were worn and tired, posters plastered over posters. Graffiti splashed violent wallpaper on storefronts and lampposts. Broken glass scratched at sidewalks in need of repair. Few people were on the streets and those who were scurried like prey. The predators leaned in doorways, smoking, owning their night turf. Petty princes in a kingdom they'd clawed apart because they had no way out.

"One question has been answered," Anna remarked.

"Yeah, what's that?"

"I know where all the poor people who used to live on the West Side went. They're being pushed into the East River."

"Just keep walking and be ready to rescue me from bad guys," Frederick said. After they'd reached the subway, laid down their tokens and waited on the platform, he said, "I bet you enjoyed that. You're an adrenaline junkie, Anna."

"I didn't," she said honestly. "When the wildlife is sad it takes the fun out of it."

There was no good way to take the subway from East Harlem to the Upper West Side. Unless one went north over the river and back, it took at least three trains. This late, trains weren't running with any frequency. "We should have hailed a cab," Frederick grumbled.

"Think they're pretty common in East Harlem after midnight?"

At least there were plenty of seats. A majority of the ride they had the car to themselves. STOPMUDP4J: the string of letters and the number tickled a seed in Anna's psyche that gave her a feeling of impending disaster. Try as she might, she couldn't coax the seed into flower. Ignorant and nervous: an all-too-human condition.

New York's underground flickered by, an

industrial strobe blackened by dirt and use. Anna considered staying on the subway downtown to follow through on her hunch. In the end she had to give it up till morning. Dead of night was no time for sleuthing in public places. One needed the protective coloration of business as usual.

E mmett called at nine a.m. Frederick had left for Columbia-Presbyterian, the engagement ring in his pocket, Tom Sawyer under his arm. Anna had been up since six, passing the time staring at the phone, pacing and harassing Rani and, until he escaped, Frederick.

"Emmett," she said, and knew she was talking too loudly, holding the phone too tight.

"Got your print results," he said shortly. "No match."

"Did you check the boyfriend, Ma—" Anna started to say "Macho Bozo," then took a second to dig up his real name: "Underwood, Michael?"

"His prints are in the system. They were run just like the others. No go. Sorry."

The "Sorry" was very final.

"Are you working back-to-back shifts?" Anna asked, to create the illusion she cared about him as a person. "You were on late last night."

"I'm on late tonight too. I came down to check this out, since you had your undies in a bundle."

Anna was on Molly's cordless. She thanked Emmett on the way to the door, left the phone on the table in the entryway and took the stairs. The elevator did not suit her need to be doing.

In the lobby of St. Vincent's Hospital in the Village, she slowed down enough to find a pay phone and punch in the thirty-three numbers required to make an AT&T credit card call. Patsy was in her office and not on the phone, a double dose of luck.

"Busy, busy, busy," Patsy said, before Anna could tell her the call wasn't social. "A zillion crates of champagne get delivered today. In the heat and the crowds, whatever 'bouquet' the stuff has is going to get majorly bruised. And a dim sum of the world. Mrs. Weinstein's got haute couture food designers doing a bunch of cuisines to celebrate the old melting pot. Hah! The 'old' melting pot never had it so good. With Ralph Lauren cushions and designer food, this ought to be the lips-to-heinies fashion event of the century."

"Yeah. Hey," Anna said, caught up in her own program. "Any word on Corinne?"

Patsy shifted gears effortlessly, unperturbed by—or accustomed to—Anna's preoccupations. "Hang on a sec. Let me ask Charlene if the Chief called the hospital this morning." Charlene, Anna remembered, was the Chief Ranger's secretary. She hadn't the foggiest idea what the Chief's name was. She would never be a political animal.

Patsy was back. "Okay. Here's the scoop."

358

A paper rustled and she continued in a voice that indicated she skimmed and paraphrased. "Corinne has been moved from intensive care to critical care. Looks like they think she has a bad brain injury. Other than that, all systems are go. In a coma. May or may not come out. If she does...ooooh. Not good. Probably suffer loss of speech and motor control. Poor kid."

Fleetingly, Anna wondered if she'd done the actress any favors by saving her life. No guilt was attached. Anna was comfortable with her role as an EMT. She had no secret desire to be either an angel of death or an angel of mercy. Her job was to get them out of the park alive. Here it wasn't even her job, but it was still her duty. One picked others up when they got knocked down. One didn't have to love them, like them or ever see them again, just set them on their feet and move on.

"Thanks," she said, and belatedly, "Good luck with the soiree."

"Keep tomorrow night free."

"Will do."

The hospital was busy in the antiseptic and diseased way of hospitals, employees either lethargic or harried depending on their case-load. Once Anna had thought of New York in terms of theater, bus exhaust and the ever-present smell of urine. From now on she would remember it as an endless maze of hospital corridors linked by subway trains.

A bored young black woman, hair high and lacquered, nails impossibly long and impossibly red, told her where she could find critical care. Anna rode the elevator up several floors with a beefy ward assistant stoically listening to a litany of complaints from an elderly man in a wheelchair.

Critical care was quieter—hushed, a library where those hovering between cured and dead were housed. Nurses seemed to stand a bit straighter, weigh a bit less and walk with more purpose than their counterparts on the first floor. Voices were muted. Overhead fluorescents spread a cold fever of light. Anna loitered by the elevators as if she were waiting to ascend or descend until the hall was nearly empty. One woman remained, a stalwart nurse in white smock and trousers seated behind a high counter. A computer screen absorbed her attention. A better chance might not present itself. Trying to look as if she had a reason to be in the ward, Anna moved purposefully down the hall, opening each door as she came to it and peeking in on misery in myriad forms. The third door was the one she sought. Having slipped inside, she closed it noiselessly behind her.

She'd never seen anyone in a coma before. Corinne didn't look dead and she didn't look as if she were sleeping. Her blond hair had been washed free of blood and lay neatly combed on the pillow. The blue eyes were closed and the lips bloodless, slightly parted. *Sleeping Beauty,* Anna thought. The actress had that death-in-life look of the fairy tale princess awaiting a kiss.

If caught, Anna knew she'd be tossed out

if not arrested. Losing no time, she moved to the bedside, pulled the field fingerprinting kit from her pack and inked the fingers of Corinne's right hand. As she rolled each one, marking the print in its proper place on the fingerprint card, she noticed how slender the woman's hands were. No strength there. In a sudden flash of anger, Anna condemned those who clubbed baby harp seals, drowned kittens and attacked fragile women.

On the positive side, she couldn't but notice how much easier it was to fingerprint a "dead" person. Small blessings. She bagged the card and got out a wet wipe to clean Corinne's hand. Voices in the hall frightened her away. She hurried out, leaving the caregivers to marvel over what medical phenomenon had blackened the digits of their new patient.

Emmett was not yet on duty. For that Anna was grateful. She'd worn out her welcome, and possibly that of Frederick, for years to come. Detective Mallow was in, a chicken-necked young officer informed her, his tone suggesting Mallow was always in and this was a bad thing.

Declining escort, Anna threaded through the jumble of cops and criminals to the corner where Mallow dwelt. Puffs of lint still held his undivided attention. To announce herself, Anna fell back on the cliché of clearing her throat.

"I know you're there," he said without

reproof. "I'm just not at a stopping place. Be a minute."

Anna drifted to the bulletin board on the wall next to his desk and read detailed descriptions of items she'd thought too ordinary to describe. Detective Mallow had broken down such homely things as a smear of Pepsodent and a chip of Pretty in Pink nail enamel to their basic components. To what end, she had no idea.

"Done," he said. "Evil laid low by a speck of lint. How do you like them apples?" His triumph was so heartfelt Anna couldn't but admit she liked the apples just fine, enjoying with him the lesson in humility the little things could teach the best and worst humanity had to offer.

"Emmett run your prints?" He pushed back from his desk and Anna followed him to a nook in the rear of the room, where he poured himself a celebratory cup of coffee and offered her one. A brief look at the tarry mess and she politely declined.

"He ran them last night," she said, watching him spoon precise amounts of Cremora into his cup with an aluminum measuring device attached to his key ring. "No matches."

"And what is it that brings you back to this garden spot on such a lovely summer morn?"

"I've got another set of prints." She trailed him back to his corner.

"I see. You want these run too?"

"No. I want to compare them with the print you lifted from the safety pin."

The detective thought a moment, blowing

gently on coffee Anna suspected hadn't been hot for several hours. "We can do that. It'll cost you, though."

The sour taste of disappointment flooded her throat. Not at spending the money, at losing respect for Mallow. "I'll want to hear the story," he continued. "I never could resist a story. I think it's why I got into this business. I've always got to stay till the end. Find out who did it. Who gets the girl."

Anna's relief was out of proportion to the incident and she realized how deeply she needed to believe that members of the human race could harbor the altruism gene.

Back in his immaculate cubbyhole, Mallow retrieved copies of the prints taken from the plastic head of the safety pin, laid them next to the card Anna had brought from the hospital and sat down, his jeweler's glass over his eye. Humming "Row, Row, Row Your Boat," he studied the two. With the end of a finely sharpened pencil he pointed out the match points. When he finished he handed her back the card and cleaned his work space. Only when all was in order did he speak.

"The prints from the safety pin were partials," he told her. "And one was smudged. But I can say with reasonable certainty that there is a match to the thumb and forefinger of the card you showed me."

"Reasonable certainty?"

"A perfectionist, eh?" Mallow leaned a skinny haunch against the desk, folded his arms and let his eyes wander as his brain engaged at full capacity. "I'd say a sixty to sixty-seven percent certainty on the index finger and a ninety-seven point three percent certainty on the thumb." He winked at Anna. "Now my story." Over unbelievably bad coffee and stale bear claws, Anna told him what she knew and what she suspected. Mallow listened with flattering intentness.

"So the lady scratched the code or whatever it is on her own arm?" he asked when she'd finished.

"It looks that way. We'd thought it was some kind of signature or message from the attacker, but the delicacy with which it was done bothered me. I've had zero experience with serial, mutilation-type murders—" A look of such pain and sorrow flashed across the detective's mild features that Anna knew the same was not true of him. "But it seemed to me a person violent enough to bash in a woman's skull would have hacked out his message in a bloodier fashion."

"You were right," Mallow said, and Anna could tell being right ranked high on the detective's priority list. "Now that you know the woman made the marks herself, what does that tell you?" He used the tone of an instructor to a promising pupil. Anna was not offended. If she was lucky, she would never know as much about man's inhumanity to everybody and everything as Detective Mallow did.

"The obvious would be that she was trying to tell us who her attacker was," Anna said, forming her thoughts carefully, not wanting to disappoint her teacher with sloppy thinking or poor logic. "If we take S T O P at face value, that leaves M U D P four J. Could be initials. M.U.D. There's a violent boyfriend in the mix. A guy named Michael Underwood. That's a start. Stop M.U."

"Underwood's the drunk with the half-alibi," Mallow said.

"Right. His Stanley Kowalski routine on Liberty could have been a cover-up."

"Could be."

"I don't buy it either. The guy had a blood alcohol content of point three five. Not exactly in any condition to be clever or circumspect."

"And there's the D P four J left hanging about," Mallow added.

Anna dumped her half-consumed coffee in the garbage and slung her daypack over her shoulder. "Thanks for everything. Are you off Fourth of July weekend?"

"I am, but I've got a few loose ends to tie up. If you need me I should be around."

The world was made up of loose ends and Mallow couldn't resist them. Total job security. "Thanks," Anna said again, and ventured out into the heat. Not yet noon and it was so hot she was tempted to stop in at one of the hole-in-the-wall groceries and buy a dozen eggs just to see if one would really fry on the sidewalk.

Cabs were out; cabs were cursed with cab-drivers. Anna hadn't seen Molly yet today, but thinking of the long subway ride from East

Harlem to the Upper West Side brought on a twinge of nerves. Not at the incarceration or the crowding but at the time. Anna wasn't sure why, she just knew she had to be moving. Ambient anxiety, panic attacks: this was the stuff she should be talking to Molly about, or at least one of her colleagues. Anna had gotten a B+ in Psych 101. She could hazard a guess as to what the psychiatrists might say: She was projecting her own fears onto a criminal case. Because she was out of control of Molly's health and her own life, she needed to control something, hence her preoccupation with Corinne, Agnes and Hatch. Because her ex-boyfriend kept proposing to her older sister, she needed to find an arena in which she was needed.

Anna wasn't interested in hearing any of that. Law enforcement believed in little voices more than they did in psychology. Anna believed in both. Today she chose to ignore Freud and the gang; she was in tune with the little voice.

From Grand Central, she called Patsy's number on a pay phone. To shut out the clamor of loudspeakers, voices and feet, she jammed a finger in her free ear. At noon on a weekday the place was as busy as Grand Central. Patsy didn't answer. Lunchtime. On the eleventh ring somebody picked up. Anna didn't recall having seen a switchboard. The secretaries probably took turns covering each other's phones. A garbled voice said, "Statue of Liberty and Ellis Island National Monuments." Poor dear had to say that every time the phone rang. Over lunch she evidently had to say it around a mouthful of egg salad. Anna let a drop of compassion soak in, then asked her, "Could you put me through to law enforcement?"

Two rings and law enforcement picked up. "Joshua?"

"He's on nights. May I help you?"

Nights. Of course. Her mind was not up to par. The voice was that of the one ugly Park Policeman. Proving she was as shallow as any regular Joe, she couldn't remember the ugly one's name. She made a mental note not to be such a pig in the future.

"Can I help you?" he repeated.

"No. Thanks, though." Anna had to tell the Park Police what she'd found out about the pin. She was not deviant—or foolish—enough to hoard information that might help an investigation. A pay phone in a noisy train station wasn't the place to do it. She'd be on Ellis in person soon enough.

The less than exquisite Park Policeman's name was Brandon. Though she hated wearing them, Anna appreciated name tags for situations such as this. Dutifully, she gave him the safety pin and both sets of prints. Dutifully, she sat through his lecture on jurisdiction, removing evidence from a crime scene and obstructing justice. When she didn't seem properly contrite he turned up the heat, making vague threats about reports to superiors. After a while he ran down, his need to be boss sated for the moment. To soften him up, she made flattering chitchat, then asked what they had on Michael Underwood.

Confidential. Pending. Police business. The man had to plow through that while Anna was the soul of patience, smoothing his feathers and bolstering his ego, survival skills denigrated as "feminine wiles." At length, to put her in her place, Brandon couldn't resist divulging a piece of information. "Your M U D theory on the M and U being for Michael Underwood doesn't hold water. Of course we checked him out first thing." By the way he said "we," Anna got the distinct impression Brandon never got anywhere near Underwood. "He's got a rock-solid alibi."

Anna said nothing, gave him no satisfaction. She merely looked dubious and bided her time.

He sweetened the pot: "He couldn't have a better one if he'd known what was going down."

"Going down," like "Let's rock and roll," was such a trite phrase Anna had to suppress a derogatory snort.

Brandon leaned back in his chair and waited for her to ask what it was so he could have the pleasure of not telling her. Ugly, like stupid, is as it does. Brandon was getting uglier by the minute.

"When does Joshua come on duty?" Anna asked, with such perfect politeness it left no doubt that she intended to go to a "real" policeman with her questions.

It worked.

"Underwood was in jail," Brandon said smugly. "He got a DUI up in Westchester County the night that actress was whacked."

Whacked. Anna indulged in a tasteful snort. Why not? She'd gotten everything out of Brandon that she'd come for. Macho Bozo was cleared of all but being a drunk and a jerk. Unless creatures of that ilk were underfoot, she tended to ignore them. There wasn't time enough in the world to deal with them all.

"Have you got a date for the big bash tomorrow night?" Brandon asked as she stood to go.

For an instant she thought he was asking her out, then realized he was trying to engage her in conversation to keep her there a little longer. It beat working.

"No hot date," she said, and shrugged into her pack. Her date with Dr. Madison was a day affair and, for reasons she couldn't put her finger on, she was morally certain it wouldn't carry over into the night. "I'm going with Patsy."

"Top brass was invited. The Super, the Chief, Trey Claypool—he won't go, he's too good for just about everything. But you weren't invited. Patsy can't invite you." The eyebrows were up, a judgment was coming down. Anna realized she'd been set up. Of course she hadn't been invited. She was nobody, and though she considered her thirty-six thousand a year rolling in dough, it wouldn't buy a day's worth of Post-it notes for a campaign such as Mrs. Weinstein was launching.

"Not invited out loud, you might say," Anna told him, and crossed to the door. "But we have got to be there. Can't have a picnic without ants." She left before he could begin a lecture on NPS policies regarding the sucking up of illicit hors d'oeuvres.

Brandon had triggered an idea. She would like a date for the Liberty doings. Patsy was still out. Anna slipped into her office to make the call. A moment's forage in her pack turned up her address book. He answered on the seventh ring: moving slow today.

"Hey, Jim, it's Anna. Got any plans for the Fourth?"

He didn't. Thirty-one years on the docks and he'd never been to Liberty Island. "I guess I'd like to see where Jimmy worked," he said. Anna was glad he didn't say "see where Jimmy died," though he must have been thinking it. She hung up smiling; she really liked the old guy, looked forward to sparring with him over pilfered Scotch and an international array of canapés. Right amongst the crème de la crème, a broken-down old stevedore and a field ranger. Partners in reality.

A good chunk of the day remained and Anna's sense of hurry had not abated, but she was out of things to hurry and do. The bottom of the barrel had been scraped and she was no wiser than before. Islands II and III held no appeal. It was too hot and she had no desire to see Billy by accident or design. People broken in their own eyes were too great a drag on the soul to be faced when not feeling particularly Herculean oneself. Manhattan, Molly, Frederick required more energy than she had. Nervous energy she was rife with, but it didn't provide emotional strength. Home would be good: a dry pine-scented wind, a cat, a view not chewed by buildings or dulled by smog.

Options limited to hiding or whining, Anna chose the former, waited patiently for the two-thirty boat to Liberty, then sought out the Keeper of the Flame. A minuscule kindness would be good on this day of heat and self-pity. She hoped he'd appreciate the thought if not the gift.

Charlie's back was still bothering him. He sat in his "office," a partially subterranean space beneath the ranger station, accessible from the alley between it and the maintenance sheds. Tucked between battered wooden storage cabinets and a wall covered in newspaper stories written over the years about him and his lady, he was sipping coffee and laboring over his pen.

"Am I interrupting?" Anna asked, squashing in beside him.

"I'm a poet," he said simply. "Working on a new one."

"Ah." Anna knew better than to ask to see a work in progress. "I got the pictures back. The ones of you turned out pretty good." She took them out of her pack and spread them on the carpenter's bench he used as a desk.

"She's beautiful, isn't she?" Charlie said. Anna admitted she was.

"I wish I could have gotten her all cleaned up for the ball," he said wistfully.

"Nobody'll notice," Anna said.

"That's the trouble. Nobody notices anymore."

Mortality was weighing heavily on the Keeper, and Anna didn't know what to say. They sat staring at the pictures, thinking their own thoughts.

"Is that the 'biner you were talking about?" Charlie asked, pointing to the snapshot of the carabiner that had been found on Hatch's body.

"That's it."

Charlie picked up the photo and held it under the light of an old bed lamp with cowboys and cacti on the shade. "Not one of mine." Anna didn't doubt him. Climbers knew their own equipment.

"Maybe fell out of somebody's pocket. Tourists here are from all over. You know, come to America, hike, climb, see the sights."

"Must be what happened," Anna agreed.

Charlie graciously accepted the photos she'd taken of him, but it was clear he considered himself only an object that obscured a portion of his lady's perfect form.

Anna left him to his poetry, walked the short distance to Patsy's house and took up residence on the couch with a battered copy of Robert Louis Stevenson's *Kidnapped* and a bag of strawberry Twizzlers.

Only once was she forced out of her cocoon of sugar and fantasy. Patsy's phone rang. Anna ignored it, but when the machine came on and she heard David Madison's voice she dragged it onto her chest and answered.

"Hey, I got a real live person," he said, sounding genuinely delighted.

"You're half right," Anna said. "I'm real. I can't swear to the 'live' part today. The couch got me. I've been clamped in its jaws half the day."

"Good. Save your strength for tomorrow. Are we still on for our date?"

"I just need to know what to wear."

"Casual. We're going kayaking."

Anna's spirits underwent an unsettling rocket rise followed by a crash. Kayaking promised relief from the crush of a city that grew hotter and heavier each day. But travel would be required. Time. She would not cancel Jim Hatchett's visit to Liberty.

"Where?" she asked. "I've got to be back in town by seven at the latest."

"Back-to-back dates? You're a popular girl."

Anna chose not to accept the invitation to explain herself. Madison took it with good grace and went on.

"Not a problem in the least. We're kayaking on the Hudson. New York has everything. There's a sports complex on the West Side in the Twenties, Chelsea Piers. Full-service. They rent kayaks. I thought I'd bring a picnic lunch. You can bring the expertise. We'll

373

paddle as long as you like and get you back to wherever you need to be with time to spare."

Details were worked out. They'd meet at Columbia-Presbyterian around two-thirty. That way Dr. Madison could do morning rounds and Anna could visit Molly. Arrangements made, they severed the connection.

Kayaking; Anna loved it. When she worked on Isle Royale she'd kayaked nearly every day. Light and unmechanized, kayaks tied one to the water, and so to the world, in a way no other boat, with the exception of a canoe, could. Kayaks were silent, responsive. Thin hulls let the cold of the water seep into legs and butt. Low profiles put the kayaker in the bosom of the swells, a leaf flowing with wind and tide.

But who wanted to be at one with the orange peels and floating condoms in the Hudson, enjoying the playful antics of the rats under the piers?

"Stop it," Anna ordered herself, but the jaded cynic within was not easy to silence.

Wine had no flavor but she drank it anyway. Food had no appeal so she didn't eat. By ten-thirty she'd wasted enough of God's good humor and Patsy's patience for one day and retired to her room. Since becoming a Park Ranger, she had spent much of her life camping out: in glorious country, on fire lines, in dormitories, on couches and floors. In comparison, Patsy's cramped spare room was luxurious. Still, it wasn't home. Mandy had become consistently and openly hostile. Anna's continued presence was driving a wedge between the housemates. Turning out the light, she focused on the glitter of Manhattan through the open window at the foot of her bed. The fairy lights had lost their glamour.

She promised herself she would book her flight home on July 6. Molly was on the mend. Frederick was beside her. Unflattering as it was, Anna was relieved not to be needed any longer. If she'd ever been needed at all.

"You were. You are," she said aloud to reassure herself. She fell asleep half believing it.

23

As it was Friday night, the eve of the Fourth of July weekend, party boats were barging a frenzy of revelers around the island. Music was so loud not only was Anna pried out of what had been a pretty good sleep, but she could make out the words of the lyrics: "Closer, closer, I gotta love you tonight." Could be any of a thousand songs. Pulling shorts over her bare behind, she soaked in the trite message. A tank top and flip-flops completed her ensemble. Worst-case scenario—or best-case—the only one who might see her was Andrew. A tryst with such a handsome fellow would be soothing to a girl's frayed nerves. Anna took a moment to run a comb through her hair and spritz herself with Patsy's Pleasures perfume, hoping it would prove prophetic.

Years had passed since she'd succumbed to the urge for sex with a casual acquaintance, presuming Andrew could be had. When she had worked on Isle Royale, she'd slid into available arms and after the brief moments of *la petite mort,* there had been tears. Hers. Not of shame or guilt—no one had been hurt, no one betrayed—but for the emptiness they had longed, and failed, to fill with each other.

This time—again assuming the delectable policeman would be hers for the asking—would probably be no different. Knowing this, she still adjusted her top to a more alluring angle. Being a perennial stranger had left its mark. Moments of purely physical release coupled with strong arms to hold her didn't look half bad.

Out of doors the air was leaden with noise, dull bass punctuated with what sounded like rapid fire from cheap handguns. Across the chop of the harbor were sparks and sputters of light: firecrackers dragged out a day early. Undoubtedly they were illegal, but on the water the worst an offender would do was destroy his own boat. Harbor Patrol might have been fairly lenient.

Night wrapped around, a warm wet blanket, as Anna wandered across the lawn Patsy and Mandy shared with the Assistant Superintendent. A waist-high chain-link fence separated the land from the short, sharp drop to the sea. Below, glittering in wavelets, rocks formed a natural jetty pointing toward the south shore of Ellis.

A spark flickered in the nurses' quarters of the infectious disease ward: fire. The instant Anna pictured the loss of the rambling derelict buildings of Islands II and III, she knew what a tragedy that would be. For many of those not native to America and not brought in chains on slave ships, Ellis and Liberty were the beginning. Every stone was soaked in family history, cultural mores, ethnic roots. America— new, robust, passionate—crammed two small islands with the stories of the nations of the world and the people who left them in hopes of a better life.

Another flicker and Anna relaxed. A flashlight; Joshua making his rounds. Unlike Hatch's, Joshua's movements were unpredictable, his routines varied. Hooking her fingers through the wire mesh, she leaned back. Cyclone fences were miserable things. The one fence that did not make good neighbors. Patience Bitner, a woman she'd known on Isle Royale, swore that's how she could tell if a neighborhood was going downhill: the proliferation of Cyclone fences.

Unexpectedly, the staunch wire gave and Anna fell back six inches before it caught again. Startled but unhurt, she noted the cause: five or six yards to her right, near a thicket of head-high bushes, the fence was down, its posts evidently undermined by the sea. Killing time, hoping the temptation to seduce Andrew

377

would pass, she followed the fence line to the break. A post had fallen over, its concrete base exposed, wire bent toward the water. Not merely sagging but bent. This breach in Liberty's token line of defense had been exploited. More than once, by the look of the trampled wire. By the light of the moon and the faint leaks from the statue's floodlights through the leaves, Anna saw a dark shape, less an object than an absence of reflections on the water. Hanging on to the wire to keep from slipping down the bank in her treacherous flip-flops, she leaned closer. A runabout with a motor too big for its frame was moored in the lee of the natural jetty.

It was the perfect place for trespass. Claypool's windows faced east and west and the overgrowth of bushes effectively screened the place from any other direction. Interlopers: weekend adventurers looking for a romantic spot, no doubt. The islands, jewels of isolation in the bustle of the harbor, would be prime targets. A pleasant thought tickled Anna's mind. She had an excuse to seek out Andrew. The gods were placing too much in the way of temptation before her. Her dubious virtue was in glorious danger. Pushing through the interlaced branches, a shortcut to the mall leading to Lady Liberty, she laughed at herself. Deep within her was a seventeen-year-old girl who steadfastly refused to be tamed by the questionable wisdom of middle age.

Stepping deeper into the brush, she watched

her feet. If she waded into a copulating two-some it wouldn't be the first time, but coitus interrupt us was not her favorite pastime.

Branches closed behind her. Leaves met overhead. In front, foliage blotted out the light. Locked in this miniature copse, suddenly, momentarily, she heard the party boats go quiet: CDs being changed, sound systems shut down in sync, whatever caused the odd hush that occasionally falls on a roomful of people when, for no explicable reason, all conversation stops at once. Overlaid on this palette of silence was the skritching of the runabout rubbing against the rocks, and a faint shush in the leaves near her.

As she stood there clasped in darkness, no flashlight, no underpants, ridiculous shoes—reality slapped Anna between the shoulder blades with a cold fishy smack. Peculiar things had been happening, things that left a trail of dead and broken bodies. In lust and boredom, she'd forgotten the world was a dangerous place. As Hatch had forgotten a predictable pattern could prove fatal.

The fog of preoccupation lifted and she stood stock-still, letting her senses sharpen. Thoughts of sex evaporated and she felt a chill despite the heat of the summer night. The racket of the party boats returned, robbing her of her sense of hearing, something she relied on when working without light.

What had alerted her? Merely the blindness of the brush? A sixth sense? Or was it the anxiety that had circled her all afternoon coming to roost? Danger rose around her with the scent of crushed leaves. And a different odor, one out of place: the mingled smell of garlic and stale sweat. Slowly, trying not to make a sound, she began backing out of the bushes. Her flip-flops scooped up leaf litter. One pulled off of her foot. She didn't stop to retrieve it. There had been a sound; the boat on the rocks and the shush. A breath. When she walked into the black of the brush she'd heard breathing. Now it was as if she could feel it on her bare skin.

A second step. A stick or thorn jabbed into the heel of her bare foot. She used the pain to help her stay centered. Maybe the leaves in front of her moved. Maybe they didn't. Through the raucous music she couldn't hear if someone moved with her. Two more steps and she would be clear of the copse, she could turn and run. Her left foot eased back, settling firmly. Now was not the time to emulate Japanese maidens being chased by monsters and fall down.

Out on the water, a Roman candle ignited. Hot-pink light flooded over her shoulders, illuminating the ground in neon. A yard away were boots; army boots, worn and scarred. She turned to run and sensed rather than saw movement from above. She was to be clubbed down as Corinne had been.

Protecting her head with her arms, she turned the meaty part of her shoulder to absorb the blow. It hit with such force that she staggered and went down on one knee. Before she could pull herself up, a flash of black, and the impact of a bootheel colliding with her temple flattened her. There followed a crushing weight that knocked the breath from her lungs and forced her face into the dirt.

The man was in a hurry. Her death was not on his agenda. She lay without moving, taking courage from the fact that there were plenty of live possums in the world. Playing dead came easy. Without breath, her brain rocking from a kick in the head, she doubted she could have risen if she tried.

No more attacks came. Breath returned in squeaking, niggardly drafts. When she was able, she pushed onto her hands and knees and crawled to the island's edge. Futilely, she tried to wipe clear eyes blurred with dirt and trauma. He'd taken the boat. Under the perfect cover of party boat music, he was motoring away.

Not because it would do any good but because she was hurting and, though the incident was over, shaken, Anna sought out Andrew.

He did not disappoint. He was strong and handsome and calm. First he ascertained that she wasn't going to die in the immediate future; then he checked the island to make sure the boatman had worked alone, Liberty's residents were unharmed and no damage had been done to the resource. The statue was locked for the night. Built on Fort Wood, she was a fortress unto herself. The lady was unhurt.

Anna waited at the ranger station. Her back

was killing her. She didn't want to stand, sit, lie down or be alone. Until Andrew returned she leaned against the wall, her feet braced on the bottom of his desk, keeping her spine, a conduit of pain, in perfect alignment. Between blows to shoulder, back and temple, she believed it to be the only thing holding her together. The wall's support lessened the pressure.

Andrew came back and she allowed herself to be helped to a chair. He retrieved the first aid kit from the basement and gently cleaned the abrasion the kick to the face had left on her cheekbone. While he worked she told him what happened. When she described the assault to her person his brown eyes glowed with an anger that warmed her heart. Come first light, he would search the crime scene, but both doubted he'd learn much.

Cotton balls streaked with blood and dirt began to pile up on the desk. "You might get away without a black eye," Andrew said, surveying the damage. "The kick didn't land square. Looks like it glanced off, taking skin with it." He held her face in his hands. Anna could smell a faint promise of cologne. Not the usual stuff, but sweet and spicy. Maybe it was just the smell of the man. As he examined her wound, his face was close to hers, his skin flawless, eyelashes long. But she knew she'd break in a million pieces if she so much as raised her arms. Andrew never knew what a near miss he had.

"Let me take a look at your back," he said.

A considerate EMT, he walked around the chair rather than making her turn. With the detachment of a physician—or a black man touching a white woman in a racist world—he lifted the tank top, clinically careful not to expose too much of her.

A low whistle, then: "You've got to see this. It's perfect. Perfect, heck—it's evidence. Stay put. I'm getting the Polaroid."

He headed for the stairs. Gingerly, Anna raised herself from the chair. An eight-by-eleven-inch mirror was hung near the door so rangers could check to see if their hats were on straight before exposing themselves to the eye of the public.

Having removed it from its nail, she propped it against the telephone on the desk. Out of deference to Andrew's sensibilities, she held her top over her bare breasts after pulling it off. Each movement hurt, reminding her how frail individual components of the body are, how fortunate she was not to live with pain on a daily basis, how it behooved her to be more careful.

Agonizing craning of the neck and twisting of the torso brought her back into view, and with it, Andrew's evidence. Below her right shoulder blade, extending nearly to her kidney, was a bruise, a bootprint, the tread blood-purple, the heel black and angry red.

"An inch higher and your shoulder blade would have shattered. Two inches lower and he would have ruptured a kidney. This is a vicious person." The words were civil, the

383

delivery icy. Andrew was cut out to defend the weak and rescue fair maidens. "Hold still." Anna obliged and he snapped half a dozen pictures.

"What do you think?" he asked. "Size ten, ten and a half?"

"Sixteen," Anna said, and he laughed.

"A work boot?"

"No." Andrew politely turned his back. Anna put her top back on. "An army boot."

The boot she'd seen in the crowd the day Agnes died.

The boot she'd seen in the subway when she was pushed.

And, she didn't doubt, the boot that had kicked the stairs from under her.

24

Anna had soaked and she had slept for a couple of hours. Patsy awakened her with a cheery "Happy Fourth of July," then, with the pronouncement "There is no rest for the wicked—or the ambitious," rushed off to work on Mrs. Weinstein's political event. The bathroom mirror gave Anna a damage report. As Andrew had predicted, she was spared the cosmetic misery of a black eye, but her cheekbone was an angry purple shot through with red abrasions, tender to the touch, battered bad enough it hurt to close her teeth.

The bootprint on her back had ripened to perfection. Bruises were blue-black ringed with red. Andrew had omitted the worst of the what-ifs. Two inches to the left and it might have snapped her spine. Soft-tissue injuries took the longest to heal. Anna would feel this boot for a long time. This morning it felt as if the son of a bitch had stomped clear through to her belly. Muscles had screamed, bones ached, viscera roiled. Nausea had racked her cells, ruling her body with toxic tides.

Today she wanted to see Molly; she had a kayaking date with the good doctor, and another with Hatch's dad for Scotch and memories. Staring at her reflection in the glass, she felt far too old for any of those things, too banged-up to face crowds, noise or Molly's angry compassion when she saw what her only sister had allowed the world to do to her. Thoughts of Robert Louis Stevenson and the sofa had nearly seduced her into canceling everybody, when Mandy's puffy face appeared around the bathroom door. "Oh," she said, letting annoyance shine through feigned surprise. "It's you. I thought by now you would have gone back to wherever."

"Soon."

"Good. I hope you've got plans for the Fourth. I'm hanging out in *my* house, on *my* couch. Maybe I can get a little privacy."

"Big plans," Anna said. "I'll be out of your way before you can say 'Miss Manners.'"

"You're a laugh riot." Mandy slouched off in the direction of the kitchen.

Mentally, Anna apologized to the couch for abandoning it to a fate worse than death.

Dressing was an ordeal. She'd never stopped to think how many muscles it took to pull a shirt over one's head.

Because of the facial contusions, makeup was out. Since raising her arms higher than her shoulders set her back to spasming, she couldn't do anything with her hair. Jamming on Agnes Abigail's spud hat, Anna decided David Madison would have to take her as she was or not at all.

Movement helped, as did the already intense rays of the midmorning sun. She knew that when she stopped she'd feel rotten, but she enjoyed the slight reprieve. Liberty Island was mobbed. It was the lady's day of tribute; she stood for the dreams formalized on Independence Day. Since joining the National Park Service fourteen years ago, Anna had worked every Fourth of July. It was a big day in the outdoor recreation business. Having no family, she'd been glad to volunteer to work the holiday. Other rangers got to stay home with their kids, Anna made time and a half, everybody won. Winding her way through the masses, trying not to get her fragile frame jostled, she realized she preferred it that way. Working on holidays, one wasn't required to have fun. There was no pressure, no disappointments. And she usually had a wonderful time. Park visitors fed her. She was part of a

dozen parties but owed allegiance to none. If
the gathering was boring, she moved on. If it
was too rowdy or offensive, she arrested everybody.

Molly made the long hot journey worth
every insult to Anna's bruised body. She was
sitting up and had color in her cheeks. A
woman's eyes could tell the blush was laid on
from without, not generated from within, but
its application bespoke a desire to live. Frederick was there, of course. It was a small
wonder his rear end hadn't grown to the
chair. Anna was glad to see him. Glad to see
his shirt was pressed and his shorts clean and
well fitting.

Easing down onto the cool linoleum, the wall
bracing her aching back, she told the story of
her adventure. With loving ears to hear, she
found herself feeling sorry for the woman
who got stomped. Molly gave her usual lecture on the benefits of getting a real job where
clients rarely tried to kill you. Frederick's
eyes glinted with a need to pulverize the man
who had battered her, and Anna felt at home.

Once her tale was digested, Molly rang for
the nurse and demanded Dr. Madison be
summoned. By the time Anna realized it was
for her, it was too late. Madison shined his pen-
light in her eyes, palpated her spine, gave
her a handful of Advil and a prescription for
Valium to help with the spasms. He was a con-
scientious physician, so the scrip was for ten

tablets, nonrefillable. Enough to get her through a few days, not enough to get her hooked.

"Are we still on for two-thirty?" he asked as he was leaving.

"Two-thirty," Anna agreed.

"Maybe kayaking is not such a good idea," he said, thinking of her injuries. "Maybe we should just tuck in for an at-home." He winked, said, "Meet me in my office. By the way, nice Idaho potato," and was gone.

Anna had forgotten she still wore Agnes Abigail's cap. She left it on. By now she'd have such a severe case of hat hair that hiding it was a cosmetic courtesy.

Shortly thereafter Frederick excused himself, pleading an errand Anna knew he didn't have. He kissed Molly tenderly on the forehead, gave Anna a pointed look and left. It was payback time.

"So. You want to marry him or what?" Anna asked after the door closed.

Molly laughed, a weak but wonderful sound. "Is it too late to pack you off to finishing school?"

"Sorry," Anna said. "The last few days I've been feeling rushed. No time. No time for niceties. No time for anything."

Using the wall, she crawled to a standing position and creaked over to the abandoned chair. The cool of the floor, so pleasurable when she first sat down, had chilled and stiffened her.

"Anxious?" Molly asked.

"Sort of. Impending doom. Just stress."

"Tell me about it."

Anna started to, the habit of a lifetime, then stopped. "You're not going to weasel out that easily. We are talking about you. So. What's the plan?"

Molly sighed and leaned back against the pillows. She closed her eyes and suddenly the rouge looked garish, her face old. "It's not that simple," she said wearily.

"Take a stab at it."

"Frederick...If I..." Without opening her eyes, Molly raised a translucent hand to her brow, pressed her temple with her fingertips. Anna stifled the urge to ask if she was okay, if she was getting a headache. This was one conversation she didn't want to derail. "I've felt...When Frederick..."

Anna had never seen her lose her sharpness of intellect. Under other circumstances it would have scared her. At present she was sure Molly wasn't suffering a stroke or early-onset senile dementia. Molly was unable to say what she needed to without mentioning the unacceptable fact that she'd fallen in love with her little sister's boyfriend. With the meat of the conversation gutted, all she had left were paltry word scraps.

"Let me try," Anna said. "You were attracted to Frederick when you first met, but since he and I were an item, you banished him to the northward of your affections. There you left him, in exile, because you liked me best."

"I still like you best," Molly said with a faint, sweet smile.

Anna wanted to thank her, respond in kind, but couldn't. She forged ahead. "Even after Frederick and I split up you continued to ignore him."

"I didn't really think about him," Molly said. "It's not like I pined away. He was just...just one of those things. Ships in the night."

"I know you didn't. He was mine, therefore he was dead to you. Buried and forgotten." Anna stopped a moment. "I really appreciate that. It means a lot." Two short sentences containing heartfelt feelings. Why did she have to dig emotional truths out of her liver with a pickax, one nugget at a time? "Can I go on with my hypothesis?" she asked irritably.

"I wait with bated breath."

"You get sick. Frederick comes running. I come running. What's a sister to do? Then Frederick turns on the charm and, underneath that charm, you sense a deep and committed love for you. The old attraction returns, grows into something more. But you still like me best. And though I say to go ahead, your shrinky training tells you this is my ego talking, me being self-sacrificing, that deep down I am hurting. How am I doing so far?"

Tears leaked from under Molly's closed lids. "You missed your calling," she said. "You'd have made a hell of a psychiatrist."

"Here's the end of the story. This is not hypothesis. This is fact. Don't analyze it, just hear it."

"Sometimes a cigar is just a cigar?"

"Right. This is a major cigar. There is no

deep down. I'm not hurting. Not only am I not hurting, I'm hoping. I want you to be happy. I want to know somebody is taking care of you—" Molly started to protest. "Not a word," Anna snapped. "I want to know somebody is taking care of you because I'm not good at it."

More slow tears. Anna felt her own eyes pricking and shoved the heels of her hands in the sockets to dam the flow. The attempt was foiled. She banged her cheekbone and water gushed from both eyes. "Damn," she muttered. Molly opened her eyes. "Hit my cheekbone," Anna said.

"Right." Molly closed her eyes again, smiling in a way that engendered in Anna a childish desire to pinch her. The second hand on the wall clock jerked its way around the numbers.

"You know why you've never been able to take care of me?" Molly asked.

"Because I'm a selfish twit?"

"Because I have never let you. I cheated you of that because I needed to feel strong, in control. When I got so sick, I wanted to go ahead and die. Not because life wasn't worth living but because I knew I couldn't fool myself I was in control. I was scared to death. I'm okay with it now."

"Psychiatrist, shrink thyself?"

Disappointment shadowed Molly's face. Anna was hiding behind cheap humor.

She tried to exonerate herself. "Thank you for telling me that," she managed.

Another spastic circuit of the second hand.

In half an hour Anna had to leave to meet David. "Do you think you were able to retire the superwoman cape because Frederick was here?" Anna asked.

"And you were here."

The exchange had tired Molly. Anna could see weariness, the words sapping her strength. Time to drop the subject. One more question: "What are you going to do?"

"I honestly don't know."

Anna left it at that. Frederick returned a quarter of an hour later looking so frightened, excited and expectant that Anna was sorry all she could give him was an I-did-my-best shrug. The two of them made desultory conversation about subjects neither was interested in, while Molly drifted in and out of a doze. At two-twenty Anna said, "I'd better go. Big date with the doctor."

When she didn't push herself out of the chair to leave, Frederick said, "You don't seem too thrilled with the prospect."

"I'm not. I should be."

"Tired from the night's fisticuffs?"

She shook her head. "General weirdness."

"What's the problem?"

"With me no doubt. He's a good guy. Too long in the city—I've come down with chronic heebie-jeebies."

Frederick drummed the backs of his long skinny legs against the linoleum. He'd taken Anna's customary place on the floor. "I wasn't going to say anything," he said. "It wasn't exactly good timing for me to be casting aspersions on your gentleman friends. Could be misconstrued, don'tcha know."

"But..." Anna prodded when he didn't continue.

"But nothing, really. You know how women can see things in other women men don't have a clue about? Like some gal's on the make, or lying about her face-lift? Men are no different. The takes-one-to-know-one thing. Madison sets off my alarms. My snake alarms."

"Nothing specific?"

"I should have kept my mouth shut. He saved Molly's life. He's probably a great guy."

"But the snake alarms."

"Buzzing."

Anna levered herself out of the chair. "It's all yours," she said. "I'd better be going."

"Anna?" She stopped at the door. "Check out the Persian Kittens web site if you get a minute."

"Sure," Anna promised, hoping there was nothing wrong with Rani.

Dr. Madison was late. Like cops and firemen and other emergency personnel, doctors' jobs started out making them late. Then late got to be a habit and the job an excuse as often as not. Anna rocked back and forth in his chair, feeling each and every bruise. Two forty-five. No David. Nothing on his desk amused her. She punched a computer key and the screensaver, a dizzying array of ever-changing geometrics, winked out, replaced by his menu. She had a minute, maybe more. Having clicked on his AOL, she went to "favorite places." Persian Kittens was still bookmarked. A scatter of clicks and computer fiddlings and she was at—or in, or on, she was never sure—the web site.

Not a kitten in sight, and near as she could tell, the rugs the "models" were posed on weren't real Persian. Cyberporn. She'd heard of it but never had had cause to give it much thought. Closing out the site, she processed what she'd seen. She had nothing against porn per se. Most of it was demeaning to women, but men liked to look at naked ladies. Politics, morality and ethics weren't going to change that. What bothered her was that Madison had been so quick to accept the accolades heaped on him when she'd mistakenly praised him for looking up kittens, going the extra mile for a patient.

Not really a big deal. Everybody took a freebie now and again. Besides, what was he going to do? Tell her, "Oh no, that was a hard-core porn site I like to visit when I'm supposed to be working"? Too much to expect of anybody human.

It was bizarre that it was in his office. The man lived alone. He could keep porn in his home without fear of discovery. That he had it in his place of business could mean a number of things. Maybe fear of discovery heightened the excitement. Discovery of the porn itself or of him doing what men traditionally do when viewing pornography? His chair was feeling less than pure all of a sudden. Keeping the porn at the office might also mean he'd developed enough of a craving for the stuff that he couldn't get through the day without it.

Or it could mean nothing. Curiosity. Porn site ad pops up on E-mail, gets opened, filed, never thought of again.

But Persian Kittens was on his "favorite places" menu. Frederick's snake alarm rattled in Anna's head. She jiggled the deep file drawer, the one where David Madison had surreptitiously deposited the folder. It was locked. Fingers quick from the practice of searching and frisking felt out the standard places keys were hidden. David's key, unimaginatively enough, was tucked under the blotter. In a second the drawer was open. The contents had nothing to do with Molly's treatment, the New York City morgue or the identity of Agnes Abigail Tucker. Printouts of nude women urinating, lactating, pregnant women. Magazines with such enticing titles as *Big Boob Orgy* and *Butt Rangers* were stacked a foot deep. A gym sock was near the bottom. Inside was evidence the doctor's hobby extended to amateur photography. What looked to be nearly a hundred snapshots of women were stuffed inside. A plain-faced woman on elbows and knees, her bare bottom in the air, her neck craned as she leered over her shoulder at the camera as if concerned any of her dubious charms would go unrecorded. Anna flipped over the snap. On the back was written: "Jew-elly, Virgin Islands." A woman fifty-five or sixty,

395

suffering from obesity, fat thighs spread, wearing nothing but what looked to be Mardi Gras beads: "Andrea, Louisiana." "Helen, Alabama." "Suzi, Little Rock." "Patty, MS." "The Blackstock sisters." "Anne, artist?" Anna had seen enough. She tucked the sock back between two videos, *Incest* and the promising title of *Horny Haitian Midgets*.

Settling the collection back roughly the way she'd found it, Anna noticed a sheet of paper with a list of names. Each was numbered. Jewelly was there and Andrea. She skimmed down. Number 44 was Sonya. The name rang a bell. For a moment Anna racked her brain; then it came to her. The silver-haired nurse who had met them on the elevator that first day Dr. Madison walked her out. "Forty-five?" she'd said. Anna looked back at the list of names. Number 45 was Anna P., followed by a question mark.

Nauseated, she slipped the list back in the drawer, locked it and replaced the key under the blotter. So much for the date. It was five of three. She took up her pack and left, taking the stairs so she wouldn't run into the doctor. Later she would thank Frederick and tell Molly. At present she felt too much of a fool, ashamed, as if the slime of Madison's secret life had rubbed off on her. She wanted to hide and lick her wounds. At the hospital's entrance, she hailed a cab. Cabbies no longer struck her as the lowest life-form in New York.

Secure in Molly's apartment, she turned up

the air-conditioning, captured Rani for fur therapy, then called Delta Airlines. Not a single seat was available on the sixth of July. On the seventh there were openings, but since she was booking so late, the one-way would cost $1,287.34. Anna grabbed it. Cheap at twice the price. Escape hatch open, she felt better. Molly would understand. Frederick would be glad to have her out from underfoot and Hills Dutton, her District Ranger at Mesa Verde, would be thrilled to have her back writing parking tickets and rescuing poodles from parked and locked cars. Summer, July, was Mesa Verde's peak season.

Clasping a compliant kitten to her chest, Anna lay carefully back on Molly's sofa. The cushions were soft but firm. Good for her back. She pulled the dead child's cap off and scratched her scalp where hair had sweated into a mat. Rani, a ball of fur with silver paws, batted at the hat. "You are a true Persian kitten," Anna told her. "Why would anybody want to look at ladies with no panties on when they could look at you?" Not yet interested in male sexuality, Rani jumped off Anna's chest and ran down the hall as if all the hounds of hell pursued her.

Anna turned the spud cap around and studied the logo. "Idaho potato," Madison had said. The words percolated in her brain. "Spud" and "Call Caroline" were two of the items on Hatch's laundry list. One of the Carolines worked at Craters of the Moon in Idaho. Was that the connection? Had Hatch guessed the cap, and therefore the kid, were from Idaho, and called the only law enforcement officer he knew there to follow up on the hunch? Or had he just thought to call an old friend to see what had happened with her poachers, Dick Head and Thomas Jefferson. No, Anna corrected herself. Andrew Jackson. Andrew Jackson Thomas.

Put the pieces in a bottle, shake 'em up and see if they fight. Idaho. Agnes Abigail Tucker. Idaho. Caroline. Idaho. Dick Head. Idaho. Andrew Jackson Thomas. There'd been one other mention of Idaho that she wasn't including, but she couldn't remember what or where so she let it go. Shake the pieces. Andrew Jackson Thomas. What had Agnes's mom called the girl's father, the father she was sure had abducted her child? A.J., that was it. A.J. Tucker. A.J. Tucker/Andrew Jackson Thomas.

Anna sat up so quickly her back went into spasm and she had to swear for a minute till it passed.

A.J., Andrew Jackson, had taken Agnes and finally ended up in Idaho with the kid, and both had been living under the pseudonym Thomas. How or why Agnes had come to New York, Anna couldn't figure, but it was satisfying to put one and one together if not two and two. She stuffed the cap in her pack. Tonight she'd return it to Jim. It had produced the one clue it had. Not much use now except for tracking down Tucker/Thomas to notify him his daughter was dead.

"Not my job," Anna said.

Having turned off the ringer on the phone, she showered and lay down on Molly's bed. It was after five when she awoke. Her mouth tasted foul and her hair had dried standing on end, but she felt much improved. Two messages had been left on Molly's machine, both from Dr. Madison, wondering where she was and what had become of their date. *Should he grow too lonely,* Anna thought, *the doctor could undoubtedly be counted on to take things in hand.* What was it the doctor at the morgue had called Madison? "A great backdoor man." At the time, Anna had thought it was some kind of proctology joke. The pathologist had a southern accent. In Louisiana a backdoor man was a lover. A married woman let him in the back door when her husband went out the front. No wonder the staff at the morgue had been so obliging. Anna punched rewind.

Because of Jim's infirmity, she was to take the subway to Brooklyn and the two of them would catch a cab back to MIO to get the staff boat to Liberty. Anna planned to leave around six. That would put them on the island after seven-thirty, when the festivities were in full swing. Patsy had said the official tour of the statue for the four hundred or so bigwigs was scheduled from seven to nine. After that everyone would assemble on the mall to park their plush posteriors on the Ralph Lauren cushions and watch the fireworks. That left Anna just under an hour to eat and shower again. Not for cleanliness' sake, but to tame her wild hair.

Hot water was a balm to her bruised back and face. Blunt trauma had its own healing schedule. Unfortunately, she was dead center of the next-day pain cycle. What had hurt the previous night and been stiff and sore in the morning had solidified into a bone-deep ache that ran from the top of her head to her right buttock.

Refrigerator and cabinets were devoid of anything appetizing. Frederick tended to eat the same way Anna did: not much, not regularly and mostly "found" foods. Another reason he and she were a bad match. Given time, they'd starve each other to death.

New York neighborhoods were grand places to forage for food. Anna would grab something, then go fetch Hatch's father. On her way out she took Molly's cell phone from the table in the entryway and stuffed it in her pack. Why she took it—even if she could make the wretched thing work—she wasn't sure. In the wilds of Texas, the backcountry of Colorado, the swamps of Michigan, she'd never felt as isolated as she did in this mecca of phones, faxes and bike messengers.

As it turned out, Molly's neck of the urban woods was rich in florists' shops and poor in fast food. On Broadway, Anna would have better luck. A clot of unpleasant-looking young men had coagulated on the sidewalk between Molly's apartment house and the corner. Though temperatures were in the high eighties, they dressed in trousers, heavy shoes and long-sleeved shirts in uniformly dark colors. One squatted on the pavement, one leaned against the building, the others loitered in orbit. Everybody smoked. The leaner had an additional cigarette tucked behind his ear for emergencies.

Daylight, not a bad part of town, cars and other pedestrians about—even with her diminished physical capacity, Anna wasn't concerned for her safety, but uncomfortable memories from adolescence welled up. Seldom could a girl pass a gang of boys without suffering crude remarks. *Sticks and stones,* she reminded herself. She also reminded herself she was no longer a girl. Construction workers were no respecters of age when it came to unseemly shouts, but teenage boys usually couldn't be bothered. One of the perks of being middle-aged.

Her guess was right. They took no notice of her whatsoever. They wouldn't have noticed if she'd been sixteen and naked. A heated discussion was in progress. "Bitch niggers" and "Fucking slopes" and a handful of racial slurs that were new to Anna but sounded aimed at Middle Easterners were batted through the air. Cowards whipping up their courage with words. Courage to do what? If it had to happen, Anna hoped it would be limited to property damage.

As she was passing gratefully out of earshot a final phrase spat into the street reached her: "Motherfucking mud people."

Anna stopped so abruptly a woman behind her bumped her, sending a spasm of pain

401

into shoulder and butt. "Watch where you're going," the woman said distractedly.

"Sorry." Mud people. She'd heard that before, though not often. People who were not "white," not "pure," not "Aryan"; people the color of mud, with muddied ancestry, from the mud. It was the most all-inclusive racism there was. Us and Them. Us was white. Us was whoever we said Us was. Them was dirt.

"Oh shit," she whispered. "Oh shit," and "Taxi!" In true New Yorker fashion she ran to the edge of the traffic flow, waved her arm, then sprinted to steal a cab stopping for a businessman, wearing a suit, briefcase in hand.

"Hey," he screamed as she jerked open the car door. "That's my cab. My client—"

"Shouldn't be working on a holiday," Anna shouted. She slammed the door and told the cabbie: "Battery Park." After looking in every mirror twice, he pulled carefully into the lane of traffic.

"I'm in a hurry," Anna said, because she had to, not because she thought it would do any good.

"Everybody's in a hurry, lady."

"This is life and death."

"It's always life and death."

The subway would have been faster but she was committed. Pawing through her day-pack, she retrieved Molly's cellular phone. Mud people. STOPMUDP4J. "Stop Mud People 4 July." That's what Corinne had tried to

tell them. Her only means of communica-
tion was to scratch the warning in her own flesh.
She hadn't been naming her attacker. She'd
lain there, her brain broken, and, with the safety
pin for a baby's diaper, tried to save others.
Because the brave little goose was an actress
and, as Zach would have said, therefore
affected, she'd put the 4 before the J in the English tradition. The futile act of heroism stung
Anna's eyes.

Not futile. Not yet.

She began punching numbers from her
address book into the cellular. For once she
was sorry she was not from here. She didn't
have the Superintendent's home number or
the Chief Ranger's or the Park Police's.

Patsy didn't answer. Of course; she and
four or five hundred others were pouring into
the statue. The cab sped up. "Hallelujah," Anna
said. The cab slowed down. She punched
911 and send. A recording put her on hold.
The cab stopped at a red light. No time; the
sensation was back in force. Anna felt as if her
skin were coming off. The light turned green.
Still on hold. Fourth of July, there were probably emergencies all over the city: kids blowing
their fingers off with illegal firecrackers,
drunks punching one another, smashing up cars.
"New Jersey!" Anna said.

"Now you wanna go to Jersey?"

"No. Never mind."

"Suit yourself."

The monument now belonged to New Jersey.
Or partially to New Jersey. That might have

screwed up jurisdictions. "What's nine-one-one in New Jersey?" she demanded.

"Same as in New York, lady: nine-one-one. A B C is A B C over there too—or so I hear."

Anna put the phone back to her ear. The wax shavings, the elephant tracks in the garden, the bruises above Hatch's kidneys, the cache under the stairs that was there, then not there, the stink in the ward, the carabiner, Charlie being tossed a can too heavy for a small man, the deaths of Agnes and Hatch, the midnight boater, the attempts on Anna—everything fell in place, painting a picture so clear Helen Keller would have seen it days ago.

Still on hold. She stabbed End and called Molly's hospital room. She got an operator. Anna had forgotten Molly was still back in ICU. No phones in ICU. She asked if Frederick Stanton could be paged. "It's an emergency," she said. The Columbia-Presbyterian operator was well versed in the handling of emergencies. Frederick was paged. No response. Supper hour. He'd picked a hell of a time to abandon the hospital cafeteria for the better fare outside. Her next choice was Dr. Madison, extracurricular activities notwithstanding, but she knew he had the afternoon off. She asked for his home number. No emergency in the world was going to pry that out of the operator. She offered to take Anna's number and have Dr. Madison return the call. Anna had no idea what the number to Molly's cellular was. It wasn't written anywhere on the flippy little phone. "Never mind," she said, for the second time in so many minutes.

"Damn, damn, damn, damn."

"Keep your pants on. It can't be that bad," was the advice from behind the wheel.

Yes it can. "Just drive."

Cursing eyes grown too old to read fine print, Anna squinted at the tiny numbers in her tiny address book and pushed the corresponding tiny numbers on Molly's tiny cell phone. James Hatchett, Sr., answered promptly. "Jim," Anna said, no time for hello. "I think I know who killed Hatch and why. I won't be coming to get you. There's something going down at the statue." *Going down.* Under stress she reverted to cliché. "I need you to dial nine-one-one for me." As the cab crept through Hell's Kitchen, Anna told Jim what she'd pieced together. From the terse grunts and a final "I'll get on it. You watch yourself," she knew she could count on him. Jim Hatchett wasn't a man easily flustered.

One more call and she would be out of ideas. The Ellis Island number was answered by a recording that droned tediously through too many options. Finally she'd poked enough buttons and was put through to the law enforcement office. Another machine fielded her call. Joshua was out—making his rounds or just killing time till the fireworks started. Even without fireworks, the boats on the harbor were a good-enough show to keep him occupied most of the night. Anna left a detailed message.

"Battery Park," the cabbie announced. "See, you worried for nothing. It's still here."

"A little farther," Anna instructed. "Drop me at the Marine Inspection pier across from the station where the four and five lines run."

"Why didn't you say so?"

The only bill Anna had was a twenty. She didn't wait for change. Taxi fares being what they were, there wasn't that much anyway. Eyes on the pier, she ran. Brakes squealed and a man screamed what she guessed was the equivalent of "Fucking idiot" in the language of men who wear turbans.

Anna forced herself to slow down mentally if not physically. Fear bred tunnel vision. Dead or crippled, she'd be no good to anybody. A security guard she'd only seen once or twice manned the kiosk at the gate to the MIO dock. A nice-enough kid who passed the time by reading paperback thrillers with blood-stained covers. Anna flashed her visitor's pass and told him to keep trying to get hold of the statue. "Tell them to get dogs in," she finished, then remembered the elephant prints, the wax, and knew dogs wouldn't do any good.

He was not pleased to participate in an adventure not contained between the covers of a book. "That's quite a story," he said, and Anna could see him choosing not to believe her. For an instant she wished she looked like Max Brand or Travis McGee. Reaching through the open window, she gently laid her hand on his shoulder. "You do *exactly* as you're told," she said kindly. He'd do it.

Whether he believed her or not, he'd do it. Maybe she couldn't emulate Brand or McGee, but she was a master at doing the dark side of mothers. Far more frightening to boys of any age than mere muscle.

"Staff boat's long gone," the kid volunteered. "Dwight'll be almost to Liberty by now. But there's an interpreter and her dad going over." He pointed down the dock. A red head and a bearded face were just visible above the planks. The remainder of the two was presumably standing in a boat. Mandy and her Castro-clone cohort; the bearded man who dressed like an action figure from a guts-and-glory mercenary magazine, right down to the scarred and worn army boots. The boots she'd seen at Agnes's death and the subway, and one of which had the imprint of its sole emblazoned on her back.

"Tucker!" she yelled. "Andrew Jackson Tucker!" The beard turned toward her and she walked at an even pace over the boards. Running would spook him. Once he got on open water, she had no way to catch him. As far as she knew, no one on Liberty knew he was coming—knew he even existed.

"It's over," she said reasonably, and turned her hands palm up in the universal gesture showing one was unarmed. "Liberty's crawling with feds. The game's lost. Mandy, you might want to step away from this guy. I don't know what line he's been feeding you, but it's not true. His name is Tucker, he's a member of a militia group from Idaho. He's the father of the girl who died at the statue." Anna had been fairly sure what she was saying was the truth. When she saw the startled irritation on the man's face, she knew it was.

Mandy made no move to leave the boat. Anna kept walking. Forty feet separated her from the boat. She needed to get to the end of the dock before Tucker started the engine. To keep him distracted she kept talking: "He murdered Hatch."

Mandy glared at Anna with such scorn it was a wonder her lip didn't curl clear up to her nose. "You're so fucking stupid," Mandy yelled. "There's no cops on Liberty. They don't know shit." She held up a radio. They'd been monitoring air traffic. "And A.J. didn't kill Hatch."

"Shut the fuck up," Tucker growled. Mandy had used his name. Anna guessed it wasn't the same as her hearing it from a known confederate. Tucker had spent some time in a court of law. He jerked the pull rope. The engine cranked but it didn't start.

He pulled again and Anna began to run. The fifty-yard dash, ten seconds in eighth grade. Forty feet, thirteen yards, how many seconds? Absurd arithmetic flickered through her mind. Tucker was too dangerous to fight with, but if she could get him out of the boat for even a few seconds, she could disable the engine by ripping off the spark plug wires and chucking them into the harbor.

"I know he didn't kill Hatch," Mandy was yelling. Her rage, always under the surface, had been loosed; flecks of foam whitened the corners of her mouth, blood suffused the fat cheeks. Anna's feet pounded the planking. Pain ricocheted up her spine. She pushed against it. The interpreter's face grew redder and redder, a party balloon about to pop.

"You know how I know, you stupid bitch?"

A fist caught Mandy square on the mouth. Blood spurted where teeth had been. Snapped back, she fell overboard. "Radio!" A.J. barked. Then: "Fucking bitch." Mandy had taken their radio with her. The engine sputtered and came to life.

Anna and the runabout left the dock at the same moment, she in the air, it on the water. She did not want to catch Tucker. She'd already caught him once—or he'd caught her—and she'd come away the loser. In the instant her feet left the pier, she knew what she had to do. She had to land on, or catch hold of, the gunwale as she fell to the water. Capsize his boat, flood his engine. Then, if the gods were kind, get the hell away before he laid hands on her.

Time proved Einstein right; it telescoped and elongated in the same space. As her feet left the dock a moccasin fell off. She was aware of the cooler air on her bare foot. She saw the shoe tumbling. Below, between the runabout and the thick pilings supporting the pier, she watched Mandy floating facedown. Red hair feathered around her head like an exotic sea urchin. Simultaneously all was a blur, passing so fast it was incomprehensible.

Straightening her legs, Anna braced herself for the shock when she collided with the boat. In a whir of movements, A.J. bent, lifted an oar, swung it like a bat. Curling into a ball, arms around her knees, Anna tucked her head. The blow fell across her shoulders. Hampered by a moving boat, the oar landed without force. But Anna was in the water and Tucker was motoring away.

"You okay? You okay?" she heard as she surfaced. July 4 and the harbor was as cold as if it remembered the melted snow of January.

"Okay," she sputtered. "Fish Mandy out." Anna hoped he'd comply. She had no desire to waste time saving the life of such a major pain in the ass. "I need a boat," she said as she floundered to a rickety wooden ladder at the pier's end.

"There's just the one," the guard called. "And you can't take that. It belongs to the Assistant Superintendent."

"Thanks." Dripping, Anna pulled herself onto the dock. A spasm was building in her lower back. Willing it away, she forced herself to her feet. The other moccasin was gone now. Belly-down on the planks, the guard was bent in two at the waist, trying to haul Mandy's dead weight from the water by pulling on one freckled arm.

"Give me a hand," he said.

Anna ignored him and ran down the pier to where Claypool's runabout was moored. A sharp pull and the engine came to life. Claypool was a careful man, his equipment in

410

good order. She commended him as she turned the stolen craft into open water. Drifting after her she could hear the guard's yell: "Come back here. Help me. You can't take that boat, it's the *Assistant Superintendent's!*"

Quarter past seven. Mrs. Weinstein's cross-cultural collection of important people would be riding elevators, climbing stairs, filling the crown. "Shit," Anna whispered, better words deserting her.

The harbor was alive with boats of every description. Brightly colored sails fluttered and dipped in an offshore breeze like the wings of butterflies. Stinkpots—the derogatory term sailors on Isle Royale used for motorboats—buzzed between the more graceful craft in an orgy of power. Yachts from up the Hudson, Long Island, Connecticut, the Carolinas, graciously allowed the lesser folk to scrabble about them. Thousands of people out to see the fireworks.

They might get a better show than they'd bargained for.

Ahead, bucking on water chopped by a dozen wakes, was Tucker. Anna had the faster boat and the distance was closing between them. His beard kept appearing on his shoulder as he looked back. Peripherally, she was aware that the holiday merrymakers were not pleased. Shouts were hurled like stones as her wake nearly capsized a canoe. A.J. sideswiped a cigarette boat with a five-thousand-dollar paint job and ruined a romantic water picnic when his wake rocked a dinghy, dumping the champagne bottle into the sea and toppling the glasses into the bean dip. Havoc was good. Somebody would call Harbor Patrol. Anna leaned forward as if this minute streamlining would increase her speed.

A disorienting sense of the surreal surrounded them. As in a war zone, there were flashes of fire and the crack of guns, but the soldiers were laughing, dressed in shorts and flowered shirts. Flares were from Roman candles, the reports from firecrackers. Pounding chop hammered Anna's back, starting muscle spasms that threatened to rip her hands from the tiller. Icy spray needled through hot air to sting her face and neck. Details were unnaturally clear. Names of the pleasure craft whirled by: *Pig Pen, Daddy's Girl, The Wife.* Anna could see separate air bubbles in trailing fingers of foam, each rivet in the hull. The red of the gas can glowed. The black of a hooded sweatshirt crammed beneath the bench was a black hole in the keel. Black sweatshirt: that's what Claypool had been wearing the night he abandoned her at MIO. The night Hatch was killed.

Dwight had alibied Mandy, said she didn't catch the staff boat that night but was marooned on Manhattan. But Patsy had said something. They were talking about vibes or karma and being able to feel it. Patsy said that the night Hatch died Mandy must have felt it too, because when she got up in the middle of the night Mandy had been awake and around. The import of that didn't register at the time,

412

but it proved Mandy was on Liberty when Hatch was pushed. Since she didn't take the staff boat, she must have found another way. If Anna could "borrow" the Assistant Superintendent's boat, so could Mandy. In the dark and the rain, wearing Claypool's hooded sweatshirt, Anna had mistaken her for him. Mandy knew Tucker hadn't killed Hatch because she had done it herself. "Damn," Anna whispered, wishing she'd not bothered to have the security guard pull her out of the sea.

Despite danger to civilians, she cranked the throttle to full open. The boat shuddered and lunged. Tucker was close: twenty yards, fifteen, ten. Like a dog chasing a car, Anna wondered what she'd do when she caught up. Killing him was out. Since she had no gun, no knife and little strength, she doubted she'd be much of a threat. Besides, they needed him, needed to know where the radio transmitter was and who was manning it.

"Stop him!" she shouted. No one heard over the sound of the engine. Everybody thought it was a game. Anna tried to squeeze more power out of the Evinrude, but it was giving its all. The only workable plan was to ram him. With luck she'd disable the boat. She hoped a responsible party had already called Harbor Patrol and there would be heavily armed good guys to take over.

An open expanse of water appeared. Tucker had maneuvered into the ferry lane. Seven yards. Five. The beard was on the shoulder. Then he was turning around, his camo-covered knees knifing up, boots over the gunwale and back. Reversed, he straddled the tiller facing her. His boat slowed, traveling blind.

He was giving up. *Thankyoubabyjesus.* Three yards. His hands went between his knees. Two yards. Anna cut power.

The hands came back in sight. In his fists was a handgun, silver and huge. A .45 at close to point-blank range, with a barrel Anna could have driven a truck into. She opened the throttle wide, jammed the tiller hard to starboard, smashing into the side of his boat. He fired. The shot was wild. Cordite stung Anna's nostrils as the impact of the collision threw her forward, both hands on the bottom of the boat. Tucker was driven back, boots in the air. She was the first to right herself. The Evinrude had died. She jerked the rope pull. It roared to life. Turning, she saw Tucker rise. He had not lost hold of the .45. Up it came, slow, deliberate, leveling at her head. Anna dove over the side and swam for the bottom. Thrumming reverberations chased her, the sound of bullets traveling through water. Cold seized her muscles. Salt water, murky with God knew what, closed pea soup veils around her. There'd been no time to breathe and her lungs expanded with need. Something cold brushed the back of her leg. Maybe the severed limb of a cadaver dumped with medical waste. Maybe her luck was improving and it was only a shark.

Lungs gave out and she kicked for the surface. No hope of stealth. Survival forced her up gasping and choking. She drank in the humid summer air with a chaser of seawater. The Verrazano Narrows Bridge, Manhattan, Ellis: she oriented herself till she faced Liberty Island. Tucker was moving on, his wake already fading. She'd lost. "Help!" she screamed. "Somebody help!" Private boats flurried and partied a hundred yards to her left. To the right the behemoth canary-colored ferry from Staten Island had started its run. Her own boat was still running. With no dead-man switch to cut off the engine when the operator disappeared suddenly, it had started the inevitable circle of an unmanned boat. Canted to the left, the propeller plowed a rough arc, circling back toward her. Had she been 007 she would have waited, bulldogged the boat like a runaway steer and hauled herself aboard. But she'd seen the scars of a ranger at Apostle Islands who had been gored by his own propeller. She struck out for the nearest boat.

Cold and trauma took their toll. With the first long reach of her arm, her back went into full spasm, pulling her head back toward her heels. Anna cried out and was gagged by salt water. Coughing bound the muscles tighter. The backs of her thighs struck in sympathy. Panic was a red glare in her mind. She beat feebly at the water with impotent hands. They could not hold. Eyes open, watching the light recede, feeling the deepening cold swallow her feetfirst, she sank.

Suffocation. Bubbles. Liquid murmuring. Cold. Molly on the respirator. Twelve in. Twelve out. Tubes trailing jellyfish tendrils. Molly fighting to open her eyes. Molly, tube in her throat, choking. Molly's hand, a starfish of white. Molly.

With the last echo of her will, Anna forced her arms up and back. Each move taking a quantity of thought, she interlaced her fingers around the back of her neck. Pulling hard, she began dragging her head down, curling her knees up toward her stomach, forcing the knots in her back to untie. It hurt so bad she screamed. Underwater the sound was faint, as if someone else, far away, was in terrible pain. Anna felt sorry for that person. Fleetingly, she wondered who it was.

Muscles stretched, cracked—she could hear it through the bones of her spine. The cramp opened its iron fingers. Anna clawed her way toward light. Though it never seemed to grow any closer, she finally burst through the green membrane and sucked in the air.

Mindlessly, the runabout was completing its prescribed circuit. Blades spinning at twelve hundred revolutions per minute cut through the water. Anna reached for an armful of water to drag herself from harm's way. Another spasm. Drown or be sliced to ribbons, then drown. The choices were not appealing. Anna wished she believed in God so she could revile Him or make peace with Him. She managed an atheist's prayer: *God damn it, do something.*

The angry growl of a much bigger dog washed over the water. The staff boat on its trip from Liberty to Manhattan bore down the ferry lane. Through the window of the pilot's cabin, she could see Dwight. His face was set, hard. He was going to run her down.

She tried to scream but drank instead. She tried to dive but back and legs rebelled. Water heaved upward and took her, turned her over and over, crushed the air from her lungs and tangled her arms and legs. Darkness spread and Anna knew she was giving up, going down. It was an oddly peaceful, if unremittingly cold, sensation.

25

No you don't. Oh no you don't."

Anna could hear. She tried to breathe, but a warm wet substance was clamped over her mouth. A blow struck between her breasts and she came up swinging. Her fist collided with slippery softness. A singularly noncelestial grunt followed and she opened her eyes. Curious faces ringed her. Dwight knelt over her, his earring stellar in the deep light of afternoon.

"God damn it, you don't give CPR to somebody that's not dead, for Christ's sake," Anna snarled.

"She's found religion," Dwight crowed. "That was a close one. What were you up to? Are you sober?"

With the captain's help, Anna sat up. "No jokes. Go to Liberty. Serious shit." There wasn't air enough to make sense, but Dwight heard the urgency behind the words and ran back to the bridge to take over from whomever he'd left minding the helm.

The *Liberty IV* turned neatly, intersecting her own wake, and the sound of engines grew in pitch. "Dwight. Good man," she whispered, then lost it in a fit of coughing that ended in vomit tasting of salt and acid.

Cal, his arms ironwood and bone, held her gently. When the heaving stopped, Anna disentangled herself from him and sat up, her back against the bulkhead. Cal's face was a foot from her own and for the first time Anna could see his age. He hid it in the black heart of warm, understanding eyes. Cal had seen too many things and had never lost heart. "Tried to run me over," she said, making no sense even to herself. She ran out of steam.

"Old Dwight wasn't aimin' at you. He was aimin' at that little boat 'bout to dice you into sausage. Hit it too. Dead on. It's kindling. Dwight saved your life and you cussed him and punched him." No censure sharpened the deckhand's words. He was just telling a story. One that, by the twitch of his lips, amused him greatly. "Dwight stopped and I drug you out." Anna noted Cal was as wet as she.

"Thanks," was the best she could do.

He nodded his acceptance and Anna knew she was safe for the moment. It was okay to close her eyes. No it wasn't. They flew open, startling Cal. "Help me to the captain," she croaked.

Without argument, Cal lifted her. Her hundred and twenty pounds were nothing to him. After a few shambling steps she found her legs worked. Cal bore the brunt of her weight till they reached the short, steep stairs to the bridge.

"I beg your pardon," he said, and Anna felt powerful hands on her rump as he boosted her up. Not sure she could stand unaided, she crawled a couple feet and braced her back against the starboard bulkhead. "Get on the radio," she told Dwight. "The statue is full of explosives. Probably C-four. Idaho militia. Racists. Skinheads." To her own ears she sounded insane, but Dwight didn't question her. While he made radio calls, Cal came up to sit next to her. The deckhand was black, a mud person, a person to kill. Rage warmed Anna and her muscles grew stronger with the heat. "Skinheads," she repeated, thinking out loud. The white boy with the shaved head, the janitor, the lunk who had a swastika tattooed on his neck, the idiot who had "accidentally" tossed a forty-pound can to Charlie, effectively ensuring he wouldn't be climbing around the statue for a couple months. The others called this lump of humanity "Idaho." That was the reference she couldn't recall. He was the one who wanted to work S-6, Miss Liberty's breasts. That's where some of the charges would be.

Tucker or Mandy would have smuggled the stuff over from the abandoned halls on Ellis where they prepared the charges, hollowing out pillar candles and packing them with C-4, then resealing the openings with wax. Anna had found the wax shavings. Early on she'd gotten a whiff of the sweet-sour stink of the explosive. The candles, the wax, were to seal the C-4 so dogs couldn't sniff it out. A long time ago, in another life, she and two other girls had brought marijuana over the border that way. The pillar candles had left the distinctive round "elephant prints" in the garden and in the dust underneath the stairs.

On one of her nightly forays to torment Billy Bonham, it made sense Corinne might have stumbled across them in their preparations. They clubbed her down and threw her in the garden to die.

The C-4 would have been taken to Liberty by boat. They probably docked on the natural jetty in the blind spot behind Claypool's and passed the materials off to Idaho.

His janitor cart would have been the perfect way to carry the explosives and the climbing gear he would need to place the charges. One night he must have dropped a carabiner. Hatch had found it, clipped it to his belt, probably never suspecting what it meant. Or dying because he did suspect.

"The cavalry is on its way." Dwight broke into her thoughts. "And I got hold of Andrew.

He's contacting Patsy, the Superintendent and anybody else he can get his hands on to start an orderly evacuation of the statue."

"Sorry I cussed you," Anna said.

"Enough said."

"Not a picnic," Cal remarked.

They knew what he meant. Stairs were narrow, elevators small; under the best of circumstances it would be thirty minutes or more before Mrs. Weinstein's people were clear.

"Call Andrew back," Anna said, remembering. "Tell him look for a thick white man. Called Idaho. On cleaning crew. May know him. Arrest him." Weariness was such that complete sentences were beyond her. In her mind's eye she saw again the look on Tucker's face when Mandy went over the side with the radio. Her guess was, Idaho was setting the charges. He would radio Tucker when he was clear and Tucker would flip the switch. Without the radio, there had to be a change in plans. Tucker now had to find Idaho, relay messages in person; then the both of them had to get clear and get back to where the transmitter was stashed so they could detonate the charges with a radio signal. "Tell Andrew to look for Castro clone," Anna said as Dwight spoke into the mike. "Armed and dangerous. Call security at MIO. If he's still got Mandy, arrest her. Police brutality requested." Energy sapped, Anna concentrated on breathing.

"These jokers couldn't have picked a worse day—or better, depending on how you look at it," Dwight said. "Everybody's on the island. They even had a tugboat land, but by the time Andrew got down to the dock to shoo it away it'd pulled out." He got back on the radio. Anna continued breathing.

When the *Liberty IV* docked, the pier was empty. Cal helped Anna ashore. Dwight told his handful of commuters in the lower cabin to stay on board and trotted off in the direction of the statue. In the distance was the chop of helicopters. The cavalry. There was nothing left for Anna to do. She didn't do bombs and didn't want to do crowd control. The monument had people for that. For once she would bow out and let others do their jobs. Molly would be proud.

Weary, sick and too sore to walk straight, she thanked Cal for saving her soggy little life and limped off down the covered dock. Mrs. Weinstein hadn't stinted on the decorations. Japanese lanterns glowed, pastel moons hung from overhead beams. Piñatas, donkeys and bulls and a pig, grazed the air between them. African masks glowered from the roof supports. Chinese dragons on paper wind socks hung limp in the still air. It would have been a great party.

Wanting to avoid adventure, Anna didn't take the wide tourist thoroughfare between law enforcement headquarters and the concessionaire's building, but turned left at the end of the dock and squeezed through the high wooden gate that hid the ugly utilitarian part of the island from the public. The alley between the headquarters and the machine sheds was filled with the directionless light of evening. No shadows, no edges, lines ran together. Anna moved as if she waded through deep fog. The only thing tethering her to reality was the smell of deep-fried rancid coming from the Dumpsters.

"Anna," said a Dumpster.

She stopped. With an effort, she engaged her mind.

"Over here."

She knew she should have been startled, but she was too tired. Moving all of a piece so she didn't twist back or neck, she faced the Dumpster that had spoken. In this shadowless world a shadow lay half under the metal bin.

Andrew. Officer down. "Jesus," she whispered. She knelt next to him, her hands feeling for cuts, blood, deformities. "What happened?"

"Shot." His voice was strong. Good sign. Not scared. Shock killed as sure as bullets.

"Are you okay?" God, she was tired. It made her stupid and careless. Too late, she looked around the alley for possible danger.

"They took off a minute ago, maybe less." Andrew was dragging his lower half from under the Dumpster. A snail's trail of blood darkened the concrete beneath him. "I was locked with Ben—Idaho you called him. Another guy shoots me in the back. In the buttock. I rolled under here. They didn't take the time to kill me. He smashed my radio. My gun's under there." He pointed to the neighboring garbage bin. "Ben knocked it out of my hand when I got shot. He said something to the other guy about getting something from Mandy, if that makes any sense."

It didn't. Mandy was on Manhattan, preferably dead or in chains. Unless he'd said *Mandy's*, Mandy's house.

"You go. I got it under control here. I mean, I'm not dying or anything. Just useless. Go now."

While he talked, Anna squirmed under the Dumpster and retrieved Andrew's gun. A Glock 9mm, a good weapon. She chambered a round. "I'll be back," she promised. Arnold Schwarzenegger had said the same thing in *Terminator 2*. It sounded more convincing with the accent.

Anna ran lightly down the alley. Her heart wanted to sprint but she didn't dare press her luck. Another back spasm would be too costly. Both shoes were at the bottom of the harbor and her bare feet made no sound. Glock first, she rounded the corner slowly, her body partially shielded by ornamental shrubs.

Patsy's house was dark but for the window in the back where Mandy slept. The kitchen door stood open. The plane tree hid the walk and half the bench where the interpreter had smoked her cigarettes. Sitting in the dusk, as relaxed as if he'd not just shot a Park Policeman and tried to shoot and drown a ranger, was Andrew Jackson Tucker. His beard was wagging and Anna could see the dull glint of a knife or metal rod belonging to whoever sat beside him screened by the trunk of the tree. Idaho probably.

Tread soundless, Anna eased closer. Tucker wasn't as relaxed as she'd first thought. His eyes darted and his hand crawled incessantly around the pocket of his trousers. For some reason he'd pocketed his .45. Two mad bombers sitting on a park bench of an evening, shooting the breeze and fondling their weapons. The scene was hinky enough that it made the little hairs on Anna's neck stand up, but she had no reason to think things were going to get any better.

Stepping from the shelter of the shrubbery, she trained the Glock on Tucker. Though she made no sound, he saw her and grabbed at his trouser pocket.

"Don't," Anna said. "Don't." She would shoot him. He heard it in her voice and his hand moved reluctantly away from his weapon.

"We were having a nice talk. Would have ended nice as pie," Tucker said.

"You behind the tree, show me your hands. Hands first. Both in view. Move out from behind the tree. Slow. Hands first."

Two hands came out, about the same height as Tucker's face. Whoever it was didn't stand up. "Get up, move out," Anna ordered.

The hands trembled. Tucker reached for them as if to help. A familiar voice said, "Anna?" Tucker's hands closed over the new arrival's and, with a short jerk, pulled the other man from behind the tree, an arm wrapped around his throat and another around his gut.

"Jim." Anna wavered. "How did you get here?"

"Tug captain owed me a favor. Looks like I stepped in it."

"Shut up." Tucker kept his head behind Jim's. Anna couldn't get a clean shot.

"You're almost as stupid as that kid of yours," Tucker said. "But more useful. Get up." He stood, dragging Jim up with him. The aluminum walker Anna had taken for a club fell over.

Jim's eyes narrowed, grew hard, chips of flint in his wrinkled face. The crippled legs kicked feebly, then stopped. His arms, the only strength he had left, hung at his sides. He didn't even try to pull Tucker's forearm from his windpipe.

Anna kept the Glock where it was, hoping Tucker would make a mistake.

"This the guy that killed Jimmy?" James Hatchett asked evenly.

"More or less," Anna replied. Her arms were beginning to shake. Normally she could hold a handgun out for a good long time. Her recent swim and the outrage to her back robbed her of control. The barrel of the Glock trembled. It would get worse. Precision shooting was no longer an option.

"Shoot, Anna," Jim said, and meant it. "Shoot right through me. Kill the bastard."

"Shut up, old man." Tucker worked the .45 out of his pocket and held it under Jim's jaw. "She can't do that. She's got to 'protect and serve.' She's a government lackey. She can't let you die even to save all those spics and slopes the government's so fond of. Hell, they're bringing 'em in by the boatload. Now they want to let the Jews make it mandatory our kids are taught to love their little mud brothers. Most Americans, real Americans, will celebrate the Fourth a little differently from now on. Freedom to be white, freedom to fight ethnic pollution. Freedom to refuse to let a bunch of Jews in Washington and New York brainwash our kids." Tucker walked backward, towing Jim along, keeping his body between himself and Anna's gun. Out from under the plane tree, onto the grass, moving toward the sea and Ellis Island, Jim's useless legs bumped pathetically over the ground. "Let's go blow up some mud pies," Tucker said. "You'll see how Liberty looks falling on a wall of subhuman mud."

"Why did Mandy kill Hatch?" Anna asked, to keep him talking long enough for the winds of fortune to blow her way.

"Stupid cunt. Nearly screwed the whole deal. Ben knocked her into the middle of next week for that stunt."

The black eye Mandy had been sporting; a small price to pay for taking a man's life. The screen door rattled and Tucker shouted, "You stay put till it's over, Ben. I got a little extra business."

"What's happening, Pa?"

"Do as I tell you." If Tucker wanted Idaho to stay put, he must be unarmed. Good to know. Anna kept pace with Tucker and his flesh-and-blood shield. He was backing toward the chain-link fence. His boat would be moored there. In the boat would be a neat plastic box. That box would send a radio signal that would set off the C-4 strapped to Lady Liberty's bones.

Anna's arms were shaking so bad she'd stopped trying to use her sights and was pointing the gun as she would point a finger, trusting in years of experience. Sacrifice the one for the many. Blow great bloody holes in James Hatchett that the hundreds of souls in Liberty's heart might live. Tucker was right, Anna couldn't do it. Good little lackeys of the United States Government didn't gun down innocent people, regardless of the temptation— or the cost. It was something she really liked about her job.

"He'll kill me, then he'll kill you," Jim said. "And blow up the thing anyway."

"He's not fast enough," she said. Maybe that was true. If she could hold the Glock steady long enough.

Tucker reached the fence. Leaning against it, he gauged the distance to the boat and the detonator. He readied himself to go down the bank. Once there was dirt between him and Anna, he'd drop Jim and kill her. Anna started to move closer, not letting him out of her sights even for an instant.

"Stop or I blow his fucking brains out," Tucker said.

"And I kill you."

Tucker moved the .45 from Jim to point it at Anna. "Or I just shoot you. What are you going to do? Shoot through this old bag of shit?

I would. He's no use to anybody anymore." The barrel moved back to Jim's temple. Tucker was having fun.

Jim fixed Anna with his remarkable eyes. "I'll give Jimmy your regards," he said with a hint of a smile.

"Shut the fuck up," Tucker hissed.

Anna knew her part, the only one left to her. The time she'd felt slipping through her hands all week. Now she must buy a little of it back. She lowered the Glock. "Easy," she said. "I like my job, but I'm not dying for it. Or for anybody's niggers." A.J. wasn't a trusting soul, but she was singing his song and he loved listening. Anna kept talking. A scarred brown workingman's hand eased to the waistband of a geriatric blue jumpsuit. Silver glinted. A strong old wrist turned expertly, his arm jerked up and back. Jim buried the fish-gutting knife deep between Andrew Jackson Tucker's ribs.

Above the beard, the militiaman's eyes grew wide with surprise. Then his finger closed on the trigger. Half of James Hatchett's head was gone, his body jerked to the side. The silver barrel of the .45 swung toward Anna. She fired four shots into A.J. Tucker before he hit the ground.

26

Regardless of how divinely inspired, New York frowned upon unauthorized persons shooting people with borrowed guns. Anna spent seven hours with three different law enforcement agencies giving statements, defending her actions, accepting congratulations, being bullied and drinking bad coffee. Drowning in polluted salt water was beginning to seem like the good old days.

It was late afternoon on the fifth of July before she got to the hospital to see her sister. Once again Molly had been moved out of ICU. For good this time, Frederick insisted, and Anna believed him. Frederick welcomed her as the conquering hero. Molly tried to scold her for old times' sake, but Anna could tell her heart wasn't in it. Multiple bypass surgery, a near-death experience, age—something had finally mellowed Dr. Pigeon. Anna could see a new and beautiful softness in her sister's eyes.

Frederick settled Anna in a comfortable chair, plied her with water and left her to tell her story in her own way. Anna had thought she'd want to but found she didn't. Living it had been enough. It wasn't a tale of high glamour, riches gained or lost. It was a nasty little story of hatred, fear and ignorance.

"I'm flying home tomorrow," she said, and felt guilty at how relieved she sounded. They were unoffended. Anna was reminded there

430

might be something called unconditional love and found the energy to go on.

"Tucker is dead—twice. Jim's knife would have killed him in an hour or so. Andrew's bullets made it happen a little sooner." Anna wasn't hiding anything. Molly and Frederick knew she'd shot the man. The whole country knew. The press Mrs. Weinstein brought in to get the political goody out of the festivities had descended on Anna et al. like ravening beasts. "Idaho—Ben—Tucker's eldest from his first marriage, half brother to Agnes Abigail, was arrested, no problem. Without Daddy around to tell him what to do, he gave up without a fight. He was working under the name Ben Thomas. When Tucker took an alias his son did too. Mandy was arrested later. The security guard let her go but she was tracked down at the apartment on the Lower East Side where the Tucker/Thomases were staying. Bad news is, she can't be made to testify against Ben or vice versa. They're married. Agnes was her sister-in-law. Mandy shoved Hatch to avenge her death, thinking it would impress A.J. and her husband. Make her one of the revolutionaries."

"What was this Ben/Idaho going into Mandy's house to look for?" Frederick asked.

Anna hoped he'd forgotten that. "A picture," she said. "He had it on him when he was arrested. I'd seen it once. I thought it was a military shot—somebody's regiment or something. There were kids and dogs around. That should have tipped me off. Military pic-

431

tures are sans civilians. The shot was of his Idaho militia group. Tucker was in it and so was Ben, though he had hair, so I might not have recognized him. Ben/Idaho was removing anything from Mandy's room that could incriminate them."

"And you a trained observer," Frederick teased.

"And me a trained observer," Anna admitted.

"I don't understand. Did Mandy get on with the Park Service and then get transferred to the statue just to set up this job?" Molly asked. "That's a little tricky. It took you years to get on permanent."

"No. Mandy was already at the statue when Ben got the job. He was the inside man. Then she was recruited. Idaho wooed and won her. Six weeks start to finish. She was easy pickings. A misfit, a malcontent. She needed a cause. Wanted to belong. Wanted to get even. A cult groupie waiting to happen. So Idaho stepped in."

"And the little girl jumped?" Molly asked.

"We think so. Her pack had to have been taken by her father. I remember his boots, he was front row center after she fell. The only thing that makes sense is she had detonators, blasting caps she was going to leave in the statue for her half brother. When Hatch took her for a pickpocket she was sharp enough to know if she got caught the plot would be exposed. So she jumped."

"Died for the cause," Frederick said.

"At fourteen it seems like the thing to do,"

Molly added sadly. "Children soldiers. We've been murdering them since the beginning of time."

"Do they know where this guy got the C-four?" Frederick asked.

"Not for sure. The speculation is he stole it from a mine or mines in Idaho. Some of the more isolated sites have pretty poor security."

They digested the precariousness of life for a moment.

"Corinne's still in a coma," Anna finished. "Even if she comes out of it, she's going to be a mess."

Nobody said anything. The room should have been thick with the sorrow of the world, but it wasn't. Molly and Frederick had a lightness about them that permeated the air, lifted Anna's spirits though she wasn't sure why.

Molly had her hands under the coverlet, as she'd had once before.

"Have you got another kitten?" Anna demanded.

Molly laughed. "Not another kitten." She took her left hand from beneath the sheet and waggled her fingers. The emerald caught the light, the gold shone.

Joy boiled up in Anna so fiercely she had to clamp her teeth hard and close her eyes so she wouldn't start crying.

"Are you okay?"

"We don't have to do it."

"Oh my gosh."

"We were only kidding."

The backpedaling made Anna smile. As soon as she had herself under control she would tell Frederick to send for the tailor. The sooner she got fitted for that peach silk tux, the better she would sleep at night.

Her sister was going to be looked after.